DOORADOYLE STOCK

L(
31

3 0012 00004324 9

B

✔ KU-067-258

THE PRICE OF FAME

Acknowledgements:
Carola Edmond and Linda S. Price, for editorial guidance.
Tanya Ossack, for assistance in research.

The characters in this book are entirely imaginary
and bear no relation to any real persons living or dead.

British Library Cataloguing in Publication Dat
Mosco, Maisie
   The price of fame.
   I. Title
   823'.914[F]   PR6063.081/

   ISBN 0-450-06108-6

Copyright © 1985 by Maisie Mosco Manuscripts Ltd

First published in Great Britain 1985
Second impression 1992

All rights reserved. No part of this publication may be
reproduced or transmitted in any form or by any means,
electronic or mechanical, including photocopying,
recording, or any information storage and retrieval system,
without either prior permission in writing from the
publisher or a licence permitting restricted copying.
In the United Kingdom such licences are issued by the
Copyright Licensing Agency, 90 Tottenham Court Road,
London W1P 9HE.

Published by New English Library,
a hardcover imprint of Hodder and Stoughton,
a division of Hodder and Stoughton Ltd,
Mill Road, Dunton Green, Sevenoaks, Kent TN13 2YA
Editorial Office: 47 Bedford Square, London WC1B 3DP

Photoset by Hewer Text Composition Services, Edinburgh
Printed and bound in Great Britain by
Biddles Ltd, Guildford and King's Lynn

THE PRICE OF FAME

Maisie Mosco

F45,909.

NEW ENGLISH LIBRARY

For
my grand-daughters
in order of appearance:
MIRANDA SELBY

JANE MOSCO

CLAIRE MOSCO

ZOE SELBY

CHARLOTTE BLAU

Part One

O what a tangled web we weave,
When first we practise to deceive!
Sir Walter Scott

CHAPTER ONE

HE FOUND the photograph while he was rummaging in the attic, where he had gone to fetch some books for which there was no space on the shelves in his room. The fascination of relics from the past caused him to linger amid the cobwebs longer than he had intended, and his eye fell upon his mother's old trunk.

It had travelled with her when her parents were touring players. Labels bearing the names of provincial railway stations were plastered upon it, like a map of her transient childhood. And on the lid, printed boldly in white, was her name: ALISON PLANTAINE.

He had often wondered what she kept in it, and was not surprised to find among its contents masses of theatre programmes. Some, yellowed with age, were from the days when she worked with her family company. Before she became the star she now was, her son thought.

Why did he mind her being famous? Because she belonged to her public, not to him. He swallowed down his resentment, as he had long since learned to do, and returned his attention to the trunk.

There was a blue georgette scarf in it, and a white glove with tiny pearl buttons. Two baby boots, tied together by their laces, lay tangled with a pair of dark-lensed spectacles. The baby boots must have been his, and it was nice to know she was so sentimental about him. But why had she kept the spectacles with her mementoes? He espied the little round cap she had probably worn when she made her stage début playing Juliet, in 1916, and had the feeling that everything in this trunk could tell a story about his mother and her life.

He picked up an embroidered silk shawl he could

3

remember covering the grand piano in the living room when he was small, and was wrinkling his nose because it reeked of mothballs, when the photograph and a German theatre programme slipped from its folds to the floor.

He retrieved them and tossed the programme back into the trunk, recalling his mother once mentioning that she had appeared at a theatre festival in Berlin, in the thirties. It must have been before Hitler came to power, he reflected, or a half-Jewish actress would not have been welcome there.

The winter afternoon was darkening to twilight. How long had he been in the attic, browsing through his mother's private treasures? And without her permission. A stab of guilt assailed him. But the deed was done now. He might as well remove the photograph from its tissue-paper wrapping and peep at it before he closed the trunk.

Inscribed on the cardboard frame, in Alison Plantaine's handwriting, was: 'My dear papa, on his Bar Mitzvah day'.

To her son, though he was two years older than her father was then, it was like looking at a picture of himself. Yet she had told him he was her adopted child.

Alison returned from a wearying rehearsal to a cold and empty house.

'Richard!' she called when she opened the living-room door and was greeted by dead cinders in the hearth, and a gust of February chill. 'Where are you? Why have you let the fire go out?'

Not until she had been in every room, looking for him, could she believe he was not there. Her son was a considerate boy, more inclined to have a cup of soup waiting for her when she arrived home than to this kind of behaviour. There was not even a note saying where he was.

This was his half-term holiday from school. Had he mentioned going somewhere today, without it registering with her? And what sort of mother was she, if that was the case? One who wasn't cut out to be a mother, as her cousin Emma had once bluntly told her.

4

What would Emma, if she were here, do now? Ring up some of Richard's friends. But when Alison did so, none of them had seen him that day.

If there was ever a time when Alison was aware of her inability to cope alone, it was now. Why did something like this have to happen when Emma was up north visiting her mother? And when Maxwell Morton, who was not just Alison's manager but her dear friend, was abroad on business? He and Emma had been her support for more years than she cared to remember. Seen her through every crisis. Helped her raise her child. Shared with her the anxieties to which parents are subjected.

Richard, though he was fatherless, was blessed with the love of two people to whom he had become a surrogate son. And they would not forgive Alison if some harm had befallen him in their absence, she thought with alarm. Supposing he had slipped out to buy a bar of chocolate and been run over by a bus? Was he lying in hospital, unconscious, unable to tell anyone who he was?

She was about to telephone the police when Richard came home.

'How dare you do this to me!' Alison flared to him. But relief expressed in anger is not uncommon in a parent.

He gave her a sullen glance, then went to the kitchen to pour himself some milk.

Alison followed him, still beside herself. 'Where have you been?'

He did not reply to the question. 'When is Auntie Emma coming back?'

'She wasn't sure. She said she'd let us know.'

Richard drank his milk and put down his glass. 'Well, I hope it's soon. I'd rather not be here alone with you.'

Alison was bewildered. When she left for rehearsal this morning everything was fine. He had kissed her goodbye. What could possibly have happened between then and now, to turn him against her? 'What have I done?' she asked.

Again she received no answer. But the look her son gave her was more eloquent than words. As though he

5

hated her. It was all she could do to remain standing where she was. Not to recoil. By the time she had recovered, Richard had gone.

She heard him walk upstairs to his room and slam the door. If she went after him, it might make things worse. A painful feeling of rejection assailed her. And a sudden *déjà vu*. When had he made her feel this way before? When he was a little boy and overheard Alison and Emma talking about sending him away, because of the impending war. Richard had thrown a tantrum, kicking and screaming at her. When he calmed down he would not let her near him. He had wanted only Emma – as he had made clear was the case now.

It occurred to Alison that whenever her son was deeply hurt about something, she was the one against whom he hit out in return. Never Emma, or Maxwell, though they disciplined him when necessary which Alison had never done. But what had hurt him today? If she asked him, he would not tell her. She would have to wait until Emma returned.

In the interim, Alison and Richard lived under the same roof like strangers. Her initial attempts to behave normally with him were rebuffed, and she retired into her shell.

During his years as a wartime evacuee with an American family, Richard had helped with the household chores and learned how to cook simple meals. Usually, when Emma was away, he stepped into the breach and Alison had looked forward, ruefully, to several more days of dining on sausage and mash, or egg and chips. But Richard pointedly cooked only for himself, leaving her to make herself a sandwich when she came home from work. Alison could not cook.

As she was at present between plays, they were at home together in the evenings, which served to emphasise their estrangement – Alison sat in the living room, and Richard sequestered himself in his bedroom.

The day came when Alison could bear it no longer, and almost called Emma to ask her to hurry back. She stopped herself from doing so. Emma had enough on her plate at the moment. She had been summoned north by her sister Clara, when their mother tumbled from a stool while cleaning her kitchen cupboards. No bones were broken, but Clara would not be losing the opportunity to try to bulldoze Emma into returning to Oldham to live with the widowed old lady – a term which conjured up quite the wrong picture of Alison's Aunt Lottie, she reflected with a wry smile. A more ebullient matriarch than Lottie Stein had never lived.

Nevertheless, thought Alison, Emma was probably having a hard time at Clara's hands. Though Emma had come to London to live with Alison in 1930, and it was now 1948, Clara had still not forgiven her for deserting the parental home. But in Clara's book, an unmarried woman was not entitled to a life of her own.

It did not enter Alison's mind for a moment that Clara's current campaign to get Emma to return north would succeed. Alison knew that Emma had fought and won the battle with her conscience and conditioning long ago. And by now, her life was too enmeshed with Alison's for her to extricate herself. Nor did she wish to, or she would have said yes to the American officer who had proposed to her during the war.

Perhaps the proposal itself had been enough for Emma, Alison mused now. Just knowing that a man had wanted her – for no other man had. Alison mused, too, on what a perfect wife and mother her cousin would have made. As Emma's late father had once said, beneath her plain exterior was a seam of pure gold.

Me, I'm just the opposite, Alison thought, eyeing her reflection in the hall mirror; after deciding not to call Emma she had remained beside the telephone, lost in her thoughts. You're still a glamorous lady, she silently assessed herself, though you'll be fifty in two years from now. Talented, too. But what kind of person are you? Hopeless and helpless, that's what. You can't even cope with your own son.

CHAPTER TWO

EMMA HAD never received such a rapturous welcome. She was kissed and hugged by Alison and Richard in turn as though she had just returned from a long and hazardous trip to the North Pole. It did not take her long to divine that both were not just pleased to have her back, but relieved, too.

'What's been going on while I was away?' she enquired after she had taken off her hat and coat.

'Nothing,' Richard replied.

'Except,' said Alison, who could contain herself no longer, 'that our boy is, for some reason, not speaking to me.'

They followed Emma to the kitchen, where she immediately donned a pinafore without which she was rarely seen.

'We'll have a cup of tea, and Richard can tell me all about it,' she said.

'There's nothing to tell.'

'Does that mean you've now forgiven me for whatever it is that I don't know I've done?' Alison asked him.

'I'll see you later, Auntie Emma,' Richard said, and left the room.

'He has been walking out on me like that all week!' Alison exclaimed. And added, after putting Emma in the picture, 'What could I possibly have done to upset him that day, when I wasn't here?'

'Where do you keep his birth certificate?' Emma enquired, after a thoughtful silence.

Alison felt the blood drain from her face. 'It's in the safe. But what makes you think his behaviour has anything to do with that?'

Though they had heard Richard go upstairs, and were speaking quietly, Emma shut the kitchen door. 'I feel like a conspirator, Alison. And I don't like the feeling. When I think of the lengths we went to – even embroiling the family up north – to protect you from scandal — '

'It was my career, not me personally, that had to be protected,' Alison cut in. 'I would never have lent myself to the deceit had I not been who I am. Do you really think I'd have willingly let my son grow up thinking I'm not his real mother?'

She tried to steady her trembling voice and found that she could not. A blast of anger shot through her. 'And you failed to mention who masterminded the conspiracy, Emma. Our friend Maxwell – who makes a packet out of every production I appear in for him and wanted to go on doing so – dreamed it all up!'

'You've had your share of flops, but Max never minded,' Emma answered. 'And it wasn't his pocket he was thinking of. He knows as well as you and I do that Alison Plantaine would fall apart if anything happened to her career.'

Emma had put the kettle on to boil, and brewed some tea. 'What's to be gained by apportioning blame, Alison? I've always felt in my bones that one day the lies we told Richard would come home to roost.'

'When he's old enough to understand, I shall tell him the truth.'

'You don't think it's possible that, somehow or other, he has found out?'

'How could he have done?'

Emma poured the tea and toyed absently with the sugar-spoon. 'I believe in God – whom you call Destiny, Alison. And I've had time to learn – as you have – that if He intends something to happen, He has His ways.'

Alison smiled bitterly. 'If it's retribution you're talking about, Emma, I have already paid in full. Wasn't losing my son's father – the only man I've ever loved – punishment enough?'

CHAPTER THREE

MAXWELL MORTON returned from his business trip to two anxious women and an uncharacteristically subdued boy.

Alison had moved from her West End apartment shortly after the war, and now had further to travel when she was appearing in a play. Morton, too, was inconvenienced by the move; he had to drive to North London when he dropped in on them. But he and Alison had agreed with Emma that a house with a back garden was a more suitable home for a growing lad. As always, Richard's welfare came first with them all.

The house was unnecessarily large for three people, but it was situated in a leafy lane close to Highgate Ponds, on the borders of the Heath, and Emma did not mind the extra housework. Here, the air was fresher, devoid of the city-centre petrol fumes she had never thought healthy for a child. And Richard was able to have a bedroom with plenty of space for a desk. He was a studious boy and they had lined the walls with bookshelves for him, but the books had overflowed to the floor – he spent all his pocket money on buying more.

Emma was also happier in the house on her own account. Where she came from, flats were a rarity and she had never felt comfortable living in one. Now she had a kitchen with a hearth in it, which had quickly become the heart of the home as her mother's kitchen was, up north.

Morton, who had no relatives, visited the three who had become for him his family immediately he arrived back in London. Though he was not part of their ménage, he spent more time at Alison's house than in his Mayfair bachelor flat. To the others – though the boy was not his son, nor either of the women his wife – it was as though the head of the family had come home. They loved and respected him. But he would never know that Emma's love for him was that of a woman for a man.

Would she ever stop loving Max that way? Emma thought, surveying his travel-weary appearance that evening. Or cease to be plagued by twinges of jealousy because he had always adored Alison, who did not want him? Max probably thought that she herself had said no to the only proposal she had ever had because marrying an American would have meant uprooting herself in middle age, she wryly reflected. But, had *he* asked her, she would have followed Maxwell Morton to the ends of the earth.

She had not dismissed Al Wiseman's proposal lightly. All Emma had ever wanted was to be cherished in the way her father had cherished her mother. But accepting Al would not have been fair to him if she could not return his devotion, and she had finally decided that her place was with those who already depended upon her. Without her, Alison's and Richard's stable home-life would cease to exist.

She took Morton's hat and coat and hung them on the gleaming mahogany hallstand.

'I'm capable of doing that myself,' he said after she had whisked them from his hands.

'Nobody would think so – as you usually just dump them on a chair!'

Such verbal exchanges between them were common, and a source of amusement to Alison and Richard. This evening, neither so much as smiled.

'So how were things on Broadway, Max?' Emma asked, though she was not interested in either the theatre or his business machinations – as he well knew. But she could not bear the tension emanating from Alison and Richard. A fine homecoming for Max, she thought.

Morton, too, was affected by the atmosphere, and replied caustically, 'As I've been to Canada, not the States, I wouldn't know, Emma. Now will someone please tell me what's wrong with you all tonight?'

'You had better ask Richard,' said Alison.

11

Emma held her tongue.

'I'll see you later, Uncle Maxwell,' Richard said, departing upstairs.

Morton thought, as he often had, that it could not be easy for a boy to live with two women, in a household without a man. Morton did his best to fill the breach, but had never fooled himself that it was enough.

Alison led the way into the living room and he went to warm his back before the fire

'If Richard's kicked his football through the kitchen window again, it isn't the end of the world,' he said with a smile.

'I wish that were all it were,' Alison replied.

Morton's smile faded to a thoughtful frown as he listened to what they had to tell him.

'Richard is behaving as though he hates me,' Alison summed up.

'There's no other way to describe it,' Emma endorsed.

'It is certainly worrying – but aren't you two being a bit melodramatic?' Morton said.

'That can sometimes be said about Alison,' Emma retorted. 'But never about me. I've seen it with my own eyes, Max. Richard has been so cold to her this week, it's a wonder, when he passes her the jug of water at the supper table, that it doesn't turn to ice.'

Morton headed for the door. 'Maybe I'll have more success than you did in discovering what this is all about.'

He returned no wiser. But an interesting detail had emerged. 'On the evening Richard went missing, Alison, he visited your stepcousins.'

Alison shot out of her fireside chair, such was her fury. 'Then we need look no further! Those despicable Plantaine twins have finally turned my son against me.'

Morton waited for her to calm down. 'I agree that they are a pair of arch-schemers,' he said with distaste. 'It's no secret in show business that conniving has got them where they are.'

'Where exactly are they?' asked Emma. The theatre-world gossip she heard Alison and Morton discussing invariably failed to register with her. 'Didn't Lucy Plantaine get married recently?'

Alison nodded, her lips curled with contempt. 'Charles Bligh has made an honest woman of her. Though his wife divorced him long ago, it took Lucy – who was the cause – years to hook him. But now she is married to an impresario, she'll be a permanent star, and her twin will get Bligh Productions' plum directing jobs – though neither of them has an ounce of talent.'

'I wouldn't say Luke Plantaine has no talent,' declared Morton, who was fair even to those whom he abhorred.

Nor, in honesty, would Alison say that. But the mere mention of the Plantaine twins was inflammatory to her. They had done their best to make her miserable when the three of them were still youngsters working with the family repertory company, and in later years had tried to capitalise on Alison's success to promote their own careers. She had not let them use her and they had become her bitter enemies, but ingratiated themselves with Richard when he was still a little boy.

'The mere fact that Richard likes the twins and I loathe them has caused trouble between him and me!' she exploded to Emma and Morton. 'But you two are well aware that I've always attributed evil motives to their befriending my son.'

She grows more beautiful with the years, Morton thought. And anger enhances her beauty. The flush staining her cheeks emphasised her sculptured features, and her eyes had darkened with feeling to the colour of her blue-black hair. For Morton, there had never been any other woman, though many had lain in his arms.

Alison toyed wretchedly with the milky pearls at her throat, which Morton had given her for Christmas. He had given Emma the expensive-but-sensible brown cardigan she had on. His gifts epitomised how he saw them – and were Emma's yearly reminder of something she knew too well.

'Stop playing with your necklace, you'll break it,' Emma said to Alison.

13

'I am more concerned with my already broken heart. And the twins are to blame for it.'

'That's pure supposition,' said Morton. 'And I doubt that even they could manage to turn a boy against his mother in the space of an evening.'

'Unless,' said Emma, 'they told him that Alison really is his mother. That she's been lying to him all his life.'

A silence followed.

'They have no way of knowing that,' Morton said.

'But that wouldn't stop them from saying it,' Alison answered. Then she laughed harshly. 'Which would fit in with your idea of God and His ways, wouldn't it, Emma? Though I would not have expected Him to employ a couple of devil's disciples to wreak His vengeance!'

She'll go to pieces in a minute, Morton thought, seeing her fingers move from the pearls to her apricot wool dress and begin plucking edgily at a pleat. It was like watching a performance, but her emotions were real, not controllable as they were when she was acting a part onstage.

'We must stop conjecturing,' he declared firmly, 'and stick to the facts. Adolescence is a tricky time and Richard is going through it at present. I can remember myself having moods I couldn't account for, or rationalise, when I was his age. Okay. So an adolescent boy takes off for a few hours without leaving a note saying where he's gone, and is in a funny mood when he gets back. What is so odd about that?'

'The way he is still behaving,' said Alison. 'As if I've done something terrible to him.'

'Which you have,' Emma told her.

'And a lot of help you are!' Morton flung at her.

Emma ignored him and addressed Alison. 'Career or not, with the benefit of hindsight, would you still agree to the cover-up you agreed to sixteen years ago?'

'No,' said Alison unhesitatingly. She gave Emma a wan smile. 'When I was younger, I believed that everything would come right in the end.'

'You mean you thought, because you were Alison

Plantaine, you had a charmed life,' Emma replied.
'But you know, now, that nobody has – not even you.
That people have to pay for the things they do. I never
agreed with the cover-up, and I told Max so, though I had
no choice but to go along with it. One lie always leads to
another – and look where we are now.'

Emma turned to Morton. 'Perhaps you remember me
saying to you when we first learned Alison was pregnant
that I would never allow anything to be done that harmed
the child? But I wasn't thinking far enough ahead, Max.
There's no way any of us can protect Richard from the
shock of discovering who he really is. If he's found out by
accident – or had it put in his mind by the twins – that's
even worse than his hearing it from Alison's lips.'

Morton poked the fire to hide his agitation. Was Emma
trying to make him the scapegoat for how she now felt?
Outwardly, she was the only one of them who seemed
calm, and was now standing with her hands in her cardigan
pockets, eyeing him with rebuke. Her tiny, birdlike appearance made her seem a meek little person, he thought. But
when necessary, she was anything but!

'Thank you, Emma,' he said brusquely, 'for telling us
what we can now see for ourselves. But might I add that in
a crisis people do what is expedient for the immediate
problem. Speaking for myself, at the time you are harking
back to I was concerned only for Alison. There was no
Richard. And — '

Morton broke off in mid-sentence when the boy entered
the room.

'If I'm interrupting a private conversation, I'll come
back later,' Richard said, hovering in the doorway.

Alison made up her mind. 'No. Come in and sit down,
darling. What we are discussing concerns you.' She was
aware that her voice sounded choked and that tears were
stinging her eyes. But her own feelings were unimportant.
What mattered was setting things right with her son. *For*
her son.

Richard did not sit down, but went to stand beside
Emma, as though he sought her support. And it struck

15

Alison that, in effect, he had been doing that all his life. Though Alison was his mother, she was someone he did not wholly trust. Emma, who was always there for him, spelled reliability – and Alison, flitting back and forth between him and her career, the opposite. After the war she had undertaken a lengthy provincial tour, and Richard had never been sure when she would next manage to get home to see him.

But there was something else that probably accounted for his distrust, she thought now: the way, when he asked her questions about the past – as children do – she fended him off and was guarded with him, lest she let slip a loose end in the web of lies that shrouded his origins.

Alison steeled herself to unravel that web. She knew that Emma and Morton were aware, without her telling them, of what she was about to do. It could not be done without causing pain to her son.

'Do you love me?' she asked him.

His reply did not bode well. 'Unfortunately I do.'

'Then I hope you'll try to understand all that I am going to say to you. And forgive me, if you can.'

Richard brought from the inside pocket of his blazer the photograph he had found in the attic, and propped it up on the mantelpiece. 'Has it got something to do with this?'

Alison exchanged a glance with Emma. Richard's birth certificate was safely locked away, but she had overlooked other clues to his true identity that were here in the house. The ways of God – or Destiny – were more simple than one supposed.

Richard was studying the photograph. 'I look exactly like him, don't I, Mother? And since I found his picture, a lot of thoughts have whirled around my mind – including the hopeful one that Auntie Emma might possibly be my real mother, since your father was her uncle.'

Alison could not have been more brutally affected had Richard slapped her face.

Morton stubbed out his cigar. 'If you realised what a hurtful thing you have just said, you would not have said it, Richard.'

16

'Yes, I would, Uncle! But I'm still waiting for my worst fear to be confirmed.'

'There seems to be an unpleasant streak in you I hadn't detected,' Morton answered.

'I wonder where it comes from,' said Richard, eyeing Alison.

'Hold your tongue!' Morton thundered.

Richard gave him a sullen glance and moved closer to Emma.

'Do me a favour, will you, dear?' she appealed to him. 'Listen with an open mind to what your mother is going to tell you.'

But Alison knew that his mind and heart had already closed against her. That he would strip the tenderness from the story of her brief interlude with a young German intellectual that had resulted in his being born.

While she told it, Alison's voice sounded false to her own ears.

And to Richard's. 'Tell me another!' was his strident reaction. Having German blood in his veins was unthinkable – like hearing that he was the son of a murderer. 'If you decided to invent a father for me, why did you have to make him a Hun? And don't bother telling me any tales about why you pretended you adopted me!'

'The decision your mother made about that was very hard for her,' Emma said quietly.

Morton, too, came to Alison's rescue. 'And you may as well know, Richard, that it was I who advised her to take the course she did.'

Richard gave him a thoughtful glance. 'Oh yes?'

'You are old enough to know,' Morton went on, 'the social stigma attached to an unmarried mother. Women who are a good deal less in the public eye than yours has always been would not have such a thing known about them. She was already a star, and the slur on her name would most certainly have damaged her career.'

This was the worst thing Morton could have said.

When, thought Richard, did her career not come before me? But Uncle Maxwell was no better than she

17

was! He had advised her and she had done as he said. The honorary uncle whom Richard had always idolised had turned out to have feet of clay. Auntie Emma was the only one left to trust.

Alison was, with difficulty, holding herself together. 'Is there anything you would like to ask me?' she said to Richard. She could not bear to see the hurt in his eyes.

'Only who my father really was.'

'I've already told you, darling. If I had a picture of him, I'd show it to you, but I didn't think of asking him for one. It's probable that he wouldn't have had one to give to me – he wasn't the kind to bother about snapshots. All I want you to believe, Richard, is that we loved each other very much.'

'Then why didn't he come to England and marry you?'

'He was engaged in anti-Nazi propaganda. It was just before Hitler came to power, and he couldn't leave Germany at such a time.'

'If you'd said he was Jewish, I might have swallowed it,' said Richard with contempt. 'But the other Germans were on Hitler's side, weren't they? Or they wouldn't have let the Nazis do what they did to the Jews.'

'There were some decent Germans, Richard, as I found out when I was in Berlin. Your father was one of them. He was a good man.'

Richard gave Alison the cliché-reply that, so soon after the war and the holocaust, was still the British belief: 'The only good German is a dead one.'

Alison's lover had died for his ideals. He had, with other young intellectuals incarcerated by Hitler, hanged himself in his cell on the night history would record as The Burning of the Books. The smoke raised by that literary funeral-pyre had signalled for Richard Lindemann that barbarism reigned in the country he loved.

This was one of the things Alison had intended to tell her son. She had wanted to tell Richard, too, of the terrible uncertainty she had suffered, not knowing if his father was alive or dead. The suicide was not confirmed

18

until after the war, when she had steeled herself to go to Berlin.

In the interim, she had lived for her child and her work. She was a passionate woman, and had not remained physically faithful to her son's father. But there was no love in the occasional sexual encounters she allowed herself. It was as though all the love she had to give to a man had been spent during those three weeks in Germany, in 1932.

'Uncle Maxwell was with me in Berlin. He met your father,' she told Richard.

'Very briefly,' Morton said.

He'd lie through his teeth for my mother! Richard thought. Then he remembered Alison once referring to their having been in Berlin together, and recalled the German theatre programme he had found in the trunk – and not strewn carelessly with the other old programmes: carefully preserved.

'Why didn't you stay there with him, if this man you say was my father wasn't able to leave?' he cross-examined Alison.

Morton replied for her. 'She was committed to appear in a play for me, Richard. Your mother has always been loyal to me.'

As you are to her, thought Richard, so you're helping her tell me this cock-and-bull story! 'Does this mythical German dad of mine have any relatives?' he enquired sarcastically.

Morton put an arm around Alison. 'If you don't change your tune, Richard, I shall have something very severe to say to you.'

The poor kid is like a hurt animal, lashing out in all directions, Emma thought. Couldn't Max see that? No! He was too besotted with Alison to see anything or anyone but her. If we were all together on a sinking ship, with only one lifebelt, Max would want Alison to have it, Emma reflected irrationally – feeling as if she were on that sinking ship at present. The close family unit they had been since Richard's birth had suddenly divided into two

19

camps – or so it felt. Max's defence of Alison was as aggressive as was Richard's reaction to what he had been told.

'I'm still waiting to hear if I've got any fairytale relations,' Richard prodded them, in the same sarcastic tone. 'Or did my Uncle Hansel and Auntie Gretel get lost in the Black Forest?'

'As a matter of fact, your German grandfather was an eminent surgeon,' Alison said.

'Did he get the Iron Cross for using Jews as guinea-pigs in the concentration camps?' said Richard snidely.

'That's quite enough of that,' Morton answered. And added, 'Your mother never met him. But I did – when I went to Berlin, after we heard that your father had disappeared. Herr Doktor Lindemann was one of the people I called on.'

'We understand that he died of pneumonia, during the war,' Alison said.

'And we know of no other relatives of your father's,' said Morton.

To the boy, the way they dispensed the information between them was as though they had rehearsed it.

'How very convenient for you,' he said. 'It means there is nobody I can check up with, doesn't it? Disappearances and pneumonia my eye! Where did you get the name Lindemann from? A German telephone directory? For some reason, you don't want me ever to know who my father was. Maybe he's married and you're scared I'll go and see him and cause a scandal for him and my mother – the one they avoided when I was born. I don't believe a word you two have said!' he blazed to Alison and Morton.

Then he fled from the room and, as always, it was Emma who went to calm him down.

CHAPTER FOUR

ON THE morning after their emotional scene, Alison rose early to breakfast with her son before he went to school.

'You look beautiful even when you've just got up, Mother,' he said when she joined him and Emma at the kitchen table.

'Thank you, darling,' said Alison, who had tossed and turned all night.

'It wasn't a compliment. Just an observation.'

Emma laughed, to ease the strain. 'It's a long time since you saw your mother at this hour, isn't it, Richard?' For Alison to rise at seven was unprecedented.

'And I appreciate the peace-gesture,' said Richard, reaching for the toast.

'I'm thankful you are speaking to me this morning,' Alison told him.

Richard gave her a smile, but there was no warmth in it. 'There's no point in my not doing, as we have to go on living together. Now may we please talk about something else?'

Emma hastened to do so. 'You haven't told me yet if there was anything special in the letter you got from Janet yesterday, Richard.'

'She sounded fed up, Auntie. Could we invite her here for a weekend, soon?'

'Certainly,' said Alison and Emma in unison. Emma's niece was dear to them both.

'It will be a break for her to get away from her parents for a couple of days,' Richard opined.

Emma dished up a fried egg and plonked the plate before him. 'A nice thing to say about my brother and sister-in-law! Conrad and Zelda are wonderful parents.'

'But I'm sure Janet doesn't exactly enjoy the way they quarrel about her.'

Conrad and Zelda Stein's differences of opinion about raising their daughter were legendary in the family. Zelda's over-anxiety amounted to an obsessive neurosis. Conrad did his best to counteract its effects upon Janet, at the expense of his relationship with his wife.

'Auntie Zelda would have liked to have a lot of children, but God only gave her one child,' Emma felt constrained to point out to Richard. 'That's why she makes such a fuss of her little girl.'

'Her little girl is fourteen,' was Richard's caustic reply. 'But what's the betting that her mother won't allow her to spend a weekend with us? It would mean letting Janet out of her sight!'

Alison agreed, but nevertheless telephoned Zelda that evening.

'Let our Janet travel to London and back on the train by herself?' was Zelda's horrified response to the invitation. 'I don't even allow her to go from Oldham to Manchester on her own.'

'Then you're storing up trouble for yourself,' said Alison, mindful of the trouble with her son that her own short-sightedness had brought her.

'Who are you, Alison, to give me advice about bringing up my child?' Zelda demanded. 'You've never been a full-time mother. Emma has done all the worrying for you.'

'Not quite all,' Alison retorted. 'But I didn't ring up to talk about me and you. I just thought it would be nice for Janet and Richard to get together. They've always been good pals, but only see each other when we come north for family occasions.'

'And there'll soon be a family wedding,' Zelda reminded her. 'I was sewing the silver beading on Janet's bridesmaid frock when you rang up. She and Richard will see each other in a few weeks' time.'

Richard appeared in the hall when Alison was replacing the receiver. 'She said no, didn't she?'

22

'Which is hardly a surprise.'

'When I think what it must be like to have Auntie Zelda for a mother, I'm glad I've got you.'

'This is certainly your day for paying dubious compliments!'

'It was just an observation, Mother. Like the one I made about you looking beautiful even when you've just got up.'

'Call it what you like,' said Alison dryly.

'And another,' Richard said, avoiding her eye, 'is that I wouldn't mind dispensing with my honorary uncle.'

Alison paled. Had he softened towards her, only to harden against Maxwell? 'Uncle Maxwell was upset last night, darling – as we all were. You must forgive him for sounding off at you the way he did.'

Richard's lips tightened. 'There's a good deal more for me to forgive him than that.'

CHAPTER FIVE

'RICHARD AND Janet will soon be grown-ups,' the family matriarch observed to Alison, while surveying her brood.

Alison glanced at the tall, slender lad and the petite, fair-haired girl wearing her first pair of high-heeled shoes, recalling them as toddlers playing together on the rug where they now stood conversing. 'One doesn't notice the years speeding by, Aunt Lottie. But oh, how they do!'

'And I'm now an old lady, with a grand-daughter getting married tomorrow.'

The clan had gathered for the event, and pre-wedding excitement mingled with the tobacco fumes in Lottie Stein's parlour. Tomorrow's bride was not present – but her mother was, and Lottie did not expect the harmony that had so far prevailed to last, on that account.

Clara did not let her down. 'Why did my daughter have to be a March bride?' she complained. 'I'll be lucky if the wind doesn't blow the feathers off my hat!'

'But if our Lila had been a June bride, you wouldn't have needed a new fur coat to wear for the wedding,' her husband pointed out.

'And I might not have been here for it,' said Alison. 'I'm hopeful that the play I'm about to appear in will have a long run.'

'We're well aware that we wouldn't have been honoured with your company if you were appearing in one now,' Clara told her scathingly. 'You didn't come to my Percy's *Bar Mitzvah*, did you?'

Her Percy, now a balding physician on the wrong side of thirty, gave her a long-suffering glance.

His uncle Conrad voiced the sentiments of the entire

24

family. 'Only Clara would still be harping on something that someone did, or didn't do, twenty years ago!'

'Eighteen years ago,' Clara corrected him. 'Don't make my son, who hasn't yet managed to find himself a wife, older than he unfortunately already is.'

Alison, who had long been Percy's confidante, comforted him with a warm smile. Only she knew that he had a Gentile girlfriend, whom he knew the family would never accept. Their attitude towards intermarriage had not budged an inch since the days when Alison's father became the black sheep after marrying her non-Jewish mother. It's remarkable that they eventually admitted me to the fold, she was thinking when Richard cut into her cogitation.

'Don't feel too bad about my mother having missed Percy's *Bar Mitzvah*,' he said to Clara. 'I doubt that she would cut a performance to attend my wedding.'

He isn't consoling Clara, he's jibing at me, Alison wryly thought. But her professionalism was something he had never understood. It was as though, since his early childhood, he had seen the theatre as a rival for her affection.

Lottie lightened the atmosphere with a joke. 'You're thinking of getting married already, Richard? So who is the lucky girl?'

The girl beside him joined in the family laughter, though she hoped it would be her. Though other boys pursued her – she had always been a beauty – for Janet Stein there was nobody like Richard. He had been special to her since they were tiny tots. And it seemed to her now that she had loved him all her life.

'Don't stand so close to the hearth, Janet,' her mother cautioned her. 'A red-hot coal could leap out and set fire to your frock.'

'It would have a job,' said Conrad caustically, 'to leap over the fireguard.'

'A person can't be too careful!' Zelda retorted.

'And if I weren't around to stop you, you'd wrap our Janet in cotton wool and then put her in a glass case.'

Janet gave her parents a placating smile, which she was

25

well-practised in doing. 'It's all right, Dad. It's too warm by the fire. I was just going to move away.'

Richard followed her to the window bay. 'How do you put up with it?' he asked quietly.

'I may not have to for much longer. I intend to audition for a place at RADA – but I haven't told anyone, yet.'

Richard eyed her with astonishment. 'The Royal Academy of Dramatic Art? But it's in London – your mother would have a fit!'

Janet absently fingered a leaf of the aspidistra that enhanced Lottie's old-fashioned parlour. 'If I let that stop me, I'll never be an actress, will I?'

'This is the first I've heard of your wanting to be one,' Richard replied.

'Your mother was here when I told the family, but she must have forgotten I said it, by now. It was right here in this room, at Grandma's seventieth birthday party,' Janet recalled. 'Before you came home from America. I did a couple of what Grandma calls my "recitations" – and your mother said afterwards that she thought I might be going to follow in her footsteps. Then everyone set upon her.'

'I bet they did, Janet! One theatrical in the family is enough for them.'

'But they're going to have another, and when I told them so there was such an uproar, I haven't mentioned it since.'

'What if you don't get a place at RADA?'

'I'll try to join a repertory company and get my training that way. Like your mother got hers with her family company. Her father trained with the company, too, didn't he?'

Richard thought of the boy in the photograph, whom he so closely resembled. 'So I understand.'

'I bet he never dreamt, when he left home to join the Players, that he'd end up marrying the great Gregory Plantaine's daughter,' Janet reflected. 'And you can't really blame him for changing his name to Plantaine, can you? It's always been an illustrious name in the theatre. They say that Gregory was one of the finest Shakespearean actors of his day.'

But Richard had not known until recently that Plantaine blood ran in his own veins; that the feeling he had for the theatre, which vied with his resentment of his mother's devotion to it, was inherited from the long line of thespians whence Alison came.

'I've never felt the urge to tread the boards, but I wouldn't mind directing,' he declared.

Janet gave him a warm smile. 'Then one day you can direct me in a play.'

'I shall look forward to that, Janet.'

It was a moment both would recall in years to come, and they would see themselves again as a starry-eyed boy and girl oblivious to the vicissitudes which were to line their paths.

'Do you visit your Grandma Plantaine often?' Janet asked.

'I've never met her.'

Janet then remembered hearing on the family grapevine that Alison was estranged from her mother, and observed: 'The nicest of people sometimes find it hard to get on with those they love. Dad told me he didn't know he had a cousin Alison until her father returned home for a deathbed scene. He also said that an occasional rift with Auntie Clara would be very welcome,' she added with a giggle.

'If I had to spend more time in her company than I do, I'd probably agree!' said Richard.

Clara was pacing the room, listing everything that could possibly go wrong with the wedding arrangements. 'If the bar dries up, I'll die of shame,' she capped it.

'Jews aren't drinkers,' Conrad reminded her. 'At your wedding, I was sent out to buy more lemonade.'

'Which wedding was that, Uncle? Her first or her second?' Percy enquired.

Though he did not know it, her first marriage, to his father, was of the shot-gun tradition and his question caused a momentary awkward silence among his elders.

27

Only his stepfather shared his blissful ignorance. 'This is a happy occasion,' that kindly man chided him. 'Not the time to remind your mam that my poor predecessor was killed in the Great War.'

'What were we saying when Percy interrupted the conversation?' Lottie hastily intervened.

'Clara was giving us her dramatic portrayal of mother-of-the-bride,' said Alison dryly.

'And a crack like that from my cousin the actress I can do without!' Clara exclaimed. 'It's a pity for my sake that your boss Mr Morton gave you time off from rehearsals to come to the wedding,' she added acidly.

'If you didn't want me to come, you shouldn't have invited me,' Alison replied in a frigid tone.

'Wanting has nothing to do with it,' Clara rapped back. 'You're family, aren't you, Alison?' she said, voicing the traditional code applied when compiling a guest list for a Jewish wedding, or a *Bar Mitzvah*. You invite your relatives whether you like them or not, she might as well have said.

'Mr Morton isn't my mother's boss,' Richard told her when he was able to get a word in. 'He's only her manager.'

'And also my dear friend,' Alison added.

Emma, who was now pouring tea, put down the pot. 'Mine, too.'

'Why are you two defending the man?' Clara said to them. 'I haven't accused him of anything.'

'Since when was it defensive to call someone a dear friend?' Emma asked.

But she had sounded defensive. Alison too – and they both knew it. Nor was this the first time in recent weeks that they had felt it necessary to counteract Richard's derisory attitude toward Morton.

Only my manager, indeed! Alison was thinking, though factually this was so.

It's as if, thought Emma, Richard is all of a sudden trying to nudge Max from his place in our life.

Clara was still looking for trouble. 'We should have

invited their dear friend to the wedding,' she said snidely to her husband. 'As neither of them has a man, we could have seated him between them at the dinner table.'

'Our Clara would have done us all a favour if she'd stayed at home to supervise her daughter's hen-party tonight!' Conrad exclaimed.

'She did my sister a favour by going out,' Percy said.

'And she would have done me a favour if she hadn't mentioned Mr Morton. That man has always been a fly in the family ointment,' Lottie could not stop herself from saying. She had met Morton only once, but had taken an irrational dislike to him long before then.

'May we please change the subject?' said Emma. 'This is supposed to be a celebration, not an inquest.'

Lottie exchanged a glance with Conrad, who was aware, as she was, of Emma's unrequited love for Morton. Was Conrad, too, thinking that if it weren't for Mr Morton Emma might now be living in Florida with a nice Jewish husband? But Emma still corresponded with her American gentleman and Lottie had not yet given up hope.

'Why don't we just talk about the price of fish?' said Clara. 'Or discuss what's on at the local cinema next week. In this family, that's the only way of staying on safe ground.'

It struck Richard, then, what dangerous ground a family gathering was. Like a minefield of secrets waiting to explode if somebody said the wrong thing. He had no doubt that his mother's secret was known by the elders in this room, and thought it remarkable that it had remained hidden from him. But he still did not know the whole secret: who his father really was. And tonight the air had been thick with all kinds of innuendo; somewhere contained within it, was there a clue?

Janet had seen his expression shadow. 'What's wrong, Richard?' She received no reply and slipped a comforting hand into his.

Richard could remember her doing so when they were little and someone had trampled on a castle he had built on Blackpool sands, during a family holiday. And in a way, he thought now, the same had happened again. Though his mother had told the lies, it was Morton whom Richard held responsible. Morton had told her to do it – and hearing Lottie call him the fly in the family ointment had finally ground Richard's image of him to dust.

He managed to smile when Emma handed him a cup of tea.

'Drink it while it's hot, it'll make you feel better,' Janet said to him, and he thought that if he could choose himself a sister, Janet would be her.

CHAPTER SIX

The Importance Of Being Earnest, in which Alison played Lady Bracknell, enjoyed the long run for which she had hoped, but, as always, she had after a while itched for a new theatrical challenge and did not mind when the play closed.

'What am I going to do next?' she asked Morton while they dined at the Ivy on a chill autumnal evening in 1949. 'Something exciting, please.'

Morton glanced at her cleavage and said lasciviously, 'With your shape, my dear, you could star in the *Folies Bergère* Revue that's on at the Hippodrome now.'

'I didn't mean that kind of exciting! And maybe I should start wearing high necklines.'

Morton averted his gaze. 'Please don't.'

He waved to an American impresario, who was in London to see if any of the West End's current offerings were worth transferring to his own territory; Morton went to see Broadway plays for the same purpose.

Alison, who had just been forcibly reminded of what she preferred to forget – that Morton still desired her – returned the conversation to a professional plane. 'How I wish we had a new British playwright of Arthur Miller's calibre, Maxwell.'

'Me, too. When I saw his *All My Sons* in New York, I thought how well you would play the role of the mother. I've heard that his *Death Of A Salesman* is a brilliant follow-up. But as I can't get my hands on it for you, Alison, and there are no new English plays worthy of you around, I'm thinking of reviving *The Vortex*.'

'With me as Mrs Lancaster – also a mother-role,' said

Alison ruefully. 'Why are you so keen for me to play a part for which I am, regrettably, so ill-cast?'

Morton patted her hand. 'I'm prepared to wager that one day Richard will realise what a wonderful mother he has.'

'If I play Mrs Lancaster,' Alison reflected, 'it will be the first time for many years that I've played a lady of my own generation.'

'Lady Bracknell is even more ancient than you are,' Morton teased her.

'Ageing-up for a role, Maxwell, is quite different from not needing to. But I've been fortunate to be able to get away with playing women younger than myself for longer than most actresses manage to.'

'I doubt that your public knows how old you are, Alison. Some women are the ageless kind, and you are one of them.'

'Then why do you want me to star in *The Vortex*?'

'Because you've not yet appeared in a Coward play. When they were premièred Gertie Lawrence had the monopoly and — '

'Never mind,' Alison interrupted. 'Ageless or not, for my own self-respect I shall have to make the transition to playing middle-aged mums like myself sooner or later. It may as well be now.'

Her eyes sparkled with anticipation. 'Florence Lancaster is a character I shall really be able to get my teeth into.'

'You sound positively carnivorous, my darling. But you will not be getting your teeth into it until you have had a good rest.'

'I don't need a rest. Nor do I want one.'

As always, when her personal life had gone awry, Alison's therapy was work.

As Morton well knew. 'Nonsense!' he said firmly. 'You look like a rag-doll, albeit a beautiful one. And the sun is still shining on the Riviera. A vacation would do neither of us any harm. I shall rent a villa for a couple of weeks. As it happens, Basil Breen, whom I'd like to direct *The Vortex* for us, is in the South of France until the end of the month; we could arrange to meet him, and discuss it.'

'Stop waving a carrot under my nose, Maxwell,' said Alison; Breen was her favourite director. 'I'm not in the mood to relax in a deckchair,' she added.

'That's exactly why you must. And Richard still has some of his school holiday left. Sunshine and sea air will do him good, too.'

Alison's expression tightened. 'Richard has already had two weeks in Blackpool, with Emma and our Oldham relatives. That's more than he deserves.'

Morton surveyed her for a moment. 'You're being too hard on the boy, Alison.'

'Am I?' she said stiffly.

The real-life drama that began in Alison's living room, eighteen months ago, was not yet resolved. Richard was still behaving as though Morton were the villain of the piece.

They rarely spoke of it – doing so was painful to both – but Morton did so now. 'Richard had to have a whipping-boy after learning he had been lied to, Alison. And I'm it.'

'That's Emma's theory, too. But why you, Maxwell, not me?'

'If he held you responsible, he couldn't respect you, could he?' Morton absently crumbled the bread on his side-plate. 'Not that I think he has rationalised his behaviour. He's too young for that. But it stands to reason, doesn't it, Alison, that a boy must be able to respect his mother. If he had to believe ill of you, I think his whole world would disintegrate. So he's attached the blame to me, as I said I made you deceive him.'

'You didn't exactly put it that way.'

'But that is how Richard has chosen to see it. Even mature adults – and he is far from that – are capable of making themselves believe the convenient thing to avoid being hurt.'

Alison smiled wanly. 'You ought to have been a psychoanalyst!'

'When you have all the pieces of a jigsaw, it isn't too difficult to put them together.'

'But one is still missing from this picture, Maxwell. Why is Richard prepared to believe ill of you, after all you have been to him?'

Morton fingered the lapel of his dinner jacket, and Alison saw his eyes sadden.

'Don't imagine I haven't asked myself that question; I wouldn't be human if I didn't. And I'm quite sure he would rather not believe ill of me. But he has to, in order to absolve you.' Morton managed to smile and lighten his tone. 'In time, he will see the whole matter in its true perspective. He'll ring me up and say, "How about coming to see a game of cricket, Uncle Maxwell?" as though nothing had ever gone wrong between us.'

'Meanwhile, he is giving you a terrible time.'

'And if I didn't care deeply for him, I wouldn't put up with it.'

Did Maxwell not know, Alison thought, that his putting up with it had made Richard realise what Alison had always known – that he was putty in the boy's hands.

There had been times in recent months when Alison had wanted to slap her son when he said something to undermine Morton. But she had remembered her mother once having raised a hand to her, and that she had never forgiven her for it. Richard has enough to forgive me for, she had counselled herself. But this made it no easier for her to witness the campaign he was waging to make Morton feel like an interloper whenever he came to the house.

'You're here again, are you?' he would say when Morton dropped in. 'Haven't you got anyone except us?' Or similar remarks, said in a joking way with serious intent.

Morton would reply with a silent, implacable smile. But the answer was no. Though Alison had not until now thought about it, he had no life outside his business but her own little family, of which time and all they had shared together had made him a part.

34

When she first met him he had been what was in the Twenties and Thirties described as 'a man about town', and a popular figure in the capital's social scene. More invitations to parties than he could possibly accept had poured through his letterbox, and he had often showed his face at several on one night.

Now, his socialising was limited to that involving business, and usually at lunchtime; more theatre deals were done at the luncheon table than at a desk. If he dined out, it was – like tonight – usually with Alison. As a man might after marriage, he had dropped out of the life that was his before Richard was born.

I ought not to have let it happen, Alison thought while they waited for their dessert to be served. But she had not seen it happening.

Because she was oblivious to the effect of her demanding nature upon those close to her, Emma would have said. There was more than a grain of truth in this. But Alison could not have been the great actress she undoubtedly was had the egocentricity she displayed not been present in her.

The personal self-doubt by which she was from time to time afflicted had never so much as touched her artistic belief in herself. Alison Plantaine had known from the time she was a small girl, watching the Plantaine Players from the wings, that she was destined to be what she had become; that she had something unique to give, and it was from this that what others called her ego had sprung.

Those with whom Alison came in contact either loved her or loathed her, and the latter were the majority. But her profession was one in which jealousies abounded and work-relationships lasted no longer than the fraught rehearsal period and the run of a play.

Though others formed lasting friendships, Alison never had. Her talent had elevated her at an early age to the plane inhabited by the very few, and she had learned to accept the respect laced with envy accorded her by those who would never achieve what she had. There were times when she yearned for the affection that theatre people

35

had for some of her peers – Sybil Thorndike, for instance. But Alison had long since faced the fact that her own charisma was not like Miss Thorndike's; that there was about herself an unapproachable quality that warned people off.

Was it there when I was a precocious child, or did I later acquire it as an armour against being hurt? she was thinking when the waiter brought the dessert. The naïve twenty-three-year-old who had come to London had trusted everyone. Several hurtful let-downs had taught her to be more selective. But if you were too wary, you ended up with a dearth of friends.

'You're miles away, Alison,' Morton said to her. 'Come back to the table and eat your fruit salad.'

'I was having one of my rare moments of self-examination,' she said, pouring cream onto the fruit. 'And it struck me that if I had expected less of people, how different my life might have been.' She gave Morton a thoughtful smile. 'Yours, too.'

'If you expected less of people, you wouldn't be Alison Plantaine. But where do I come into it?'

'It was thinking about you that set my mind on that track.'

Was this an oblique way of saying that had she married him, though it would not have been for her a love match, both of them might have been happier? Morton wondered. If so, it wasn't too late for them now.

Alison's next words snuffed out his flicker of hope.

'If you hadn't devoted yourself to me and Richard, to the exclusion of all else but your work, Maxwell, you might have found a woman who could have made you happy and given you the children I know you always wanted. You might even have had a son to eventually take over Morton Theatrical Enterprises, as you did from your father.'

She sipped some water, and Morton saw that tears were in her eyes. 'I ought not to have let you shoulder my burdens the way you have.'

She paused and put down the glass. 'If I'd had a circle

of friends, as most people have, there would have been others in London I could turn to, apart from you. But I'm not the sort who makes friends easily, and it has rebounded on you. On Emma, too.'

Remorse, like anger, enhances her beauty, Morton reflected. But whereas anger set her vivid appearance alight, emotion had lent a soulful purity to her face. Her hair, drawn back severely into a chignon, seemed fitting for the picture of penitence she now was.

'There is nothing for you to be conscience-stricken about, my dear,' he told her gruffly. 'I entwined my life with yours and Richard's of my own accord. You didn't trap me into it.'

'If I hadn't needed you, there'd have been no reason for you to do so,' Alison answered. 'But there was nobody but you and Emma. There still isn't.'

Morton patted her hand, as one might comfort a child standing alone in a playground full of children. 'Nobody has more than a handful of true friends, Alison. Those who think they have find out otherwise when they are in trouble.'

'I made that discovery in relation to myself a long time ago.'

'But the difference between you and most people – especially in the theatre – is that you let that discovery stop you from encircling yourself with acquaintances and calling them friends. A good many so-called friendships are nothing of the kind – but they are a means of keeping loneliness at bay, and for the majority that's what counts. You, on the other hand, demand depth and integrity in all your relationships, which is why you have so few.'

'Tell me something I don't know!' said Alison.

Morton paused while the waiter poured their coffee, before continuing what was beginning to sound to Alison like a lecture.

'Nor are you the sort, Alison, to make allowances for the shortcomings of others. To say, "Oh well, nobody is perfect," which, human nature being what it is, we are all required to say or think occasionally about those with whom we mix.'

'That doesn't mean I think I am perfect.'

'Heaven forbid that you should be! You would be a very boring lady,' said Morton with a smile. 'Instead of the most capricious one I know. But you are exemplary in the matter of integrity, and apply your own high standards to everyone else, which is the root of what we've been discussing. You are loyalty personified, too, my dear. When I think of all the offers you've received over the years to play plum roles for other producers — '

'How could I desert you, Maxwell?' Alison cut him short. 'It was you who brought me to London from the sticks.'

'As you are Alison Plantaine, you would have got here anyway.'

'That's beside the point.'

'But your loyalty to me through thick and thin isn't. We've shared a few flops in our time, haven't we?' Morton reminisced.

'And put a good face on, right here at the Ivy, when the curtain fell on them! But you always managed to get us back on the crest of the wave, didn't you, Maxwell?'

'I'm glad to see you are smiling again, my darling,' he said. 'And please don't let the arrival of your stepcousins ruin your evening.'

Alison looked up and saw that the Plantaine twins had just entered the restaurant. With them was Lucy's husband, Charles Bligh.

'How could it fail to?' she had time to reply before the trio stopped to speak to them, *en route* to their table.

In this theatreland mecca, Alison had no option but to submit to their false kisses. The gossip columnist seated within hearing distance would have a field day if Alison told the twins and the oily Mr Bligh to go to hell – which she felt like doing – and she thought, as she often did, that in public an actress could never stop playing a part.

Lucy was still playing the ingénue she was when

her widowed mother married Alison's uncle Oliver Plantaine, thirty-odd years ago, Alison noted with distaste. And Luke dispensing the boyish charm that hid the self-seeking individual he really was. Having them smile fondly at her was to Alison like being confronted by a couple of snakes.

'By the way, Alison, we've asked that lad of yours to join us on my yacht,' said Bligh, shifting his cigar from one side of his loose-lipped mouth to the other.

'The poor dear boy is fed up of mooning around with too much time on his hands,' Lucy said. 'So we thought we'd give him a treat for the rest of his school hols.'

Bligh pinched Lucy's over-rouged cheek. 'My little sweetheart is never happier than when she's making others happy.'

You mean than when she's making me unhappy! thought Alison. 'Richard didn't mention it,' she said.

'Probably because we only mentioned it to him when he dropped in to see us last night, but he'll get around to it,' said Luke.

Alison had not known Richard had seen the twins last night. Nor had she laid eyes on him today – he had left the house before she got up. But one could not keep a boy of sixteen under lock and key. He came and went, as his schoolmates were allowed by their parents to do, and Alison would not have had it otherwise. She and Emma had assumed it was schoolfriends with whom he spent his time. But he was probably seeing a good deal more of Luke and Lucy than Alison had supposed.

'Charlie's found me a smashing play, Alison darling,' Lucy cut into her thoughts. 'That's why he's taking me on a cruise, before rehearsals begin.'

'To fatten her up for a long run,' Bligh chuckled, slapping her behind.

Lucy gave him a little-girl pout that went with her frilly tulle frock. 'Isn't my Charlie naughty?'

Alison, who found him repulsive, managed to smile. How could Lucy bear to go to bed with so tasteless a man? But doing so had made her a star.

Morton would have liked to enquire what Lucy's new play was, but if Bligh had wanted him to know he would have told him. Like as not, it was one Bligh had deviously snatched from under some other impresario's nose, as he once did to me, Morton recalled. Bligh would wait until all was signed, sealed and delivered before making an announcement – but was already mentally rubbing his hands over the money he would make.

The man was known to be a shark in more respects than one, but fortune had, nevertheless, smiled upon him throughout his shady career. Morton could not remember Bligh ever having an outright flop.

'If you see Richard before we do, tell him we'll let him know what day we're leaving for the cruise,' Lucy said to Alison, 'and arrange to pick him up.'

'I'm afraid Richard will not be able to accept the invitation,' Alison replied.

'Oh, you're not going to play the heavy-handed mother, are you, darling?' said Luke with a reproving smile. 'It's time you stopped it, my love. Where do you suppose it's going to get you?'

'It really is time,' said Lucy, 'that you let that poor boy have a bit of fun.'

Alison could imagine what kind of fun it would be. Booze and girls, to turn a boy's head. What went on aboard Bligh's yacht was common gossip.

Morton was having similar thoughts, and said politely, 'I don't think it's quite the sort of vacation for a lad of Richard's age. But the invitation is appreciated nevertheless.'

'One would think old Maxwell were the boy's father!' joked Bligh, who did not care if Richard went along or not.

'As he hasn't one, and Alison appointed me his godfather, I've made it my business to watch out for him,' Morton coolly replied. 'But he is accompanying us to St Raphael for the rest of his school holiday – which puts paid to the matter.'

'Maxwell is renting a villa, so we can all soak up some

sunshine,' said Alison, though she had not, until that moment, had any intention of going to France. But it would now provide a valid reason for Richard's not joining the yacht party. Just a flat refusal to let him go would cause more trouble between herself and her son.

'As we shall be moored at Cannes, we may see you around,' Bligh said before departing.

'Maybe we should go to Italy, not France,' said Alison when she and Morton were recovering from the encounter.

'It will still be blazing hot there.'

'I would rather frizzle than risk Richard's setting foot on that yacht!'

'We shall have to forbid it, and hope that the way we've raised him will stand us in good stead,' Morton replied. 'You can't protect him for ever from the twins or any other bad influence, Alison. In the end, it's up to him and I don't see Richard letting us down.'

CHAPTER SEVEN

'IF YOU don't mind, I'd rather stay at home,' said Emma when she learned of the coming trip to France.

'When wouldn't you rather stay at home!' Alison exclaimed.

'I always come to the opening night of your plays, don't I?'

'And oh, what a favour that is,' said Alison with chagrin. 'You'll never change, Emma.'

'One gallivanter in the family is enough.'

'And only you could call the sporadic socialising I do nowadays gallivanting.'

Emma went on clearing the breakfast table. 'Stop getting at me, will you, Alison.'

'You need getting at. What will you do all alone here, for two weeks?'

'Things I don't have time to do when I'm busy with my usual routine. When you get back, you'll find three kinds of homemade jam, and a shelf full of pickles I've bottled myself — '

'You are impossible!' Alison interrupted her. 'Who needs three kinds of homemade jam and a shelf full of pickles?'

'More to the point,' said Emma, 'is what do you need me in France for? You said that a maid who also cooks comes with the villa.'

'Is that how you think we see you?' said Alison, sounding shocked.

Emma did not reply.

'You'd better believe, my dearest Emma, that you are a good deal more to the rest of us than how you seem to see yourself. And one good reason for you to come is they say travel broadens the mind,' Alison teased her.

'Living with you has already taken care of that.'

Alison smiled wryly. 'I suppose it has.'

'You suppose right! And I don't need another holiday. I've just had one at Blackpool.'

'With Conrad and Zelda – some holiday! How many rows did you have to referee?'

'Only one big one, when Richard let slip that they'd been on the Big Dipper the night Conrad took him and Janet to the Pleasure Beach. Zelda threatened to divorce Conrad if he ever took such a risk with Janet's life again.'

'I'd like to shake some sense into Zelda,' Alison declared. 'But I pity her, too. Thinking back, she was always a candidate for what she has become. Remember when she got so desperate to have a baby she snatched one from its pram?'

That incident had coincided with Alison's own need of a foster-mother for Richard during the first year of his life, and she had let Zelda have him. Fortuitously, Zelda then became pregnant: Conrad had feared she might refuse to give Richard back.

That was one time when Destiny was kind to all concerned, Alison reflected now, remembering how well it had finally worked out.

Emma returned her to the present. 'About coming to France, foreign travel isn't for me, Alison. When I went with you to America, the time you appeared on Broadway, I was seasick there and back.'

'The English Channel is a millpond compared with the North Atlantic,' said Alison, who was never seasick. 'And the crossing will be over before you know it.'

'I also get badly bitten by insects,' Emma added to her protesting.

'They find Maxwell tasty, too. You can take some calamine lotion with you, to stop the itching, like he does.'

'I'd rather prevent the itching. By not going. Clara told me that when Lila went to Paris on her honeymoon she got bitten. And the weather wasn't even warm in March.'

'It must have been a bed-bug,' said Alison with a giggle.

'Lila and her husband also got ill from drinking the

water,' Emma relayed, 'and had to stay cooped up in their hotel room most of the time.'

'On their honeymoon, they would have done anyway.'

'Really, Alison!' said Emma, as she did whenever Alison made a risqué remark.

Close though we are, there are levels upon which Emma and I can't communicate, Alison reflected. Because Emma had never slept with a man, nor was she as broadminded as she believed. But she had managed to stretch her mind to accommodate what went against her conventional conditioning when Alison conceived Richard, and Alison was thankful for that.

'Have you finished listing the reasons why you're not coming to France?' Alison asked her.

'How many more do you require?'

'Only the real one.' Alison had sensed that there was more to Emma's wish to opt out of the trip. 'If you wanted to come, you would, despite everything you've said.'

'All right. I don't want to come.'

'Could it be because you don't relish being under the same roof as Maxwell and Richard?'

Emma sat down at the table and said bitterly. 'Who would?' She smoothed a wrinkle in the gingham table-cloth that complemented the blue-and-white willow pattern china on the dresser. 'Max isn't a young man. And he's had a heart condition for years.'

'It is only what they call a murmur,' Alison tried to reassure her. 'My uncle Oliver has that condition too. So far as I know, it has caused him no trouble, or the twins, who spare me no anxiety and know how fond of him I am, would certainly have told me. And I've never known it bother Maxwell.'

'But even a man with a perfect heart could be made ill by what Max is being subjected to by Richard,' Emma declared with concern. 'And I'm afraid of how it's going to end, Alison.'

'Being dramatic and over-imaginative, darling, is my prerogative, not yours.'

'Are you saying you're not worried about it?'

44

'You should know better than that. But I've come to think that Maxwell's attitude – painful though the matter is to him – is the only one possible. We must just sit tight and wait for Richard to get what's eating him out of his system. After the chat Maxwell and I had about it over dinner, last night, I'm more hopeful that all will come right.'

'In my opinion,' said Emma, 'what's eating Richard is he thinks Max has you under his thumb, that Max is stopping you from telling him who his father really was. Richard still doesn't believe he is the son of a German.'

'He doesn't want to believe it.'

'And who can be surprised? The Nuremberg trials weren't that long ago. I can remember Richard reading the newspaper reports – and the look on his face. He's an impressionable boy; and I'm a sensible woman, but if I didn't know what Richard Lindemann went through at the hands of the Nazis, nobody would get me to accept there's such a thing as a good German,' said Emma with feeling.

She was not given to delivering diatribes. Alison could recall her doing so only once before: when Emma learned Alison was to appear at the Berlin festival she had tried to convince her that it was wrong for her to entertain audiences in which there would be Nazis, from whom those German Jews with foresight had already begun fleeing.

It was on our thirty-second birthday, Alison remembered. They were born on the same August day, and Morton usually gave them a shared celebration. On the one Alison was now recalling, he had ordered a hamper from Fortnum's and taken them for a picnic on Hampstead Heath. But the outing was marred by Emma's insistence that Alison was putting professional commitment before personal principles by appearing in Berlin.

Not until Alison arrived in the German capital and saw the burgeoning barbarism for herself did her own Jewish blood rise to the surface and make her feel as Emma did.

'Did I ever tell you that I walked out of a big party in Berlin, though I was the guest of honour, when I discovered that the host was a Nazi?' she said to Emma now.

Emma shook her head.

'I was introduced to Goering there,' Alison said with a reminiscent shudder. 'I ought to have spat in his eye!'

'On behalf of your Jewish father.'

'No. On my own account – though until I went to Berlin, I felt the sting of anti-Semitism only on my father's account. That's why I shall never forget that party, Emma. It was the night I found out I am my father's daughter in every sense of the word. If I'd listened to you and not gone to Germany, I might have lived out my years without ever knowing.'

'If you'd listened to me, you wouldn't have met your Waterloo.'

'I prefer to think of Richard Lindemann as the love of my life. Which returns us to my son not wanting to believe his father was a German,' said Alison with a sigh.

'It's going to take generations for that nation to regain the respect they've lost,' was Emma's reply.

'I doubt that it will take that long for Richard to regain his for Maxwell.'

'If it does,' said Emma, 'Max will by then be kicking up the daisies. I just hope the way Richard is treating him doesn't hasten the day.'

Emma, who could never remain idle for long, rose to begin peeling vegetables for the stew she was making for their evening meal, which she would put to simmer in the oven all day.

'Shall you make us some dumplings with the stew?' Alison asked irrelevantly.

'No. They're Richard's favourite and I don't feel like giving him a treat.'

Alison had to smile. 'A moment or two ago, you were pleading his case.'

'That doesn't mean I forgive him for distressing Max. Or for what he said to me the other day.' Emma put down her vegetable knife and stared through the window at a squirrel clambering up the apple tree in the back garden. 'I wasn't going to tell you, Alison, but I had better.

Richard said he would find a way of making Max pay for what he'd done.'

'That's just kid talk, Emma.' Alison helped herself to a carrot and bit into it. 'I'm no happier about the present situation than you are, but I haven't got into the state you have about it – which I don't recall you doing about anything ever before. You must come to France – you definitely need a break.'

'What I definitely need a break from would be going with me. So if you don't mind, I'll stay here.'

Thus it was that Richard set forth on his first trip alone with Alison and Morton. It was also his first continental holiday and he approached it with mixed feelings.

'If we had more time to spare, we could have stopped over in Paris. But we'll take Richard there sooner or later,' Morton said to Alison on the Channel steamer.

'I'm grateful for the two weeks in St Raphael you are allowing my mother to spend with me,' Richard said. And added, 'She and I have never had a holiday together before.' What a pity you have to be with us, his glance implied.

'Wherever,' said Morton, 'did you get the idea that I allow, or don't allow, your mother to do things?'

'If you don't know the answer to that, I must leave you to figure it out,' Richard replied.

They were seated on deck and Alison wrapped her cashmere travel-cape closer around her, against the wind and brine. She had had to bite her tongue in order not to reprimand Richard for his rudeness. Her promise to Morton that she would behave as though nothing was amiss was difficult to keep. He was huddled in his overcoat, trying to keep his cigar alight. Richard was sprawled in the deckchair between them, staring out to sea – and spreading a pall of gloom on either side of him, Alison thought with asperity. How was Maxwell managing to sustain that unruffled veneer?

She thought it must surely crack when Richard said, 'I would much rather have accepted Mr Bligh's invitation. It is only to please my mother, Uncle Maxwell, that I'm going to stay in your villa.'

But Morton let the insult wash over him. 'So long as you enjoy yourself, Richard, it isn't important who you are trying to please,' he said pleasantly.

'And the way for me to do that,' said Richard, 'is to spend most of my time in Cannes. Luke told me I can get there from St Raphael by bus and visit them on the yacht.'

Morton gave him a friendly smile and kept his tone even. 'We would prefer you not to go anywhere near that yacht, Richard.'

Richard stiffened. 'When I rang up to say how sorry I was that I couldn't join them, Lucy told me they'd be happy to have all of us go aboard for a drink whenever we felt like doing so.'

'That was most kind of her,' said Alison. 'But, as I'm sure you are aware, Uncle Maxwell and I have no intention of accepting the invitation.'

'And what,' Morton inquired, 'is all this about you going aboard for a drink, my boy?'

'Whenever he calls me "my boy", I know I'm in for a lecture!' Richard exclaimed to Alison.

'You obviously require one, as you seem to think it's all right for you to begin imbibing alcohol at your age,' she replied.

Richard gave her the first long-suffering smile she had ever received from him. 'I've been imbibing alcohol for some time, Mother dear.'

'I beg your pardon?' said Morton.

'The Plantaine twins aren't stuffed-shirts,' Richard informed him. Like you, his accompanying glance said. 'They gave me my initial nip when I was fourteen. It almost choked me, of course – but it doesn't any more.'

Alison could cheerfully have choked the twins.

'I have a whisky-and-soda with them quite often, nowadays,' Richard revealed.

'I'm relieved to hear that you only have one.' Morton told him. 'And if you'll take the advice of a chap who got nauseously ill from having several, when he was your age, you'll stick to one.'

'Aren't you going to forbid me to have any at all?'

48

'Since when was I the forbidding kind?'

'Since I found out you forbade my mother to tell me I'm her son.'

'Advised would be a better word,' Alison said.

Richard gave her a tortured look. 'What does the word matter? It came to the same thing in the end. I grew up not knowing, didn't I? What matters is cause and effect.'

He got up and went to lean on the ship's rail.

'For one so young, he has a succinct way of putting things,' said Morton.

'I've always known he has his father's intellect,' Alison forlornly replied.

Morton smiled. 'He certainly didn't get his ability to whittle things down to their bare essence from you.'

'I wonder,' Alison mused, 'when his education is completed what Richard will do.'

'Join Morton Theatrical Enterprises,' Morton replied. 'What else?'

Alison realised, then, that this had long been Morton's dream. A shiver of foreboding rippled through her. 'I wouldn't count on it, Maxwell dear.'

But Morton, for once, preferred to be an ostrich. 'By the time Richard is ready to begin his career, his present resentment will be long forgotten. Meanwhile, as you and Emma and I agreed, we must just sit tight and wait for it to pass.'

While you go on turning the other cheek, thought Alison – of which she was forcibly reminded that evening.

Morton had arranged for them to travel to the Côte d'Azur on the Blue Train, which he considered suitably luxurious for Alison and her image.

'You'll find the food second to none,' he told Richard in the dining car.

Richard put down the menu which he had been perusing. 'Is there nowhere you haven't eaten? And nothing you haven't done?'

It was one of the moments when Alison felt like slapping him; but Morton's mask of implacability remained intact.

49

'In my line of work, Richard, a man gets around. And it gives me a lot of pleasure to be retracing some of my footsteps with the two people for whom I care most in the world.'

Richard averted his gaze to the window and watched the countryside through which they were speeding merge into the gathering dark, as night fell. What a mealy-mouthed hypocrite Uncle Maxwell was, saying what he just had after what he had done!

'What would you like for your first course?' Morton asked him.

'You can decide. Like you do about everything else,' Richard replied.

But during the meal he managed to put Morton's treachery from his mind, and allowed himself to fantasise that he was no different from any other boy. Going on holiday with his parents, like the pimply French youth across the aisle, whom he had heard call the stout couple with him 'Maman' and 'Papa'.

He probably thinks I'm with my parents, Richard thought. And how he wished that were so. That he was part of an ordinary family – but he had always wished that, and been embarrassed when a schoolmate once asked him why his mother called herself Miss Plantaine.

Richard had replied that this was customary among actresses, be they married or not – which was true. But he would have liked his mother to be a married lady, and as he grew older became puzzled about why she was not. She was famous and beautiful, and a warm and loving person, and Richard was sure that many proposals must have come her way. Why had she chosen not to marry?

These were still his thoughts while they waited to be served with coffee, and he saw Morton silently gazing at Alison, with something akin to worship in his eyes. Uncle Maxwell is in love with her, Richard realised with a sud-denness that almost caused him to knock over a water carafe the steward had not yet removed. The realisation was followed, in a blinding flash, by the idea that Morton might be his father.

CHAPTER EIGHT

EMMA CAME home from shopping in Highgate Village and found her brother pacing the garden path.

'Conrad! What are you doing in London?'

'Can't a chap visit his favourite sister?' Conrad eyed her with affection and kissed her cheek. 'I'll tell you why I'm here while you make me a cup of tea, our Em.'

'I didn't think it was just a social call – on a working day. And without letting me know you were coming,' Emma replied.

Conrad took her laden basket while she opened the front door. 'What on earth are all these plums and lemons for?'

'To make jam and lemon cheese. Anything else you'd like to know!'

'Only why you haven't reported your out-of-order telephone. I did it for you, by the way. Not being able to get through was why I'm here unannounced,' said Conrad as they entered the house.

'The phone isn't out of order. I left it off the hook,' said Emma.

'What on earth for?'

'Haven't you ever felt you didn't want anyone or anything to bother you?'

Conrad hung up his raincoat and gave her a bleak smile. 'That's how I feel most of the time.'

'But I'm glad to see you,' Emma assured him.

'And I you, our Em.' He replaced the telephone receiver on its cradle. 'No point in leaving it off, now your peace has been disturbed.'

'This might be Alison's house,' he said, following her into the kitchen, 'but it has your inimitable touch.'

51

'I like things spick and span.'

'And homely,' Conrad added, 'which was what I meant.' He watched Emma put the kettle on to boil and get out some cups and saucers, in her unflurried, efficient way, and thought, There's nobody like her. Just being with Emma always made him feel better.

'I still miss having you around,' he said, 'though you've been gone from Oldham for nearly twenty years.'

They exchanged a sibling smile. As a boy and girl they were always close and the bond was still there.

Emma warmed the pot before spooning tea into it. Like their late father, her brother was the kind who thought the family business could not function in his absence. Why had he left the store, to come to London? Something must be wrong.

'I have to talk to Alison,' he said, divining her thoughts.

'What about?'

'My darling daughter,' he answered. 'Whom I've just found out is not the straightforward girl she has always seemed.'

'I find that hard to believe, Conrad.'

'Me, too. But I have to believe the evidence of my eyes. I found an application form to audition at a drama college, in Janet's room. I'd run out of notepaper and went to borrow some from her desk, while she and Zelda were out.'

'But as she hadn't hidden the form where you couldn't possibly find it, she is not as underhand as you are making out,' Emma defended her niece, though she was shocked by what Conrad's discovery implied.

'Deceit is deceit, Emma, and, thanks to Alison, there's been too much of it in our family.'

Emma ignored the reference to Alison. 'Applying to audition doesn't mean Janet will get a place, Conrad. She is probably keeping it to herself rather than upset you and Zelda now about something that might not happen.'

'But applying without so much as mentioning it to us proves how deep she is,' Conrad tersely answered. 'I had no idea she was even thinking of it. That's what hurts the most.'

'Do you really expect to share all your daughter's secrets?'

'I didn't think our Janet had any.'

'So you've been proved wrong.' Emma brewed the tea. 'And in a ménage like yours, with an only child who has always had to tread carefully so as not to upset her mother, or cause trouble between her parents, it's inevitable that the child keeps a lot to herself.'

'What you're saying is that Zelda and I have asked for what we've got. Maybe there's something in that – but it isn't my fault.'

'I'm not apportioning blame, Conrad.'

'But in the matter of Janet wanting to be an actress, I am! This whole damned mess is Alison's doing,' Conrad exclaimed. 'And I've come to ask her to try to undo the damage she's done. She must tell Janet that the stage isn't for a homeloving girl like her. Janet wouldn't even be considering it if Alison hadn't encouraged her.'

'So far as I know, Alison has done no such thing. But you'll have to discuss it with her when she gets back from France. She's on holiday at the moment, with Richard and Max. I'm afraid you've had a wasted journey.'

'No, I haven't, love. I've seen you. But why didn't you go with them, Emma?'

'You know me, I'm a real stay-at-home,' she said with a shrug.

Emma turned away to pour the tea, but Conrad had seen her expression shadow. All was not well with her, but he was not surprised. Our Em tries to fool herself and the family up north that she's happy with her lot, he thought. But even an angel – and Emma was not quite that – would find it hard to live, year in, year out, with Alison Plantaine. Sooner or later, one way or another, the rot was bound to set in. Had that process begun? Emma was the sort who thrived upon being needed – but there was a difference between being needed and being used.

'If you ever get fed up with living with Alison, our Em, you can always come back to Oldham,' he told her with feeling.

'If I haven't got fed up yet, I'm not likely to,' was her cryptic reply. 'If I strike you as being a bit down in the dumps at present, Conrad, it's because our little family is going through a difficult time.'

Conrad had not, until then, viewed Emma, Alison and Richard as a family.

'Alison and Max and I are having a bit of trouble with Richard,' she went on.

Morton is part of their set-up, Conrad registered. And what an odd set-up it was. Given the precarious triangular relationship of unrequited love contained in it – Emma's for Morton, and Morton's for Alison – Conrad marvelled that it had lasted for so many years. What would it take, he wondered, to detonate such a potentially explosive situation? Had one of the two women been anyone other than his selfless sister, it would surely have exploded long ago.

'What's Richard been up to?' he enquired with a smile that masked his thoughts.

'There's nothing you could do to help if I told you, and right now, you seem to have enough trouble of your own,' Emma answered.

Then the telephone rang, and Conrad saw her tense. As though she is expecting bad news, he thought when she went to the hall to answer it.

She was gone for several minutes, and returned looking immensely distressed.

'It was Alison,' she said. 'Max is in hospital. And I'm not surprised.'

'Was he ill before they went to France?'

'He's been under a lot of strain, and I saw something like this coming,' Emma replied. 'He collapsed late last night, and Alison feared it was a heart attack. Thank God it wasn't – just over-exhaustion, the doctor told her. But they are keeping him under observation and making sure he rests.'

54

Emma kept the details of Morton's collapse to herself. Conrad would be shocked to hear of Richard's part in the matter; that Max had had to forcibly remove him from Bligh's yacht, the worse for drink.

'I'm amazed that you haven't rushed upstairs to pack your case and fly to France,' Conrad could not stop himself from saying.

'So am I,' she answered. 'But that wasn't a nice thing to say, was it, Conrad? It makes me wish I'd never told you how I feel about Max.'

'You didn't tell me. Mother got it out of you and I happened to be there at the time. But I had guessed long before then.'

'Just so long as Max never guesses,' said Emma wanly. 'Alison would like me there, and I nearly said I would go. Then I thought, what's the point? He's being well looked after in the hospital and his condition isn't serious. And Alison will visit him. What would he want me there for?'

Poor Emma, Conrad thought. 'You've made the right decision,' he said. And added, 'Would you like me to stay here and keep you company for a day or two? Until you pull yourself together?'

Emma smiled. 'I haven't fallen apart – I've had too much practice in not doing.' She went to kiss her brother's cheek. 'But I'm touched by the offer.'

'Thank goodness you didn't accept it, or in my absence the business could fall apart.'

CHAPTER NINE

'IF YOU hadn't stormed out of the villa when Uncle Maxwell said he was looking forward to you punting us on the river at Oxford, none of this would have happened,' Alison said to Richard.

They had briefly left the hospital to stroll on the sunlit Croisette, and Richard gave her a surly glance.

'Are you saying I have to sit the Oxford exam, and go there if I get a place, just because he wants me to?'

'What he wants for you, Richard, is the best of everything.'

End of conversation! thought Richard – so far as his mother was concerned, but he had more to say. 'That doesn't give him the right to dictate to me, Mother. You've allowed him to do so for as long as I can remember. Also to you, if I may say so.'

'You may not say so!'

'That won't stop me from thinking it.'

He wants me to side with him against Maxwell and I can't, thought Alison wretchedly. What a stressful week this had been. An uneasy peace had reigned at the villa until last night, when Morton unwittingly brought it to an end. Unwittingly, because he had taken it for granted that Richard wanted to go to Oxford.

But nothing could be taken for granted about Richard any more, Alison was discovering – except that he would run for comfort to the Plantaine twins, who were ever lurking in the wings.

'Your trouble,' she told him, 'is you don't appreciate who your real friends are. And you will never have a better one than Maxwell Morton.'

'If you say so, Mother,' Richard replied enigmatically.

The idea that Morton was his father was by now firmly rooted in his mind; a father who did not wish to own him.

It was a fantasy lent substance by facts and Richard had spent the week mooning on the beach, considering them. That Morton had arranged his education and his wartime evacuation to America was not the least of it, he thought now, stealing a glance at his mother as they strode along.

He curbed the impulse to ask her if Uncle Maxwell paid his school fees and said instead, 'I've sometimes wondered why he takes such a great interest in me.'

Alison halted at a pavement café near to the Casino Municipale. 'Because you are very dear to him, Richard. Your lack of perception astonishes me,' she added when they had seated themselves at a table beneath the striped awning.

What a pity, thought Richard, I can't tell her I am a good deal more perceptive than she would wish. 'But why am I so dear to him?' he enquired. It was like playing a game of cat and mouse with her – but what she deserved!

Alison gave him a cold glance. 'I have recently had cause to wonder that myself. A boy who behaves as you have to him would not be thought endearing by anyone. And to crown it by boarding that yacht and getting drunk, as you did!'

'I wasn't drunk, I was only a bit tipsy. And I'm entitled to visit my friends.'

'If they were your friends, they would not be encouraging you to drink at your age.'

'They didn't encourage me. I helped myself to the whisky. And I'd have got back from Cannes to St Raphael under my own steam. You and Uncle Maxwell didn't have to come and fetch me.'

Alison thought it more likely that he would have spent the night on the yacht – in the arms of one of the girls from whose midst Morton had found it necessary to physically remove him. She had remained on the quayside, but had witnessed the degrading scene.

'What a fool he made of me in front of my friends!' Richard re-lived it.

'If you'd gone with him quietly, your dignity would have remained intact,' Alison answered. 'Given that you were in your cups.'

She gave the English couple eyeing her with interest from a nearby table her dazzling, public smile and smoothed a wrinkle from her white linen skirt.

She was wearing a black silk blouse with it, and a crimson straw hat tilted fetchingly over her eyes. 'That outfit becomes you,' Richard digressed.

'Thank you. But being a troublemaker does not become you. You are responsible for that dear man being in hospital,' Alison crisply replied.

'I'm sorry he was taken ill, but I refuse to accept responsibility for it. The chain of events that led to his collapse was begun by him – not me. And if he goes on trying to organise and supervise my life, it will lead to further trouble.'

He rose from his chair. 'Now if you'll excuse me, I've had enough of your recriminations.'

'Sit down,' Alison hissed. She waited for him to do so. 'How dare you stalk off and leave me sitting here? I have already been recognised, as I am wherever I go. Upset though I am, I have to maintain my image – and you must not display the disrespect you just did.'

'The price of fame!' said Richard sardonically.

Just part of the price, thought Alison wanly. Richard would never know how dearly she had paid for her success. Wasn't she paying now for the long-ago lie she had told to protect her career?

Richard, too, she thought, with a surge of love for him.

'What's all this?' he said when she tenderly touched his cheek. 'A public show of affection, lest my attempt to depart abruptly gets reported in the *Daily Express*?'

'No, as a matter of fact. But when I think what could be made of Maxwell dragging you protesting from that floating den of vice, I go cold!' Alison was stung to retort. 'And you are never to put us in such a scandalous position again.'

'Who do you mean by "us", Mother? You and me?

Or you and him? And it strikes me that that man would go to any lengths to avoid a scandal.' Or he would have acknowledged his son, instead of only treating me like one, Richard reflected.

Alison, though she was seething with anger, managed to keep her voice low. 'I won't have you referring to Maxwell as "that man". Who do you suddenly think you are?'

The trouble is, I suddenly know who I am, thought Richard. But I daren't tell you I know. Nor are you ever likely to admit it to me, and there's always going to be this terrible, unspoken thing between us. Like an abyss we are unable to cross – created by that man!

Alison ordered another *orange-pressé* for Richard, and some more *café-filtre* for herself. She had not slept a wink last night, most of which was spent at the hospital while Morton underwent medical tests – with her hiccuping son beside her. She felt like a limp rag – but the culprit looked fine, she noted sourly.

Richard was watching the passing parade. Was the overdressed lady escorted by a young man in a yachting cap his aunt? Or he her gigolo? The variety of imponderable and improbable relationships abounding on the Riviera had not escaped Richard, nor the flattery paid him by females old enough to know better, aboard Bligh's yacht.

'If only you would try to be your old self again with Uncle Maxwell,' Alison appealed to him.

Richard wished he could tell her that his old self could not be resurrected, now he knew who his real self was. That the affection he still had for Morton made losing respect for him the more hard to bear.

'If only you could see things from my point of view,' he countered.

'You have yet to convince me your point of view is reasonable.'

'Is it unreasonable to object to someone who has no rights over me acting as though he has?'

'If that is how you now construe Maxwell's devotion

to you, I must wait for you to recover your senses,' was Alison's sad reply.

And that's that, thought Richard. She had failed to grasp the opportunity to tell him the truth. She was probably scared that Morton would really have a heart attack if she revealed their secret – and such a weary expression was in her eyes, Richard could not help feeling sorry for her.

'It's all right, Mother,' he said. 'It's him I'm angry with, not you.'

Alison sipped some coffee and managed to smile, though she felt like weeping. 'You are doing him a dreadful injustice, Richard,' she declared. 'In the whole world there could be no finer man.'

'If you think so much of him, I'm surprised you haven't married him,' Richard dared to say. And having said it, in for a penny! he thought. 'I'm not too young to have noticed he's sweet on you, Mother.'

'Where did you get that expression from?' said Alison to cover her confusion.

'It's a relic from my spell in the States,' Richard told her. And there were times, like now, when he wished he could turn back the clock to those happy years with the Baxter family.

Alison was wishing Richard would stop giving her such piercing glances, as though he was trying to read her mind. 'A number of men have been what you call sweet on me,' she said lightly.

'I don't doubt it. You're a good-looking broad.'

'And that is enough American jargon for one afternoon! But before we change the subject, Richard, you might like to know that the only man I've ever really loved was your father.'

Richard let the reference to the mythical German pass, with the contempt that trying to pull the wool over his eyes deserved.

Alison noted his curled lips. 'You still don't believe he was your father, do you?'

'No. And I never shall.'

60

A short silence followed, then Alison paid the bill and glanced at her watch. 'It's time for us to go back to the hospital – and please don't upset the patient when we get there, Richard.'

'But I shall have to upset him soon, when I tell him I'm not going back to school.'

'I beg your pardon?' said Alison.

'There's no point in my plodding through two years of sixth-form studies if I'm not going on to university,' he told her, voicing the thought that had just crystallised in his mind.

Alison snapped her handbag shut and pulled on her immaculate white gloves. What would her headstrong son present her with next? She had not known he was headstrong until recently. He had obviously inherited that trait from her, and now she must try to put the brakes on *him*.

'You have never been a plodder, Richard,' she declared. And added, feeling as though she were onstage playing a Victorian mama, 'Nor are you yet of an age to make your own decisions, or to know what's good for you. You must be guided by those who do.'

'Uncle Maxwell, you mean!'

'In his opinion, you are bright enough to get to any college in the land.'

'I don't care what he thinks.'

'Nor what I think, apparently.'

'Not when you sound like his mouthpiece, Mother. Which, when it comes to me, is how you sound most of the time. Whatever he says, goes, and you can't deny it. You haven't even asked me what I intend to do instead of going back to school.'

'You can tell me while we walk back to the hospital.'

'I can tell you now – in one sentence,' said Richard. 'I want to direct plays.'

They had begun the return stroll along the Croisette and Alison stopped in her tracks.

Richard took her arm and they resumed walking. 'Is that such a strange ambition for someone with Plantaine blood in his veins?' he said with a wry smile.

61

Since returning from America at the age of twelve he had shown no inclination toward a career in the theatre – and now this! Alison had not yet recovered from her astonishment. 'Well, well,' was all she was capable of saying. But she felt like jumping for joy.

'I've always been interested in how a production springs to life,' Richard told her. 'It isn't just the acting that makes it happen, is it?'

'You had better not say that to any actor or actress but me! Or you won't be a very popular director. Artistes are egotistical and temperamental, they need careful hand-ling, Richard.'

'I've had plenty of practice,' he said with the cheeky, lop-sided smile that had not lit his face for some time.

Richard Lindemann's smile – but Alison did not risk ruining this rare moment of unity by saying so.

While Richard went on talking, revealing a theatrical insight she had not known he possessed, they drew closer in spirit than they had ever been before.

'But you must surely understand, darling,' said Alison when he paused for breath, 'that sixteen is far too young for you to begin directing.'

'I don't expect to be allowed anywhere near a stage at first, except perhaps to sweep it,' he answered. 'Which I wouldn't mind doing, if necessary. I'll take any menial job that's going, to get my foot in the door.'

Alison could feel the excitement emanating from him and laced her fingers through his as they neared the hos-pital. 'When Uncle Maxwell hears about this, I'm sure he won't insist on your staying on at school. He'll probably find a niche for you in his organisation.'

Richard removed his hand from hers. 'You're still talking as though I require his permission, Mother. As though, if he says no, I won't be allowed to leave school.'

'It won't arise, Richard. I'm certain he will say yes.'

'I don't care a fig what he says.'

They had halted on the hospital steps, their brief close-ness gone.

Alison averted her gaze from her son's hostile face to the

two Catholic priests who stood conversing in the foyer. 'Uncle Maxwell could help you get started, Richard. It would do no harm for you to spend some time in his office and learn how a production gets put together from start to finish – which few directors bother to interest themselves in.'

'The last thing I'm prepared to do is take a leg-up from him. But what you just said isn't a bad idea,' said Richard thoughtfully. 'And Uncle Maxwell isn't the only impresario I know.'

Alison's hand fluttered to her throat. 'You're not thinking of asking Charles Bligh for a job?'

'Why not? All's fair in love and war, Mother.'

CHAPTER TEN

CONRAD'S CONFRONTATION with Alison was delayed
until the summer of 1950. In the interim, Janet had won a
place at RADA, and Richard had joined Bligh Productions.

'I'm surprised Richard didn't go to work for Mr
Morton,' said Conrad on the humid Sunday he travelled
south to see Alison.

She gazed through the living-room window at the glint-
ing sliver of Highgate Ponds visible between the trees in
her front garden.

'That is what I would have wished, Conrad. But you
must surely know by now that parents don't always get
their wishes granted.' Alison turned to look at him and
noted his haggard appearance. 'Or you wouldn't be in
London now, would you?'

Emma had brought them some coffee and left them
alone. But Alison did not blame her for not wanting to get
involved in their differences. When Conrad telephoned to
say he was coming, she had steeled herself for a battle –
and the silence in the room, now, was like the calm before
a storm, she thought.

'This visit is a last stand on your part to use me to curtail
Janet's career, isn't it?' she challenged her cousin. If there
was going to be a set-to, she wanted to get it over.

'What career?' he answered tersely.

'The one she will surely have in the theatre. I recognised her talent years ago.'

'And if you hadn't opened your mouth and said so,
none of this would have happened,' Conrad flashed.

'If that's what you wish to think, go ahead and think
it,' Alison answered. 'But as I am an actress myself, I
know differently. A gift like Janet's – and that's what it

64

is – is like a flame burning inside one. A fire that requires no fanning — '

'Stop giving me a performance, Alison!' Conrad interrupted impatiently. 'You never say a word without sounding as if you're on the stage. And lately, there are times when my daughter sounds the same. Since she got that scholarship, Janet isn't the same girl.'

'What you mean is you've suddenly discovered there is more to her than you thought. And that she has a mind of her own.'

'Well, she certainly never showed it before.'

'And you should ask yourself why.'

'She's turned out to be a dark horse is why,' said Conrad with distress.

'But why did she have to be one?"

'I didn't come here for you to give me a grilling, Alison.'

'I know why you came – as I've already said. But it's time you opened your mind to what you and Zelda have done to your daughter.'

'I beg your pardon?' said Conrad icily.

'Instead of wringing your hands over what you think she is now doing to you,' Alison went on. 'Janet has spent her whole life subjugating her feelings to her parents' – like a chameleon that has no choice but to be one. What I'm saying, Conrad, is that she adapted herself to her situation, which isn't an enviable one for a young person. A less considerate girl than Janet would have broken loose long ago.'

'She could hardly have left home any sooner than she's thinking of doing,' Conrad retorted defensively.

'A youngster doesn't have to leave home in order to break loose,' said Alison with a wan smile. 'One need look no further than my son's defection for proof of that. Richard has gone his own way, though he is still living under my roof.'

'What defection? And why did you let him?' Conrad wanted to know.

'The details are too painful for me to talk about,' Alison

replied. 'Suffice to say that the man Richard is working for is no friend of mine, or of Maxwell Morton's. He's a rival impresario, though that is the least of it.'

'I wouldn't have thought Richard could be so disloyal.'

'Nor would I. But that proves we don't know our own children, doesn't it, Conrad?'

'You can say that again!'

Alison absently straightened the chintz curtains in the silence that followed, then went to sit beside Conrad on the sofa.

'I'd have bet my life that our Janet would never do anything to hurt me and her mother,' Conrad said.

'But it isn't the kind of disloyalty Richard is guilty of.'

'I think I'd have booted him out if I'd been you, Alison.'

'That's what I felt like doing,' she revealed. 'But Emma wouldn't have it. Nor would Maxwell.'

'It hasn't escaped my notice,' said Conrad, 'that he can twist them both around his little finger. But one would have thought his going to work for a rival would have brought Mr Morton up short. If I were him, I wouldn't want to look at Richard again.'

'I hope you won't take that attitude with Janet.'

'She hasn't upped and left us yet. And you're the one who could change her mind.'

'How, exactly?'

'By painting things black to her. Tell her the truth, Alison, about how hard it was for you before you made it. You're the only actress she knows, so she thinks the theatre is all glamour, that following in your footsteps she'll end up like you – a star.'

'I happen to think Janet has what it takes to become one.'

'But you can't know for sure. And think what my little girl would have to go through between now and then! Also, I've seen what your career has done to your personal life, Alison – and I don't want that for my daughter.'

'I'm also the only actress that *you* know, Conrad,'

Alison answered. 'And it might reassure you to hear that many lead stable and happy family lives. My chaotic personal life is because I'm me, not because I am a star.'

'That I'm prepared to accept, knowing you as I do.'

Conrad got up and stood with his back to the hearth, which Emma kept filled with greenery in summer.

'It's too late to lecture me about it,' said Alison with a smile, 'if that's what you're about to do.'

'But not too late to stop my kid from leaving home. If she does, Zelda will go to pieces.'

'And that's your real problem, isn't it, Conrad? How you'll cope with Zelda when Janet has gone.'

'I wouldn't want my daughter to go on the stage even if her mother weren't neurotic about her,' Conrad retorted. 'Show me the Jewish father who would.'

'How about my father?'

'He turned his back on our way of life, didn't he? – and the stage was responsible, which strengthens my argument, Alison. I don't want our Janet to go off and forget who and what she is.'

'It may surprise you to know,' said Alison, 'that in spirit my father never left the fold. Though he didn't practise Judaism, he was a Jew to his dying day. Nor did he ever break his emotional link with the family. He once told me that he'd thought he had succeeded in doing so, but found out that it couldn't be done; that even though he took my mother's family name, he had remained who he was when he was born.'

'I must say I was surprised that he had asked to be buried in a Jewish cemetery,' Conrad said gruffly.

'It was no surprise to me,' Alison replied. 'And when I visit the cemetery, on my pilgrimages to Oldham, I think how sad it is that Papa and his parents, lying peacefully side by side in death, were so bitterly estranged for much of their lives.'

'Why did you call your trips to Oldham pilgrimages?' Conrad wanted to know.

'That's how they feel to me, Conrad. In view of my rootless childhood, I've latched onto my father's roots, I

67

suppose. A Plantaine I may be, but I tend to think of your mother's house as the ancestral home,' said Alison with a smile. 'Which might account for me feeling a good deal more Jewish than I do Christian.'

'I didn't know that.'

'You do now. And I've not yet finished defending my father and the stage,' Alison said. 'You hold the stage responsible for Papa's doing what you call turning his back on the Jewish way of life – but the real cause was the family's attitude to his leaving home. And I rather think it's up to you, Conrad, whether or not Janet cuts herself off as Papa did. If you give her no cause for bitterness, all will be well.'

'Spare me the performance,' said Conrad. 'I'm not here to see you play Portia pleading a case. If you're not going to help me talk Janet out of it, say so and have done with.'

'Did you really think I would?'

'It was worth a try – but I ought to have known better.'

'And I would be wasting my time trying. Janet is made of stronger stuff than you think, or she would not have taken the matter this far. All I can do for you, Conrad, is promise that when she comes to London I'll take her under my wing.'

'*If* she comes, Alison – not when. And I can't think of anyone under whose wing I'd rather she weren't,' was Conrad's response.

'Are you casting aspersions on my morals?'

'Let's just say that your moral attitudes are not mine, Alison, and leave it at that.'

'Aside from the necessity to maintain my public image, I'm not hidebound by conventions, like you are – if that is what you mean,' Alison retorted. 'If I'd lived my private life hemmed in by social hypocrisy, I should have known no happiness at all – and I've known little enough,' she added with feeling.

'And would you want your son to live his life your way?'

'I believe in grasping happiness while one may, Conrad.

It is an all-too-fleeting thing. The answer to your question is yes.'

'Then I definitely wouldn't want my daughter under your wing.'

A strained silence followed.

Then Conrad made one more try. 'If you told Janet you were just being kind when you said to her she is very talented – or whatever it was you said the night you started all this off – it might take the wind out of her sails.'

'Aren't you dismissing too lightly that the Royal Academy of Dramatic Art has confirmed what I said, by accepting her?'

'And you are to blame for the whole damned thing!'

Alison let the reiterated recrimination pass. 'Be that as it may, Conrad, my advice to you – for what it's worth – is, let Janet go without a fight. Though I am heartsick about Richard's disloyalty to Maxwell, and sometimes find it hard to contain myself, I know that Maxwell and Emma's words to me on the subject are true: Nothing is worth causing a rift between oneself and one's child.'

She paused only for breath, before continuing her impassioned plea. 'That's what you have to make Zelda see, Conrad – because I'm sure you can see it for yourself. That is what your present dilemma boils down to – as mine did. Janet will go with or without your blessing; but if you don't stand in her way, you may be sure she will come back.'

Once again, Conrad felt he had been witnessing a performance. There was an ache in his throat – but his actress cousin was capable of moving a stone to tears.

'For the first time ever,' he said to her, 'I have to admit you are talking sense.'

'And how paradoxical it is that one must let one's children go in order to keep them,' she replied.

'There's more to you,' said Conrad, 'than meets the eye.'

'It has taken you far too long to find that out,' said Alison, giving him a cousinly hug.

Conrad straightened his tie, which she had sent askew. 'But it won't be easy to make Zelda accept the inevitable. Not to mention what our friends and neighbours will think about our Janet going on the stage.'

'We are back with social hypocrisy,' said Alison with a dry smile. 'But when Janet is famous, your friends and neighbours will set aside their attitude towards the legendary fast theatrical life, and be proud to say they know Janet Stein. Half of them are probably swapping husbands and wives behind the lace curtains themselves!'

'Not in Oldham and Manchester they're not! You really are outrageous, Alison.'

'Getting back to Zelda: it might help if you told her that Janet would be very welcome to live here.'

'That sounds like a good idea.'

'Despite your misgivings about your daughter being under my wing?' said Alison dryly.

'I can rely on that being counteracted by her also being under Emma's eagle eye.'

CHAPTER ELEVEN

THOUGH ALISON had advised Conrad not to fight Janet, she had fought Richard hard, and had initially forced him to stay on at school.

Recalling that period now, it seemed to her that her house had not been a home, but a battleground. She had not laid down the cudgels easily, for it was not just her own battle she was waging but Morton's too – though he had begged her to let Richard win.

How did I live through it? she sometimes asked herself. Her work, usually therapeutic, had this time had the opposite effect. The mother-son relationship in *The Vortex* was too close for comfort. Onstage, Alison's own emotions had mingled with those of the mother she was portraying, whose self-absorption had, in Coward's drama, almost pushed her son over the edge.

The playwright had opened his mother-character's eyes in time to avert disaster. But in life, Alison had thought, awakenings were not always so fortuitously timed and, all too often, came after the event.

Long afterwards, when she was again between plays, she wondered if portraying Mrs Lancaster had equipped her with a perception she had not formerly possessed, brought home to her what Emma and Morton had declared to her, and she to Conrad: that no issue was worth fighting for if it meant the end of one's relationship with one's child.

Acquiring that parental wisdom had not made applying it more palatable. If Richard ended up the most distinguished director in England, Alison's pride in him would be marred by his rejection of Morton.

Meanwhile, he had a long way to go before achieving

distinction, and her present relationship with him could be happier – on her side, at least, Alison thought listening to him talking to Janet at the dinner table on Christmas Day.

Though RADA was closed for the holiday, Janet had chosen to stay in London, and Morton was spending the festive day with them, as he habitually did.

Alison shared a glance with him over the young people's paper hats, while Emma served the plum pudding and brandy-butter. Was he thinking, as she was, that Richard's hat – a silver-foil crown – matched his opinion of himself nowadays? The way he was lecturing Janet on stagecraft, one would think him already a director!

Her son had got too big for his boots, though the work Bligh had found for him was that of a junior clerk in his office. One term at drama college would have taught Janet more about stagecraft than Richard had learned behind his desk in a year; but Janet was giving him the attention he didn't deserve, Alison noted, observing the rapt expression on the girl's lovely face.

Bligh had promised to send Richard on tour as an assistant stage manager as soon as a vacancy with one of his touring shows occurred, and Alison hoped it would be soon. It would be a relief to get Richard from under her nose for a while. How could someone so dear to her also be such a thorn in her side?

Stay calm, she counselled herself. All will come right in the end. But it was hard to keep hoping so, with her son changing into an over-confident smoothie. And how could he not, when the people he mixed with buttered him up and made him think he was a god?

'Lucy says she can't wait for me to direct her in a play,' Richard told Janet.

This was for Alison an illustration of the flattery Richard so eagerly lapped up. 'She's going to have to wait a long time,' she said to counteract it.

'Why are you always putting me down, Mother?' was Richard's response.

'Because it does you no good for people like Mrs Bligh to be constantly building you up.'

'I see. And why have you begun calling Lucy by her married name?'

'As she worked so hard to acquire it, why not?'

'I bet you didn't know how catty my mother can be, till you came to live here,' Richard said to Janet.

Emma hastily interceded. 'We haven't pulled the crackers yet. And don't tell the family up north, Janet, that your Auntie Emma cooked a Christmas spread.'

'Why not?' asked Morton, who had eaten more Christmas dinners cooked by Emma than he cared to count. 'It was a kosher turkey, wasn't it? I got it from that butcher in Golders Green for you, like I always do.'

'Didn't anyone ever tell him that Jews don't celebrate Jesus' birthday?' Richard said to Alison. 'Though I would have expected him to know it without being told.'

He loses no opportunity to belittle Maxwell, Alison thought with distress – as though his electing to work for Bligh were not, for Morton, humiliation enough.

'I've never had a Christmas dinner before,' said Janet. 'But I'm enjoying myself very much.'

'As your aunt has,' said Morton, 'for the past umpteen years, on Christmas Day.'

'Which only adds to my guilt,' Emma answered. 'But we do light Chanukah candles here, too, Max – as you may have noticed – as well as decorating the Christmas tree,' she said, glancing at the window bay where it stood in tinselled splendour. 'All I hope, is that none of our relations from up north ever walk in on us at this time of year, or they'd do what the Catholics call excommunicate me!'

'I don't see why,' said Richard. 'This happens to be a two-religion home.'

'And Emma has just reminded me that I was raised a Catholic,' Morton said.

This was news to Richard and Janet.

'Don't you ever go to Mass?' Janet asked him.

'I stopped being a believer very many years ago, my dear.'

'But you didn't have to tell the children so!' Emma rebuked him.

'Shall you and I go and play in the nursery, Janet?' Richard quipped, and added to Morton, 'Aren't you afraid of eternal damnation – or whatever it is that sinful Catholics are threatened with by the priests?'

'I have to admit that I suffer the occasional qualm,' Morton dryly replied.

And not going to Mass, thought Richard, is the least of your sins!

'Formal prayer is only the trappings of religion,' Alison opined.

'Don't say that to Grandma Lottie,' Janet said. 'She goes to synagogue every Saturday.'

'Yet I'm sure,' replied Alison, 'she'd be the first to agree that the trappings are less important than honouring the basic creed. A good Christian or Jew, whichever, does not bear ill-will toward his fellows,' she declared, hoping her son would take her point.

Richard used it to make one of his own. 'Then why don't you show some goodwill toward the twins?'

'For that, I would have to be not just good, but a saint!'

'We still haven't pulled the crackers,' Emma again intervened. 'Let's do it now.'

And avoid another round of verbal fireworks, Morton thought, offering one end of his cracker to Alison. Sitting tight until Richard came to his senses – and Morton still hoped that he eventually would – was for him like reclining voluntarily upon a bed of nails.

Richard shared his cracker with Janet.

Emma was left dangling hers in the air. But that, she reflected wryly, is the story of my life. Only two could pull a cracker – and the same went for a good many other things. She glanced at the youngsters whose creature comforts and welfare were her responsibility, recalled the old nanny-song about being everyone's mother, but nobody's wife, and could not stop herself from giggling.

'You ought not to have given Emma that big glass of sherry, Maxwell,' said Alison with a smile.

'What are you laughing at, Auntie?' Janet wanted to know.

Myself. And laughing is better than crying, Emma thought. 'Do I have to share my private jokes?' she said, stemming her hollow mirth. Then she glanced at the Shetland granny-shawl Morton had given her for Christmas and began giggling again.

Alison fingered the piece of glamorous costume jewellery with which he had presented her. 'I'm pleased that you're having such a merry Christmas, Emma dear.'

'That sherry,' said Morton, 'has really gone to our Em's head!'

'A chocolate with a drop of liqueur inside it would go to Auntie Emma's head,' Richard said.

And would that the same applied to you, thought Alison. Though she had not seen Richard the worse for drink since the incident in Cannes, liquor fumes were detectable on his breath when he returned from wherever he spent his evenings.

Alison did not need to ask with whom he spent them. The twins had succeeded in what they had set out to do. Richard had progressed from dropping in on them to being part of their intimate circle. Lending a sympathetic ear to a boy who thought his mother did not understand him had drawn him closer to them, as working for Lucy's husband had. Alison feared that total alienation from her might be the next stage, and knew she must tread carefully to avoid it. But doing so was not easy.

'I hope the production Mr Bligh sends me on tour with will be one of Luke's,' Richard was saying to Janet. 'I might get to watch some of his rehearsals. He's a terrific director and I could learn a lot from him.'

Just so long as you don't emulate him in other ways, Alison wanted to say, but held her tongue.

Emma observed her expression. 'Come and help me make the coffee, Alison.'

Alison followed her to the kitchen. 'It's as well you got me out of there!'

'Why do you think I did?' Emma got out the percolator

her American suitor had given her during the war, after despairing of the boiled-in-a-pan coffee she had offered him. 'Running down the twins to Richard will get you nowhere, Alison. Every word you utter against them pushes him further away from you.'

'I know it.'

'Then why don't you make yourself stay *shtum*, like you just managed to, all the time?'

'The times I find it hardest to stay *shtum*, Emma, are when Richard insults Maxwell.'

'Me, too. And I don't know how Max manages to. But all three of us agreed it was the only way, didn't we?'

'In theory, I still agree,' Alison replied. 'But sustaining what we agreed upon is becoming what our old pal Colonel Clark would call a pain in the ass!'

'That sounds like my impression of your American boyfriend,' said Emma. 'He was never a pal of mine.'

Alison had to smile at her prim expression. 'It takes two to tango, Emma dear.'

And to pull a cracker, Emma harked back.

'I wanted what he did,' said Alison, 'as I made plain to you at the time.'

Alison did not lack partners for whatever purpose, but Emma did not want to believe that satisfying animal lust was one of them.

'I just hope you'll never do it again,' she said.

'I'm afraid I already have – as I warned you and Maxwell I might, when you were both so upset about my carefree little affair with the colonel. I'm not yet in my dotage, Emma, and on the rare occasions when someone I really fancy comes along, reminding me I am a woman, not just an actress and a mother, it harms nobody for me to have a brief fling.'

'I don't understand how you could, with someone you're not in love with,' was Emma's shocked response.

'Believe it or not, darling, a woman is as capable of enjoying sex without love as a man is. But I didn't know it until I met Colonel Clark.'

'It's a wonder your goings-on haven't got into the gossip

columns!' Emma tartly exclaimed. 'Though you've managed to keep them hidden from Max and me.'

'There has only been one fling since the colonel, Emma – with a Swedish airline pilot who was staying at my hotel in Paris, when I went there to buy some evening gowns last year and — '

'I don't want to know!' Emma cut in.

'If you'd gone with me, as I wanted you to, there'd have been nothing to know,' said Alison with a laugh. 'But it's Richard's goings-on, not mine, that are a matter for concern,' she added, returning to the present.

'And I keep telling myself,' said Emma, 'that the Richard we're seeing now isn't really him. That sooner or later the lovely considerate boy he used to be will take over again.'

'I wish I had your optimism.' Alison watched Emma set their late grandmother's Crown Derby coffee set on a tray. 'Do you recall me predicting a long time ago that the twins would do something really terrible to me one day?'

'You've always had that feeling about them, Alison.'

'And it has strengthened with the years. You used to tell me I was being melodramatic. What can they possibly do to you? you said. If I could have forgotten their existence, I would have, but they haven't let me. I can remember likening them to a couple of snakes – and you telling me not to be daft, Emma. But that's how they've always made me feel, as though they were waiting for the right moment to strike. Only I know, now, that they haven't just been waiting. They've engineered things to make that moment come.'

Emma was filling the cream jug and paused in the act. 'You're giving me the creeps, Alison!'

'Now you know how I've felt all these years – as though a creeping menace has been hovering over me. And now I see it clearly for what it is. A careful plan to hurt me where I am most vulnerable – through my son. They must have made up their minds to do it the first time they saw me with Richard, when he was just a little boy. Thinking

77

back to that afternoon, what they have done, and how they've done it, is quite plain to me. They set out to charm him there and then, and he thought I was being unfair when I refused Luke's offer to take him for a spin in his new sports car.'

Alison stared into space and saw a picture of herself hauling Richard in a reefer coat and sailor hat out of Fortnum's, to get him away from the twins.

'I must have had a premonition of things to come,' she said to Emma. 'I remember shivering in the taxi home, though I had on a fur and it wasn't an especially cold day. I also recall Richard bleating defiantly that he liked the twins, even if I didn't.'

She smiled grimly. 'So you see, Emma, he was only about six when they inserted the tip of the wedge between us. The next day, they drove it in a little further by sending him a gift they knew he would adore and I wouldn't want him to keep. Richard begged me not to return it – and I was too soft-hearted to stick to my guns. Fool that I was!'

'When I got back from up north and found he'd scraped the hall paintwork with that motor car they sent him, I nearly had a fit,' Emma recalled.

'It was bigger and shinier than the one Maxwell had given him – so he abandoned Maxwell's gift, as he has now rejected Maxwell!' said Alison with asperity.

'Any child would have done that.'

'But Richard is no longer a child.'

'He still hasn't forgiven Max for advising you to raise him as your adopted son.'

'And I am beginning to think he never will – and that your optimism, Emma, is clouding your vision. There's no doubt why Richard went to work for Bligh Productions, but punishing Maxwell is by now only the half of it. He's having a wonderful time being made to think he's a god by the twins and their set. Richard has got so big-headed, he has completely lost sight of what Maxwell once was to him.'

She paced the kitchen restlessly. 'I don't like the person

my son has become. But it's the twins' doing – and I won't let them take him from me.'

Emma transferred the coffee from the bubbling percolator to a gleaming silver pot. 'Then you must play your own cards more skilfully than you have been doing, Alison.'

When they returned to the dining room, Richard was not there; and Janet looked dejected, Alison noticed.

'Had a good gossip, girls?' said Morton, who had envied them their brief respite from Richard's company. 'Our young man got fed up with waiting.'

'Richard went upstairs to freshen up for the party he's invited to tonight,' Janet said.

'When isn't he invited to a party?' Alison replied. But she had expected him to stay home on Christmas night, and had to stop herself from saying so, when he returned to the room.

'Do you mind if I skip the coffee?' he asked, glancing at the clock.

'Of course not, darling,' said Alison, and managed to add pleasantly, 'You go wherever you are going and have a good time.'

Richard gave her a surprised glance. 'I'm off to the Blighs', as a matter of fact, and I thought of taking Janet to the party, but when I mentioned it to Lucy she said she was already expecting more people than the flat can accommodate.'

'Please don't feel bad about leaving me sitting at home,' Janet said to him. Any more than you would if it weren't a festive time of year, she privately added.

'You probably wouldn't enjoy it anyway, kiddo,' he told her. 'Curling up with a book is more in your line.'

And used to be more in your line, thought Alison, recalling the days when Richard was rarely without a book in his hand.

'Fare thee well, then, kiddo!' he said, stroking Janet's hair as though she were a child and he a man.

Having her live with them was to Richard as if his wish that she were his sister had materialised, and it was like a sister that he treated her. The pet-name he had bestowed upon her was a constant reminder to Janet that his affection for her was not the kind she wanted it to be.

Like Alison, she could act offstage as well as on, and masked her feelings now, matching Richard's style. 'Fare thee well, also, young Lochinvar! Hasten thee to the cab that shalt be thy steed!'

'Alas! I venture forth by Tube,' said Richard, whose salary did not yet run to taxi fares, and added, after kissing Alison and Emma goodbye, 'Get thee to thy beds when thou wilt, lest this errant knight tarry till morn.'

Alison was about to tell him he had better not stay out all night, but a kick from Emma under the table froze the words on her tongue.

'We wouldn't dream of waiting up for you if it's going to be a late party,' Emma told the thorn in their sides.

A flat silence followed his departure.

'I hope you'll be so easy-going if I want to stay out all night,' Janet said to Alison and Emma.

'We won't,' they replied in unison.

'Because I'm a girl! Richard gets away with murder.'

They were unable to tell her that allowing him to do so was part of the policy they called 'sitting tight'.

'When RADA reopens after the holiday, Janet, you must start inviting some of your friends home,' Alison said. 'Those who don't have family in London would enjoy a home-cooked meal.'

'Especially one Auntie Emma has cooked. But Richard doesn't bring his friends home, does he?' Janet remarked. 'I wonder why?'

The kind he likes to mix with he wouldn't dare bring here, Alison silently replied.

'Shall we play Monopoly?' asked Janet when she had finished drinking her coffee. 'I'll go and fetch it.'

Emma had no interest in board games and wanted to get on with washing the dinner dishes. But for some reason her niece seemed in need of cheering up. 'A game of Monopoly would be very nice,' she said.

'And a good deal less strenuous than the charade we

are playing for Richard's benefit,' Morton added when Janet had left the room.

'I'm amazed that an intelligent girl like Janet hasn't seen through the show we're putting on for him,' said Alison.

'But you missed your cue, Alison. When Richard told us whose party he was going to, you should have said to him, "Wish the Blighs a merry Christmas from us all." You are not nearly cunning enough,' Emma declared.

'Emma is stage-managing me, Maxwell,' said Alison. 'Don't you think that's funny? But there are all the ingredients of a rip-roaring farce in this entire situation. If I were watching it, instead of being part of it, I'd laugh myself silly. And I'm far from certain the comedy won't, before the final curtain, turn into a tragedy.'

Alison was pacing the room, as she had in the kitchen.

'You'd better calm down before Janet comes back,' Emma said to her.

'We're putting on a show for her, too, aren't we?' she said, halting beside the hearth, and adjusting a greetings card that had slipped askew amid the collection on the mantelpiece. 'Pretending we couldn't care less about Richard cavorting till all hours.'

Morton stubbed out his after-dinner cigar. 'If there is one thing I've learned, Alison, it's that Shakespeare was spot-on when he wrote that all the world is a stage and all the men and women merely players. In my experience, for one reason or another – and even when they are unaware they are doing it – everyone puts on a show for everyone else. Tell me the person who would go naked and unashamed before his fellows.'

'Really, Max!' Emma exclaimed, though she knew perfectly well what he meant. Hadn't she been play-acting for years to hide her love for him?

As Janet was doing, to hide hers for Richard, but her elders had yet to learn that.

'So on with the show, girls!' Morton summed up with a sigh. 'The one we three are jointly engaged in is in a good cause.'

CHAPTER TWELVE

RICHARD SAW her eyes kindle with interest the moment he entered the Blighs' Belgravia apartment. On the Tube train, he had experienced his customary pang of guilt about deserting Janet. Now, as always, thoughts of her were dispelled by the heady scene to which the twins had introduced him. Women like the one now watching him over the rim of her champagne glass were part of it.

'Who's the stunning redhead standing beside your lovely new pedestal?' he asked Lucy, who had greeted him rapturously in the hall.

'If you like that marble pedestal, poppet, I'll give it to you.'

'That's really nice of you, Lucy, but what would I do with it?' he said with a laugh.

'Put it in your bachelor flat. When you get one – and it's time you did,' Lucy took the opportunity to plant in his mind. 'I'll keep it here for you, until then.'

Richard had only to admire something of Lucy's and it was his. But it was not the pedestal he was interested in, but the gorgeous creature beside it. 'I haven't seen her around before, Lucy.'

'And she's giving you the eye, isn't she, poppet?' Lucy teased him. 'You shouldn't be so devastatingly attractive!'

'And you look absolutely ravishing tonight,' said Richard, though he thought she looked anything but.

Lucy had this evening abandoned her ingénue image in favour of a flowing white chiffon gown which was not for a woman of her small stature. And the matching turban she was wearing with it made her round face look

like a pudding tied in a cloth, Richard thought. His
mother, on the other hand, had impeccable taste – but
Lucy's lack of it did not diminish Richard's affection for
her.

'Kindly tell me who the redhaired lady is, Lucy darling,'
he persisted.

'The poor thing is recuperating from a broken marriage.'

'And probably looking around for husband number
two,' said Luke who had joined them.

'Meanwhile, she is giving our dear boy predatory
glances, like all my girlfriends do. If he weren't my little
cousin, I should be after him myself!' Lucy continued
teasing Richard.

Richard laughed, but there was no denying what Lucy
had said. It was invariably mature ladies who made a
beeline for him, rather than girls of his own age.

His mother could have told him that the little-boy
appeal that had attracted her to his father was present in
him, and that it had nothing to do with his youth, but
would always be his special aura.

Alison was thirty-two when she met Richard Lindemann,
and he twenty-six. She had initially thought him even
younger, and had asked herself why she was so drawn to
him, but could find no answer. Intellectuals were not her
kind, and he was not a conventionally handsome man.

Nor was Richard, who apart from his engaging crooked
smile bore no physical resemblance to his father. But both
were the kind who drew older women like a magnet.

'How old do you suppose the redhaired lady is?' he
asked Luke when Lucy had drifted away to the drawing
room.

'Late twenties, I'd say,' Luke assessed her. 'She's
American, by the way – and an heiress to boot. Her papa
is reputed to be one of the wealthiest men in the States.
And that pendant she has on looks as if it could be the
Kohinoor diamond!'

Something his great-aunt Lottie had once said in his
hearing returned to Richard's mind: that money could

not buy happiness. He had noticed that in repose the lady's face was sad.

'Is she a pal of yours and Lucy's?' he asked Luke.

'Not exactly.'

'Then what is she doing here?'

'Aren't you forgetting whose flat this is, old chap?' said Luke, glancing to where Charles Bligh was chatting with the leading man in Lucy's current play.

'I tend to think of it as yours and Lucy's place, as you are the ones I drop in to see,' Richard answered with a smile.

'Then let me give you a tip, Richard,' said Luke. 'Never underestimate the importance of our mutual benefactor. Lucy and I would not be foolish enough to make that mistake. And you must always bear in mind that the one who makes it possible for us to make things possible for you is Charles Bligh.'

Richard was assailed by disquiet, though he knew not why. As though he were part of a conspiracy and had just been warned not to let down his fellow-conspirators.

'Charlie would be most upset if he thought you had forgotten his existence in his own home,' Luke added, smiling at Richard with the frankness and fondness he always displayed towards him. 'And we've got your brilliant future to think of, haven't we, old chap?' he said, giving Richard's arm a playful punch.

Richard brushed his disquiet aside. Luke cared about him and just didn't want him to put a foot wrong. 'Thanks for sorting me out, Luke. I'll remember what you said.'

'Make sure you do, my lad.'

The redhead had emerged from her momentary sadness and was again eyeing Richard contemplatively – which neither he nor Luke failed to observe.

'She could have any man in the place, if she set her cap at him,' said Luke. 'Even me or Charles – but don't tell my sweet sister I said that!'

Richard's eyes met hers over the head of a squat gentleman who was one of the several around her. 'I won't.'

'But she has obviously selected the only boy in our midst,' Luke declared with mock chagrin. 'When you are around, Richard, the rest of us don't stand a chance.'

Richard blushed. 'I wouldn't say that.'

'I would. And as you are one of the family, you had better be nice to her, old chap. Charles met her at a Broadway opening, last spring, and she mentioned that she wouldn't mind putting some cash into a show.'

'Is that why he invited her to the party?'

'You catch on quick! The lady is alone in London, and Charles asked her to eat Christmas dinner with us, *en famille*, before the party began. But Mr Morton must have told you that the first move in a deal is often a friendly social overture.'

Richard's expression tightened, as it did whenever Morton's name was mentioned. 'He has never discussed his business affairs with me.'

'Which goes to show that he doesn't trust you,' Luke did not miss the chance to say.

The words were to Richard like salt upon an unhealed wound. He had succeeded in convincing himself that he did not care about Morton, but there were moments, like now, when the hurt of Morton's not acknowledging him as his son returned full force.

'I hope you will have the good sense never to allow your mother to persuade you to leave Charles and work for her friend,' Luke said.

'She tried to talk me into working for him, before I joined Bligh Productions,' Richard revealed.

Luke would have been surprised had Alison not done so. But he and Lucy had noted that Richard did not talk to them about his mother, and they had been careful not to question him. This was not to say that they refrained from continuing to subtly poison his mind.

'Poor, misguided Alison,' Luke sighed. 'One would have thought her first consideration would be for you to do what you thought best for yourself. But, regrettably, loyalty to you-know-who is her first priority, and her kith and kin have suffered as a result. She was the first blood-Plantaine ever to desert the family company, and it was Morton who lured her away.'

This was one way of putting Morton's having offered Alison the chance to appear in the West End.

In Richard's present frame of mind, the word 'lured' in relation to Morton and his mother equated with his supposition that Alison had, in a weak moment, allowed her manager to seduce her. Morton probably had a wife somewhere, and had been unable to marry Alison, thought Richard. Catholics were not allowed to divorce. But the biggest sin Morton had committed was lying about Richard's parentage, to save not just Alison's reputation but his own.

Luke cut into his painful cogitation. 'From the day he whisked her away from the family, your mother and Morton have been thick as thieves. It distresses me to use that phrase with regard to my dear cousin Alison. But I've always made a point of being honest with you, Richard, old chap. And my advice to you is stay with those you know you can trust, who trust you.'

'I intend to,' said Richard tersely.

'And now to matters more pleasant.' Luke bathed the redhead in a smile as she detached herself from her admirers and came to join them. 'Allow me to present my cousin, Richard Plantaine,' he said to her. 'This lovely lady is Mrs Lee Taylor Colville, Richard.'

'I'm delighted to make your acquaintance, Mrs Taylor Colville,' said Richard.

'What olde-worlde charmers you Plantaine males are,' she replied in a husky drawl that sent a tingle down Richard's spine. 'You may call me Lee, and I guess I'll call you Rick.'

'I got called Rick when I lived in your country, during the war,' Richard told her.

'Honey and sugar, too, I bet! By all the girls you dated.'

'I wasn't old enough to date girls.'

'And that sure puts me where I belong,' she said with a rueful laugh.

'If you two will excuse me,' said Luke.

Lee seemed to notice neither the wink he gave Richard, nor his departure.

'How did you like living in the States?' she asked Richard while a waiter topped up their champagne glasses.

'It was great while it lasted.'

'That's a somewhat profound statement from someone so young.'

They shared a long glance and Richard thought her green eyes the most eloquent he had ever looked into. It was as though she was telling him something about herself that could not be said in words on so short an acquaintance. As if she wanted him to know that she too had learned that the good times don't last. But Richard doubted that many made that discovery as early in life as he had.

He could not have been more than six when it was first illustrated to him. Emma was up north and his mother had devoted herself entirely to him for a whole week. She had taken him with her to the theatre each night and let him watch her from the wings. During the day they had gone sightseeing in town, the way other mothers did with their small sons. For a brief while he had felt that she belonged to him and had wished it could always be that way.

Lee returned him to the present. 'I'm feeling a little guilty about leaving my father alone at Christmas. Daddy has nobody but me. But I guess I wouldn't be such great company for him right now.'

Richard recalled her broken marriage and gave her a sympathetic smile.

'And it was Daddy, bless his heart, who made me take this trip,' she went on. 'Some friends of mine have a place at Klosters and asked me to join them there. Do you ski, Rick?'

'I've never been what you'd call the athletic type. As my wartime hosts found out when they took me ski-ing in New Hampshire.'

'Me neither,' said Lee. 'But the après-ski parties in

Europe are great fun, I'm told. And I had a yen to see some snow. In Hawaii, I'd have spent Christmas Day lying by the pool, just like any other day.'

'Is that where your home is?'

'One of them. We have an apartment in New York – I lived there with my ex. Daddy rarely uses it. Then there's our old family home in Philadelphia, the house I was raised in, which since my mother died Daddy keeps staffed with servants and refuses to put up for sale – he's a sentimental old guy. We also have a ranch in the mid-West. If you ever eat prime-rib in the States, Rick, it's liable to have come from one of our herds.'

'If raising cattle is your father's business, why did you live in Philadelphia?' Richard was curious to know.

'It was my mother's hometown and she didn't want to leave it when she married Daddy. Who isn't, by the way, what I may have just made him appear. Though he's what we call in America a "beef-baron", the only time he puts on a cowboy hat is when he visits the ranch for meetings with those who run it for him. His first million was made on the stock market; when he bought the ranch he had never been astride a horse. But why am I telling you all this?' said Lee with a laugh.

'I asked if Hawaii was your home.'

'And as it's where Daddy now lives, I guess the answer is yes. My mother loved the island of Maui, and spent the last months of her life on our vacation estate there. She's buried on the island, so Daddy has made it his home. He wanted to stay close to her, and rarely leaves Maui for longer than it takes to make a flying business trip.'

Lee smiled up at Richard and toyed with her fabulous pendant. 'So here I am, Rick, all alone in London. I've never been here before, so I decided to stop over for a day or two on my way to Switzerland. I'm leaving tomorrow.'

'But it's still tonight,' Richard daringly said, and saw Charles Bligh give him a wink.

Like the boss telling an employee he's doing a good job, Richard thought, remembering Luke's asking him to be nice to Lee – and why. But the rapport between

Richard and this exotic woman had nothing to do with any of that. Nor was it just her looks, that would enthrall any male. The vulnerability he had detected beneath her sophistication matched something within himself.

'How old are you?' she enquired, surveying him.

'Seventeen-and-a-half.'

'Too young by far to make the enigmatic remark you just made. Are your parents here tonight?'

'I have only my mother. And if she were here, you couldn't help but know it – she's Alison Plantaine.'

Lee looked distinctly awed. 'I saw her in Pygmalion on Broadway, when I was a child. We were staying at our Park Avenue apartment on my ninth birthday and my parents took me to the theatre for a special treat. It was Alison Plantaine who showed me at an early age how exciting good theatre can be.' Lee laughed wryly at her own expense. 'Who would have thought that twenty years later I'd be cradle-snatching her son!'

It was an outright admission of Richard's attraction for her. 'Girls my own age aren't my style,' he replied.

'And young boys are not as a rule mine.'

'Where are you staying in London?'

'Are you thinking of escorting me back there?'

'If you'd like me to.'

The ball was now firmly in Lee's court. A passing waiter refilled her glass, enabling her to avoid replying.

Richard declined to have his glass topped up. This was no time to get drunk.

'Are you all set for a stage career yourself?' Lee asked him.

She sipped her drink while he told her what he hoped to be, and said when he had finished speaking, 'As you are a Plantaine, it shouldn't take you too long.'

'That wasn't Luke's experience,' Richard answered. 'He was in his thirties by the time he got his West End break. There are many more talented young directors around than the number of plays that get staged.'

'But your mother will be able to help you on your way,' said Lee.

'I would rather she didn't.'

'I see.' Lee fixed a Turkish cigarette into a jewelled holder, handed Richard a gold lighter and waited for him to apply the flame. 'Not many guys in your position would hesitate to take advantage of it, Rick.'

'I'd prefer to make my own way.'

'And I'm sure you will. All it takes to stage a production is money.' Lee smiled dryly. 'And Mr Bligh, along with a number of other producers, is hoping to avail himself of some of mine.'

She's shrewder than people take her for, thought Richard.

'He was telling me over dinner tonight about a couple of new plays that have landed on his desk that are worth doing.'

'One of them is a first play by a girl called Marianne Dean. I'm working in Charles' office at the moment,' said Richard. 'One of my jobs is to read all the unsolicited manuscripts that come in and shortlist them. Miss Dean's play is the best I've read for some time.'

'Then maybe I'll help Charles give her her break.'

'Just on the strength of my opinion?'

'If Daddy doesn't talk me out of it.'

Richard's impression of 'Daddy' did not make him too hopeful on Marianne Dean's account. As though the beef-baron were present, he seemed to be ever hovering at his daughter's elbow. Whenever Lee mentioned him, a picture of a big, powerful man was conjured up.

'It will depend upon what kind of mood he's in when I discuss it with him,' said Lee. 'Sometimes he is indulgent about my interest in the arts, and sometimes he isn't.' She gave Richard a warm smile. 'But I shan't let him talk me out of backing a play for you to direct in the West End when you're ready, Rick. That's how we got on this track, I guess. When I said all it takes to stage a production is money, I was going to tell you that you can count on me when the time comes.'

Momentarily, Richard felt older and wiser than her. 'Isn't that rather a rash promise?'

90

'Probably. And Daddy would be cross with me for making it.'

The powerful man scowled in Richard's mental image of him. 'Then why did you make it, Lee?'

'Why not? When you're famous, I'll get a big kick out of it if I gave you your start. And I couldn't use up all the dollars my mother left me if I lived to be a hundred. There'll be more when Daddy's gone. I'm already helping a group of promising painters in New York to keep body and soul together. And if their promise doesn't materialise, I won't miss what it's costing me. It's only money, Rick.'

'But I'm not sure I could let you help me.'

'What an independent guy you are! But I sure admire you for it. Will you promise not to be so independent with me?'

Again they shared a glance, then Richard's gaze strayed to her cleavage.

'You scamp,' Lee said with her husky laugh. 'There's something about you that gets me, kid though you are – and you darnwell know it!'

'The feeling is mutual.'

'Yes. I guess it is. But returning to the future, and it won't be next year, or the year after, all you need do is contact me if you need me to back a play.'

Lee finished her champagne and put down the glass. 'Meanwhile, it's been nice chatting to you, Rick. I wish you well.'

Richard got the message. 'You don't want me to take you to your hotel, do you?'

'I wouldn't put it that way,' she said with a smile and went to join Bligh, leaving Richard wondering if and when they would meet again.

CHAPTER THIRTEEN

EARLY IN 1953, Alison appeared in her first post-war flop. It was also the play in which Janet made her West End début, and its failure was the more distressing to Alison on that account.

Janet accepted the disaster with a shrug and a smile. As though, thought Alison, her none-too-happy homelife with her parents had conditioned her to take philosophically whatever came.

Or had she inherited the family trait her great-grandmother, Alison's Grandma Shrager, had displayed? It was present in Emma, too. The capacity to come to terms with disappointments that others would not easily accept. As if, when things went well for them, they must think themselves fortunate.

These were Alison's ruminations on the night the play closed. After removing her stage make-up and changing, she had hastened to Janet's dressing room to comfort her and found her calmly brushing her hair, instead of shedding bitter tears as Alison, in her position, would surely have done the moment she was alone.

'I wish I had your nature, Janet dear,' said Alison. 'And I feel as though I've let you and the rest of the cast down.'

Alison's first thought when a production in which she was starring failed was for her fellow-actors.

'I feel bad about the author, too,' she added with chagrin. 'How hard on him it is that this has happened to his first play.'

'If you couldn't make the play succeed, Alison, nobody could,' Janet replied.

'Maybe not. But I shall always feel responsible for your first West End appearance being the fiasco it has been.'

'I've got lots of time to live it down.'

Again Alison marvelled.

When Morton announced the bad news to the cast, that evening, everyone else had been dismayed. Though the play had been slated by the critics, to close after only a week was ignominy indeed.

Janet put down her hairbrush and gave her mouth the light touch of lipstick that was the only cosmetic she wore offstage. 'It was lovely of Mr Morton to launch me, Alison, but I ought not to have let him. The people I was at RADA with are still getting experience with provincial reps, and think themselves lucky to be in work. What has happened serves me right for not waiting until I'm ready,' she added wryly.

Alison thrust her hands into the pockets of the black mink jacket she was wearing over her evening gown and said emphatically, 'Let me assure you of something, Janet, and you had better believe it. Neither Maxwell nor I would have allowed you to make your début now had you not been ready, and right for the role.'

'Be that as it may, Alison, because I'm related to you I had the edge over the other girls who auditioned. I should have listened to Richard.'

'What did the oracle say?'

'That I ought to make my own way, without help from Mr Morton or you.'

Alison watched Janet pull on a yellow beret. 'That seems to me odd advice from someone who is not above accepting a leg-up himself.'

Richard had progressed from Bligh's office to stage-managing productions directed by Luke.

'Do you suppose Richard would now be Luke Plantaine's protegé, had he followed the counsel he gave to you?' Alison said. 'A great many talented young men would give their eye-teeth to be where Richard is now – en route to getting the chance to direct while they are still young. Most will have to wait until their youth has fled – if they ever make it at all.'

'Please don't try to turn me against Richard,' said Janet stiffly.

'Is that what you think I am doing?'

'Aren't you?'

'Why should I, Janet?'

'I've lived in the same house with you and him for five years, Alison – excluding the periods he, or I, was away working, which were a welcome relief from the strain. I would have to be blind, deaf, and completely insensitive,' said Janet, 'not to know how things are between you and him. And it's all because he went his own way, isn't it? Instead of yours and Mr Morton's.'

'Nothing is ever quite so black and white,' Alison said.

A silence followed and she fingered her pearls, aware of Janet watching her through the mirror, then averted her gaze. 'In every situation, Janet, there are factors unknown to those who observe it from outside.'

Janet got up to put on her camelhair coat. 'I'm not prying, Alison.'

Alison noticed her sensible shoes, like a housewife might wear to go shopping, and reflected upon the difference between the new generation of actresses and her own. The contrast between her own evening attire and Janet's casual appearance epitomised for Alison the change in social attitudes wrought by the war. The days when evening dress in the stalls was *de rigueur* were long gone. And young actresses dropped their glamorous image when they were offstage. As though they were ordinary members of the public doing a job, Alison thought now. But, till the day she retired, her own nightly exit from the stage door would maintain what her public expected of Alison Plantaine.

'I didn't mean to upset you,' said Janet, tying her coat belt around her tiny waist. 'Nor is it necessary for you to explain. It isn't my business.'

'If I tried to, I wouldn't know where to begin. Suffice to say, Janet, that it distresses me deeply that Richard and I have drifted apart. I love him very much.'

'So do I.' Why had Janet let herself say it? But it was like a great weight being lifted off her to share her secret with someone at last.

For a moment, Alison did not take in what she had just been told. That her son and her cousin's daughter cared for each other was taken for granted. Not until she saw the expression in Janet's eyes did Alison understand. 'Oh, my dear child,' was all that shock and compassion allowed her to say.

'Did you never suspect?'

Alison shook her head.

'Then I'm obviously a better actress than I thought,' said Janet, giving her a bleak smile.

But in the light of her new knowledge, times when she had sensed that all was not well with Janet returned to Alison. Nor had there ever been any boys among the college friends Janet brought home in her RADA days. And when she managed to get to town during her work stints in the provinces, she had always come alone.

Hoping Richard would be there, Alison realised now. But he rarely came home for the weekend when he was on tour, and if he did, spent his time with the twins.

'You're a pretty girl, and Richard is not the only boy in the world,' Alison declared.

'He is for me,' Janet replied.

The words filled Alison with foreboding. Though her German lover had been dead for many years, no man since had engaged her emotions. But someone might have, had she never known Richard Lindemann, and she did not delude herself that there was not a good deal she had missed that other women had. Artistically fulfilled though she was, in other respects her life had been wasted.

Was it to be the same for Janet, because of Richard? 'You think him the only one for you now, but your life is only just beginning,' Alison told her firmly. 'And the lack of consideration Richard has displayed in recent years does not make me envy whoever will one day be his wife. Nor his lack of principle,' Alison added.

'Couldn't that just be that his principles are different from yours?'

'If he has any, they most certainly are! But there are not two ways of doing the decent thing, Janet. The only way is to do it. Richard didn't show up for your début night, did he?' Alison deliberately twisted the knife in the wound his absence must have been to Janet. Though it distressed her to have to do so, she must try to remove Janet's blind respect for Richard.

'He's in Leeds with a production,' Janet defended him.

'My dear girl, you know as well as I do that, unlike the cast, stage-managers don't have to be dying to get someone to take over on the odd occasion. And may I remind you that Richard did that, in order to be at the première of Lucy Plantaine's new play.'

'Lucy is his boss's wife, and Mr Bligh invited him to the première.'

'And there we have it!' said Alison. 'He would not want to upset Mr Bligh – indispensable though I'm sure he thinks he is to the production he's touring with. But he didn't mind upsetting you.'

'You certainly are trying to turn me against him!' Janet flashed.

And for your own sake, Alison thought.

'But you won't succeed,' Janet declared.

'Then I must hope that before too long you'll see for yourself what I am trying to make you see, and give your heart to someone more worthy of you, my dear.'

'How,' demanded Janet, 'can a mother think that way about her own son?'

'When he gives her no option but to do so,' Alison answered. 'And when you are a mother yourself, Janet, you'll discover as I have that maternal love is not, like romantic love, necessarily blind.'

'I wish I hadn't told you. And if you don't mind, I'd rather we didn't speak of it again.'

'As you wish,' said Alison kindly. 'But if you ever feel like crying on a sympathetic shoulder, you know where to come.'

'I'll bear that in mind. But we shan't be seeing too much

of each other if I get back into repertory, and I intend to try.'

'You must do whatever you think best for yourself, Janet. And your room will always be there for you, in my house.'

Janet gave her a hug. 'I want us always to be friends. I admire you so much.'

'Thank you, darling. But it would pay you to confine your admiration to my professional achievement,' said Alison with a dry smile. 'I would advise you most strongly not to model your personal life on mine.'

Janet appraised her for a moment.

'To what do I owe the sudden scrutiny?'

'I was thinking that you're still as beautiful as I thought you were when I was a little girl.' Janet paused. 'But you've never been happy, have you?'

'When did that sudden insight strike you?'

'When you told me not to model my personal life on yours: it was how you looked when you said it.'

'Perhaps because this conversation has caused me to look backwards in time. Moments of happiness have come my way, Janet – nobody's life is entirely devoid of them. But most people are prepared to settle for what passes for happiness. Marriages are made every day between couples who will never know the heights of joy I once briefly experienced. The old saying that what you've never known you never miss is well founded, and they are more fortunate than I.'

Alison fingered the clasp of her evening bag and paused to reflect. 'My trouble, Janet, is I've never been able to settle for less than perfection. Professionally, I'm never completely satisfied with my own performance. And on a personal level – well, let's just say that I'm a bit like a butterfly-catcher who lets the ordinary variety flit by, because once for a short while I held an extraordinary one in my grasp.'

'It's men we're talking about, isn't it?' said Janet. 'Not butterflies!'

'What we are really talking about, my dear, is my hope

that you will make none of my mistakes. Now, how about joining Maxwell and me for supper at the Ivy – instead of going home to brood about my son?'

'I can't go to the Ivy dressed like this,' was Janet's excuse for declining.

Alison did not try to persuade her otherwise, and envied her the luxury of going directly home. The failure of a play was something its star and producer felt like hiding their heads about, she thought. But the tradition was to do the opposite.

'I have a distinct sense of *déjà vu*,' said Alison to Morton, when they had smiled at commiserating acquaintances in the restaurant. 'Every flop I've been in was a new play.'

'Which accounts for your having been in relatively few,' Morton replied. 'The new work that has come my way – especially since the war – has rarely been worth staging. The same, in my opinion, applies to some that others have staged. Now if I could have got my hands on Rattigan's *The Deep Blue Sea* for you — '

'How I envied Peggy Ashcroft her role, when I saw that play,' said Alison.

'But we mustn't sit here wringing our hands, my dear,' Morton said. 'We'll have you back on the boards soon, don't worry.'

'In another revival no doubt. But I long to get my teeth into a challenge. I wouldn't mind trying a contemporary thriller, Maxwell – and from your point of view they're good box office. That one of Agatha Christie's that opened not too long ago at the Duchess — '

'*The Mousetrap*,' Morton cut in.

'It will probably run for most of this year.'

'I doubt it,' said Morton. 'But pedestrian thrillers are not for you, Alison.'

'Then kindly find me a new play that is.'

'Unfortunately, Alison, the post-war British equivalent of Arthur Miller has yet to emerge.'

'So you have said *ad nauseam*, Maxwell. And when he does, Charles Bligh will probably nab him first,' said

Alison sourly. 'If ever there was an illustration of the devil taking care of his own, it's Mr Bligh's never getting his fingers burned!'

'How can he, when he never puts them into the fire?' snorted Morton. 'I have never known him once do what the rest of us sometimes do; back a play for art's sake at the risk of losing one's shirt.'

'Like you just did.'

'And I still think the writer has promise and hope he won't give up. I heard on the grapevine, by the way, that Bligh has finally relinquished the option he kept renewing on that woman-writer's play. He was hoping to get most of the finance from an American backer, also a woman, but in the end she didn't cough up.'

'One really has to be sorry for young playwrights trying to get ahead,' said Alison. 'Between the critics who slay them with the stroke of a pen, and impresarios who keep them on a string, it's remarkable that any of them survive to make their name. I heard Richard telling Janet the saga of that poor girl waiting in hope for her play to be staged – I think he said her name was Marianne Dean. Why don't you do her and me a favour, Maxwell, and try to get hold of that manuscript for me to read?'

'For a very good reason, my dear. Your flop must be followed by a sure-fire success.'

'Miss Dean,' said Alison tartly, 'ought to send her play to Joan Littlewood, who isn't in it for the fame or the money!'

'Who is that crack levelled at, Alison? You or me?' said Morton with a grin.

'I have never been in it for either,' she retorted. 'The fact that my art has brought me both is a bonus. So what is my next revival to be, Maxwell? As you've said no to a thriller.'

'I've said no to a pedestrian thriller – which Emlyn Williams's *Night Must Fall* cannot be called. How would you fancy it, Alison?'

'There is no need to ask me twice!'

Alison's dark eyes were now alight with anticipation,

like a kid who's been told it is to have a treat, Morton thought. A moment ago he had been wondering how to prise her from the doldrums, but he ought to have known that nothing raised Alison's spirits more than the prospect of exciting work.

Though Richard still lived under her roof, he had in effect gone from her. Morton, who missed the boy's affection no less with the passage of time, wondered when Alison's nerves would snap and felt that only her work was holding her together.

The charade they were still playing with Richard had long since become second nature to them, as though Alison and Morton, Emma too, were past caring what Richard did. But nothing could be further from the truth. The truth was that it was for them a like-it-or-lump-it situation, in which Richard held the upper hand and always would, Morton thought. The three who had raised him loved him too dearly to risk pushing him further from them than he had already strayed.

It was an ever-present sadness to Morton and the two women. But he no longer discussed Richard's defection with them, and doubted that they talked about it with each other. Little by little, a torpor of resignation had enveloped all three of them, Morton was thinking when the waiter served their soup.

'It would be lovely if Basil Breen were available to direct *Night Must Fall*,' Alison said.

'I'll call him tomorrow, my dear,' Morton answered. Thank God she has her career, he thought.

CHAPTER FOURTEEN

WHILE *Night Must Fall* was in rehearsal Alison's days were blessedly full, but the house echoed with emptiness when she returned in the evenings. Janet was doing another stint with a provincial repertory company, and Richard still touring.

'With both of them away from home, I don't know what to do with myself,' said Emma over dinner one night.

'Then you can imagine how Zelda feels – and would even if she weren't neurotic,' Alison answered. 'You and I tend to forget, Emma, that this isn't Janet's home.'

'But that doesn't alter how I feel now. When I don't have either of the kids to look after, I have too much time on my hands. And please don't tell me,' said Emma before Alison had time to reply, 'like you did during the war, to find myself a canteen to work in! I'm past that kind of thing.'

'If you say so, darling. But I'm sure there must be a Jewish soup kitchen or something of the kind in London, where your services would be appreciated. Past it, indeed – you're the best cook I know.'

'It's me that's past it, not my cooking,' Emma wryly replied.

'Nonsense!' Alison retorted. 'You're the same age as me, and the day I think I am past it they can bury me. Your trouble, Emma dear, is you have always put all your eggs in one basket.'

'You're wasting your breath lecturing me, Alison, because I can't be any different from the way I am. My trouble isn't what you say it is. It's that I have to be needed – and who needs me now?'

'I do, darling, and always shall. So does Maxwell.

101

There is more to being needed than ministering to people's creature comforts, and you know it. And one day, maybe Richard will wake up and realise he still needs us all.'

'We should only live that long! And you certainly need me to answer the telephone,' said Emma, when it rang and Alison did not stir herself to answer it.

The change in Richard is probably even worse for her than it is for me, thought Alison when Emma had hastened to the hall. Emma had devoted herself to his raising, while Alison pursued her career – and how painful it must be for Emma to see how he had turned out; as though she had personally failed. Now, she was left with little to do but brood about it, and – like Alison – was angry and distressed at one and the same time. But Emma's anger did not stop her from maintaining Richard's empty room as though it were a shrine. Or from laundering the soiled shirts and underwear with which he presented her whenever he came home.

How dare that boy treat Emma like a laundry service and this house like his London hotel, Alison was thinking hotly when Emma returned to the kitchen.

'Percy's on the phone,' Emma told her. 'He wants to speak to you – and didn't crack a single joke while he was talking to me, which isn't like my nephew. Also, he said he's calling from his surgery. What would he be doing there at nine o'clock at night? And on a Wednesday, which is his half-day off?'

'Never mind the soup kitchen, Emma,' said Alison with a smile. 'You should offer your services as an assistant to the modern equivalent of Sherlock Holmes.'

'I can smell a family crisis a mile off. And the worst ones always seem to involve you,' Emma declared apprehensively as Alison went to take the call.

Emma's nose for impending trouble had not let her down. Percy had telephoned to tell Alison he was going to marry his Gentile girlfriend.

'It's about time,' was Alison's response. 'I'm absolutely delighted to hear it, Percy dear.'

102

'But you're the only one who will be,' he gloomily replied. 'And I probably would never have done it, if Beth hadn't said she can't go on seeing me if it's never going to lead to anything. She's thirty now, and was only twenty-five when we met. I've kept her on a string for long enough.'

'Like your mother has you,' said Alison. 'Her apron string! And I'm glad for your sake, my dear, that you've made up your mind to break free.'

'You and my mother have never liked each other, have you?'

A picture of her cousin Clara ruling the roost in the Stein household in her teens rose before Alison. It was followed by another – of Clara the young war-widow in 1917, embroiling her parents and Conrad and Emma in her vicious feud with her in-laws.

Percy had been under his mother's thumb, one way or another, all his life. She had used him as a pawn in her spiteful punishment-game with his paternal grandparents, and he had not met them until he grew up.

As I've kept Richard away from my mother, Alison reflected with a pang of guilt, while she listened to Percy pour out his feelings on the telephone. But spite played no part in Alison's estrangement from her mother. Each was to the other as a red rag to a bull. Old resentments, spoken and unspoken, were responsible, she thought now. A brief reconciliation had occurred when they met by chance during the war. But neither had suggested meeting again. Both knew that the only way to maintain peace between them was for them to remain apart.

'I didn't want to be a doctor, but Mam wanted me to be one,' Percy was bitterly saying. 'And I don't blame you for not liking her, Alison. She takes it for granted, and always has, that everyone will dance to her tune.'

'That's why she doesn't like me,' said Alison. 'Because I never have. I am a bit that way myself, I suppose,' she admitted.

Emma would have called that the understatement of all time.

'But I'm not in the habit of imposing my will on everyone,' Alison added, 'whether what I want them to do will make them miserable or not.'

'Like Mam does. You couldn't have put it better. So she isn't a very nice person, what can you do? But she's still my mother and I love her in spite of everything.'

Alison knew that feeling all too well. It was an inner conflict she had lived with since her youth. And on her birthdays, she always thought of Hermione Plantaine and shed a tear for their wasted years.

'But Mam's entitled to fly off the handle about me marrying Beth,' said Percy. 'It's the worst sin a Jew can commit, and nobody's committed it in our family since your father did, Alison. Mam will faint with shock when I tell her – she doesn't even know that Beth exists.'

'You'll be there with your medical bag, to bring her round,' said Alison dryly.

'And after I do, she'll either chain me up so I can't get married, or tell me never to darken the door again.'

'The latter is highly probable,' Alison agreed.

'That's why I've spent my half-day pacing the surgery trying to screw up the courage to tell her. I made my decision after Beth and I had lunch together, then I couldn't bring myself to go home.' Percy paused miserably. 'Being exiled like your dad was for most of his life isn't a pleasant prospect, Alison.'

'You will not be exiled by Emma and me. And once the deed is done, I don't see my cousin Clara cutting herself off for ever from her doctor-son. How could she go on boasting about you, if she did?'

'That's an encouraging thought!'

'When is the wedding to be?'

'It's up to you, Alison. We'll get married whenever it's convenient for you to be there.'

'For you, I'll take a day off from rehearsals, though we are now in the thick of it,' Alison was moved to say. 'My favourite doctor doesn't get married every day. But a Saturday would suit me best.'

104

'That's the one day it can't be. Jews don't marry on the Sabbath.'

'Not even when they're marrying out of the faith?' said Alison with a laugh.

Percy laughed too. 'I know it seems daft, but to me, it would be like committing an extra, unnecessary, sin. And from God's point of view, it would probably make me even more of a criminal.'

'But I hope you won't go on thinking of your marriage as a sin for the rest of your life,' said Alison.

'That's what I'm hoping about Beth. Her family are devout Methodists and will hit the ceiling when she marries me. There's no chance of them coming to the wedding, which will be in a register office, needless to say. And afterwards,' Percy added sardonically, 'we'll be living in sin so far as both our families are concerned.'

'It would be advisable not to tell your mother which register office,' Alison said. Clara was capable of marching in on the ceremony and causing a scene.

'And it may as well be in London, Alison, as that's where you are,' said Percy.

'You make me sound like a raft to which you are clinging in turbulent waters!'

'That's what you've been to me since I was a kid. But Beth is somewhat in awe of meeting you.'

'I am looking forward to meeting her. And I shall treat you both to a super wedding breakfast at the Ritz,' Alison promised.

She returned to the kitchen humming a merry tune, but Emma's reaction to hearing Percy's news was a good deal less cheerful.

'I knew he had a Christian girlfriend, but I hoped it wouldn't come to this.'

'How could you have known?' Alison had not breathed Percy's secret to a soul.

'I'm not as green as I'm cabbage-looking,' was Emma's withering reply. 'For years Percy's been whispering to you in corners at every family get-together we've been to.

What else could it be about but the matter he daren't discuss with anyone else in the family?'

'Your powers of detection,' said Alison, 'continue to astound me.'

'How much of a detective does a person need to be,' Emma demanded, 'to put two and two together when an eligible Jewish chap of thirty-six is still single? A doctor, too, whom all the girls and their mothers have been trying to catch. The reason has to be a Gentile nurse.'

'But your two and two has just made five,' said Alison. 'Beth is a librarian, not a nurse.'

'And much good that will do my poor sister,' Emma declared with distress.

'Knowing Clara,' said Alison, 'it will probably put her off reading books!'

'I have no more respect for her than you have,' Emma replied. 'But I have to be sorry for her now. Since the war, there's been more intermarriage than there used to be, and it isn't quite the disgrace to a family that it once was — '

'Are you saying that people are growing more tolerant?' Alison interrupted.

'No, just resigned to the possibility,' said Emma. 'But it's still a Jewish mother's worst fear.'

'Nevertheless, Emma, I took the liberty of assuring Percy of your support.'

'I don't intend making an outcast of him, if that's what you mean.'

'But his mother might and Percy knows it. It would be a comfort to him to have you at his wedding, as well as me.'

'Clara would kill me!'

'I haven't noticed you being afraid of her before.'

'All right! You've talked me into it – but she will never forgive me when she finds out.'

Thus it was that on a rainy April day, Emma in her best brown outfit, and Alison, elegant as always, in a Dior suit, stood beside Percy and Beth while they became man and wife.

Emma was thinking of her sister, whose wrathful presence she could feel hovering as though Clara were in the room.

Alison's thoughts were of love, that had lent radiance to a weary, balding man and a plain young woman on their wedding day. She had no doubt that the union she was witnessing was a genuine love match. What did the displeasure of their two families matter? she reflected as Percy placed the ring on Beth's finger. What mattered was that Percy had not let the bright butterfly of happiness slip from his grasp.

CHAPTER FIFTEEN

A FEW DAYS after Percy's wedding, Alison and Emma travelled north for a funeral.

That Lottie Stein would not be there to greet them when they arrived in Oldham was inconceivable to both. They were eating breakfast when Conrad, who dropped in to see his mother each morning on his way to work, rang up to tell them that the old lady had died in her sleep.

Alison emerged from the daze she had been in since they received the news. 'How I dislike train journeys,' she said, gazing gloomily through the compartment window as they sped through Staffordshire.

'Probably because you did so much travelling by train when you were a child,' Emma replied, briefly brushing aside the guilt and regret that mingled with the pain of losing her mother.

Alison sipped some of the coffee a steward had just served them. 'But the Plantaine Players didn't travel first class.'

'Nor did I,' said Emma, 'until I moved into your world. Some of your extravagances still shock me, Alison. Though I'm thankful today to be travelling in comfort, and that we have the compartment to ourselves.'

'If Maxwell weren't abroad, he'd have driven us to Oldham, like he did when your father died.'

'I wouldn't have wanted him to.'

'Your mother was very rude to him that day,' Alison recalled. 'It wasn't like her.'

But she had guessed how I feel about him and was upset on my account, Emma mentally replied.

'And on another occasion, she said something about

108

Maxwell being the fly in the family ointment,' Alison went on. 'As though she held him to blame for something, the way Richard does.'

'Drop it, will you, please?' Emma said edgily.

Alison put a comforting hand on hers. 'We can't not talk about your mother, darling, as if she had never been here and part of our lives.'

'You seem to have succeeded in doing that with regard to your own mother,' said Emma with uncharacteristic sharpness, 'though she is still alive.'

Alison withdrew her hand.

'I'm sorry. I shouldn't have said that, Alison.'

'You were perfectly entitled to say it. It's true. But that doesn't mean I never think about Mama.'

'There is no need to tell me that.'

They lapsed into silence, each with her private thoughts.

Emma voiced some of hers. 'When I think of how Clara made it clear to me that if Mam ever needed looking after it would be my responsibility, because I'm single, well, I don't know whether to laugh or cry! In the end, Mam didn't trouble either of her daughters, did she?'

'And she would be pleased that she didn't.'

'That,' said Emma, 'is the aspect that makes me want to cry. Has it ever struck you, Alison, how unkindly life is arranged? It begins with the parents looking after the children, and ends the other way round. But the parents do it willingly and the children don't.'

'I wouldn't include you in that last sweeping statement,' Alison replied. 'Had your mother needed you, you would have devoted yourself to her.'

'But she would have seen herself as a burden to me – and I'm sure that's what old people dread being, no matter how devoted their children are.'

Emma glanced through the window at the rural scene that would soon be replaced by the industrial panorama of her childhood, and remarked, 'The cows are lying down in the meadows – that means it's going to rain.'

'And I will forecast something else,' said Alison. 'That

Clara will set about us for standing by Percy, the moment she sets eyes on us. Her silence so far is distinctly ominous!'

They had expected a tirade from Clara over the telephone. Or that she would come hurtling to London to give them a tongue-lashing face to face. But they had heard not a word from her.

Percy's sister, Lila, who had sent him a congratulatory telegram though she had not dared flout her mother by going to the wedding, had told Emma that Clara had taken to her bed. Nobody expected her to take the matter lying down for long.

She appeared to be still doing so verbally when she let Alison and Emma into the house, and mystified them further by kissing them both.

'We expected you to shoot us down,' said Emma bluntly. 'And if you're going to, please get it over now, before the house fills up with people coming to the funeral.'

'It's what you both deserve,' Clara answered. 'But as Mam would have said, what's done is done,' she added resignedly.

Then she and Emma held each other close in a moment of shared grief for their departed mother.

Clara dabbed her eyes and put away her handkerchief. 'It's best to let sleeping dogs lie,' she declared.

Alison and Emma exchanged a glance. Were they dreaming this? Clara was more at home with a dagger in her hand than an olive branch.

She must have something up her sleeve, Alison thought. On the rare occasions when Clara was nice to someone, they usually paid for it later.

'There's nothing to be gained by recriminating,' the arch-recriminator said.

And something to be gained by holding your tongue, thought Emma, who was as suspicious of Clara's civility as Alison was,

Clara, though her eyes were swollen with weeping for her mother, was quite composed.

110

Too composed, Alison observed. As though she had carefully rehearsed the scene now taking place in Lottie's parlour. Like an actress awaiting her cue.

Alison unwittingly gave it to her. 'I'm longing for a cup of tea – is anyone around to make us some?'

'Zelda has slipped out to buy some groceries; Mam's larder wasn't stocked for the crowd of us there's going to be,' Clara answered. 'And I asked Conrad to collect the mourning chairs and prayerbooks from the synagogue. Perhaps you would make the tea, Alison. I'd like a private chat with my sister.'

That's why you got your brother and his wife out of the house, thought Alison. Clara wanted something from Emma she might not get if Conrad and Zelda were there to put their oar in. What a cunning creature she was!

'What I'd like to do is go upstairs and pay my last respects to my mother,' said Emma. 'Whatever you want to say to me privately can wait, Clara.'

'I'm afraid it can't,' Clara replied. 'Conrad will be back before long, and it's none of his business,' she confirmed Alison's suspicion. 'Also, for what I have in mind we've got to move fast, Emma. Before the funeral and the week of mourning begins.'

'I'll go and make the tea then,' Alison said. If she stayed in the parlour a minute longer, she would ask Clara how she could be thinking of anything other than her bereavement right now, and it would spark off a row that Emma could do without.

'Stay where you are, Alison,' said Emma. 'Clara can say whatever it is in front of you.'

'Anyone would think you need a witness!' Clara exclaimed, showing a flash of her usual self.

Emma made no bones about it. 'Maybe I do. Does what you want to discuss with me by any chance concern our mother's will?'

'As a matter of fact it does. I've had a peep at it, and — '

'I bet you have!' Alison cut in.

Clara ignored the interruption. 'The house was Mam's only asset, and she's left it to you, Emma.'

111

'And you don't think that's fair, I suppose?' Emma answered. 'Though your husband is wealthy enough to buy you a handful of houses, as well as that palace in Prestwich you live in.' Her lips curled with contempt. 'I can read your mind, Clara. I always could, so you need say no more. You're thinking that as I live in London, I'll sell this house – and why should I have the money the sale will bring? You've always been money mad.'

Clara allowed the insults to wash over her – and there had to be a reason for that, both Alison and Emma thought.

'The house won't bring any fortune, Emma,' she declared. 'But if you do what I tell you to, it could be a very different matter. If my husband weren't wealthy, I wouldn't be in a position to help you.'

'And if you want to help me,' said Emma, 'it must be a way of helping you to make money.'

'So what's wrong with both of us making something out of it?'

'Out of what, Clara? Our mother's death?'

'I'm referring to the sale of the house.'

'Isn't that the same thing?'

'As the house has to be sold, you're splitting hairs, Emma. And you haven't yet heard all I have to say. It's the third house from the avenue corner, isn't it? And you may have noticed when you passed by in the taxi that the corner one, and the one next door to it are both up for sale.'

'Alison and I had other things on our mind when we turned into the avenue,' Emma said with disgust.

'Those two houses have been on the market for some time,' Clara went on. 'Families are smaller nowadays, and modern housewives don't want these big, old-fashioned homes to look after. I could probably buy them for a song – which is all you'd get for this one. But the land from all three houses would be worth plenty to a developer. Luxury flats are catching on in the north, but there's a shortage of available land.'

She gave Emma a sisterly smile. 'You're welcome to

112

what Mam has left you. I don't want to share your inheritance, so you were wrong about that. All I'm asking for is your co-operation in something that could do us both some good.'

'Why didn't you just buy the other two houses and offer them to a developer – instead of waiting for Mam to die?' said Emma curtly.

Again Clara turned a deaf ear to the insult. 'I thought of doing so,' she replied pleasantly, 'and the people I'm negotiating with now came from Manchester to have a look. They said the plot wouldn't be big enough to make it worth their while, but if I could persuade my mother to sell, we could do a deal. Mam wouldn't hear of it, when I mentioned it to her.'

'And I can imagine how she felt!' Alison exploded. 'Being asked to get out of her home, so her daughter could profit from it!'

'This is nothing to do with you!' Clara said vehemently. 'But it might interest you to know that I would have arranged for my mother to live in the best apartment — '

'How very considerate of you,' Alison interrupted.

'With a marvellous view of Oldham,' Clara went on regardless, 'and no stairs to climb up and down, like she had here. In a posh, eight-storey block, with a lift and a caretaker.'

'And no garden to plant her seeds in like she did every year,' said Emma.

'There'd have been a communal one, with a gardener to look after it. Mam was too old to plant seeds and water the flowers. But that's beside the point now. And if we're going to do it, Emma, there's no time to waste. It would be just my luck for the other two houses to be suddenly snapped up by someone with the cash to convert them into bedsitters.'

'You're out of luck anyway,' Emma told her. 'Because I'm not going to sell this house.'

The mask of pleasantness dropped from Clara's face. 'What are you going to do, then? Let the place rot, empty, until the day you find out what a mistake you

113

made by going to live with Alison, and come running back here?' She picked up the poker and gave the fire an angry poke. 'Because that's how you're going to end up, our Emma! Seeing through the person who took you away from us.'

'You said that to me years ago, Clara, and I warned you never to say it again.'

'But that day has to come – mark my words. And when it does,' Clara added nastily, 'I'll slam my door in your face if you ask for sympathy from me.'

'Instead of assassinating my character,' said Alison, 'why don't you take a good look at your own, Clara? It's time you did – though even if you were to miraculously change it's too late to undo all the hurts you've inflicted. To whom, in your whole life, have you given any lasting pleasure? Except yourself! And your mercenariness, even on the day your mother breathed her last, shocks even Emma and me, who know you too well.'

'Don't give me one of your performances, Alison. I'm not in the mood for it!'

Clara swept from the room, leaving the aftertaste of her presence behind her.

'What shall you do with the house?' Alison asked Emma.

'I don't know. And it isn't just the house I care about.'

Emma gazed through the window at the laburnum by the garden gate. Opposite, a copper beech glistened with raindrops from the April shower that had preceded the sunshine now flooding the room.

'Can you imagine, Alison, what a block of flats would do to this peaceful backwater? A great big building that would blot out the sky for those living opposite? And the noise of the flat-residents' cars, coming and going, like they do in London, would drown out the chirping of the birds, and the lovely sound of the wind rustling the leaves on the trees.'

'But as your dreadful sister said, Emma, flats are catching on in the north. There isn't enough land to go on and on building houses. It had to happen.'

114

'All the same, I'm not going to help it happen to this part of Oldham.' Emma gently fingered one of Lottie's treasured ornaments that had stood on the window ledge for as long as she could remember. 'I'd rather let the house to people who will take good care of it, so it will go on being a home. My mother would have liked that.'

'Then why not offer it to her grandson?' Alison suggested. 'Beth said at the wedding that they would have to live in furnished rooms until they found a house. Is Percy's surgery far from here?'

'It's much nearer here than where he was living. By the time he got out of prisoner-of-war camp and was rehabilitated and demobbed from the army, all the suitable vacancies in Manchester had gone. Percy works with an elderly doctor in Failsworth. But Clara raised a rumpus when he wanted to leave home to live where he works.'

'No doubt she wanted to keep him within the Jewish community,' said Alison. 'And much good it did her! If there's one thing I've learned by being a mother, it's that parents can't impose their ideas upon their children. What they daren't do in one's presence, they'll do in one's absence – and Percy is a prime example of it.'

'Since when were you qualified to speak for parents?' Clara said from the doorway. 'It's my sister who brought up your son.'

'How long have you been standing eavesdropping?' Emma acidly inquired.

'Long enough to hear that callous idea Alison put into your head. Only the family troublemaker would suggest that you offer the house to Percy.'

'She must have been lurking outside the parlour for several minutes,' said Alison to Emma with distaste.

'And it's as well I did!' Clara retorted. 'It gave me the chance to nip in the bud what you want Emma to do to me.' She put a tragic expression on her face and appealed to Emma, 'Isn't it enough that my son married that girl, without the agony being piled on for me by him bringing her to live in my dead mother's home?'

115

'There are times,' Alison crisply told her, 'when I think that you too should have been an actress. Were I not so sick with disgust, I should have to applaud the show you just put on for Emma's benefit. But like it or not, Clara, Beth is now your daughter-in-law. If you had any sense, you would accept a situation you can do nothing to change.'

'Have you finished?' said Clara.

'Not quite. You are a fine one to accuse me of being callous, Clara, after the proposition you put to Emma before Aunt Lottie has even been laid to rest. And in my opinion, Percy and Beth coming to live here is the poetic justice you deserve.'

Emma's mind was racing ahead. 'And won't it be lovely, Alison, for another generation of the family to grow up in this house?'

Clara knew when she was beaten, and inserted her vengeful verbal dagger where it would wound her sister most. 'But they'll be my grandchildren, not yours, Emma. Nobody is ever going to call you Grandma.'

'As the Bard said, what's in a name?' Alison swiftly countered. 'Emma will share the role of grandmother with me, as she has shared the mothering of my son.'

Part Two

Fame and tranquillity can never be bedfellows.
Montaigne

CHAPTER ONE

'IT'S TIME I directed a West End play,' Richard said at breakfast one Sunday morning.

Alison put down her teacup. 'My dear boy, you are still only twenty-three.'

'The same age you were when you made your London début,' he reminded her.

'But I wasn't responsible for the entire production, only for my own supporting role.'

Emma was at the cooker, refilling the teapot, and telegraphed Alison an eye-message to say no more.

Alison ignored the warning. 'You'd be well advised, Richard, to do what Janet is still doing – broaden your experience before exposing yourself to West End audiences, not to mention the critics. And Janet's doing so is a good deal less necessary.'

'Is that your way of taking me down a peg?' Richard flashed.

'Is there nothing I can say to you that you won't construe that way? If the play flopped, the failure would be attributed to its young and inexperienced director: the cast would join with the critics in that respect. I'm trying to save you from the ignominy and repercussions of a disastrous début in the capital, Richard darling.'

'Because I'm Alison Plantaine's son, and the ignominy would rub off on her?' Richard crunched some toast and gave Alison a cold glance. 'If you had your way, Mother, you'd never let me take a chance that may push my career forward, lest the opposite happens and sullies your own distinguished image. But I have to be my own person – and I'm starting now.'

Emma thought it time to intercede. 'You started a long

119

time ago, Richard. And when did your mother ever try to stand in your way? You have come and gone and done as you pleased since you left school. The things you just said are unfair.'

And much good our policy of letting him do as he pleased has been, Alison thought.

'Whose side are you on?' Richard said tersely to Emma.

Emma brought the teapot to the table and refilled the cups. 'So far as I'm concerned there are no sides, Richard. We're a family, and your mother and I care about you.'

'But my mother cares about her career more. She always has.'

Who could blame him for thinking so? Emma reflected. 'Have some more toast,' she said.

'I don't want any more toast!'

A strained silence followed, then Richard gave Emma an affectionate smile. 'Sorry for snapping at you, Auntie. I know you like to feed me up when I'm home for the weekend.' His smile disappeared. 'Which sums up the difference between you and Mother. Your feeling for me is a good deal more maternal than hers.'

'Would you mind,' said Alison, 'not talking about me as if I'm not here?'

'In effect, while I was growing up you weren't,' Richard answered. 'You were a sort of fairy princess who drifted in and out of my life, while Auntie Emma scolded me if I was naughty, and made me wash behind my ears. And the theatre was my rival for your love.'

'But you are now grown up and should know better,' said Alison.

'It isn't easy,' Richard replied emotionally, 'to rid oneself of feelings implanted when one is a child.' And you've yet to prove to me that I was wrong, he thought, and added, 'When I think back to my childhood, it's remarkable that I myself have ended up in the theatre. That I've joined the enemy camp!'

The enemy camp is Bligh Productions, not the theatre, thought Alison, but she managed not to say so and said instead, 'I'm glad you allowed heredity to win, though in that respect you might have followed your father's intellectual path.'

Richard gave her an icy stare. 'Are you still hoping I'll swallow the story of that mythical German writer?'

The subject had not been raised since their eventful holiday in France, in 1949, and it was now 1956.

'Where is your friend this weekend, by the way?' Richard inquired. 'It's unusual for me to come home and not find him ensconced in an armchair.'

'You arrived in the early hours,' Alison answered ignoring his cutting tone. 'Maxwell isn't in the habit of dropping in for breakfast.'

'But he'll be here for lunch,' Emma said.

'In that case,' Richard told them, 'I shall go out for mine. Lucy will be happy to give me lunch. She's interested in doing the play I want to direct for the West End.'

Alison was relieved that the conversation had switched to a topic less personal, if no less contentious. 'But what matters, so far as the play's being staged, is whether or not her husband is interested in it, Richard. The finance will have to come from Mr Bligh.'

'Not necessarily,' he replied. 'If Charles will put up some of it, I can get the rest.'

Alison prickled with apprehension.

'I could probably get the whole sum required,' Richard went on. 'But if Charles wants to come in on it, I shall be delighted. He's given me the chance to make my own way. And Luke, to whom I'll be eternally grateful, has taught me all I know.'

'If you're thinking of landing yourself in debt, to back a production you're not yet ready to undertake, I implore you to think again,' Alison said. 'And Maxwell, whose experience as a producer you cannot deny, though you've turned against him personally, would tell you the same.'

'Of course he would!' Richard retorted. 'He has his reasons for holding me back, and you have yours. And one of yours is loyalty to him. The two touring plays I've

121

already directed for Charles are making money for Bligh Productions – and how painful that must be for you and your friend, Mother dear.'

'Do you suppose that profit has anything to do with what I've said to you? Money has never been my be-all and end-all, Richard, and the same goes for Maxwell.'

'I'm prepared to accept that regarding you, Mother,' Richard conceded. 'About him, I am less sure. But setting aside that aspect, for Alison Plantaine's son to direct a West End play for someone other than Maxwell Morton would be for you two public ignominy indeed.'

'If that's why you are doing it, go right ahead,' Alison told him witheringly.

Emma's face was creased with distress. 'When you were still a schoolboy, Richard, you told me that one day you would pay Max back – for whatever you think he's done to you. I know it was no idle threat, you've been punishing him for years – and, believe it or not, he is still your friend, though you don't deserve him to be. But learning that you want to deliberately hurt your mother has come as a big shock to me.'

'You've got it wrong, Auntie. If I could make my way without hurting her, I would — '

'Fair enough, Richard,' Alison cut in stiffly. 'But let me assure you that any ignominy I might suffer, were your West End début a disaster, would be nothing compared with yours, not to mention the damage to your career when it has barely begun. My concern about this stems solely from the maternal love you seem to think is not in me.'

'I stopped expecting you to be any different from how you are many moons ago, Mother.'

Emma managed to laugh, to ease the tension. 'You've not yet seen that many moons!'

But it would be a blue-moon phenomenon for Alison to put anyone, even her son, before her own career, Emma thought when Alison switched to the topic of her next play. As Richard had just said, she would never change.

'Kitchen-sink drama isn't for you,' was Richard's reply

to Alison's saying that she would not mind appearing in one. 'It would be like casting yourself as Sally Hardcastle's mum in *Love On The Dole.*'

'I wasn't yet playing middle-aged roles when that play shocked everyone with its stark realism,' Alison answered wryly. 'But twenty years on, I know my place.'

'Take my advice, Mother, and let the new genre wash over you,' said Richard. 'You'll still be here when it has gone.'

'Maxwell doesn't expect it to last for too long, either.'

'Though I hate to have to agree with him, I must.'

'But he was glad when something that could be called a new trend came along,' Alison replied. 'Though their settings are drab, and their themes depressing, plays like the new crop have something important to say, and have given British drama a shot in the arm.'

'*Look Back In Anger* is the one that's really done that,' Richard declared. 'It's like a cry from the wilderness that speaks for the playwright's generation.'

'Something similar was said when Noel Coward's work first appeared, in the Twenties,' Alison recalled.

'Please don't compare John Osborne's work with Coward's,' Richard said. 'You might just as well compare a nourishing meal with a soufflé.'

It was then that Alison realised that a chasm existed between herself and her son, professionally as well as personally. Her views on theatre were to Richard 'old hat', and he thought her incapable of stretching her talent to encompass a new genre role. In a minute we'll be quarrelling about drama, from our relative attitudes, she thought. The generation gap that was making itself overtly felt in family life, as it never had when she was a girl, could – if she allowed it to – affect her already strained relations with Richard. A time had come in her own youth when she had found herself questioning the artistic ideas of her elders in the Plantaine Players, but she had not dared to voice her thoughts. Nowadays, young people spoke their minds, and be damned to respecting their elders.

123

As the play *Look Back In Anger* did. Alison returned full circle to the point from which she had begun her reflection. Its working-class hero and top-drawer heroine mirrored the younger generation's changed attitude towards class since the war – as Shakespeare and Shaw had held up a mirror to society in their work.

'Young Osborne will go a long way,' Alison pronounced to Richard.

'He would probably consider that an accolade, coming from you. The play I'm hoping to do in the West End is a comedy, by the way.'

'Then I hope you are an expert on timing,' Alison replied. 'In comedy, timing is all. Would you mind telling me where the finance you spoke of is to come from?'

'Don't worry,' said Richard. 'You won't have to rescue me from financial disaster, should I be faced with a flop. The answer to your question is I've found a fairy godmother, who would comfort me with a smile and tell me it's only money.'

Alison and Emma were momentarily speechless.

'I met her a long time ago,' Richard enjoyed telling them.

'How old is she?' Emma wanted to know.

Alison had not yet found her tongue.

'Not too old and not too young,' said Richard mischievously. 'But you'll meet her at the première – if you'll both do me the honour of being there!'

'I wouldn't miss it,' said Emma.

'Nor I – unless I'm appearing in a play,' Alison managed to say.

'And there you have my life in a nutshell!' Richard told Emma. 'She wouldn't hand over to her understudy even to sit beside her son on the most important evening of his twenty-odd years,' he said before departing.

Emma began clearing the breakfast table. 'Sometimes you shock even me, Alison. What will it take to make you see what really matters?'

Alison toyed pensively with a teaspoon. 'And what will it take for my nearest and dearest to realise how hard it is for me to be two people? Alison Plantaine the actress, and Richard's mother? Since the night he was born I have lived with that conflict.'

'But you never let the mother in you win.'

'And now my son, to whom I was once a fairy princess, has a fairy godmother. I don't like the sound of that at all.'

CHAPTER TWO

'HAVE YOU seen a rehearsal of Richard's production?'
Morton asked Alison when what she had tried to prevent
was under way. Morton, too, had cautioned Richard,
though with no hope of his warning being heeded.

'Would he be likely to allow me to?' Alison replied.

She was currently appearing in *The Cherry Orchard*,
and Morton had dropped in to her dressing room after the
evening performance.

'Madame Ranevsky's troubles are nothing compared
with mine,' she said of the character she was playing. 'As
if what is probably in store for Richard were not enough,
Janet too is involved in it. I fear her second appearance in
the West End may last no longer than her first, Maxwell.
That girl needs her brains tested for accepting the part.'

'Youth puts its faith in youth,' was Morton's reply.

And Janet is still in love with Richard, thought Alison
unhappily. The chance to work with him, untried though
he was, must have been irresistible. How different she
is from me, Alison reflected. Janet had proved herself
single-minded about love: her art came second.

Put to the test – and how long ago it seemed – Alison
had taken the opposite course, returning to England to star
in a play, instead of remaining in Germany with Richard
Lindemann. Nor had it just been loyalty to Morton that tore
her from her lover's arms, but devotion to her art, too.

It had since occurred to her that Richard Lindemann
had known only one side of her, and briefly at that. Had
they married, he might have found her other side the
painful enigma their son did. But it was equally painful
for Alison. The loving human being she was did not live
comfortably with the dedicated actress driven by some

126

inner force to strive eternally for a perfection she could never quite achieve.

Last night, when she had arrived home from the theatre too exhausted to eat, Emma had told her that it was time she stopped doing one play after another. 'Rest on your laurels for a while, you're famous enough,' she had said.

Laurels indeed! Alison thought. Fame and the necessity to sustain it once you had achieved it sometimes felt like wearing a hair shirt that allowed you no peace.

Morton was watching her remove her stage make-up. 'You're looking very pensive, Alison.'

'I was thinking that when I look back I seem never to have had a private life.'

'That's the price of having become a star while you were still young.'

'One of the prices,' said Alison, recalling her conversation with Richard in Cannes, on the subject of fame. 'There've been several, Maxwell – and I could wrap them up and tag them with a single label. Despite the warmth you and Emma give me, and the adulation of my public, inside myself I am lonely.'

'That's the chill wind at present blowing towards you from Richard, but one day it will pass,' Morton assured her.

'What makes you so sure?'

'You are his mother. And he is your son.'

Alison got up and went behind the screen to change into her evening gown. 'Were you close to your mother, Maxwell?'

Morton stubbed out his cigar and nodded. 'She was the only person, apart from our Em, who called me Max. And like Emma, she was a great little cook.' Morton's eyes misted with remembrance. 'Though she died when I was very young, I remember her vividly.'

'My son would probably prefer to forget me,' said Alison bleakly. 'And who could blame him?'

'If you're going to launch into one of your self-denigration sessions, I'm leaving!'

'Please don't.'

Morton could hear the rustle of taffeta from behind the screen. 'Need any help with your zipper?'

'No thanks. Nor do I need you to suddenly begin getting fresh with me.'

'I would – if I thought it would get me anywhere. Have you ever considered, Alison, how different Richard's life might have been if you'd married me?'

'He wouldn't have been Richard. He'd have been your son – if we'd had one.'

'I meant if you had married me when you discovered you were pregnant. He'd have thought himself my son and so would the world. We should all have been spared what he is putting himself and us through because he won't accept who his father was.'

Alison emerged in a black silk sheath and returned to the dressing table to put on her pearls. 'You didn't ask me to marry you at that point in our lives,' she reminded Morton.

'Because Richard Lindemann was still alive and part of the scenario. Had he not been, I would certainly have proposed to you – for the umpteenth time. By the time we confirmed that he was dead, it was a number of years too late for us to marry and pretend our boy is mine.'

Morton fidgeted with his chin and avoided Alison's eye. 'But a terrible thought has occurred to me recently.'

'You had better not share it with me. I have enough terrible thoughts of my own.'

'I must,' Morton replied. 'Because it could be the answer to Richard's animosity toward me lasting so long. I think Richard has got it into his head that I am his father.'

Alison paused with her lipstick halfway to her mouth. 'What makes you think that?'

'I've been around all his life, haven't I? And, except when he was evacuated to the States, it was I who fulfilled the father-role for him.'

'That's no reason for him to think that you actually fathered him.'

'As Emma would say, I should only have had the

pleasure!' Morton allowed himself to joke. 'As things are, I no longer even have the pleasure of being what I once was to Richard,' he went on. 'And for the most ridiculous of reasons: he now thinks I am what I would have been proud to be, and despises me for not owning up to it.'

He paused to absent-mindedly smell some of the roses with which Alison's dressing room was, as always, filled. 'When a person doesn't want to accept the truth, they clutch at an untruth that seems feasible. That is what Richard has done, Alison. I feel it in my bones. Presumably he would rather have a Canadian father who won't acknowledge him as a son, than a dead German one.'

'I'd forgotten you were born in Canada,' Alison said for want of anything else to say. Momentarily, she was dazed by Morton's theory, then questions that Richard had asked her about herself and Morton returned to her mind. Including why they had not married, she recalled.

'The sooner you and I clear this up with him, the better, Maxwell,' she said.

'How impulsive you have always been and still are, my dear,' he replied. 'What I've said to you is supposition – and if I am right, what good could it do to discuss it with Richard? Since he didn't believe the truth when it was told to him, why would he now, when the fiction with which he chose to replace it has had years to entrench itself in his mind? It's possible he imagines you and I have been sleeping together all his life.'

'Then he ought to be writing fantasies, instead of directing plays!' Alison snapped.

'If there was ever a man who received all the approbation and none of the pleasure for the sins accredited to him, it's me,' Morton said with a hollow laugh.

'But as you yourself said, it is only supposition.' Alison surveyed Morton's weary countenance. How old was he now? She had lost count, but he was much older than herself – and beginning to look it. The vigour that had once emanated from him was all gone, though he worked no less hard than he always had. 'How many shows have you got touring at present?' she asked him.

'Four – but who's counting?' he said with a smile.

'I am, because you look worn out. You've got another play besides mine in town, and one in rehearsal, haven't you?'

'Also a co-production on Broadway. And one being tried out in Boston, which I'm none too happy about and must pay a flying visit to. Every silver hair on my head was probably put there by a show, Alison.'

But it's always my problems we talk about, never his, she thought with contrition and went to kiss his cheek. 'You must have gone grey very early, Maxwell dear,' she said, brushing the silver mane away from his brow. 'You already were when our paths first crossed, or I should think myself responsible for that part of your distinguished appearance.'

'But my business stopped being my *raison-d'être* the day I admitted to myself that you are,' he told her.

'I don't deserve to be, Maxwell.'

'Who gets what they deserve?' he joked, helping her on with her cloak.

'I'm afraid,' said Alison, 'that Richard will, with regard to his West End début.'

'In some respects he is like you. And it isn't always possible to stop a runaway horse from rushing headlong to its fate.'

'Which in his case will be a panning from the critics. There's no way he could be ready to do what he's doing, but he won't be able to say we didn't warn him.'

'And that fairy godmother of his is all set to lose her pantees,' Morton declared.

'I would rather you hadn't put it quite so graphically!'

They were about to leave the dressing room, and Morton paused with his hand on the doorknob. 'So that's what you think, is it?'

'Which mother wouldn't?'

Alison had not yet met the lady, who was due in London for the première, but had felt from the first that there was more to Mrs Taylor Colville's interest in Richard than he had revealed.

130

CHAPTER THREE

JANET KNEW while Richard's production was still in rehearsal that it was doomed, but refrained from saying so when Alison quizzed her. Love and loyalty were for her twin emotions, but that did not prevent her from seeing her loved-one's work with a critical eye.

The play was about an impoverished upper-class family determined to maintain their traditional lifestyle, and with a more experienced director could be a tongue-in-cheek social comedy of the times, Janet thought one morning while awaiting her cue in the drab and draughty rehearsal room.

Why had Charles Bligh let Richard plunge in too soon? Probably because Lucy had fallen for the star role and it was not her husband, but Richard's fairy godmother, who had taken an option on the play and was backing it.

Janet brushed aside her shadowy fears about that unknown American lady, and thought with feeling that had Bligh's money been at risk, he would be sitting watching these rehearsals, instead of sunning himself in Australia where Luke Plantaine was at present rehearsing a play.

In the absence of both, Lucy, Janet had noted, was taking advantage of Richard's professional inexperience and his respect for her. She was the kind of star who cared only about her own performance, and needed a strong director, like her brother, to ensure that her selfishness did not ruin the production.

An example of this occurred when Janet made her entrance. Lucy was playing the lady of the manor, and Janet the one remaining servant in the ancestral home. They were rehearsing a dinner-table scene and using improvised props.

131

'You may serve the entrée, Withers.'

'Yes, milady.'

'What is the entrée this evening, Withers?'

'Baked beans, milady.'

Lucy stopped acting. 'How dare you try to get a laugh at my expense!' she snarled when Janet lifted the lid off the dish to reveal the sparse course to the audience, with an accompanying droll facial expression.

'This production could use a few laughs,' said the playwright, who was seated gloomily at the back of the room.

Lucy rose from the rickety stool that was serving as her gilded dining chair. 'Richard! We had better settle this here and now, darling. This is either my scene or it isn't.'

The actor playing her husband gave her a sugary smile that did not match his tone. 'Forgive me for butting in, Lucy dearest, but I was under the impression that this was my scene.'

'As written it's the servant's scene,' said the playwright. 'But in performance, the play I wrote is rapidly disappearing.'

'And should you ever write another – which heaven forbid you to do – it would pay you to bear in mind that those whose names appear below the title on the programme and billing do not have scenes,' Lucy informed him.

'Why don't you just appear in monologues, Miss Plantaine, and have done with it?' he retorted.

Richard unfolded his lanky figure from a chair and joined the cast. 'May I get a word in now?'

'It's time you did,' the playwright snapped.

A real-life scene of this kind was not unprecedented during rehearsals of any production, and less so when a play was being premièred and its author as yet unknown.

Richard dealt first with the author. 'Instead of sitting in on rehearsals, biting your nails, Pete, why not find yourself something useful to do?'

No greater insult than that dismissive suggestion could be made to a playwright, though their superfluity once the manuscript is out of their hands is a painful fact of life to

132

dramatists in general, and responsible for the precarious author-director relationship common in the theatre. Each is aware that the other must be handled with kid gloves, but neither Richard nor Pete had yet had time to acquire that art.

The most useful thing that Pete felt he could do right now was attack Richard and Lucy with a sledgehammer to put them out of action and save his brainchild.

If the author would stay out of it, all would be fine! Richard was thinking with an asperity he must keep bottled up. 'Go and have a chat with the designer, Pete,' he said soothingly. 'There's a small problem about the set – there's a meeting about it going on now, at Charles' office.'

'And I wish Mr Bligh were there himself. I need some-one to complain to! What sort of problem? And why wasn't I invited to the meeting? Whose bloody play is this?' was Pete's heated reaction.

'You can't be in two places at once, can you, my love?' Lucy caustically told him. 'And everyone, including the designer, is aware by now that you've chosen to honour the cast with your constant company.'

'But you'll still make the meeting if you hurry,' said Richard hopefully.

The playwright was torn by indecision. He would be as unwelcome at the meeting as he was here – though every-one concerned was currently earning their bread because of his play. 'I wish I'd been born without the gift God gave me,' he exclaimed, thrusting his hands in the pockets of his shabby raincoat. 'I'd be happier driving a truck.'

'And that is how you will probably end up, sweetie, if you don't let those who know better than you do get on with it,' Lucy snapped.

'I think the best thing I can do,' said Pete, 'is get drunk and stay that way until the torture I'm being made to suffer is over! And I include in that the première and the reviews, which will probably be as agonising for the rest of you as for me. If I'm required – that will be the bloody day! – you'll find me next door in the pub, Richard.'

A moment of silent relief followed his departure. Only Janet felt sorry for him.

'Now we can get down to work without sparing that poor lad's feelings,' said Lucy, who spared nobody's. She gave Janet a cold stare. 'I won't have my performance affected by the antics of my fellow-players, Richard.'

'All I did was roll my eyes and raise my eyebrows,' Janet said.

'At a moment when I am supposed to be expressing pathos,' Lucy retorted.

'What's wrong with pathos and comedy side by side?' Janet enquired.

Lucy turned her back on her. 'Who is directing this play, Richard darling? You or Miss Stein? Was it your idea for her to do what she did, or hers?'

Richard avoided Janet's eye. 'It wasn't mine.'

'And if you'd rather I didn't do it, I won't,' Janet said.

'Fine, kiddo. We'll leave it out.'

Lucy had won. But how could she not when Richard always allowed her to win? Janet thought.

As the opening night drew nearer, Janet had no option but to watch Richard go on blindly steering his ship of dreams towards the rocks he was surely heading for.

When the day's work ended, they usually travelled home together and spent their evenings by the fire with Emma; but Janet knew that had Alison not been appearing in a play, Richard would have made himself scarce.

The best that could be said for his present relationship with his mother was that they had agreed to disagree. He avoided Alison's company and never mentioned his work in her presence, nor did she raise the subject.

The tips that Janet sometimes dared to offer him were dismissed with tolerant amusement.

'As you're in the play, kiddo, you can't see the overall production,' he told her on one such occasion.

'I see it better than our star does, as she sees absolutely nothing but her own performance.'

134

'We both live with a star, kiddo – and I for longer than you have. We know how they tick,' was Richard's response.

'And nobody knows better than I do,' said Emma, who was knitting while she listened to them.

'But Alison is a true professional,' Janet declared. 'I was once in a play with her, remember, and she shows the same consideration and respect for her fellow-actors and the director that she expects from them.'

'You don't like Lucy, do you?' said Richard.

'She isn't exactly likeable.'

'Now, now, kiddo!' he said with a smile. 'I hope you're not turning into one of those actresses who is jealous of the star.'

'You should know me better than that.'

Richard gave her a brotherly hug. 'And you should know when you're being teased. You're the nicest girl a chap could have around – or I wouldn't love you as much as I do.'

But in quite the wrong way, Janet mentally replied.

'And from what I know of Lucy Plantaine, I pity anyone who has to work with her,' said Emma. She had sat tight and kept silent for too many years in that respect, and felt it necessary to support Janet.

'But you only know Lucy from Mother's point of view,' Richard answered.

'From Janet's, too, now.'

'But that isn't knowing a person, is it, Auntie? If I had allowed myself to be swayed by Mother's judgement of the twins, I'd have been deprived of a friendship that's been instrumental in my becoming what I am.'

That you can say again, thought Emma.

'What are you knitting?' Janet said to change the subject. 'It looks like something very special,' she added, fingering the ball of white silk Emma was using.

'As a matter of fact, it's a silk muffler for Richard to wear with his evening suit, on his opening night.'

Richard went to kiss her cheek. 'And how like you to think of knitting me one.'

'You haven't got one, have you? I don't want you to catch cold on the way to the theatre.'

'As yet, I haven't got an evening suit, either.'

'I heard your mother offer to buy you one,' Emma said.

'You also heard me refuse the offer.'

'So you'll have to wear my scarf with that old corduroy jacket you wear all the time,' Emma replied. 'And everyone will wonder why the director hasn't bothered to dress up for his big night.'

'I thought you might lend me the cash to get my evening togs, Auntie.'

Emma went on calmly knitting. 'I'd gladly give you the cash as a present, Richard, if you hadn't refused your mother's offer. But I once told you, didn't I, that I don't take sides – and that includes deeds as well as words. For me to enable you to get the suit without your mother's help would be like helping you thumb your nose at her.'

'Fair enough, I understand,' Richard said. And added with a grin, 'But one of these days you're going to fall off that fence.'

Emma could have told him that it was not a comfortable place on which to perch, but the only position from which she could maintain a semblance of peace in the household.

'The answer to your problem, Richard, is to hire your togs,' said Janet.

'Good old kiddo! Now why didn't I think of that?'

Because your head is in the clouds, Janet thought. But who could keep their feet on the ground when it seemed to them that success would be handed to them on a plate? As the money to stage the production had been.

Alison was not alone in conjecturing about Lee Taylor Colville's interest in Richard. Janet had learned via Lucy that the lady was young enough not to seem ancient to Richard. Nor had Janet failed to divine the charm he had for older women.

An actress in the cast, who must have been at least thirty-five, had done everything but actually make a pass at him, Janet was thinking when he returned to the subject of Lucy.

'If our star didn't care about me personally, she wouldn't be taking the interest in the direction that she does, kiddo. I'm lucky to have her in my first West End production.'

Let's hope it won't be your last, Janet thought, that the critics don't banish you to the sticks for all time, and your American heiress tell you to go take a running jump for wasting her money.

CHAPTER FOUR

THOUGH MORTON'S presence was usually a reason for Richard's absence, on Janet's birthday he stayed home for Sunday lunch.

'Would you mind answering it?' Alison requested when the telephone rang.

'Not at all,' Richard replied.

When we're not having a difference of opinion, we're like over-polite strangers, Alison thought bleakly.

Richard returned to tell her that the call was for her. 'And my first conversation with my great-aunt Ruby Plantaine,' he added.

Alison prickled with apprehension. There was no love lost between herself and the twins' mother; if Ruby was calling, something must be wrong.

'Has Uncle Oliver been taken ill?' she asked her aunt, after the barest of greetings had passed between them.

'Fortunately, my husband remains in relatively good health. I wish the same could be said for my sister-in-law.'

'What is wrong with Mama?' Alison asked with a fluttering heart.

'I'm surprised that you sound as if you care,' was Ruby's reply. 'As you've allowed your uncle and me to be responsible for her in her declining years and ours.'

'My mother is a proud lady, Aunt Ruby. If I had sent her money – which I'd willingly have done – she would have returned it. I didn't insult her by putting her in that position.'

'Sending money is not the only way of caring for an ageing parent, Alison. I'm sorry to have to tell you that Hermione is now a sick woman. Too sick for your uncle and me to go on nursing her as we have been doing.'

138

'And I'm immensely grateful to you both,' Alison said with sincerity. 'But as I knew nothing of this, that you and Uncle Oliver have borne that burden is hardly my fault.'

'Did Lucy and Luke not tell you?'

'They certainly did not. I rarely see them. But they could have told my son.'

'They probably didn't wish to upset him,' Ruby defended the twins, who for her could do no wrong. 'And I expect the reason they didn't bother telling you, Alison, was they thought it would be a waste of time.'

'A waste of time to let me know my mother is dying? That's why you've called me, isn't it?'

'If you want it straight – and why should I spare your feelings? – I'll give it to you, Alison. The doctor told us a year ago that Hermione's condition was hopeless. He didn't put a time limit on it, but I can recognise death approaching when I see it. I saw it with my first husband and the signs are there with your mother. Hermione is not long for this world. Your uncle didn't want me to telephone you, but not to do so wouldn't be right.'

'I'm thankful you did,' said Alison, trying to control the tremble in her voice.

'It's Hermione I'm thinking of, Alison, not you,' her aunt replied. 'Though she and I have never got on, her rift with her only child has grieved me, and I have many times compared her lot with my own good fortune in having the considerate children I have. Luke and Lucy visit me as often as their work commitments permit.'

Alison knew that this was true. The twins had not neglected their elderly mother and stepfather. But one redeeming feature didn't make them the angels Ruby thought them. On the contrary, Alison had no doubt that they had kept from her what they knew about her mother for their usual calculating reasons – which in this case was to ensure she would feel as she now did, when she found out. Guilt, anxiety and pain summed it up, mingling with the daughterly love she had never lost.

'I shall come to Hastings immediately,' she told her aunt.

'And you had better do some thinking on the way, Alison. Your uncle and I are worn out from nursing your mother and I must ask you to consider us.'

Alison returned to the dining room and burst into tears.

The others eyed her in consternation. Alison Plantaine weeping was like seeing a lofty edifice suddenly crumble to the ground, and it rendered them momentarily speechless.

Alison took Morton's monogrammed handkerchief from his breast pocket and blew her nose. 'You must all forgive me. I am shattered by the news I've just received.'

'You'll feel better when you've shared it with us,' Morton said. 'Then Emma will go and make you some of her shock-relieving brew.'

'I need something stronger than tea.'

'Pour your mother some brandy,' Morton said to Richard.

'Would you mind not giving me instructions in my own house?' Richard replied.

'Stop it!' Alison cried. 'I now have something very real to grieve over, and you'd be doing me a favour, Richard, if you would put your imaginary grievance aside.'

'Would that it were imaginary, Mother,' he said, avoiding looking at Morton.

Alison had not let herself dwell upon Morton's theory that Richard thought him his father. But if Maxwell was right, how ironic it was that when she finally unveiled the truth for her son, he had imposed upon it an untruth that was causing him unnecessary hurt.

'And would that I understood the machinations of your mind,' she said while he poured the brandy.

After she had sipped some of it, she relayed the gist of her conversation with Ruby.

'You must bring your mother here,' said Emma unhesitatingly.

'Wouldn't a nursing home be a better idea?' Morton put in.

140

'How dare you suggest that my grandmother be packed off to somewhere, as though she were an unwanted old parcel!' Richard flashed.

Janet, who knew that Alison's estrangement from her mother was the cause of Richard's never having met Hermione, understood how Richard felt.

Morton, too, but his practicality had prevailed. 'I am trying to be helpful, Richard. Sensible, also. Which you must be with regard to your grandmother's welfare, and the effects her being here would have upon this household.'

'As you're not part of it, you have no right to interfere.'

'Let's leave me out of it, shall we?' said Morton evenly. 'And think of your mother and your Aunt Emma. Alison's current play has two more weeks to run and she requires all her strength and energy to fulfil that professional commitment — '

'Trust you to put her career first!'

Morton ignored the interruption. 'Auntie Emma, though you may not have noticed it, is not as young as she used to be, and the same applies to your mother. Nursing your grandma, and with the devotion they would both give to her, would drain them emotionally and physically.'

'It won't be for too long,' said Alison. 'And not only is it the least I can do for my mother, I want to do it.'

'In that case you must.'

'Is there nothing,' said Richard, 'for which my mother doesn't require your permission?'

Morton turned a deaf ear to the jibe.

'I must do what my heart tells me to,' Alison said tremulously.

'But Emma will bear the burden.'

Emma was touched by Morton's concern for her. He rarely revealed it and she was always newly surprised when he did.

'Bearing the burden has always been our dear Emma's lot,' said Alison, giving her a wan smile. 'How could it not have been, when she's been my companion for so many years?'

Alison had never denied her own failings, but that, thought Morton, was part of her charm. 'I'll drive you to Hastings,' he offered.

'You'll do nothing of the kind,' Richard told him vehemently. 'This is a family matter and need not concern you.'

Emma came down from the fence. 'Everything that goes on in this family concerns Max, Richard. He is closer than a brother to your mother and me.'

'I won't tell my dad you said that,' Janet said wryly.

'Conrad is up north, Janet. Max is here, where my life is,' Emma answered. 'And I'm thankful for him.'

'But he isn't taking Mother to Hastings. I am,' Richard declared.

'As you wish,' Morton said with a shrug, and a smile.

How does he go on taking this from Richard? Alison and Emma asked themselves. But both knew the answer was Morton's deep love for the boy.

'Take my car, Richard,' he said.

'No thanks. I'll call a cab.'

Alison lost her temper. 'Will you please stop this childishness, Richard! Either take Maxwell's car and drive me to Hastings, or don't – and he will!'

'I left the keys on the hall table,' said Morton.

Richard ignored him and escorted Alison from the room.

'What a lovely birthday Janet is having!' said Emma after they had heard the front door slam. The reverberation left them in no doubt as to who had closed it.

It was a birthday Janet would not forget. Though Richard's coolness towards Morton was nothing new, the overt rudeness he had displayed today had shocked and embarrassed her. He must be even more jealous of his mother's close friendship with her manager than Janet had long since divined.

'We must put down Richard's edginess today to the drawing nearer of our première – only two-and-a-half weeks to go,' she felt constrained to say. 'It was sweet of you to be so understanding with him, Mr Morton.'

142

Morton gave her a smile and remained silent.

What people put up with for love – every variety of it – someone should write a book about, Emma thought.

Then she and Janet went upstairs to prepare a room for the dying lady they had never met. It would not have occurred to either of them to shirk the harrowing task Alison's bringing her mother here imposed upon them, but such were the women of the Stein family.

CHAPTER FIVE

WHEN THE curtain rose, Richard was gripped by a feeling peculiar to directors: tension, anticipation, and resignation, in equal parts. Until the final curtain fell he would be unable to relax, lest something went wrong onstage. He was nevertheless looking forward to seeing the result of his work. But he must now leave it to the cast to do their best or worst; which it would prove to be was out of his hands.

The pre-performance gathering in the theatre Green Room had done nothing to steady his nerves.

The playwright, whose ill-fitting evening attire was more obviously hired than Richard's, had skulked alone in a corner, as though he were practising for the ostracism he felt would be his lot after tonight.

Alison and Lee Taylor Colville had reacted to each other like cats with sheathed claws. And Morton had, in Richard's hearing, told Janet's parents who were in town for the opening not to be too disappointed if the play had only a short run.

Emma, whose presence was always a comfort, was not there. She had insisted upon remaining at home with Alison's mother, though everyone, including the patient, had seen no reason not to engage a nurse for the evening.

For Richard, this was yet another illustration of the difference between Alison and Emma. The only thing that would have kept Alison away from the première was her own appearance in a play, as she herself had said. And her condescension toward Lee had caused Richard to wish that *The Cherry Orchard* had not ended its run in time for her to be present, he was thinking when Lucy made her entrance onstage.

He was aware of his mother's light perfume drifting from his left, and Lee's exotic one from his right. They could no more blend than the two women wearing them could be friends, he thought with one part of his mind. The other part was registering that the laughter he had expected when the star spoke her first line was conspicuously absent.

No more than a few polite titters were wrenched from the audience as Act One progressed, and Richard felt Lee's hand creep into his. By contrast, his mother's profile appeared stony to him in the darkened auditorium.

'I think I shall just stay here during the interval,' he said when the lights went up.

'That wouldn't be a good idea, Rick,' said Lee. 'And I guess your mother would agree.'

Alison did, though she was reluctant to agree with Mrs Taylor Colville. 'You must come and put on a face, Richard.'

There was no necessity to say why.

'Let's all go and have a drink together,' Morton said helpfully.

'As this isn't your show, you're not required to put on a face,' Richard replied. 'And all is not lost yet,' he added. 'Lee and I will go and mingle with whoever. There's no need for you old folks to stir yourselves.'

'We've just been relegated,' said Morton wryly when Richard and Lee had departed.

'You would do yourself a favour,' Alison answered, 'if you'd accept, as I now have, that the relegation was effected a long time ago – and probably for keeps.'

The rest of the evening was a strain for the audience, and agony for the author and director and those present who cared for them personally.

Nothing conspires to produce stilted performances from actors more than lack of reaction from those for whom they are performing. As the final act neared its end, the cast seemed to Alison like puppets mouthing words. Her only consolation was that Lucy was one of them. The others, Janet in particular, did not deserve this fate.

Only a few moments of genuine – and grateful – laughter punctuated the boredom. Janet, desperate to help Richard, risked Lucy's wrath by including the droll facial expressions he had told her to exclude. But nothing could save the play, as she and her fellow-players well knew.

At the party that followed she was required to go on acting, in company with all concerned, be they thespians or not. And never had the necessity to do what Alison called 'put on a face' been better illustrated than it was that night.

'Stay close to me, Rick. We'll get through this together,' Alison heard Lee say to Richard, as she and Morton entered Bligh's apartment in their wake.

'I'm astonished that you agreed to cross this threshold, Mother,' Richard told her.

'She has put in an appearance for your sake,' Morton answered. 'I, too. You're going to need all the support you can get, Richard.'

'Which is your way of saying "I told you so!" I suppose.'

Alison watched Richard gulp the whisky a waiter had just handed him and take another glass from the tray. 'Instead of drowning your despair, it would be more constructive to ask yourself why your production fell flat.'

Richard downed the second whisky and said to Lee, 'That's my mother. Always the professional! Work comes first and feelings last.'

'Feelings can be a quagmire to wallow in that drags one down,' Alison replied. 'If it is up that you want to go, Richard, you had better be prepared to learn from your mistakes. I am equipped and willing to help you do that.'

'You're taking tonight's little misfortune too seriously, Miss Plantaine,' said Lee lightly. 'As one swallow doesn't make a summer, the failure of his first West End production doesn't herald disaster for Rick's future.'

146

She linked her arm through Richard's, and went on, 'It sure needn't with me around. Since it was my dollars that staked the play and I'm not weeping, he doesn't have to either.'

She and Alison then appraised each other for a moment, as they had when they met in the Green Room.

What an imposing lady Alison Plantaine is, Lee thought; her black gown and white fox cape enhanced the impression. Rick had probably been dominated by her all his life.

Alison, though not a flicker in her expression revealed it, was filled with foreboding. This lovely creature was going to part her from Richard more completely than the twins had succeeded in doing, in the way that only a woman can come between mother and son. Lee Taylor Colville, in a shimmering emerald sheath that matched her eyes and set off her glorious titian hair, was everything a man could desire, and one as young as Richard would be flattered by her interest in him. Her wealth was an added attraction, thought Alison, noting the costly black opals around Lee's milky neck.

Briefly, it was as though they were alone in the room assessing each other. Then Lucy left a group of people who had been mouthing the inevitable 'absolutely marvellous' platitudes to her, and came to join them.

Her husband, who had returned from Australia to attend the première, was having no difficulty in smiling, Alison registered. Though Bligh's company had staged the play, he would not lose a penny – and would make sure that everyone knew he had only lent his name to the production to pander to his dear wife's whim.

'Come into the library, poppet,' Lucy said to Richard, 'and we'll put through a call to Melbourne. Luke will be waiting to hear from us.'

'Would you mind if I stayed here?' Richard replied.

'It's like that, is it, poppet?' said Lucy, eyeing Lee, who still had her arm linked through Richard's. 'Oh well,' she added with mock chagrin. 'But I never thought the time would come when you wouldn't want to chat to Luke.'

Nor had Alison. But Richard's loosening of his bond with the twins would not benefit her, and meant he was about to begin the next chapter of his life. If the woman now smiling up at him was as possessive as Alison judged her, it would not include his mother.

CHAPTER SIX

THE AFTERMATH of the première was for Alison like a bad dream from which she could not awaken. Hovering over her, too, was the ever-present knowledge that her mother lay dying in the house.

She was scanning the predictably scathing reviews of the play when Richard, still in his evening attire, arrived home.

'You're doing some gloating, I see,' he said, eyeing the morning newspapers on the kitchen table.

Alison took off the spectacles she now required for reading. 'If you really think that, we have drifted even further from each other than I'd painfully supposed.'

'We've drifted as far as there is to go,' he replied.

Alison felt the blood drain from her face.

'I realised that last night, when you didn't utter one word of comfort to me.'

'I'm sure Mrs Taylor Colville did not allow you to go short of comfort,' Alison unwisely said.

'What kind of crack is that?'

'You may interpret it as you wish.'

'And there's no doubt about how you interpret my staying out all night! But you happen to be wrong.'

'I'm sure my interpretation of the lady's interest in you isn't wrong.'

'I'm equally interested in her.'

'That isn't surprising. She's extremely attractive.'

'And who are you to cast aspersions on other people's morals?' Richard asked tersely. 'The proof that you're in no position to do so is me.'

Alison had not thought to see the day when her son would taunt her with his illegitimacy – and she had Mrs

149

Taylor Colville to thank for it, she thought, putting on her spectacles to busy her trembling hands.

'Now you look like the prim and proper person you're not,' Richard said. 'And may I remind you that I'm no longer a child?'

'I need no reminding. And it would be a foolish mother who did not expect her son to have affaires before settling down,' Alison replied. 'But the one you are on the brink of embarking upon is not confined to your private life.'

'Because Lee has faith in me, which you haven't! She has already offered to back another production for me to direct and — '

'You'll be wasting your time and her money,' Alison cut in.

'And you certainly know how to kick a chap when he's down!'

Alison steeled herself to tell him what she had finally allowed herself to recognise, after a sleepless night spent dissecting his production. 'I would rather kick you from the bottom rung of the wrong ladder, Richard, than watch you climb to the mediocrity that is the most you could hope to achieve.'

'How can you possibly have arrived at that conclusion, after seeing only one play I've directed?'

'Even your inexperience, my darling, could not account for the unrelieved drabness of what we saw last night. If you had what it takes, a spark or two of your creativity would have blazed through. In time, you would learn to handle leading players like Lucy, who if she were a football player would be concerned only with the goals she herself might net, and never mind if the team wins — '

'Spare me the analogies!' Richard interrupted.

'What I am trying to tell you is that technique alone is not enough.'

'And I thank you for your encouragement, Mother.'

Richard went to stare through the window and left Alison to address his stiff back.

'If I thought you would be satisfied with mediocrity, I should have kept silent. But I know you wouldn't be. In that way, Richard, you are like me. And I know that what I've said to you is painful to accept.'

'I haven't accepted it.'

'But you will have to one day.'

Why does it have to be me, thought Alison with distress, who tramples upon his dream? But nobody else would and it had to be done. Now.

'I've known too many people in the theatre,' she went on, 'whose aspirations have come to nothing. Our world is one in which few make it to the top. For those who do, it is rarely achieved overnight. Nor was it for me, though I got there sooner than most.'

'With Maxwell Morton's help!' Richard flashed. 'But you disapprove of Lee's helping me.'

'She can stake you from now until doomsday, darling, but her money can't buy for you what you lack: it can't be bought. Maxwell gave me the chance to exploit what was in me. And great directors, like great actors, are born not made, Richard.'

'So speaks the great Alison Plantaine,' said Richard from the depths of the misery she was inflicting upon him.

'It's neither my fault nor yours, my darling, that you were not blessed in that way.'

'And if you've been saying things like that to Janet – which I wouldn't put past you – it's no wonder that she left the party even sooner than you did, last night,' Richard answered.

Janet had pleaded a headache, but Alison knew that it was the sight of Richard and his benefactress together that had impelled her to leave. That lady's entrance into our lives will do Janet no more good than me, thought Alison. 'I recognised Janet's gift while she was still a child reciting monologues,' she said.

Then Richard sat down in the fireside chair and put his head in his hands. 'I can't believe this is happening.'

'And how I wish it were not.'

Richard looked up and gave her his appealing little-boy smile. 'Tell me you didn't mean it, Mother.'

The plea, and the way he was looking at her, tore at

151

Alison's heartstrings. If things were ever to be put right between them, she must tell him a lie now. Or at the very least pretend there was a chance of him achieving what he hoped to achieve. She would then have to watch him over the years tread the path of the third-rate, until disillusion stared him in the face. By then, Lee Taylor Colville would be long gone. Nobody loved a loser for long – except his mother, Alison thought.

'I'm not in the habit of saying what I don't mean,' she said.

Richard sprang to his feet. 'And I've heard enough of what you have to say! I came home to tell you I was going to take your advice – get some more experience in the sticks. But you would prefer me to give up directing, rather than have me make it without the help of you-know-who.'

'I sometimes wonder from where you got your twisted mind,' Alison replied.

'Probably from exercising it to fathom out the truth from all the lies and half-truths I've been told by you,' said Richard, striding from the room.

It was now Alison's turn to put her head in her hands, and thus that Emma found her.

'In all the years I've known you, Alison, I've never before seen you look the picture of despair.'

Alison told her why, and added, 'I've reached the end of my tether.'

'The end of your tether,' said Emma, 'is when there's no hope left. If Richard won't take your advice, he'll have to learn from his own mistakes.'

'Exactly,' Richard said, re-entering with a hastily packed holdall. 'I'm sorry to upset you, Auntie, but I have to cut loose from my mother.'

Alison quailed. 'Would you mind saying that to me? There is no need to use Emma as your go-between.'

Richard gave her an icy glance. 'I've said all I'm going to say to you. Except for one final word. Goodbye.'

He kissed Emma and was gone from the house before they had recovered their breath.

Alison sat listening to the clock ticking in the silence that followed his departure. Then Emma put a comforting hand on her shoulder and she managed a wan smile. 'No prizes for guessing who he'll run to. Mrs Taylor Colville has taken over where the twins left off.'

Emma began clearing the breakfast table. 'Nonsense, Alison. The twins took Richard under their wing to hurt you: though I thought you were being melodramatic when you first said that, I no longer do. But this American lady has no reason to be malicious towards you.'

'What you're saying, Emma, is that her motive is different from theirs, and I don't need telling that. But Richard is now under her influence, and even if it were a good influence I should find it distressing. What I would like to see is my son being his own person.'

Alison pensively fingered the sugar bowl and emerged from her reflection when Emma removed it, to put it in the cupboard. 'Richard thinks he has gone his own way, but in reality he has done no such thing. Is he to go through life being putty in the hands of one scheming person after another?'

'The boy is only twenty-three, Alison.'

'That's a man, not a boy. And the portents are already there,' said Alison.

'But for the moment,' Emma replied, 'you must try to forget you are a mother and concentrate upon being a daughter – while you still have the chance to.'

'Was Mama awake when you looked in on her?'

'If you can call it being awake, with all the sedation she's having,' said Emma compassionately. 'I shall never understand how you became estranged from such a dear, sweet lady, Alison.'

'Nor can I – from the person she is now. And I worshipped her when I was a young child. She was so fragile and beautiful.'

'Fragile she still is.'

'But her beauty has fled and it's heartbreaking to see. Though by then she had fallen from the pedestal on which I'd placed her, I can remember myself at the age of twelve – a great, hulking creature who looked ridiculous in little-girls' frocks – wishing I looked like Mama. My looks are the very opposite of the patrician Plantaines and always have been,' said Alison wryly.

'I should only have your looks!' Emma replied.

'But in my childhood it was a mystery to me where they came from,' said Alison.

'From my late mother,' said Emma unnecessarily. 'As I resemble your father. The first time Mam met you, Alison, she came home and told us that if you and I had been born under the same roof she would have thought she and her brother had got mixed up about which child was whose.'

'And what a shock it was for me to meet Aunt Lottie,' Alison recalled. 'Like seeing a picture of how I would look when I grew up, when I hadn't known until that night that Papa had a family. Or that he was a Jew.'

Alison paused, re-living the scene in her father's dressing room, when the company was playing *Macbeth* in Oldham in 1914. Lottie had come to the theatre to tell him their father was dangerously ill.

'Papa was as shaken as I was,' she said to Emma. 'They hadn't seen each other since their teens, and he knew that the secret Mama had made him keep from me was about to come tumbling out. As for me, I had never encountered any Jews and there I suddenly was with a Jewish father. It was like having to get to know him all over again. Myself, too, since I was no longer who and what I'd thought myself.'

'The way our people were looked upon in those days, and by some we still are, it couldn't have been easy for you,' said Emma.

'It wasn't. For me, every Jew was Shylock, and I've never forgiven the Bard for creating him. *The Merchant* is one play I shall never appear in, though as Conrad once said, I'd have made a good Portia when I was young.'

'But you seem to have sorted out your youthful confusion,' Emma dryly said.

'And once I had, it was as though the night I met your

mother had brought another dimension to my life. Not just finding that I had you and the rest of the family, Emma, but being part of a heritage more meaningful than the Plantaines'. The theatre is in my blood, but cannot warm my heart – and it was warmth that I had craved and missed.'

Alison's expression clouded. 'The other side of the coin was Mama's trying to keep me away from what I wanted to be part of. I was a lonely kid, and finding I'd got cousins to be friends with – from which I exclude Clara! – was a joy. Once I'd sat by your parents' fireside, with all that implies, I was hooked. That's what caused the trouble between Mama and me.'

Tell me something I don't know, Emma thought. But Alison had never spoken of it in detail before.

'Mama hated Papa's family sight-unseen, for not accepting her,' Alison went on. 'It was why I never felt able to talk to you about her.'

'But didn't it ever occur to you, Alison, that she behaved about our family the way she did because they had hurt her? That she, too, has a point of view?'

'No. But it does now – when it's too late. And it must seem as ironic to her as it does to me that two members of the Stein clan are helping to nurse her.'

'Janet and I felt strange at first calling her Aunt Hermione.'

'She told me the other day that she has grown fond of you both.' Alison smiled wryly. 'So one could say that Destiny has had the last word.'

'I'd prefer to think God has,' said Emma, 'by reuniting her with you.'

Richard came each day with fresh flowers for his grandmother, but said not a word to Alison. Emma and Janet shared the vigil with her. The sick woman was never left alone as her life flickered to its end.

One afternoon when Alison was seated by her bed, Hermione opened her eyes and smiled. 'I was dreaming of

155

your papa, my dear. How lovely to wake up and find you holding my hand.'

'Don't talk, Mama, it will tire you.'

'I've been doing too much sleeping.'

'It's the new drugs the doctor has prescribed.'

'And I must thank him when he comes again. They are keeping the pain at bay. Would you like to brush my hair, Alison? – invalid or not, I mustn't neglect my appearance!'

Alison fetched the brush from the dressing table, but did not bring the hand mirror. It would do her mother no good to observe her yellow complexion. Hermione was dying of cirrhosis of the liver; the drink with which she had eased her lonely widowhood had finally taken its toll.

'That boy of yours could not be more dear to me were he my blood grandson,' Hermione said.

But Alison could not let her go to her grave without knowing that Richard was a Plantaine. Would Hermione's Victorian upbringing mar her joy when she learned her family line would not end with Alison?

Alison was surprised that it did not.

'Oh, how absolutely splendid,' she declared. And added, 'But how very sad for you that his father did not survive the war. I had often wondered why you hadn't married.'

'I'm a one-man woman, Mama.'

'As I was, my dear. Despite the little flirtations I indulged in during the Great War, while your papa was in France.'

She watched Alison return the brush to its place. 'You still haven't forgiven me them, have you, Alison? Though you've since learned for yourself how lonely a woman without her man can be. But your father was everything to me.'

'I know that, Mama. But why are we talking about the past?'

'Perhaps because that is all we have in common, my dear, and have never been able to agree.'

Alison went to gather Hermione close. 'But we're mother and daughter, and I don't want to lose you.'

'If you weren't about to, you would not have brought me here, Alison. Nor would I have agreed to come.'

But why did it have to be like that? And oh, the wasted years, Alison was thinking when her mother died in her arms.

Conrad and Zelda came from Oldham to pay their last respects to the aunt-in-law they had never met. To Alison's amazement, Clara was with them.

Clara answered Alison's unspoken question. 'I haven't forgiven you for putting it into Emma's head to offer Mam's house to Percy and his wife, so don't imagine I have.'

'I understand they are now settled in – and that before the summer will have made you a granny,' Alison replied.

'So I hear.'

Would Clara's heart soften toward Percy then? Alison wondered.

'Our Lila is now expecting, as well, so I don't have to rely on my son to give me grandchildren,' Clara said.

Conrad and Zelda exchanged a glance with Alison. What can you do with Clara? it said.

Though they too disapproved of intermarriage, they were not the kind to cry over spilt milk, Alison thought.

'But one thing has nothing to do with another, Alison,' Clara went on. 'Or I wouldn't be here. At times like this, a family have to do right by each other – and when did ours ever not?'

Alison was moved and amused at one and the same time. Clara hated her guts, but family feeling had won. Jewish family feeling, in which hypocrisy played no part, born of the insular way of life history had made necessary for a race determined to stick together and survive. It's there in me, too, Alison thought. She and Clara did not pretend to like each other, but each would be there with the rest of the clan if the other were in trouble.

157

Clara was appraising Alison's Balenciaga dress and coat.

She's thinking that my outfit must have cost a fortune, and in a moment will ask why I'm not wearing black for my mother's funeral, Alison silently wagered.

'Dove-grey was Mama's favourite colour, so I decided to wear it today,' she replied when the question came. And could not resist adding, 'I see that your husband has bought you another fur coat, Clara – you'll soon have one for every day of the week.'

Clara smoothed her Persian broadtail. 'I'd have worn my mink, but for funerals I don't like to overdress.'

'Come off it!' said Conrad. 'You're wearing more jewellery than my wife would wear for a wedding.'

'Why should we turn up here looking as if we're Alison's poor relations, when we're not?' Clara flashed. 'But Zelda isn't even wearing her engagement ring, is she? And she could have found something smarter to put on than that plain tweed coat.'

'Unlike you, Clara,' Conrad retorted, 'Zelda doesn't think of a funeral as a fashion parade.'

'Exactly,' said Zelda. 'But let's not turn this one into a family rumpus – for Alison's sake.'

But where the Steins gathered, a rumpus there always was, thought Alison dryly. And how her Plantaine relatives would react to them she would not let herself conjecture.

'Where's Mr Morton?' said Clara. 'Isn't he coming?'

'No.'

'Don't tell me you two have fallen out? I thought you couldn't live without him.'

'You could be right.'

'Oh yes?'

'But not in the way you think.'

They were standing in the hall, in readiness for the funeral cortège to leave for Hastings, where Hermione would be buried in a churchyard beside her parents. As Alison's father lay beside his in a Jewish cemetery. When a Jew and a Christian marry, they are parted by their separate creeds in the end, Alison reflected.

She could see through the window her mother's coffin inside the hearse. Among the wreaths adorning it was one bearing the words: From the family up north. A family whose elders, now gone, had refused entrance to Hermione while she lived, and in death she and her husband had returned to their own. Religion, not Destiny, had the last word, Alison bitterly thought. But if there was such a place as Paradise, her parents who had loved each other deeply would surely be together again there.

'Have you had a row with Mr Morton?' Clara persisted curiously.

'No, but he'll probably have one with me for not letting him know my mother is dead. He's in Boston, ironing out some problems with one of his productions. Emma and I saw no point in fetching him back. There's nothing he can do.'

'Except console you,' said Clara snidely.

'Even at a funeral, our Clara can't help being herself!' Conrad exclaimed.

'One can always rely on her to supply some light relief,' was Alison's way of putting it. 'Though of the kind I can do without today. I am not short of people to console me,' she told Clara.

'But the house isn't what I'd call brimming over. There's nobody here but us.' Clara glanced at her diamond wristwatch. 'And the cortège is due to leave soon.'

Alison managed to keep her patience. 'My Plantaine relatives – and there are only my uncle and aunt and Lucy, as Luke is still in Australia – will be at the cemetery when we get there.'

'But where,' asked Clara, 'are the famous actors and actresses I expected to be here?'

'You're standing next to one,' Conrad reminded her.

Clara glared at him. 'I meant Sybil Thorndike, and Laurence Olivier – people like that.'

Alison, despite her feelings, had to smile. Clara's disappointment at not rubbing shoulders with the big names of the theatre was plain to see. 'Everyone with whom I am acquainted or have worked is not an intimate friend, Clara. There are those who would have come along today had I invited them. But I wanted a family funeral for Mama, and it's what she would have wished. It's many years since she appeared onstage and most of her own professional contemporaries are gone. But I'm sure you didn't come here autograph-hunting,' Alison could not stop herself from crisply adding.

Then the hall clock chimed two and it was time to leave – or there might have been another rumpus, thought Alison. Richard emerged from the living room and avoided her eye. He had been closeted in there with Emma and Janet. Had they been giving him a piece of their troubled minds?

If so, it was to no effect. His stony silence was maintained in the limousine in which he, Alison, and Emma followed Hermione on her last journey. At the cemetery, he placed himself between Lucy and her mother. Next to Lucy was Oliver Plantaine.

Alison found herself standing opposite them, with her Jewish cousins – as though, she thought, my two families are ranged against each other to the very last, and I am with the one I chose. As Richard's loyalty is no longer to me.

All was symbolism and nostalgia to Alison that bleak, January afternoon in 1957, as grief for her mother, and for the seeming death of her relationship with her son, mingled with remembrance.

She and her Grandfather Plantaine had once walked through this churchyard reciting one of Shakespeare's sonnets, on their way to a Christmas morning service. Her mother and grandmother, dressed in their finery, were strolling ahead of them. And oh, the head-turning when we all entered the church, Alison recalled. In the days of the Plantaine Playhouse, the family were local celebrities.

Though Alison had itched to widen her artistic horizon, and the twins had endeavoured to make her life a misery, those long-ago days were part of what she had become.

Now, only Oliver and Ruby were left to epitomise them for her; there was about them the ambiance of a bygone age. Oliver still looked every inch a gentleman of the theatre and Ruby, the one-time melodrama-queen, had not lost her flamboyance.

Why aren't I thinking only of Mama? Alison asked herself. Because it wasn't possible to think of her mother outside the context of the life they had once shared. Hermione was right when she said that all she and Alison had in common was the past – which included that Hermione and Ruby had loathed each other. Yet Ruby had done her duty by Hermione, until the time came when it was necessary to remind Alison of hers.

Emma took Alison's hand as the coffin was lowered to its resting place – as Lucy had taken Oliver's, Alison saw, and with a tenderness she had not known the twins had for their stepfather.

Sorrow was serving to heighten Alison's perceptions, as it had purged her soul of bitterness towards her mother; opening her eyes to what she had not hitherto recognised. At the funeral repast provided by Ruby, she noted the absence of non-kosher food that might offend her Jewish cousins: her aunt was more considerate than Alison had thought her.

It was that afternoon, too, that she realised that the twins' affection for Richard was not simulated.

'How's my poppet doing?' Lucy said to him at the table, with love in her voice and her eyes.

Accomplished actress though Lucy was, Alison knew this was no performance.

'This dear boy is too busy to drop in on me nowadays, and oh, how I miss him,' she told her mother. Then she rumpled Richard's hair and slipped an arm around his shoulders. 'But he's still my little pal and always will be, won't you, poppet? Luke said on the phone that he misses you, too, and that the three of us will have a grand reunion night-out when he gets back to England.'

'Alison said your brother is in Australia,' Clara diverted her. 'You should ask him to bring you an opal ring, set with diamonds; they say you can get them for next to nothing there.'

'I've been admiring your jewellery,' Lucy replied. 'Was that brooch specially designed for you?'

'I was wondering that about the one you're wearing.'

Alison was too busy sorting out her own thoughts to listen to Lucy and Clara discuss the artistry of their respective jewellers – which was the ground upon which she would have expected their minds to meet.

Lucy still had her arm around Richard. Had Alison maligned the twins' motives in befriending him? She was sure she had not. They had used him as a pawn in their game, and had ended up under his spell.

There was something about Richard that sooner or later disarmed even those who sought to use him. Only he could have managed to melt the twin blocks of ice that were where Lucy and Luke's hearts should be, Alison thought.

Now, Lee Taylor Colville was using him – in a more earthy way. Alison blotted out the picture of her son in bed with his benefactress that had risen before her eyes. Though she was far from a prude, that aspect of the situation sickened her. It was as though Richard had been bought for however much his next production would cost to stage, and to Alison it was the equivalent of the casting couch on which Lucy had fornicated her way to stardom.

The difference was that Lucy and those of her ilk knew what they were doing: Richard did not. Though he no longer trusted Alison, he was by nature trusting to the point of naïvety, and would suffer the more for it when he was let down.

'It's time we set off for home,' Conrad said to his hostess, who had seated him beside her at the table.

Alison emerged from her cogitation and registered that everyone but Clara and Lucy, who were now discussing hats, was feeling the strain of the two families coming together.

'It has certainly been a stressful occasion,' said Ruby,

when Richard went with Oliver to fetch the visitors' coats.

Alison surprised her by going to kiss her warmly. 'And I'm grateful to you for trying to make it less so, Aunt Ruby.'

'I'll call on your milliner next time I'm in London,' Clara told Lucy.

'Tell him I sent you.'

'I will. And don't forget to tell your brother to bring you an opal ring.'

Thankfully, each of her families had a thick-skinned member whose prattling had filled the awkward silences, was Alison's final thought as the cathartic experience this afternoon had been for her came to an end.

Two days later, desolation of spirit sent Alison tramping alone on Hampstead Heath in the January drizzle. She had not heard from Richard, and being between plays without one in rehearsal allowed her too much time to brood.

She returned home to find Emma and Janet seated at the kitchen table. Emma's expression was grim, and Janet's filled with pain.

'If something terrible has happened, tell me and get it over,' Alison said.

'Richard has just been to say goodbye to Janet and me,' Emma said. 'He's flying to New York tomorrow — '

'With that woman!' Janet cut in with contempt. 'They're going to be married.' She could no longer restrain her tears and allowed them to course down her face. 'I can't bear it, Alison. And now Auntie Emma knows what a fool I am, too.'

Emma handed her a handkerchief. 'Some detective I am! Why didn't I see what was under my nose? But you're a lovely girl, Janet,' she comforted her niece. 'And there are plenty more fish in the sea.'

'I told her that some time ago,' said Alison. She took Janet by the shoulders and held her until her sobs petered out. 'You must try not to think about Richard, my dear. And the way to do it is to bury yourself in work. As I shall have to do.'

'But it won't help, Alison. Any more than anything can help you, now.'

'Did Richard mention me?'

'I'm afraid not.'

'But if he thinks taking a wife will allow him to forget he has a mother,' said Emma, 'that boy is in for a rude awakening.'

CHAPTER SEVEN

THE EARLY weeks of Richard's marriage were bliss. Lee had suggested honeymooning in Bermuda, but he had opted to remain in New York. The city had him in its thrall from the moment he set eyes on the Manhattan skyline.

They would rise early and spend the day roaming the wintry streets, hand in hand. Richard wanted to see and sample everything. He was captivated by Chinatown and Little Italy, and though Lee was partial to neither Chinese nor Italian food, she refrained from saying so and in the evenings they usually ate there.

Richard was charmed, too, by Greenwich Village and would not have minded living there instead of in his father-in-law's Park Avenue penthouse, but kept that thought to himself.

In the beginning, there was much that they kept from each other. Though they came together in bed without inhibition, in other respects they proceeded with care and caution. Browsing in the bookshops near Columbia University, and eating hotdogs in Central Park in mid-winter, was not Lee's idea of pleasure, but Richard could not have known that.

She indulged his every whim and he hers – though he was rarely required to do so. Making him happy had become her *raison d'être*, a vulnerable situation for a woman. But Lee could be no other way when she loved.

Richard had sensed her vulnerability when they first met, though he was still then a lad, and was the more aware of it now he was a man. But the six-year interim had not equipped him to detect its cause.

He assumed that she had been deeply hurt by her first

husband. But she had told him nothing about it and he felt unable to ask. As she did about Richard's rift with his mother.

Each respected the other's privacy with regard to the past, as if they had tacitly agreed to put it behind them and only their shared present now existed or mattered. Richard had yet to discover that marriage is not a rebirth, and the future never a clean slate. Lee could have told him, but was hoping the love she had for him and he for her would withstand the outside influences that had wrecked her first marriage.

After a while, Richard became aware that she was constantly asking him if he still loved her; that her vulnerability was sometimes expressed in words. He gave her the passionate reassurances she seemed to need, asking himself why she needed them, and only once made a joke about it.

'How could I not love you? You're devastatingly beautiful, darling. And think of all you've done for me!'

They were having a drink in the penthouse before going out for dinner, and Lee sprang from the white leather sofa on which she was reclining. 'Is that why you married me? Because of what I've done and can do for you?'

Richard stiffened. 'I'd expect that kind of talk from my mother, but not from you.'

It was the first time he had mentioned Alison since the night he left home to seek solace from Lee. Since his marriage, he had managed not to think about her – until now – and was suddenly prey to mixed emotions, one of which was the guilt he had not allowed himself to feel.

As Lee had no idea of what Richard was thinking, she remained prey to her own emotions. Fear of losing him mingled with the doubt he had just raised. Had she let herself be duped? He was not yet twenty-four, and she almost thirty-six. Was their marriage just a convenient stepping-stone? That Richard wanted no help from Alison was the sum total of Lee's knowledge about the trouble between them.

'If you're using me to get even with your mother for whatever, and to help you on your way, we may as well call it a day now,' she said.

'How can you possibly think that?'

'How can I possibly not, if you give me reason to?'

'It was meant as a joke, Lee.'

'Then why aren't I laughing?'

Only then did Richard realise how invidious his position was. Lee was rich and he hadn't a bean. The clothes he was wearing she had bought for him – because the ones he had weren't her idea of how her husband should dress, he thought. Nor did they fit in with living on Park Avenue. He had protested about the expense, but Lee had laughed it off with her usual, 'It's only money.'

They eyed each other like two strangers across the vast expanse of white, wall-to-wall carpeting, faced with the sudden knowledge that strangers were what they were. Three weeks of love-making, shopping, and strolling the streets of New York could not make them otherwise.

'Say something,' Lee demanded.

'What is there for me to say, except that I adore you.'

A moment later they were in each other's arms. Love had bridged the gap. But Richard found himself treading ever more warily along his marital path.

It was not too long before he tripped over another hidden hazard. They were dining at Sardi's on the last night of their official honeymoon. Tomorrow, Richard was to begin working with a small theatre company financed by Lee.

'New York has revitalised me,' he said glancing around the smart restaurant at the elegantly gowned socialites – whose beauty did not compare with Lee's, he thought.

'You didn't need revitalising, honey!'

'But I am almost as much in love with New York as I am with you.'

'Just so long as my only competition is a city,' Lee replied.

She had noted Richard appraising the women diners and Manhattan was crawling with predatory females. It was to one of them that Lee had lost her first husband, after forgiving his transgressions with a number of others.

'What did you mean by that?' Richard asked.

'Nothing more than I said,' she answered with a smile.

But to Richard, it had sounded like a veiled warning, and went with her reluctance to let him out of her sight. He chided himself for the thought. He wanted her with him all the time, too. But once the honeymoon period ended, their being together night and day would not be possible.

He was to find that for his wife anything and everything was possible.

CHAPTER EIGHT

THE RAMBLING old house in Highgate, that was meant to reverberate with the sounds of family life, again echoed with emptiness. Janet had joined a repertory company in Cornwall, as though she wanted to distance herself as far as possible from all that reminded her of Richard.

'Dusting bedrooms nobody sleeps in, and living for Richard's letters, will do you no good,' said Alison to Emma.

'That's all fine for you to say!'

'If it were possible to share with you what keeps me busy, I would.'

Alison had just changed into her housecoat after returning home from the evening performance. She was again appearing in Shaw, and looking forward to a successful run. The West End theatre was thriving, but no new play Morton thought right for Alison had come his way and, though she would not have told him so, it had struck her that maybe the new young dramatists were not sending their manuscripts to him because he seemed biased towards revivals of sure successes.

Charles Bligh, however, had a more adventurous reputation and had again taken an option on a play by the still-unknown Marianne Dean; though, thought Alison, he was as liable to keep her dangling on a string as he had the last time without ever producing the play.

'What are you thinking about?' Emma asked.

'Charles Bligh and a woman playwright.'

'Does Lucy know about it?'

'My dear Emma, your mind is getting as bad as your sister's! And I was only thinking about it because I don't want to think about Richard, I suppose.'

169

'But you accuse me of living for his letters.'

'As they are not to me, I try not to.'

'One came from him today. It's on the mantelpiece. And what is experimental theatre?' Emma enquired while Alison got the letter and searched for her spectacles.

Alison smiled. 'Since when were you interested in theatre?'

'Never, which Richard knows as well as you do. But that's what his letter is mostly about. The ins and outs of his work. As he knows it's double-Dutch to me, it isn't really me he's writing to. It's you.'

'You're playing Sherlock Holmes again,' said Alison. But it was an interesting thought.

'Your glasses are in the dresser drawer, by the way.'

'What on earth are they doing there?'

'I was tidying up.'

'But I like them handy, like the ones I keep at the theatre. You having too much time on your hands, Emma, is doing me no good, as well as you!'

'Read the letter already – I polished your glasses for you.'

'Now I am convinced that you are going round the bend.'

'And I sometimes wonder,' said Emma, 'which of us will get there first.'

They exchanged a glance, then averted their eyes. Life without Richard was impossible for them both. Emma's therapy was endless cleaning, and Alison's her art, but nothing could cure what ailed them. They could not even look forward to his return, and neither was suffering only on her own account. It was a heartache truly shared, but the sharing made it no less painful.

Alison gave her attention to her son's lengthy epistle. 'He seems to be getting along well with the people he works with,' she remarked after perusing a couple of paragraphs.

'And he says he's fine, which is all I care about,' said Emma. 'He wouldn't sound so happy if his work wasn't going well,' she added.

170

'There goes the family detective again!'

'Maybe you were wrong, Alison, about him not having what it takes,' Emma persisted.

'Nobody would be more delighted than me if I were proved to be wrong, Emma. Now may I please read this in peace?'

Emma complied, but briefly. 'You could also be wrong about the kind of woman you think his wife is,' she said hopefully. 'Richard seems to be her whole life. Have you reached the part of the letter where he says she goes with him to rehearsals?'

Alison had, and viewed it rather differently from how Emma did. It was an illustration of the possessiveness she had detected in the woman who was now her daughter-in-law. And demeaning for Richard, thought Alison with distress. What could be more so than having the company's patron, who was also his wife, breathing down his neck while he worked? Not just demeaning, but inhibiting, and to the rest of the company, too.

Alison read on and elicited that Richard was not yet directing, but sitting in on a colleague's production. With Lee at his side! she thought hotly. As though he were a pet who could not be allowed off the leash. Alison would not have been surprised to learn that the same applied in his personal life. How long would it be before the marital collar to which the leash was attached began to chafe?

She replaced the letter in the envelope and returned it to the mantelpiece. 'Are we eating tonight, Emma? Or have you decided it isn't worth bothering to cook for just you and me?'

'If you can't smell the chicken casserole in the oven, there must be something wrong with your nose! I often feel nothing is worthwhile, nowadays, but the day I stop bothering to do what I have to do you can chalk up as the end of Emma Stein. It would help, Alison, if you didn't take out your feelings on me.'

'If I sounded sarcastic, I'm sorry, Emma.'

'These days you're always making cracks like that, which provokes me into snapping at you like I just did.

171

And you may have noticed, Alison, that Max doesn't drop in here as often as he used to do. He doesn't like being the butt of your feelings any more than I do.'

'You'll both have to forgive me,' said Alison contritely. 'Not that my temperament is anything new to either of you.'

Emma served their meal and sat down at the table. 'What's new, Alison, is your making Max and me pay for how you feel. Our threesome has not been without a few sharp words over the years — '

'To put it mildly!' Alison cut in. 'I have very distinct memories of you and Maxwell going at it hammer and tongs about what was good, or not good, for Richard when he was a child.'

'But, as I was going to say when you interrupted, that was disagreement, Alison. We weren't taking it out of each other.'

'Maybe I should go out and buy myself a punchball.'

Emma surveyed Alison's forlorn expression. 'We've had bad patches before, love, and managed somehow or other to get through them.'

'You'll be handing me the old cliché about there always being light at the end of the tunnel, in a minute. But from my standpoint I see not a glimmer, Emma.'

Alison stopped eating and poured herself some water. 'I'll get used to being without Richard, like I had to accept losing his father. Time will take care of that. But there is a big difference between losing someone because they are dead, and knowing your loved one is alive but gone from you.'

CHAPTER NINE

RICHARD'S FIRST meeting with his father-in-law did not augur well. Bradwell Taylor let himself into the penthouse on a Sunday morning and strode through to the bedroom as though he owned the place, which reminded Richard, who had not yet risen, that he did.

'I guess you know who I am, young man? You must be the new husband.'

'A fair conclusion, sir,' said Richard. 'As I am in your daughter's bed.' The smile he had managed to summon felt like starch on his face.

'This time she's married a smart-ass,' Mr Taylor told the air. 'The last time it was a philanderer,' he informed Richard, 'who also started out calling me "sir".'

Richard could imagine what his predecessor had ended up calling Taylor. 'How would you like me to address you?' he asked, feeling at a disadvantage lying down.

'BT will do fine, we won't be seeing that much of each other,' Taylor briskly replied. 'My trips to New York are brief and infrequent. And my little girl only comes home to Daddy when she's in trouble.'

'I don't intend to give her any.'

'I guess you'll have me to reckon with if you do. Where is my sugar-baby?'

'Taking a shower.'

'Go tell her that her daddy has dropped in.'

Who the hell do you think you are? Richard wanted to say. But he made himself get out of bed and obey the command – a request it wasn't.

Lee rushed from the bathroom to her father's arms, barely pausing to put on her robe.

'How's my sweetie-pie?' said BT, fondly slapping her rump.

'All the better for seeing her darling daddy,' she said, covering his face with kisses.

'You're dripping water on your father's shoes,' Richard cut into their reunion. 'And his suit will be ruined,' he added when BT lifted Lee as if she were a child to carry her into the living room and cuddle her on his lap.

Seeing them thus was to Richard distasteful. What kind of family had he married into? This was like something from *Cold Comfort Farm*!

'Daddy has a whole closet full of suits here,' Lee replied while nuzzling her father's cheek. 'He hates travelling with baggage.'

'The only baggage I don't mind travelling with is the one on my lap!' BT quipped.

'Daddy has a great sense of humour, Rick,' said Lee with a giggle.

'But they say the limeys haven't – and my new son-in-law isn't amused,' BT observed.

'They also say he who laughs last laughs best,' Richard responded.

'And a smart-ass your new husband sure is,' BT told his daughter, adding his guffaws to her giggles.

To Richard, it was as though they were laughing at his expense. And with a man like Taylor, who could have the last laugh? Before Richard met him, he had seemed like a powerful offstage character in a play. A day never passed without Lee calling him, or him calling her. 'Daddy' rarely failed to crop up in her conversation whatever the topic, as he had on the night Richard first met her. What Richard had divined about her father then had strengthened since his marriage. All that was at odds with his pre-impression of a powerful and influential man was Taylor's appearance. Instead of the imposing figure Richard had expected, BT was a reedy little man. But his demeanour, and the flinty grey eyes behind his spectacles, left one in no doubt that he was accustomed to calling the tune. And would doubtless have done something to prevent the marriage, Richard thought, had Lee not presented him with a *fait accompli*.

174

Nor was her father at her first wedding, Richard had learned, and was now able to understand why. She would do nothing her father told her not to do, and had not given him the opportunity to say no. Both her marriages were to BT bolts from the blue. Lee's relationship with Daddy was that of a devious child, who loved and feared him at one and the same time.

Richard's conjecture was not far off the mark. What he had yet to discover was that the powerful beef-baron's world revolved around his daughter.

Meanwhile, Richard was finding it difficult to relate his sophisticated wife to Lee's little-girl behaviour in her father's presence, and he was relieved when Taylor left.

'Daddy's always in a hurry, he never stays for long,' Lee said while Richard made some coffee.

'Why didn't he let you know he was coming?'

'He never does, honey. He likes to give me a nice surprise.'

Richard was dismayed. 'Do you mean he's in the habit of walking in on you, like he did today?'

'Why shouldn't he? It's his place, and he's welcome by me.'

The same could not be said for Richard. 'Supposing we'd been making love when he came into the bedroom?'

Lee shrugged, 'I guess he'd have shut the door again and gone to sit in the living room until we were done.'

But not, thought Richard, without instructing us to make it fast! In future he would ensure the bedroom door was locked – but what a way to have to live. 'I'd like us to move from here,' he said. 'Wouldn't you like us to have a place that's really our home?'

'Sit down, honey,' Lee said to him. 'You don't have to stand up to watch the coffee percolate and I want to sit on your lap, like I did on Daddy's. You don't have to be jealous of him,' she declared when Richard had obliged. 'I love you both.'

'Was that why you made such a fuss of him? So he won't be jealous of me?'

175

'Sure.'

But jealousy was not the feeling BT had evoked in Richard. Jealousy was a hot emotion and Richard's reaction to his father-in-law was chilled by foreboding.

'You know there's nothing I would refuse you, honey-lamb,' Lee said in her husky voice, that had from the first time he heard her speak had a thrilling effect upon him. 'But if we moved out of here, it would upset Daddy. It makes him feel good to have us make use of his apartment.'

'But it doesn't make me feel good,' Richard answered.

Lee unwound her arms from around his neck and went to lean against the chromium and leather bar. 'You don't like Daddy, do you?'

Richard evaded the question. 'What I don't like, darling, is living in a place that looks as if nobody lives in it.' And to which your father has *carte-blanche* access, he silently added.

'Have you any idea what it cost to fix up this apartment?' said Lee.

'What has that to do with anything?' But Richard was fast learning that Lee's values were very different from his own.

'What it has to do with it,' she replied, 'is that Daddy paid the best interior designer in town a fortune to give the penthouse the look it has. Daddy did it for me and I like it. And even if I didn't, to move someplace else would be ungrateful to Daddy.'

And you've just mentioned him three times in the space of a couple of seconds, thought Richard, wandering to the vast expanse of glass he was sure must be the biggest window in the world. Through it, he could see the sky-scrapers blotting out the sky. A marginally smaller window at the opposite end of the room overlooked Central Park from the terrace, but Richard had no head for heights, and had only once stood gazing briefly downwards.

'It would be nice to live in the Village,' he said, return-ing to the bar to unplug the bubbling-over percolator

176

which Lee had not thought to do. 'In one of those brownstone apartments, where we can look through the window and see the street without it being a birds'-eye view.'

'Forget it, honey,' said Lee. 'What do you suppose Daddy would say if I not only moved from here, but I lowered my lifestyle?'

'You're not married to Daddy,' Richard answered. 'You're married to me – and you'd better make up your mind, darling, which of us matters to you most.'

Lee covered her ears with her hands. 'Stop it!' she shrieked, then she ran to their bedroom and locked herself in.

Give or take the details, she had played that scene before. And while she stalled, torn between the two men in her life, her husband had busied himself behind her back with the other women in his. Which went to prove, she thought now, that only her father would never let her down.

Richard pounded on the door. 'Let me in.'

'Go away!'

'You win, darling. We won't talk about it again.' The sound of her sobs was breaking his heart.

'Do you promise, Rick?'

'I give you my word as an Englishman,' he said, hoping to make her laugh.

Lee opened the door, smiling through her tears. Richard kissed them away and afterwards they made love with the special tenderness that follows a quarrel.

'Oh God – I forgot about my diaphragm!' Lee said when they lay side by side and she was lighting a cigarette.

'Too late now,' said Richard wryly.

Lee gave him a smokey kiss. 'I guess so.'

'Put the cigarette out. I want you in my arms.'

They held each other close, their differences briefly forgotten. But Richard would not forget the circumstances under which his daughter was conceived.

CHAPTER TEN

JOSH BAXTER came home from the office and poured himself the pre-dinner Bourbon that was his one drink of the day.

He took it into the kitchen, where his wife was busy at the stove, his daughter laying the table, and his son slicing tomatoes for the salad. 'Guess who our wartime evacuee has married?'

Mary Baxter stopped stirring the clam chowder. 'Rick is married?'

'And living in New York.'

Mike and Maggie's surprise was as plain as their mother's – and there was about them the same hurt air Mary was displaying, Josh noted, sitting down in the fireside rocker.

'How did you come by this news?' Mary asked.

'Maxwell Morton called me from London about some business he's transferring from his New York lawyer to me.'

'It was through him that Rick came to be our guest, wasn't it?' Mike remembered. 'Rick used to talk about his Uncle Maxwell a lot.'

'Also about his Aunt Emma,' said Maggie.

But he rarely mentioned his mother, Mary recalled. 'So who has Rick married?' she returned to the point.

A long whistle was Mike's reaction to hearing the lady's name, which to an American had the same connotation as Rockefeller.

'I can remember reading about her in the society columns when I was still at high school,' Maggie said.

'And since you're still only nineteen, her coming-out ball – or whatever those socialites have – must have been before you were born,' Mary exaggerated – though not by too many years.

Josh had to grin. 'Why don't you two just come out with it and say she's too old for Rick?'

'But Rick doesn't agree with them,' said Mike.

'Obviously not,' his sister replied, and added with mock chagrin, 'There goes my dream! When I was little I had a crush on Rick. Mike used to tease me about it, and I hated the plain kid I was.'

'But you've turned into quite a good-looking broad,' he recompensed. 'Except you've still got carroty hair.'

'Which is the same colour yours is!'

'And mine was,' their mother reminded them. 'Before my family turned it grey.'

She resumed stirring the soup, and Mike and Maggie their interrupted tasks; but the thoughtful expressions of all three told Josh that, as he had expected, his news had turned back the clock for them to the time when Richard had been like one of this family.

'I once saw a picture of Rick's wife in a magazine,' Maggie said after a silence. 'It was taken in Hawaii, not long after she divorced her first husband. And I thought if I had to have red hair, why couldn't God have made it the same shade as hers — '

'But I bet you didn't think she'd ever come into our lives,' said Mike, deftly transferring the sliced tomatoes from the board to the salad bowl.

'I wouldn't put it that way,' his father said.

'Me neither,' Mary endorsed. 'If the marriage was announced in the papers – and with someone like her it would have been – I guess we missed seeing it. And if Mr Morton hadn't called up Dad, we still shouldn't have known.'

She dished up the chowder and they began the meal.

Then Josh answered the unspoken question hovering in the air. Why hadn't Rick called them from New York? 'Twelve years is a long time,' he told his family and himself. 'And it's almost that long since Rick returned home to England.'

'He and I used to write each other often,' Mike recalled.

'But it petered out, didn't it?' said Josh.

'I never meant it to, Dad. And I guess Rick didn't, either.'

'But it was bound to happen, Mike. And by now, Rick's only link with us, and ours with him, is the time he spent here as a kid. I'm sure he still thinks kindly of us; he's never failed to send us a Christmas card, has he? Did we remember to send him one this year, Mary?'

'Of course. And I'll let you all into a secret: when I write Rick's card, it's always with tears in my eyes.'

'You let yourself get more attached to him than you should have,' Josh replied.

'Feelings don't have brakes – except maybe for lawyers who see everything clinically, like you do!'

'Your mom may've gone grey, but she still has her fiery temper,' Josh said to Mike and Maggie with a grin.

'Rick was a lovable boy, and I missed him a helluva lot after he left,' Mary declared and added poignantly, 'It wasn't long afterwards that I had to accept that my elder son was never coming back from the war.'

She went to serve up the main course – New England boiled-dinner, which most people ate for Sunday lunch, but the Baxters preferred for a weekday evening meal – and remembered it being Richard's favourite.

'In a way, Rick's going home, and Josh junior being declared no longer missing, but dead, was as if I'd lost two sons, not one. Though Rick was just my wartime foster-child, he needed a lot of real mothering.'

'And you sure gave it to him,' said Josh.

'He thought a lot of Mom,' Mike put in.

'And I'd have bet my life,' said Mary, 'that when he grew up and got married, he'd invite me and all of us to his wedding.'

'Morton said he had eloped, so maybe that explains it,' Josh answered.

'But it doesn't explain his not bothering to call us now he's living in the States,' Maggie declared.

180

'Why did he have to elope?' Mike wondered aloud. 'He's not under age.'

Josh gave his attention to the plate of steaming meat and vegetables his wife had just put before him. 'Morton didn't volunteer an explanation, Mike, and I didn't want to pry.'

'Maybe his mother didn't approve of the marriage,' Maggie conjectured.

Mary plonked her dinner in front of her. 'Don't even mention his mother to me!' Her feeling about that lady had returned full force with the memory of Rick.

'I guess your mom still hasn't forgiven Alison Plantaine for not missing a theatre performance, to see Rick off when he left England to come and live with us,' said Josh.

'And I'll never forget his face when I asked him if his mom had wept when she waved him goodbye, and he told me she wasn't there,' Mary told them. 'But that was just the starting point of my dislike for that woman. By the time Rick left us, I'd divined that there was a lot more to forgive her for than that.'

Josh observed that his wife's usually smiling face was tight-lipped. The subject of Alison Plantaine, not raised in this house for many years, had always been to her as a red rag to a bull.

'But you have something to thank her for, don't you?' he said quietly. 'That homey weekend in London she gave Josh junior, before he was shipped into battle.'

The last letter they had received from their son, which did not filter through to them until after his death was confirmed, had told them of Alison's warm hospitality.

'My brother said she was one swell lady,' Mike recalled from the letter, and added, 'Why do we call him Josh junior now, when we just called him Junior when he was alive?'

'I guess because he's only a memory now,' said Maggie with sadness.

'And unless Rick gets around to calling us, let's leave *him* that way,' Josh requested.

'If that's your way of telling me not to call him,' said

181

Mary. 'I have to say I was intending to. You could get his phone number from Mr Morton, Josh.'

'But I'm not going to. If Rick wants to come back into our lives he'll be more than welcome. But it's up to him. He's moved into the top drawer now. I wouldn't want him to get the idea I'm looking for the business his father-in-law could put my way.'

'Dad's right,' said Mike, who worked in his father's law practice.

'Two clinical minds in this family,' said Mary, 'is too much for me! What's your non-legal opinion, Maggie?'

'You're forgetting I'm a chess-player, Mom. I guess the first move has to come from Rick.'

CHAPTER ELEVEN

RICHARD WAS relieved when pregnancy kept Lee away from rehearsals. Nor was he unaware that her absence had removed the strain of her presence from the company.

He was directing his first production for them, and happy to have the guidance of a veteran director who had taken him under his wing. But Lee would not have her husband subordinated in a group sustained by her money; Richard's protestations that he still had much to learn – which he no longer required telling – had got him nowhere with his wife who construed professional criticism from his colleague as a personal affront to herself.

'Hank keeping an eye on what I do is no different from how Luke used to be with me,' Richard told her over breakfast one morning. 'And the work the company does isn't the traditional theatre I cut my teeth on in England. Off-Broadway theatre is a world apart from what I'm accustomed to and — '

'If you want to get involved on Broadway, all you need do is say so,' Lee cut in.

'And repeat my experience in the West End? No thanks!'

'Then what are you complaining about?'

'Nothing. What I'm involved in is very exciting and will teach me a lot, darling. I'm grateful to you for making it possible, but you seem to forget that Hank Rosen was top dog before I joined the company, and still is so far as I am concerned. I haven't been with them for very long.'

Lee glanced at her thickened waistline with distaste. 'Long enough for me to now look as I do! And never mind what I seem to forget, Rick. What you have to remember is more important – that I can't have my husband kow-tow to a guy whose wages I pay. You'll have to excuse me now — '

'Where are you rushing to in the middle of a conversation?' said Richard, as she left the breakfast bar and sped away.

'To indulge in my morning sickness! – and if you leave for rehearsal before I get back, bear in mind what I just said,' she called.

Richard's approaching fatherhood was not exactly a joy to him. He had learned of it not from his wife, but from his father-in-law, which was not an auspicious beginning.

Lee had telephoned the news to BT in Hawaii from her doctor's office, before going on to an appointment at the beauty parlour. Richard had arrived home before she did, and suffered the humiliation of not knowing what her father was talking about when BT called to congratulate him.

Nor had his wife taken kindly to the idea of maternity and what it would do to her shape. Because she was willowy, and her style of dress clingy, every extra inch was immediately noticeable, and she now spent most of her time thinking of her appearance and trying to camouflage her condition fashionably, though it was not yet far advanced. The nausea she was experiencing compounded her misery.

'You must try to eat something, darling,' said Richard when she returned from the bathroom, her milky complexion tinged with grey. The colourful Hawaiian garment she wore in the mornings made it seem more so.

'I'm not hungry, Rick. And if I force myself to eat I'll throw up again – I probably will anyways!'

'You should try all the same. Think of the baby,' Richard said.

'The baby won't think of me – unless it's female and eventually has one of its own. If I'd known what I do now, when my poor momma was alive, I'd have been more considerate to her than I was.'

'If you were as considerate to her as you are to your

father, she could have had no complaints,' Richard replied.

'You just can't resist getting in a wisecrack about Daddy, can you!'

And here we go again, thought Richard.

'Why don't you just go play at being a director and let me alone?' Lee said.

'Is that what you think I'm doing? If so, when I've finished the play I'm working on now, I'll resign from the company.'

'And do what?'

'Try to get work with a company you're not financing.'

Lee burst into tears.

'If I seem ungrateful, I'm not,' Richard said stiffly. That he was feeling the strain of eternal gratitude he refrained from saying.

Lee dried her eyes and stemmed her tears. Once more, there was for her a terrible familiarity about the scene now taking place, as there was with many she had with Richard. Pregnancy apart, it was almost as though she was re-living her first marriage. Was Rick playing around, like husband number-one? She would not let herself begin thinking that maybe he was. But in other respects, everything was following the same pattern. Her 'ex' had worked in advertising, and Lee had enabled him to have his own agency. In the end, he had thrown it all back in her face and returned to his old job.

Richard surveyed her tear-stained face. Stress was not good for her in her condition. Nor was it for his work. They should be looking forward to having the baby – but neither was.

He swallowed his pride and his feelings and went to kiss her before leaving for rehearsal. And managed to say lightly, 'Hank said this is a trying time for both the expectant parents.'

'I don't want to know what Hank said.'

'I promised to eat with him tonight, by the way. There are some things he and I have to sort out and we don't have time during work hours.'

185

'Where are you eating?'

'We haven't yet given it a thought.'

'Call me when you decide,' said Lee. 'If I feel better, I'll join you. Or why not invite Hank to eat here, instead of leaving me to sit alone?'

'If you're not feeling too good, you won't want Hank around. And there's nothing to eat here,' Richard replied. Nor would it do him any harm to have his first night-out without her since becoming a married man, he thought.

'I'll have a meal sent in,' she answered.

'Why go to the trouble, Lee? You'd be bored by what we'll be discussing – lighting effects and that sort of thing. They're extra important in a production that has no set.'

'I offered to pay for a set, didn't I?' was Lee's response.

As though, thought Richard, the lack of a set were what they were debating. But sooner or later, every debate focused on Lee's money calling the tune. If she wasn't intentionally making that point, it cropped up indirectly.

'The production is devised to be played in acting areas, on an empty stage, darling,' Richard said, managing to keep his patience.

'That's what you said when I offered to pay for a set,' she reminded him. 'But everyone who sees the play and knows I'm the company patron will think I've been tight with the budget.'

'Oh, my God!' Richard exclaimed. 'Do you tell those painters whose patron you are to hang their work in opulent gilt frames when they exhibit – whether the work should be simply presented or not?'

'I'm not married to them.'

End of conversation, thought Richard. 'Have as good a day as you can, dear,' he said. And added, 'Don't wait up for me,' as he headed for the apartment door.

Lee's coffee cup bounced off his shoulder and hit the wall, such was the force with which she had flung it at him.

Richard retrieved it from the floor and returned it to her saucer. 'Thank heavens it was empty, darling, or

Daddy would have had to buy us a new carpet – it's hard to get coffee stains out.'

He could hear his wife weeping as he left the penthouse. But after five months of living with her, her sobs no longer moved him as they had in the beginning.

Was it only that long? he ruminated while riding downwards in the elevator. June sunlight was bathing Park Avenue when he stepped outside and strolled for a few yards in the fresh air, before hailing a cab. There'd been snow on the ground when he arrived in New York. The time between then and now had sped by: why did he feel as though he had aged years?

Probably because in experience he had. Gone from being responsible for nobody but himself to the status of husband and expectant father in less time than it had taken him to read *War And Peace*.

'I'm in a hurry,' he told the cab driver.

'In this burg, who ain't?'

Richard would not be travelling to work by cab were he not already late. When Lee was with him, they used the brown Rolls her father kept in New York – the one BT had in Hawaii was white, Richard had learned. There was a chauffeur for each, and Richard could have called the New York driver to take him to rehearsal. But he preferred to go by subway, when he was alone.

As though I'm trying to assert the little independence I have, he reflected as the cab carried him across town.

When he arrived at the rehearsal, Hank had begun working on a scene that was causing problems, and stopped to greet Richard warmly, as he had welcomed him to the company.

Hank Rosen was what Richard's Jewish relatives called a *mensh*; a person of integrity, who judged people for the kind they were, not who or what they were. He and Richard had taken to each other immediately, and were by now firm friends.

'I hope you don't mind us not waiting on you, Rick,' he said, pulling down the shabby grey sweater that was always riding up over his middle-aged paunch.

187

'We didn't think it right to sit around wasting your old lady's *gelt*, boychik!' said Marvin Lieder, the other Jewish member of the company.

'Enough with the jokes, Marv,' Hank answered. If nobody else had realised Rick was sensitive on that subject, Hank had.

'Who's joking?' Marvin retorted. 'If it hadn't been for Lee, some of us would have been on the breadline in those troubled times I would like to forget.'

'So why are you remembering them?' Hank said. 'Right now we got more important things to do, like get this play into shape, and the director has now arrived.'

'Me, I never forget the good things people do for me,' Marvin declared. 'And I hope the same goes for everyone else in this room who was in on the start of the company. But I guess your wife told you how she saved us from near starvation when we were on the blacklist,' he said to Richard.

'As a matter of fact she didn't.'

'Don't hold up the works, Marv,' Hank protested. 'I'll tell Rick the story when we eat dinner together, tonight.'

But Richard's curiosity was aroused. The blacklist Marvin had referred to had kept people thought to be communists out of work, during the McCarthy witch-hunt of the early Fifties. Richard could not imagine Lee getting involved in anything political.

'If nobody minds, I'd like to hear about it now,' he said with a smile. It would be pleasant to hear something uplifting about his wife.

'There ain't much to tell,' said Marvin, 'except that we'd have suffered artistic starvation, as well as the other kind, but Lee made it possible for us to form ourselves into a company, and work.'

One of the other actors spoke up and Richard noted the bitterness in his voice. 'I wasn't a Party member, like Hank and Marv were, though they're not anymore. But I got axed from the radio show I'd played in for a long time, because my brother was once in the Party.'

'I have to say,' declared Richard, 'that this gives me a new slant on my wife.'

'I'll never forget what she said when we warned her she might get blacklisted, too, for helping us to work,' said Marvin, with a chuckle. 'She said, "What are they going to blacklist me from?" And that there was nobody in the world who could tell her what to do, or not to do, with her money.'

As ever, the discussion had returned to that, Richard thought.

'Okay. Let's get to work,' Hank said, noting that Richard's expression had clouded.

That evening in the warm intimacy of a downtown trattoria, Richard's depression was evident to Hank. He had briefly emerged from it while they talked about and settled the production problems that were the reason for their after-work meeting, but was now toying dully with his food.

'There was a time,' said Hank, trying to prod him from his thoughts, 'when the actors in off-Broadway shows were just using it as a way to get to Broadway. That's how it was when we formed our group, in 1952.'

Richard gave him a polite smile, as though he were not really listening.

'And some of those shows did transfer to the big league,' Hank went on. 'But plenty didn't and were staged on shoestring budgets, with all concerned working for a pittance – like we had to, before Lee came slumming with some of her buddies to see one of our plays and offered to back us.'

Hank drank some of his chianti and said with a smile, 'If she hadn't, I guess the company would have folded sooner or later. Once the un-American Activities Committee stopped victimising us, using political blackmail to stop anyone from employing us, we'd have gone our separate ways.'

'And you might have been a bigshot Broadway director by now.'

'It was on the cards, before my career got interrupted,'

Hank answered. 'And I guess I was bitter about that, as well as about the reason it was interrupted. But once off-Broadway became a theatre scene in its own right, not just a stepping-stone for those hoping for better things, it stopped seeming a retrogressive step to me and began to excite me. It's become a place where new ground is broken and it's good to be part of that, Rick. Of what amounts to an alternative-theatre movement.'

'You're a real crusader,' Richard said.

Hank smiled. 'But just one of the standard-bearers of the revolution we're talking about. And oddly enough, it didn't establish itself with an experimental production, but with one of Shakespeare's plays.'

Richard was intrigued. 'How come?' His mother would be interested to hear this; he briefly allowed himself to think of Alison. 'And which play?'

'*Coriolanus*. When the Phoenix theatre company took over the old barn on lower Second Avenue, that used to be the Yiddish Theater. John Houseman was the director, and if my memory serves me correctly, Robert Ryan starred. It brought people flocking off-Broadway – I think it was in 1953.'

'But they played safe with their first production,' said Richard.

'And went on to become a thriving alternative-theatre company, as they set out to be.'

Richard laughed. 'The Bard would turn in his grave if he knew he'd been used to lure audiences off the straight and narrow!'

'That's no way to talk about the greatest exponent of art for art's sake!'

Richard's humour faded. 'Which is what my wife thinks she is, I guess.'

'She's done plenty to prove it,' Hank replied. 'Have you met the cellist she's helping on his way?'

Richard smiled sourly. 'That's one I didn't know about. But as she prefers boogie-woogie to Bach, I'd find it amusing – if she weren't my wife.' He forked some lasagna into his mouth and chewed it, as though it were

190

the next best thing to gnashing his teeth. 'If there's one thing Lee isn't qualified to be, Hank, it's a patron of the arts. And it strikes me that all a person has to do is excite her interest and they can take her for a ride.'

Hank wound some spaghetti expertly around his fork. 'I hope you don't think our company is doing what you just said.'

'Would I have said it to you, if I did? Nor was I deriding the cellist you mentioned – he could be a budding Pablo Casals for all I know. But, more to the point, Lee is certainly no judge of the presence or absence of artistry of whatever kind.'

Richard drank some wine and simmered down. 'I've been letting off a little marital steam, Hank. Please forgive me. Lee can do what she likes with her dollars. I'm just trying to understand her better than I do.'

'That takes time, Rick.'

'But I shall never understand how she comes to be a patron of the arts, when her knowledge of them is so limited.'

'Admiring those with talent you wish you had yourself is the usual reason, I guess.'

'Whatever, I'm glad for my sake and the company's that she's backing you,' Richard declared with the appealing smile that had, from the first, made Hank want to befriend him.

Since then, Hank had divined that Richard needed a friend. The rarified stratum he inhabited with Lee prohibited the casual socialising other theatrefolk enjoyed with their own kind.

When the company heard that Richard was to join them, Hank, like his colleagues, had not looked forward to having a stuck-up limey in their midst. His being their patron's husband, and the son of a distinguished British actress, had helped form that preconception. Everyone was surprised when Richard turned out to be quite the opposite.

They had learned via the theatre columns that his West End directorial début was a spectacular flop, but could not have known that Richard had suffered a sharp lesson in consequence, which accounted for his willingness to learn.

'Hank was still not sure if his pupil had what it took, but hoped Richard would prove more innovative than he yet was, and thought him a bright and friendly young guy who deserved to go far.

'You and Lee must come and sample one of my wife's Shabbos dinners, and meet my kids, Rick,' he said warmly. 'Friday night, with the candles lit and everything, is a big occasion in our house.'

'A homemade meal would be a real treat for me,' Richard answered. But he couldn't imagine Lee in the setting Hank's invitation conjured up.

Nor could Hank, and thought it unlikely to be accepted. How had this lad got into Lee's sophisticated clutches? A more mismatched pair could not be imagined. And Richard's saying a homemade meal would be a treat had dismayed Hank.

Richard was recalling that the last one he had eaten was cooked by his Aunt Emma. A surge of homesickness assailed him. But home was where his mother was, and he had put her behind him and must look to the future, not to the past.

CHAPTER TWELVE

ALISON WAS awakened at dawn by the telephone shrilling downstairs in the hall.

Emma came into the room huddled in her dressing gown. 'I know you keep the bell on your bedside phone switched off, Alison, but now you're awake, please answer it. I'm scared to – at this hour it has to be bad news.'

It proved, in this case, to be the opposite.

'Hello, Mother,' said Richard awkwardly.

Alison's heart leapt with joy. 'Hello yourself! What time is it in New York?'

'Almost midnight – on the last day of 1957.'

'In England, 1958 is already here. And I wish you a Happy New Year, my darling.'

'And I you.'

Alison hugged the phone as though it were her son. 'Mine is already happier than I dreamed it might be – thanks to your call.'

'I hope the reason I called will make you even happier. It didn't seem right not to tell you without delay that you're now a grandmother.'

Alison was momentarily speechless. Richard had not mentioned in his letters that his wife was pregnant. There was, too, for Alison the emotional reaction to his news.

'Say something,' he demanded.

'How are Lee and the baby?' she managed to ask tremulously. 'Is it a girl, or a boy?'

Emma digested Alison's words and had to sit down on the bed.

'Lee had a long labour, but she's fine now,' Richard

replied. 'And Miss Amy Plantaine was yelling lustily when I saw her.'

'That's a nice old-fashioned name,' said Alison.

'It was Lee's mother's name.' Richard could not resist adding, 'I didn't suggest giving her yours, as there's only room in the world for one Alison Plantaine.'

It's what I deserve for putting my career before him, Alison thought. 'I should love her whatever her name,' she said. 'And immediately my play closes, I shall come to New York to see her and you.'

But she had just reconfirmed the sin for which she was now paying, or her son – in his present emotional state – might not have said what he now did. 'I'd rather you didn't come.'

She wouldn't be Alison Plantaine if she'd said she'd leap onto the first available plane and let her play go hang, Richard was bitterly thinking. But if she had stepped out of character in that respect, he would probably have welcomed her with open arms.

Meanwhile, they were briefly silent, each with their private reflections, the static on the transatlantic line echoing in their ears, and a yearning for each other in their hearts.

'As you wish,' Alison eventually replied. This wasn't the telephonic reconciliation she had hoped. Just her son doing what he felt was due to his mother. 'Would you mind if I sent Amy a gift?'

'There's nothing she's short of,' Richard answered brusquely. 'But one of Auntie Emma's handknitted shawls would be nice to have.'

He had shut Alison out the more by what he had just said. Was it deliberate? If so, she probably deserved that, too. 'Thank you for letting me know,' she said.

Then they said goodbye with the politeness that befitted a duty call.

Alison got out of bed and went with Emma to the kitchen. Neither could return to her slumbers after the bombshell Richard had just dropped.

Emma poked the fire – before retiring she banked up

the last glowing coals with slack so it could be stirred to life in the morning, a north-country custom she had never abandoned.

Alison filled the kettle and put it on the stove to boil. Though she usually left such mundane tasks to Emma, she needed to busy herself now.

Neither had uttered a word since Alison replaced the telephone receiver. When Emma found her voice, what she said was typical of her, Alison thought.

'With Lila's baby boy, and Percy's baby girl, the new generation of the family now numbers three – and all born in the same year, though Richard's baby only just made it.'

'You and the family!' Alison moodily exclaimed.

'And there you go again, lashing out at me for how you feel,' Emma answered.

'You'll have to forgive me.'

'This time I will.'

'There's no need to tell you, is there, Emma, that Richard prefers me not to visit my grandchild?'

'Whom I remember you promised to share with me when you got one.'

Alison was putting crockery on the table, while Emma sliced bread for toast, and paused with a cup in her hand. 'You'd be welcome to share her, Emma – but Amy will be my grand-daughter only in name. The same will apply to her place in the family – that's why I reacted as I did to what you said.'

Alison placed the cup on a saucer and sat down at the table, her expression forlorn. 'If you had answered the phone, Emma, Richard would just have asked you to convey his news to me. He wasn't expecting to give it to me personally, since he knows I sleep with my bedside phone switched off – and that you're a light sleeper and would hear it ringing downstairs.'

'I'm supposed to be the family detective, not you!' Emma managed to joke, though she agreed with Alison's deduction. 'And it's surprising that either of us heard it ringing, after drinking the champagne Max brought round to toast the New Year with.'

195

And what an empty toast it seemed to all of us, thought Alison, with Richard gone from our lives.

'I only had a thimbleful, but when my head touched the pillow I was out for the count,' Emma said, and added, 'Max will be thrilled about the baby.'

'What is the point of any of us being thrilled,' asked Alison bitterly, 'if we are never to know her? I shall think myself fortunate if I ever set eyes on her. But I'm now counting the cost of my own folly.'

'Which particular folly?' said Emma drily.

'The one that's responsible for everything – and I don't mean having a child out of wedlock. I almost told Richard that I'd hand over to my understudy and go to New York right now — '

'Why didn't you?' Emma interrupted.

'It's too late now, Emma. My son wouldn't expect that of the mother I've been to him. That's the folly I was referring to. But if I had my time again, Richard would come first in every way, and to hell with my career! You once asked me, Emma, what it would take for me to see what really mattered. Losing Richard was the answer. I know now that I've lived my life with an upside-down set of values.'

'It might help to put things right if you said that to Richard.'

Alison smiled wanly. 'It would take more than mere words, Emma dear. And my chance to prove what he means to me is long gone.'

CHAPTER THIRTEEN

FOR A brief while following Amy's birth their shared parenthood drew Richard and Lee closer. It was as though the joy their baby daughter was to them had papered over the cracks in their relationship.

Richard was from the outset first and foremost a family man, endowed by nature with the true sense of values to which Alison had just awakened, and would never experience the conflict she had in that respect.

This was not to say that his work was now unimportant to him. But ambition, since Amy's arrival, no longer had him by the throat.

His first production for the company had been more Hank's than his, and he was prepared to admit it, and declined to undertake another until Hank pronounced him ready. Meanwhile, at rehearsals he remained at Hank's elbow, occasionally directing minor scenes, and appeared on the theatre programmes as associate-director.

Lee would doubtless have objected to this had she not been too wrapped up in the baby. She would not have wanted her husband to be what she called a 'side-kick' indefinitely, and Richard had now been with the company for more than a year.

But time had tempered his urge to run before he could walk. With increasing maturity he had acquired a patience of which he would not have thought himself capable. Richard at twenty-five was a different person from the headstrong twenty-three-year-old who had eloped to New York. Amy's coming had instilled in him the responsibility for another that his life had previously lacked, which marrying the woman he had could not have done.

His character had since broadened beyond his years, and the man he would henceforth be was formed, for better or worse. Which it would be was dependent upon outside influences, for there was in him the ability to live a well balanced life if Destiny allowed him to do so.

Unfortunately for Richard, Destiny in the shape of his powerful father-in-law still loomed large on his horizon; and Bradwell Taylor's adoration of the grand-daughter who bore his departed wife's name brought him to New York a good deal more often nowadays.

Since BT's visits remained unheralded, Richard never knew if he would find him at the penthouse watching Amy being bathed, when he returned from rehearsals. The nightly anticipatory pleasure of going home to his wife and child was consequently marred by a feeling he had come to recognise as dread.

Added to this was Richard's distaste for the extravagant gifts BT showered upon Amy. Her teething-ring was adorned by a solid gold pussy cat with emeralds for eyes, which Richard found repulsive, as he did the white mink cot coverlet her grandfather had given her.

It was not the objects themselves that sickened him – the gold cat was delicately moulded and the fur rug exquisitely designed – but what they represented. Both were custom-made, as though the baby-things available in even the best stores, which would not include such exotic items, were not good enough for BT's grandchild.

Amy, in her babyhood, had already been elevated to the billionaire plane, where the realities of life would not touch her. This was the rarified atmosphere she was breathing in – and such, thought Richard, would be her conditioning if he allowed it.

The shawl Emma had lovingly knitted by the fireside in the house in Highgate had never been wrapped around its tiny recipient. To Richard, it was the equal of those included in the layette BT had supplied from Saks, and a good deal more meaningful.

But it meant nothing to his wife, who apparently judged everything by its material worth though money was meaningless to her. For this, Richard blamed the man who had raised her, but he would not have his daughter shaped in that mould.

At ten months, Amy was already displaying an imperiousness unusual in so young a child. Her grandfather had taught her to raise her forefinger and beckon – a basic requisite for a member of BT's family, Richard thought, though seeing her do it made him smile. He was not amused when she began employing it in her play-pen to summon her nanny, and flew into a rage if the command was not immediately obeyed.

Though his mother was not given to issuing commands, Richard recognised her temperament in his daughter. Amy was also uncannily like Alison in appearance, which had not helped Richard's resolve to put her from his mind.

BT's remedy for a nanny's concern that her charge was being spoiled was to replace her. Richard was not consulted – but when was he ever? he reflected angrily when he returned home one evening and found a new nanny bathing Amy.

'Mrs Plantaine is at the beauty parlour, sir,' the girl said after introducing herself. 'I was free to take charge of this little darling immediately, so your father-in-law sent his chauffeur to fetch my things.'

To Richard it looked as if the little darling had taken charge. The nurse's uniform was soaked, and Amy was throwing at her the assorted toys and sponges with which she played in the bath.

'Why are you letting her do that?' Richard asked the girl.

'I instructed her not to upset my grand-daughter,' said BT from the bathroom doorway. 'What my sugar-baby needs is plenty of loving kindness. And I guess it's a good thing I have a key to let myself in here and make sure she gets it.'

'I am well accustomed to you crawling out of the woodwork!' Richard retorted.

Then Amy hit the nanny in the eye with a celluloid duck and gurgled her glee while the girl winced with pain.

Richard put his foot on the bath, grabbed his child and turned her over his knee. 'Thanks to you and her mother, what your sugar-baby needs is what she is about to get!' he thundered to BT before slapping Amy's wriggling little bottom.

He wrapped the baby in a towel, impervious to her howls, and handed her to the nanny. 'I'm sorry if all this embarrasses you, but it couldn't be helped.'

The girl gave him a resigned shrug, as though she were well used to the ways of wealthy families and their spoiled kids. Since one apparently went with the other – and who but the wealthy employed nannies? – she probably was, Richard thought, going to join his irate father-in-law who had stomped to the living room.

BT's fury was the ice-cold kind, Richard had had time to learn, and he was not surprised to be confronted by a steely stare.

'You're not just a smart-ass, you're a fool as well,' BT said very quietly.

Richard had never heard him shout. Others raised their voices in anger. BT lowered his, and to greater effect.

'You were extremely foolish to do what you just did to Amy in front of me,' he went on in the same tone. 'I'm not the kind to forgive or forget.'

'I am not asking for your forgiveness,' Richard replied.

'Which makes you even more foolish than I thought.'

Richard ignored the ominous note in his voice. 'What I must ask is that you stay out of my family life.'

'As your wife is my daughter, and your child my grand-daughter that's an impossible request.'

'And I should have known better than to waste my breath making it,' said Richard. 'Lee has never told me why her first marriage broke up, and I've never asked. I no longer need to.'

'And the sooner this one breaks up the better,' BT answered dismissively.

'The better for whom? You?' Richard was stung to retort.

'For all concerned. Including you. If you'd known

what's good for you, which side your bread's buttered, kept your thoughts and ideas to yourself and left things to me, we might eventually have been friends.'

'After my probation period had proved satisfactory to you, you mean,' said Richard with contempt. 'That list of qualifications for acquiring your friendship seems to me a suitable epitaph to be engraved on your tombstone,' he could not stop himself from adding. 'And above your name, "Here lies a lonely man" would surely be apt.'

Only a slight flicker in BT's expression revealed that Richard's assessment of him was correct. 'You obviously prefer me to be your enemy,' he said. 'But you've made the wrong choice.'

'Any man married to your daughter would find you his enemy. Choice doesn't enter into it.'

'It does for my daughter.'

'But there is such a thing as love winning the day.'

'And more than one kind of love,' said BT before he left.

Richard mopped the perspiration from his brow and went to the bar to pour himself a stiff whisky. Both were invariably necessary after a verbal ping-pong match with his father-in-law. Today's was more intense than any that had preceded it. And Richard had played as dexterously as his opponent, though BT had got in the final stroke, he was thinking when Lee arrived home.

How extraordinarily beautiful she looks, he thought as she came towards him with her sinuous walk. She had on a russet tweed suit that toned with her rich-hued hair, and the autumn wind had whipped some colour into her cheeks.

'Where would you like to eat tonight?' she asked after she had kissed him.

'Perhaps we should have something sent in – or I'll fix us an omelette. As this is the new nanny's first night with us, I'd like to be sure she's reliable.'

Lee smiled. 'Hank did me no favours when he gave you those cookery lessons while his wife was visiting with her folks in Florida!'

'I knew how to fix an omelette before I left England, darling. But he'd do me a favour if he gave you some.'

'Are you kidding, Rick? A homebird I'm never going to be and a nightbird is what I am. If I wanted a homey lifestyle, I'd employ a cook as well as a daily maid. As for making sure the nurse is reliable, how can she not be, when Daddy was here while I interviewed her. He checked her references himself.'

'And I,' said Richard, 'came home to a *fait accompli*.'

'Is this what you've been leading up to?' Lee sat down on a sofa and crossed her shapely legs. 'You left early this morning, or you'd have been here when Daddy advised me to fire the other nanny, after he heard her speak sharply to Amy.'

'Never mind. It doesn't matter,' Richard said, though it did. But there was no point in prolonging what he knew was a futile conversation. If he did, he and Lee would be plunged into their first quarrel since Amy was born, which Richard had managed to avoid only by not discussing her father or his effect upon their married life.

Any argument concerning BT was one Richard knew in advance he could not win. For Lee, Daddy was always right. But sooner or later Richard would have to stand fast by what was right for his daughter, and the day might come when Lee must make the choice BT had confidently brandished before Richard. Prior to Amy's birth, Richard would not have given much for his own chances. But there was now a bond between himself and Lee that, if it came to it, would surely tip the scales his way.

The crisis came sooner than he had expected, and was evoked by a matter far removed from Amy's welfare.

'I have something to tell you that you're not going to like, honey,' Lee said over dinner a few days later. 'I've been plucking up courage to say it since Daddy called me before you got home this evening.'

Richard stopped eating, and noted that his wife was now avoiding his eye.

'I have to withdraw my financial backing from the company. Daddy's thinking of running for Congress, and me

202

supporting people who were on the blacklist wouldn't be good for him, he says.'

'The witch-hunt is long gone, Lee.'

'But the American people still don't like reds, Daddy said.'

'There's only one guy in the company who's still a Party member,' Richard told her, though he knew he was fighting a losing battle. What Daddy said, went.

'Personally,' she answered, 'I don't give a damn if the whole lot of them march through Times Square waving the red flag. It wouldn't do me a nickel's-worth of harm. But if my backing the company could harm Daddy, I can't go on doing it.'

'You'd rather let Hank and the others down, bang in the middle of a season, because your father is thinking of running for Congress!' Like hell he is, thought Richard. This is just a tactic to put the wedge between Lee and me.

'I'd much rather not do it, but that's the way it is, honey,' Lee said with a shrug.

But the members of the company, Richard reflected, would not be able to shrug off being put out of work; or the disbandment of the group.

'This won't affect you, Rick,' Lee said. 'We'll set up a new company, with people who weren't on the blacklist. There must be plenty of resting actors around and you could audition them yourself. It would be your company from scratch – which would please me more than what you've been doing.'

Richard had not given a thought to himself, as his smile of contempt showed his wife. 'You will have to tell Hank and the others this yourself. Don't expect me to do your father's dirty work for you.'

Had they not been in a restaurant a blinding row would have followed. Instead, they faced each other across the table in hostile silence.

'Daddy warned me that you would be overly loyal to your friends,' Lee said when she could contain herself no longer. 'And that you were capable of turning nasty.'

'I have sometimes wondered,' Richard tautly replied,

'if – apart from your whims to lend patronage to the arts – you have ever had a thought in your head not put there by your father.'

Lee got up and left the restaurant.

Richard made no attempt to follow her. Even if they shared a cab they would be going their separate ways in spirit.

Later, he wandered aimlessly along Fifth Avenue, past the brightly-lit Plaza Hotel where some elegantly gowned socialites like his wife were alighting from a limousine with their tuxedoed escorts, and into Central Park, losing all sense of time so immersed in misery was he.

It was after midnight when he arrived home. Lee was not in the living room and he half-expected to find himself locked out of the bedroom.

Instead, Lee had vacated it. Her perfumes and cosmetics had gone from the dressing table, and the evidence of hasty packing was everywhere.

In the nursery, the cot was empty. With one fell swoop, Richard's life had been stripped of all he held dear.

Why did he feel no pain? A terrible numbness had him in its grip.

He returned like a sleepwalker to the living room and it was as though he had entered a vast white vacuum. Only marriage and fatherhood had enabled him to call this impersonal apartment home.

A feeling of isolation seeped through the numbness. The glint of lights on chrome furniture momentarily blinded him and he stumbled to the bar to pour himself a whisky. Propped against the decanter was a note: 'Amy and I are going where we belong. Daddy's lawyers will be in touch with you. I called Hank.'

And so far as Lee was concerned, that was that, Richard thought dully. So bald was her note, she might just as well have written: 'It's over. Forget it.' As if everything they had shared could be neatly packaged and dumped. She had even tied up the loose end in having called Hank.

But they still shared a daughter, and the thought of

Amy now blotted out all others. BT had skilfully wrought his revenge, and would use his money and influence to stop Richard from getting Amy back.

Richard knew in his bones that his only hope of watching Amy grow up rested upon his wife returning to him. There was no hope of that. Lee had made her choice, cut her losses, and run. And the pain of losing the woman he loved would be unbearable when shock's anaesthetising effect wore off.

Richard gazed through the window at the lit-up skyscrapers in this city that never went to sleep, that now seemed for him the loneliest place in the world.

Mirrored against them was a mental image of the succession of futile marriages Lee would probably embark upon and abandon, always blaming the man. She would not see that she herself was caught in a revolving door manipulated by her father.

'Amy and I are going where we belong', she had written in the bold scrawl that epitomised her sophisticated veneer. But beneath it she was Daddy's little girl.

And Amy would now be Grand-daddy's little girl. Over my dead body! Richard thought as a spurt of anger shot like a flame through his numbness. Even BT was subject to the laws of the land, and a father had his rights in the raising of his child.

The next morning he found himself a lawyer, who was none too sanguine about Richard's chances, after hearing who his father-in-law was.

'This is going to cost you,' was just one of Joe Lasky's pronouncements. 'Take my advice, Mr Plantaine, don't bother to fight it. Your predecessor didn't, I heard.'

'There wasn't a child involved.'

'That's the angle that's really going to cost you.'

Every penny I haven't got, Richard thought. 'I want my daughter back,' he said firmly.

'Just so long as you know what you're doing.'

'Even if I don't get her back immediately, I shall never stop trying, Mr Lasky.'

The hardboiled divorce-lawyer folded his arms across

his paunch and appraised his pale-faced young client, and felt an unprecedented lump rise in his throat. As Hank Rosen had, Lasky briefly pondered upon the incongruity of Richard being married to the worldly Taylor heiress – who had made mincemeat of him. But the lad seemed wide open for it.

Lasky returned his mind to business. 'If your wife sues for divorce, Mr Plantaine — '

'Not if. When,' Richard cut in.

'I was about to say we'll try for a substantial settlement for you.'

'She can have her freedom without paying me off,' was Richard's quiet reply.

The cool dignity with which he said it – not to mention the dollars he was turning down – took Lasky's breath away.

'All I want is my daughter,' Richard declared.

There's more to him than meets the eye, thought Lasky. 'I'll do my best for you,' he said warmly.

'Thank you. I'm counting on that.' Richard rose to leave and glanced at the booklined walls that reminded him of his room in the Highgate house. 'I like your office, Mr Lasky.'

'You'll probably be seeing more of it than you'd care to, Mr Plantaine,' the lawyer answered cryptically. And added, 'I guess we may as well call each other by our first names. Custody battles being what they are, by the time yours is over – if it ever is – you and I are going to be old friends.'

Richard emerged onto Wall Street with Lasky's parting words echoing ominously in his ears. But his impression of Lasky was that he was a man one could rely upon, unprepossessing though his weary blue-jowled appearance was.

Richard's wartime host had recommended him, and Josh Baxter was someone Richard knew he could trust. And solid as a rock, like the family life I experienced under his roof, he thought now, with the pang of conscience that had assailed him when he called the Baxters' home early this morning, to catch Josh before he left for his Boston law-practice.

Once there, Uncle Josh would be swallowed up for the day in meetings, Richard had thought, and no time must be lost to set in motion whatever was necessary to get Amy back. Ought he still to address him as 'Uncle Josh'? He had found himself doing so instinctively, and Mary Baxter as 'Aunt Mary', and had reflected that the link they forged with him, and he with them, would never be broken. He had been as a son to them, and they as parents to him for a quarter of his life so far.

Richard wandered down Wall Street heading nowhere, and thought it a fitting ambience for his own predicament. Though lawyers, too, had their offices here, this street symbolised the mighty dollar, and what but that, and the power it lent to men of BT's ilk, was in effect responsible for Richard's plight?

He switched his mind to Mary Baxter's warm greeting when she answered the phone – though Richard had not bothered to call until he required Josh's advice.

Josh had been at law school with Lasky and had no hesitation in recommending him; he had fixed up an immediate appointment despite Lasky's heavy schedule, and said when Richard thanked him, 'What are friends for?'

'Come and spend the weekend with us, Rick,' both Mary and Josh had urged. But Richard had not promised to do so. Why not? he asked himself now. Because the togetherness of their family would emphasise his own solitariness. And their sympathy make him want to weep. As for why he hadn't contacted them until things went wrong, suffice to say that his marriage had been like a temporary madness – or so it seemed in retrospect – rendering him unable to see the wood for the trees. But that didn't mean he no longer loved Lee.

He felt an icy wind whip his legs and saw that he was approaching the East River. How long he had been walking he had no idea. But time is of no importance to me now, he mentally told the Statue of Liberty whose face

207

was gleaming benevolently in the sunlight, and time would stand still for Richard until he got Amy back.

Meanwhile he would fill in the meaningless hours as best he may. He wouldn't mind seeing John Osborne's *The Entertainer* tonight. It was playing on Broadway, with Olivier as Archie Rice; his mother's forecast that Osborne would go a long way had proved right, and how long ago that seemed, though it was only two years.

Richard blotted out remembrance of himself and Alison discussing plays in the cosy kitchen in Highgate, and reminded himself that he couldn't afford a ticket for *The Entertainer*.

Luckily, he'd already seen the smash-hit of 1958 – Dürrenmatt's *The Visit*, with Alfred Lunt and Lynn Fontanne, he thought with grim humour; the days when he arrived in a Rolls at every Broadway opening had ended with the ending of his marriage.

His growling innards told him it was past the hour when he usually ate lunch, and his wristwatch confirmed it. He bought a hotdog from a handy stall and ate it without tasting it, as though all his senses had been dulled.

Later, he went by subway to the company's venue, reflecting *en route* that like those with whom he had been working he was now out of a job, and would find it harder than his colleagues would to find work.

When the money in his pocket ran out he could get some from his mother, but would not dream of asking her. Nor would he yet let her know he and Lee had parted. All Richard needed right now was Alison Plantaine telling him dramatically that she'd told him so, or words to that effect.

Only Hank was in the rehearsal room.

'You got here too late to see everyone crying into their beer,' he said, booting an empty can onto the chalked-out acting area. 'We've been having ourselves a wake and the others have gone home to sleep it off. I'm about to lock up and do likewise.'

'How can you be so philosophical, Hank?'

'From long experience in a very precarious business,

Rick. We were lucky to last as long as we did. I don't blame Lee for putting her father's interests first – but maybe I'll emigrate to your country, where nobody looks for reds under the beds!'

'I've been having a wake of my own – the corpse is my marriage,' said Richard.

'If the cause of death was Lee withdrawing her support from the company, you need your brains testing, kid!' Hank exclaimed.

'It wasn't the cause – only the catalyst,' Richard answered. 'Sooner or later, she'd have walked out on me with the baby anyway.'

'Now who's being philosophical?'

Richard managed a smile and a shrug.

'Don't give me that, Rick – you must be hurting like hell, inside. But in my opinion, apart from her taking the baby, you're better off. That lady and all she stands for wasn't for you.'

Hank pulled down his sweater and put on his overcoat. 'Nor is directing for you. And I wouldn't be a friend of yours if I didn't give it to you straight. This must feel to you like being dealt one blow on top of another, but if I don't tell you, who would?'

My mother, thought Richard, re-living the devastating moment when Alison pronounced what Hank just had.

Hank put a comforting hand on his shoulder. 'So maybe now is the time for you to make a fresh start in more ways than one, Rick – though you don't have to trust my judgement.'

'Unfortunately, I do,' Richard replied. He had questioned his mother's motive, but Hank had no axe to grind.

He watched Hank lock up the rehearsal room, and it was as if a door had closed on another of his hopes. If he ever attended a rehearsal again it would be as a guest. As the next time he went to a wedding his own would be for him the spectre at the feast. And if he didn't get Amy back, seeing other men with their children would be his painful lot.

CHAPTER FOURTEEN

ALISON WAS in her dressing room, changing for the third act, when the stagedoor-keeper knocked to tell her she was wanted on the phone.

'I can't possibly take a call now, Albert! Please ask whoever it is to leave their name and I'll ring them after the show.'

'I would've told 'em that, Miss Plantaine. But I thought it might be urgent – it's the Bellevue Hospital in New York.'

Alison froze. Then she threw on a wrapper and fled down the passage, grabbed the dangling receiver and managed to speak into it, though her tongue felt paralysed in her mouth.

'This is Dr Roberts,' said a voice with a nasal twang. 'As your son is alone in New York, and very sick, I thought it right to let you know.'

Alison's legs would barely support her. 'What is wrong with Richard?'

'Nothing that time and a supportive family can't cure. He's had a nervous breakdown.'

'Where are his wife and child, Doctor? You said he's all alone.'

'It seems they're no longer with him, Miss Plantaine.' The doctor paused. 'I assume that's why he tried to take his life.'

Alison mouthed to the stagedoor-keeper to fetch her a chair. If she didn't sit down, she would fall down, such was her shock.

'I'll be with Richard as soon as possible,' she said to the doctor, while Albert helped her to lower herself onto the chair.

'And I'm sure that will help pep him up,' Dr Roberts replied.

She pulled herself together and handed the telephone receiver to Albert, to replace on the hook. 'How long have we got before the curtain goes up?'

'Seven minutes, Miss Plantaine.'

'And I'm not yet fully changed. Call Mr Morton for me, would you please? He said he was dining at home tonight. Tell him I'd like him to come to the theatre immediately,' said Alison as she sped back to her dressing room with the stagedoor-keeper at her heels.

'Are you sure you're all right, Miss Plantaine?' the old man asked anxiously. 'It was bad news, wasn't it?'

Alison nodded. 'But I'll be fine, don't worry, Albert.' She gave him the warm smile that had won the heart of every stagedoor-keeper she had encountered in her long career. 'You know me!'

Albert did, but admired her anew when she presented herself on time for her entrance cue.

How she managed it, Alison would never know. Nor could her audience have known that the actress playing comedy so superbly was weeping inside herself, in the grip of her private tragedy.

The few minutes she was offstage during the final scene allowed her a brief respite. By then Morton was in the wings. When he learned why he had been summoned, he too had to sit down.

'I want you to get me a seat on the first possible flight to New York, Maxwell,' Alison said. 'My understudy is about to get her break and can play my role for however long it takes me to get my son well.'

To Morton, that didn't sound like the Alison Plantaine he knew. But in the final analysis, he thought with feeling, her maternal instinct had won its longtime battle with her professionalism. And that was the way it should be. Though Richard thought otherwise, it was she, not Morton, who had fashioned the pattern of her life. But I'm guilty of helping her, by bowing to her wishes, he thought, and with the benefit of hindsight would behave very differently.

211

Nevertheless, he reflected, watching her re-assume the character she was playing and make her entrance on cue, only a trouper like Alison could have gone back onstage after receiving such news.

The following morning, Morton saw her off at the airport, and said wistfully, 'I should have liked to go with you. But it's better that I don't.'

'And you'll do more good staying here to hold Emma's hand,' Alison replied. 'She was devastated when I told her, and still in pieces this morning.'

'I could do with someone holding mine! When I think of Richard wanting to put an end to himself — ' Morton added with a shudder.

Alison wrapped her fur coat closer around her, and picked up her dressing case, as her flight was called. 'Don't think of that, Maxwell dear. Think, as I am doing, that when I bring Richard home maybe all that went wrong between him and us will come right.'

Alison's reunion with Richard was not the private moment she had hoped for. When she entered his room, his wartime foster-mother was with him.

'I didn't expect you so soon,' Richard said after Alison had kissed him – with a restraint she would not have displayed had there not been a stranger present.

'I told Dr Roberts I would come as soon as possible, darling,' she replied with a smile.

'So he said. And I said that with my mother that could mean next year, if the play she's appearing in has a long run. Did it close last night?' Richard quipped.

Alison did not let the smile leave her face, though she felt as if Richard had just slapped it. 'No, it did not, my darling. My understudy is filling in for me – and I must thank Mrs Baxter for doing so here, until I arrived.'

'I need no thanks, Miss Plantaine,' Mary said.

'You have mine, all the same. Also for everything you did for Richard during the war.'

'And my melodramatic act has finally brought you two

together!' said Richard with a bravado both women were aware was just a veneer for the misery deep within him.

The same applied to his prattling on and on, thought Alison, listening to him do so. But it was punctuated by brief silences, like a talking machine that has to be rewound.

'Why don't you and I go and get us some coffee?' Mary Baxter said to her during one of them.

She wants to talk to me, Alison registered. And I'd welcome a word with her. 'That's fine with me, Mrs Baxter.'

'Me too!' Richard joked. 'It's like a mothers' meeting in here, this afternoon. I wouldn't mind a little break.'

'I guess it is a mothers' meeting,' said Mary when she and Alison had left the room. 'I never expected to meet you, Miss Plantaine.'

'I had always wanted to meet you. But not under circumstances like this,' Alison replied with a wan smile. They were walking along the corridor and she halted beside a window. 'Never mind the coffee, unless you really want some?'

Mary shook her head.

'Then let's just stay here and talk. All I know is the little the doctor told me on the phone. Would you mind putting me in the picture?'

Mary did not spare her the details – and Alison had the feeling she was enjoying torturing her with them.

'Rick washed down a jarful of aspirins with half a bottle of whisky – and it wasn't a spur-of-the-moment thing. He took a room in a hotel and locked himself in. He'd left the radio blasting away and a guy in the next room called the desk to complain about the noise. When the manager couldn't get in, they forced the door open and called an ambulance. But for the radio, it would've been too late to save Rick. By morning he would have been dead.'

'Oh dear God,' Alison whispered.

'Which he wanted to be,' said Mary in a clipped tone. 'And when they got him here, I understand it was touch and go.'

213

'Did he do it on the day his marriage broke up?'

Mary eyed Alison with something akin to contempt. 'His wife left him last fall, Miss Plantaine. Six months ago.'

Why is this woman so hostile to me? Alison wondered. She had felt a cold breeze waft toward her the moment they met. 'I knew nothing about it, Mrs Baxter.'

Mary thrust her hands into the pockets of her matronly tweed coat and appraised the glamorous lady that Alison, though her hair was streaked with silver, still was. 'Obviously not.'

'Richard kept it to himself.'

'You mean he kept it from you.' Mary gazed through the window at the East River. 'While he still clung to the hope of getting Amy back, I managed to persuade him to spend a weekend with us. And when I saw how he looked, I wanted to keep him with me, try to bolster his spirits and build him up, but he wouldn't stay. Afterwards, I called him often. I couldn't get him out of my mind. We asked him to spend Christmas with us. He said he wouldn't be celebrating it.'

Mary fell silent and they watched a stretcher case being rushed along the corridor.

Alison shivered, though sunlight was streaming through the window. 'This place reminds me of a workhouse.'

'Bellevue is a very old hospital,' said Mary. 'Rick was in a big ward when Josh and I got here. We managed to have him moved to the room he's in now.'

'I'm grateful to you beyond words,' Alison told her warmly.

Mary's reply was like being doused with icy water.

'Your gratitude, Miss Plantaine, is less important than Rick's well-being. When he's fit to leave here, I'd like to take him home to West Newton. Maybe you're planning to take him to England, but that isn't what's best for him.'

'What, exactly, are you saying, Mrs Baxter?'

'What I've wanted to say to you for years.' Mary could contain herself no longer. 'If you'd lost a son, as I have, it might help you to see yourself as I see you. Rick was one of my family long enough for me to divine he had hang-ups about you. But he was happy with us, and I wasn't surprised when the time came that he was reluctant to go home.'

Mary paused only for breath. 'All the blame for the state Rick is in can't be laid at his wife's door, Miss Plantaine. Wives walk out of marriages with the children every day, but the husbands don't take an overdose. They go on living. Rick did it after the custody hearing which – needless to say – he didn't win. It must have seemed the final straw to someone who's always had a raw deal.'

'I have never thought myself the ideal mother,' Alison said after a silence.

'You ought not to have adopted Rick if there was no room in your life for him,' Mary told her cuttingly.

Alison gave her a poignant smile. 'I had better tell you the truth, Mrs Baxter, which Richard now knows. The part you played in raising him, and your continued devotion, entitles you to know. I didn't adopt him. He's mine, and I value him more than you seem to think.'

She waited for Mary to recover from her surprise, and added ruefully, 'I make no excuses for my own deficiencies, Mrs Baxter. Suffice to say I did the best I could – which you don't have to tell me wasn't enough.'

'Thank you for confiding in me,' Mary said quietly. 'It makes a lot of things easier for me to understand.'

'What, for instance?'

'Let's just say that I'd always thought of you as a famous actress without a care in the world. But you must have had a lot of heartache, having to live that lie.'

'It was because of who I am that I did – that and no other reason,' Alison replied. 'But fame and tranquillity can never be bedfellows in any respect,' she added wryly. 'And would that having me for his mother had not rebounded on Richard.'

Alison toyed pensively with her pearls. 'If his father had lived to become my husband, my career might have mattered to me less. My son and I would both have had happier lives.' Nor were they yet out of the woods in their relationship, she thought. Richard still didn't believe who his father was. Nor would he until he was able to believe in her.

Mary had not anticipated feeling sorry for Alison Plantaine, but softened towards her now.

'So you see nothing is ever quite the way it seems,' Alison responded to her sympathetic glance.

'And if it seems to you that I'm competing for Rick's affection, I'm not,' Mary answered.

'It had crossed my mind.'

They exchanged a smile.

Then Mary patted Alison's hand, in her comforting way. 'I guess we both want what's best for Rick.'

'And if you think my looking after him would do him no good, I'd rather he stayed with you for a while,' Alison said.

'What I really think,' Mary declared, 'is that what Rick needs above all else is to set things straight between him and you. Then he'll face up to his broken marriage the way any other guy would.'

'That's what I'm hoping for.'

'Okay. I won't offer to take him home with me. And I guess I may as well go back to my neglected family today. He's all yours, Miss Plantaine.'

They returned to Richard's room and Alison thought with an ache in her throat that her son had never been all hers. Mary Baxter, who was now fixing his pillows, had shared his mothering, as Emma had. Zelda Stein, too, for the first nine months of his life.

But Alison did not resent the special affection Richard had for them. Maternal love was one thing he had not gone short of. But it hadn't provided the simple security of which she had deprived him.

She now had the chance to undo the damage, and her career could go hang.

Part Three

Life may change, but it may fly not;
Hope may vanish, but can die not;
Truth be veiled, but still it burneth;
Love repulsed – but it returneth!
                                                  Shelley

CHAPTER ONE

IN THE summer of 1967, the family gathered at the Midland Hotel in Manchester for Clara's ruby wedding celebration.

For once, Clara did not mind Alison stealing the limelight, but basked in the reflected glory of introducing her famous cousin to her friends.

'Auntie Clara has worn very well,' Richard remarked during the champagne reception.

Clara was nobody's idea of a septuagenarian, as she stood sheathed in white satin and bedecked with jewellery beside her portly husband, greeting their guests.

'The same can be said for you, Mother,' Richard added to Alison with a smile.

Alison patted her silver chignon and said drily, 'But Clara is still blonde and I am no longer brunette.'

'If there was no such thing as peroxide, my mother would have invented it,' Percy chipped in. 'She also spends a fortune at health farms. You've stayed trim from hard work, Alison.'

Percy's little daughter came to join him and Alison saw Richard's expression shadow. She was aware that Janet had noticed it, too. When was that girl going to stop thinking of Richard, and find someone else to love?

'You look lovely in your party dress, Lottie,' he said to the child, who was Amy's age.

'But my cousin Lionel calls me specky-four-eyes,' she said, gazing up at him from behind the spectacles she wished she did not have to wear.

'Children! Save me from them!' Lila exclaimed.

'You should have said that to yourself before you got pregnant again,' Percy joked, giving her a brotherly kiss.

Lila smoothed the blue, accordion-pleated smock that did nothing for her present egglike shape. 'It took me ten years, and it just had to happen so I'd look like this for my parents' big day! And when I think of the aggravation my Lionel gives me – I've told him a thousand times not to make fun of Lottie's glasses – I must be out of my mind wanting another kid!'

'There are times when Percy and I would agree with you,' said Beth, watching her daughter join Lionel at the buffet and help him scatter peanuts on the floor.

'Did we behave like that when we were ten?' Lila asked her brother.

'No. But this is the swinging Sixties, remember. We should be thankful, I suppose, that our kids are not yet teenagers, that they are only misbehaving with peanuts!'

'I blame the whole thing on television,' Lila's barrister husband pronounced.

'You could be right,' said Percy.

'But instead of discussing the cause, go and deal with the effect,' Beth instructed him.

Richard detached himself from the group. 'Let me have the pleasure.'

'Family occasions must be when Richard misses Amy most,' Lila said to Alison.

'And it wasn't very tactful of you to say what you did,' her husband told her. 'About being out of your mind to want another kid. From Richard's point of view, you were grumbling about what he wishes he had.'

'How I wish I hadn't made that thoughtless remark,' said Lila contritely.

'I'm guilty of having agreed with you,' Beth said.

'Neither of you is guilty of anything,' Alison put in. 'If everyone were careful what they said in Richard's presence, he would be aware of it and feel worse.'

'He must absolutely detest his ex-wife,' Percy opined. 'If you took Lottie away from me, I'd want to kill you,' he said, putting a fond arm around Beth's stringy waist.

'There's no danger,' she replied with a contented smile.

'But I sometimes wish Alec would take Lionel away from me,' said Lila. Her small son was now pelting Richard with the nuts.

Janet, who had listened quietly to the conversation, went to Richard's aid, though he appeared to be enjoying what he was being made to endure.

'Janet would make a much better mother than me,' Lila declared. 'And Richard a super dad. They don't seem to mind what one has to put up with from kids.'

'But she shows no sign of wanting to settle down, and he's had his kid taken from him,' Alec succinctly said. And added, 'In England, they say the law is an ass, and I've sometimes had occasion to agree. But compared with what's happened to Richard, under American law, ours has much to be said for it. It couldn't have been done to him here.'

'If the case had been heard in Manchester, my Alec would have seen that Richard got fair play,' Lila said, patting his somewhat equine face.

'Custody probably not,' Alec declared. 'It is usually awarded to the mother. But Richard was granted access, and his right would certainly be enforceable in this country.'

'American law differs from state to state, Alec,' said Alison, who by now knew more of its intricacies than she would have wished to.

'But I still find it difficult to accept that if a child is taken by one party out of the state where custody and access were settled, there is nothing the other party can do to enforce his rights.'

'How cold and impersonal this sounds,' said Beth. 'Nobody would think it was human lives we were talking about.'

But Richard had tried to end his because of it, thought Alison. When Lee flew to Hawaii with Amy immediately after the hearing, his New York lawyer had told him of the loophole in the law by which his wife could deny him access to his daughter; and that with her father's power behind her, Richard could forget seeing Amy until she grew up and wanted to see him. But by then her mind would be poisoned against him, he had thought with despair. His life had not seemed worth living.

Did it seem worth living now? Alison wondered, watching him and Janet play a game of ring-o'-roses with the two little members of the family's younger generation, of which his absent daughter was part. Almost a decade had passed since his crisis, but the spark that had once lit his personality had not yet returned. As though resignation to his lot had snuffed it out, Alison thought.

'Richard has had no option but to accept the situation,' she resumed her conversation with Alec.

'I'm damned if I would!' Percy said with feeling. 'Me, I'd go to Hawaii and swipe my kid from under my ex-wife's nose.'

'You would not find that easy, if your ex-father-in-law were who Richard's is,' Alison replied. 'Amy is being raised on her grandfather's estate, and from what Richard's told me about that gentleman, it is probably surrounded by guard-dogs, to protect him from all his enemies!'

Alec had mentally donned his barrister's wig, and said thoughtfully, 'Removing Amy from the country might constitute an offence — '

'But removing her from Hawaii to another state apparently could be got away with,' Percy interrupted. 'What's to stop Richard from doing that?'

'His livelihood is in England,' Beth replied. 'And a man has to live where his living is.'

While the young people continued their concerned discussion about Richard's plight, Alison's mind swooped backward to her telephone conversation with Dr Roberts.

There was nothing wrong with Richard that a supportive family could not cure, the doctor had pronounced. And just how supportive his extended family could be had moved and surprised him, when Alison brought him home.

From Percy's medical advice, to Alec's offering free

legal consultation, and Clara cash to help pay his US lawyer, each in their own way his relatives up north had rallied around him.

Alec was the only one whose offer he had taken up. Morton's Harley Street physician had supervised his recuperation, and his litigation costs were settled by Alison – as Clara had known they would be. But the old cliché, 'It's the thought that counts,' had served to strengthen Richard's spirits.

Back in England, he had no longer felt himself fighting a lone battle to come to terms with what life had meted out to him. Alison had been absent from the stage for a year, and his constant companion, though he had pleaded with her to make a comeback before the fickle public forgot her.

She had not agreed to do so until an afternoon when the twins dropped in to see Richard. Though Alison liked them no more than she ever had, the bitterness in which she had once held them was gone. Nor did she feel the sting of their malice directed at her.

'We are all getting too old for feuds,' she had wryly responded to Richard's surprise that she was prepared to let Luke and Lucy cross her threshold. There was, too, an element of the victor and the vanquished in Alison's deigning to have them in her home. Figuratively speaking, she now had the cake, and Richard's removal from their scene had, because they loved him, left them pathetically eager to accept the crumbs.

On that particular afternoon they had tea in the garden, and Alison had waited with bated breath for Richard's reply when Lucy told him there was a place for him on the business side of Bligh Productions, since he no longer wished to direct.

Alison had carefully avoided asking him what he proposed to do instead, and had almost dropped her teacup when Richard replied casually to Lucy that he was thinking of asking his Uncle Maxwell for a job.

Though he had, since returning home, been pleasant to Morton she had not dared to hope that her dear friend's dream of Richard working with him might now come true.

After the twins' departure, she had said to Richard, 'I'm delighted about the decision you've made – so long as it isn't to please me.'

'It's what I want to do,' he answered. 'Make use of my sense of theatre the way he has used his. If Uncle Maxwell will have me.'

'I'm sure he will.'

'Me, too. I would have liked him for a father – and I'm now old enough and wise enough to have figured out that it could have been that subconscious wish that made me think that he fathered me.'

Alison held her tongue and let him get it off his chest and finally out of his system.

'I probably wanted to think it – and I beg your forgiveness, Mother,' Richard went on. 'Uncle Maxwell's, too, though he doesn't know how I maligned him.'

Alison allowed him to keep that illusion. 'I appreciate your telling me.'

'I had to. And I now believe you about who my father was. I'm sorry you lost him, Mother.'

'But I gained you. And I'm happy you've decided what to do from now on. Work is a necessary part of life,' Alison replied.

'Of yours especially,' Richard said with a dry smile.

It had not taken long for Morton to discover that Alison's son was a born impresario. His sense of theatre was an essential requisite, his natural charm a surefire sealer of deals, his sharp brain enabled him to wheel as well as deal when necessary, and his youth and enthusiasm heralded a new era for Morton Theatrical Enterprises.

On Richard's first day at the office, Alison had begun rehearsing her comeback play. Her maternal task was completed and the actress in her again emerged. But that side of her split personality would never again take over, she was thinking when Percy prodded her.

'You're miles away, Alison!'

'So I was,' she said with a poignant smile. 'Travelling backwards in time, but I'm back at the party now,' she added, noting that Emma and Clara had joined the group. 'And how nice it is for us all to be together.'

'My actress cousin,' said Clara, 'is getting sentimental in her old age!' She surveyed Emma's attire. 'And my sister has never learned that brown doesn't do a thing for her. The first time I told her that she was only sixteen. Where's Janet, by the way?'

'Right behind you, Auntie. And if you've found a nice young man to introduce me to, forget it!'

'What can you do with this girl?' Clara exclaimed. 'If we let her, she'll end up like Alison, with nothing but a career.'

'My mother also has me,' Richard interceded with a grin.

Clara pretended not to have heard and went on, 'But at least Alison and Janet have their work – which is more than can be said for poor Emma.'

Clara went to mingle with her guests, leaving, as always, the ripples her verbal pebbles created in the family pond to settle as best they might.

'I sometimes wish Mam had never forgiven us,' Percy said to Beth, 'then we'd have been spared her presence. Nor would she have done, were it not for our naughty daughter's charm.'

'That's no way to speak of your mother,' Emma lectured him, though Clara's remarks had caused her to blush with embarrassment.

Janet was trying to smile.

'Nobody takes Auntie Clara seriously,' Richard said. 'Just take it from where it comes, kiddo,' he added affectionately to the woman he still thought of as an honorary little sister.

'But on this occasion, Auntie Clara is right,' Janet heard herself say. 'About me, that is. I don't want to live my whole life with nothing but my career.'

'So when's the wedding?' said Percy with a grin.

'First she needs the man,' Lila reminded him.

Janet excused herself and returned to the two children, whose sticky fingers were preferable to the sticky situation from which she had just extricated herself.

'Suddenly, Janet has no sense of humour,' said Lila.

Nor would you have under the circumstances, both Alison and Emma were thinking. But only they knew that the man Janet loved was standing beside her when Lila made her tactless remark.

Janet was now based in London and living under the same roof as Richard again. The easy companionship of their youth had been resumed as though time and events had not separated them. But they were not the same people. Richard lived only for business, and the day when he might see his daughter. And with each passing year Janet's hope that he would miraculously fall in love with her became harder to sustain.

'While you were busy playing with our kids, Alec and I were wondering why you don't just go to Hawaii and snatch yours,' Percy said to Richard.

'My brother-in-law is trying to get me disbarred!' said Alec. 'That was entirely Percy's idea, Richard.'

'And what I'm thinking of doing,' Richard replied. 'Because I'm never going to get Amy back any other way.'

CHAPTER TWO

RICHARD DISEMBARKED from the inter-island plane at
Maui thankful not to be greeted by a gorgeous wahine saying Aloha! and draping an exotic lei around his neck. That
traditional Hawaiian welcome had seemed altogether too
festive when he arrived at Honolulu, though he hoped to
feel otherwise when he left.

Meanwhile, he had no idea of how he would achieve
what he was setting out to do, and felt like the criminal he
knew he was not.

In the small terminal building, a Californian who had
chatted to him during the flight was being kissed and
hugged by the wife and child he had said he was joining on
vacation. Richard had long since written off the woman
who had been his wife, but had the same right to his child
as his fellow-passenger did. Divorce meant the end of a
marriage, not of fatherhood – and the hell with the law!
he thought.

To give the law its due, it had granted him the right to
see Amy once a month, and have her with him for two
weeks each summer. Richard would, somehow, have
made his life in the States in order to avail himself of those
meagre privileges, had Lee not made use of the out-of-
state loophole which allowed possession to be, in practice,
a law unto itself.

Richard's New York lawyer had begged him never to
do what he was now doing. Joe Lasky had seen too many
confused children made pawns in their divorced parents'
custody games, and had said bluntly that a child's most
important need was stability.

Amy was then little more than a baby, and Richard
had managed until now to set aside his own feelings and

227

take Lasky's advice for her sake. But at ten, she was old enough to understand what he intended saying to her. That he loved and wanted her, and she would from now on be with him all the time.

Amy's life with her mother was the opposite of stability, Richard reflected. One had only to read the gossip columns to know that Lee spent most of her time in Europe – and was again between marriages, after three further attempts.

Her father has probably by now bought her a divorce-pad in Reno, Richard thought cynically as he waited in the hot sunlight for a cab to take him to the beef-baron's island home. In readiness for the future marriages BT's existence ensured would not last.

Richard's bitterness toward his ex-wife had changed to pity for her. If ever there was a poor little rich girl, Lee was her. But he would not have his daughter become one at BT's hands, he thought, getting into the blessedly air-conditioned cab.

'Where to, mister?'

'The Taylor estate, please. It's at Napili.'

'Everyone knows where the Taylor estate is,' the driver said with respect. 'But Mr Taylor, he usually send his Rolls when he expectin' business gentlemen flyin' in.'

Richard smiled – a business gentleman was what he had, loosely speaking, become. He glanced down wryly at the well cut, lightweight cream suit he had rushed out to buy before leaving London. Last time BT saw him he was wearing his would-be director image, casual slacks and a creased corduroy jacket.

'Mr Taylor, he don't get no other kind of visitors,' the friendly cabbie cut into his thoughts.

'You seem to know a lot about him,' Richard replied.

'Napili's a small place. I used to live there, but my kid – he's very clever – wants to go to the Lahainaluna High School, so we moved into town, ready for when he do. My wife – what a worrier! – she don't want our Wikoli cycling into Lahaina every day with the traffic. Women!' the cabbie exclaimed while lighting an acrid cigarette.

228

To Richard, traffic on Maui was conspicuous by its absence; but to people who probably never left the island two cars and a truck must seem like a traffic jam. Everything was relative. The narrow road they were traversing looked like a pathway to peace – though for him personally the opposite might prove to be the case.

'Our Wikoli,' said the driver, 'he got big ideas for a boy of ten. He want to go to college, he says, an' he not started High School yet!'

'Wanting an education is no bad thing,' Richard answered.

'Sure. But how we goin' to pay for it? His father a cabbie, not a bigshot like you goin' to visit, mister.'

Richard eyed the man's thickset back, garbed in one of the colourful shirts that epitomised the islands, and allowed himself to briefly dwell upon the inequalities of life.

'You got any kids, mister?'

'One – a little girl.' And Richard must try to find out the layout of the estate in which she was being kept from him. 'Is the Taylor place near the beach?' he inquired casually.

'Sure thing, mister. The house an' the pool, they right above the beach. An' the grounds, they meet with it, ' he was informed by his unwitting collaborator.

'I expect there are lots of servants to take care of the place,' Richard conversationally voiced his probable problem even if BT was not there.

'Only the housekeeper,' the cabbie replied. 'Mr Taylor, he don't like too many people around him, Malia told my wife.'

'Who is Malia?'

'She the housekeeper. Malia been with the family since before Mrs Taylor died. She a nice lady.'

Richard was pleased on his daughter's account to hear that. But if BT was absent, he would still have that nice lady to contend with.

He had not until now allowed himself to face up to the difficulty of abducting his daughter. His mother, Emma and Morton had all tried to dissuade him from trying to.

Janet too. But when he remained adamant, she offered to accompany him to Hawaii. As she was currently appearing in a Morton production, permission to hand over to her understudy was readily given.

Richard was grateful for her moral support, but had insisted that it be no more than that. The actual 'crime' must be his alone – and Janet would now be pacing her room at the Royal Hawaiian Hotel in Honolulu, waiting to hear if Richard had pulled it off; or landed in jail, he thought grimly. Though the loophole in the law allowed for a free-for-all between divorced parents, BT would undoubtedly call the police if Richard trespassed on his estate.

'Does Mr Taylor keep a dog?' he asked the cabbie.

'You scared of dogs or somethin', mister?'

'Allergic to them,' Richard replied. It was the first of the several lies he would find himself having to tell the man, but it was in a good cause and slipped glibly from his tongue. 'They make me sneeze,' he added for good measure.

'Well you won't do no sneezin' today – unless you allergic to orchids also. They everywhere on Maui. Mr Taylor, he don't like dogs, Malia told my wife.'

Despite his edginess, Richard could not but drink in the scenic beauty of the route as they skirted Lahaina, once the capital of Hawaii, and headed towards Napili. When they got there, he would just have to play it by ear – and all might depend upon BT's presence or absence.

'You Hawaiians have a lot to feast your eyes upon,' he said to the driver.

'Sure. But I'm not a true Hawaiian, mister, though I was born here.' He lit another of his malodorous cigarettes. 'I guess you'd have to look hard to find one; these islands, they's a meltin' pot it sometimes seem to me. Most of my blood is Filipino, an' my wife, she part Portuguese.'

The driver laughed lustily. 'Lahaina was once an important whalin' port an' my old grandmother – she a true Hawaiian – tell me she not surprised we a people of mixed blood. An' since the war the islands been flooded with Filipinos an' Japanese.'

He glanced through the window at the unspoilt coastline, and the palm trees swaying in the strong trade wind. 'Here, we don't get too many tourists. Me an' my wife, we wouldn't like it if a whole lot of hotels was built along here, so we can't see the ocean from the highway. They say it's goin' to happen to Waikiki Beach, on Oahu.'

'But without hotels for tourists, Maui can't be prosperous,' said the businessman in Richard. The other part of him agreed with the driver.

'An' with them I would earn more money. Don't tell me, I know,' said the driver. 'But I am already better off than those who break their backs for next to nothin' in the sugar-cane fields. It's by sugar an' pineapple most people here earn their bread, mister.'

He rolled down the car window to toss out his empty cigarette packet, and could have chosen a better moment to do it. They were driving through a sudden cloud of thick black smoke and Richard felt a searing pain in his left eye, as some of it entered the vehicle.

'Is there a rubbish dump or something around here?' he asked crossly. 'Some grit from whatever they're burning has found its way under my eyelid!'

'Don't rub it, mister – it will only make it feel worse.'

This was all Richard needed right now! – and was probably an omen that all would go wrong with the plan he hadn't yet got.

'September is one of our harvest times,' the driver told him. 'Harvest comes twice a year here an' that's when they burn the sugar cane. See all those black bits flyin' in the wind? I'm sure sorry you got one in your eye.'

'Me too!'

He was still trying to stop himself from rubbing it when they reached Napili and the Taylor estate, which even with only one good eye Richard could see was idyllically situated – and for his purpose, would not be easy to penetrate.

A high stone wall, thick with bougainvillaea, shielded

the house from view, but Richard could glimpse its mellow frontage between the Norfolk pines beyond the huge, iron gates.

'The gates, they always locked. You going to have to ring the bell,' said the cabbie knowledgeably.

Richard paid him double the fare, and said with a smile, 'Would you mind hanging around for a while?' It had just occurred to him that he would need to make a hasty return to the airport, with or without Amy, and taxi ranks were not part of Napili's scenario.

'Whatever you say, mister. How long will you be?'

'I'm not sure – but I'll pay you for your waiting time.' Richard reached into his imagination for a possible reason for his reappearance with Amy, and came up with, 'I'm not a businessman, as you assumed. I'm a doctor. As you may know, Mr Taylor's grand-daughter lives with him, and I've come from New York to examine her tonsils — '

'I guess you forgot to bring your medical bag,' the observant driver cut in.

'Oh Lord! I must have left it on the plane,' was Richard's off-the-cuff answer to being caught out. 'But I'll know just by looking at her throat if she requires surgery. An experienced ear, nose, and throat man sees all too many of such cases.'

Alison would say that the Plantaines' thespian blood had risen to his aid in an emergency, Richard thought, continuing to act his part. 'If necessary, I've been instructed to take the little girl back to New York with me for treatment.'

'Lahaina Hospital was where my Wikoli had his tonsils out – but nobody would expect Mr Taylor's grand-daughter to have hers done there,' the cabbie said without resentment.

'My appointment book is so full, I just promised Mr Taylor I'd come when I could, and I didn't let him know it would be today,' Richard lied like the trouper he had just discovered he could be when necessary.

'I want you to wait in case he's out somewhere for the day in his car,' he told the man with an easy smile. 'He

232

said if he were to be, I should just go ahead with what we arranged, so I'll need you to take us to the airport. But would you mind parking your cab in the shade?'

'On this part of the road, there is no shade at this time of day, mister.'

'But there is around the bend we just turned,' he pointed out. From there, the driver would not see what Richard was about to do. 'It will do me and the child no harm to stretch our legs and walk to the car. And I don't want it to be like an oven if I have to take her back with me – she's been running a fever.'

The cabbie, whose garish shirt had soaked with sweat after standing for only a minute or two in the baking heat, looked anxious – on Amy's behalf. 'Even in the shade, a parked vehicle gets pretty damn hot on Maui, mister. Maybe I should just stay right here with the engine an' the air conditionin' switched on.'

Richard wanted to laugh – at himself and the earnest Hawaiian engaged in this ridiculous debate – but stemmed his mirth. 'I could be hours. So let's do it my way.'

'Whatever you say, mister.'

He waited for the cab to disappear from sight and thought, feeling like an actor in a crime movie: So much for the getaway plan. If Percy had come with him, as he'd wanted to, they would probably have played the whole thing like Abbott and Costello!

Such was Richard's sense of unreality. But the crime had yet to be perpetrated, and he noted the barbed wire atop the gates and the wall. Had BT strengthened his fortress against this day? Or was he afraid not just of Richard snatching Amy, but of any outsider sullying his billionaire paradise?

A paradise it surely was. The view of Napili Bay was shut out by the house, but as the car turned the bend Richard had seen the breathtaking loveliness of the beach below.

He recalled the cabbie saying the estate adjoined it, but would have to approach it from the other side of the house, if his innocent accomplice was not to see him.

233

He walked along the road in the opposite direction from which they had come, and came upon a steep path that led down to the shore. Once there, the house was again visible through a fretwork of imposing trees, and Richard could see a gleam of blue water that must be the pool.

He had expected to find a private beach, too, bordering the estate, but the glistening sands seemed open to all.

Only a small boy and girl occupied them now. Richard was studying the steep incline between himself and the house when the two children approached him. When he turned to look at them, his heart skipped a beat. The girl was the image of Alison.

'You won't tell my grand-daddy you saw me playing on the beach, will you?' she said, confirming her identity.

'You can count on me not to,' he said huskily. For once, Destiny had made things easy for him. Even if he didn't pull it off, he had seen his daughter.

'If you've come to visit him, I'm afraid he isn't here today,' she went on, giving him his mother's smile.

'What makes you think I have?'

'You have on a suit, and only Grand-daddy's visitors dress like that, around here.'

She was quick on the uptake, too, Richard thought with pride. And such a beautiful child; her olive skin had honeyed from the sun, her hair, which she wore in a pony-tail, was like black silk, and she was looking up at him with her soft, dark eyes.

'If Amy's grand-daddy was at home, she wouldn't be allowed to play on the beach,' her little Hawaiian companion said, giving Richard a friendly grin.

'This is Kimo,' Amy introduced him. 'His mom is our housekeeper – and she would sure be in trouble if Grand-daddy found out I play down here when he's away.'

'Is your mother here?' Richard inquired and saw her face cloud.

'No,' was all she said.

What she didn't say told Richard more than had she related the story of her life since he last saw her. He took her hand and led her to the water's edge. Kimo remained where he was, but was watching them carefully.

Richard resisted the urge to gather Amy close. 'What would you say, Amy, if I told you I am your father?'

The child froze. 'My father is dead.'

It was now Richard's turn to freeze.

'Grand-daddy said he died when I was a baby, and it's best not to talk about him.' She eyed Richard warily. 'So how could you be him? If you said you were, you'd be lying.'

Richard thought of the birthday and Christmas gifts he had sent to her over the years, obviously consigned to the rubbish bin by her elders. He had realised they were not being given to her when she was old enough to write a thank-you note and did not. But for BT to have told her he was dead! Was there no treachery that Lee would not deem allowable because her Daddy had plotted it? More than that, she had aided and abetted him.

'Your name is Plantaine, isn't it?' Richard said to Amy. 'Yes.'

'Mine, too.' He took out his passport and showed it to her. 'Would you like to see a picture of you and your mother and me, taken when you were six months old? It's the only photo I have of you, and I treasure it,' he added, handing it to her. 'Though you look somewhat different now!'

'But you and Mom don't,' she said, studying it. Then she looked up at him and added, 'You're one of her divorced husbands, aren't you?'

'Yes, my darling.'

'Which number were you?'

'Two.' What a conversation to be having with one's daughter, Richard thought poignantly.

'You and number-one are the only ones I didn't know,' she said with a flat resignation that tugged at Richard's heart.

'But you know me now,' he said gravely. 'And I am the only one who is important in your life.'

Amy's face lit with happiness, 'I've got a daddy!' she

called to Kimo. 'And I didn't know I had one – isn't that wonderful?'

Kimo came to join them by the water, still regarding Richard suspiciously.

Richard ruffled his hair and gave him a reassuring smile. 'It's all right, Kimo, I'm not a ghost! I really am Amy's father.'

'Kimo's daddy is really dead,' Amy told Richard.

'I'm sorry to hear that,' he said kindly to the little boy. And to Amy, 'Now you know you've got me, how would you like to come and live with me, in England?'

Kimo looked panic-stricken. 'That's the other side of the world!'

Amy ignored the interruption and said to Richard, 'What would Grand-daddy do, without me, if I did?' Obviously, her mother did not enter into it.

'You are my little girl, not his,' Richard answered. 'I loved you when you were a baby and we lived together in New York. I love you just as much now, Amy, and I want you with me.'

'Is England really the other side of the world, Daddy?'

Hearing her address him thus was sweet music to Richard's ears.

'It's trillions of miles away,' said Kimo. 'And I don't want you to go.'

'What's the matter with your eye, Daddy,' Amy asked irrelevantly.

'I got a bit of burning sugar cane in it, on the way here. It still seems to be there.'

'Then I'd better try to get it out for you. Kneel down, so I can reach. And let me have your hankie.'

Richard did as he was bid and gave her a hug when she had deftly removed the sliver of grit.

When he got to his feet, she stood appraising him, as though she were assessing him and her own future. 'I would like to go with you,' she decided. And told Kimo, 'You can keep Grand-daddy company after I'm gone.'

Tears began cascading down Kimo's nutbrown face.

'Boys aren't supposed to cry,' Amy chided him. 'I shall

236

write you lots of letters from England. And you can have all my toys to play with; you won't have to share them with me any more.'

'You may not like it in England,' Kimo warned her.

'But I'll like being with my daddy and I guess I'm going to give it a try.' She clutched Richard's hand and said urgently, 'We ought to leave now. While Grand-daddy isn't here. If I wait to ask his permission, he's sure to say no.'

'I am the one who says what my little girl may or may not do from now on,' Richard replied. 'But I dislike angry scenes, and would certainly prefer to avoid one.'

'Okay! Then let's go.'

That she was as impulsive as her actress granny, Richard was left in no doubt.

'I'm going to miss you, Amy,' said Kimo pathetically as Richard bore her away.

They paused to wave to him, when they had climbed the steep path to the road, and Richard felt sorry for the little figure in swimming shorts, alone on the beach.

'Kimo will have nobody to share lessons with now,' Amy said guiltily as Richard hurried her past the estate gates. 'I guess he'll have to go to school. Grand-daddy let him share my tutor, to please me.'

'School won't do him any harm,' Richard replied. Being protected from the rough and tumble of growing-up was in his opinion good for no child. 'In England, school is where you'll have the rest of your education,' he told his daughter. 'You'll make lots of friends there.'

Amy's eyes sparkled with excitement. 'Except for Kimo, I've never had a friend.'

This is a big adventure for her, thought Richard, as it would be for any kid. And like her grandmother, she was the adventurous kind – was that why she was going with him willingly? No. There'd been an immediate rapport between them. She wanted to be with him.

He had the presence of mind to tell her before they reached the cab that it had been necessary to play 'let's pretend' with the driver.

237

Amy gave him a conspiratorial smile. 'You knew Grand-daddy wouldn't let you take me, didn't you?'

'I know him very well,' was all Richard allowed himself to say.

It was as well that he had primed her.

'How's your throat feeling?' was the cabbie's sympathetic greeting.

'She is unable to talk at present,' Richard said, managing not to smile.

It was more difficult not to do so when Amy fingered her neck dramatically and sank limply against him, with a tragic expression in her eyes. She was Alison to a T!

'When my little boy had his tonsils out, they fed him ice cream afterwards,' the cabbie tried to cheer her up.

They were by then *en route* to the airport and he slowed down and grinned at Richard through the mirror, 'Maybe I better turn the car around, Doc. It's just hit me that you forgot the little lady's baggage, like you left your medical kit on the plane.'

'Drive on,' Richard said smoothly, though he was desperately trying to dream up another fib. 'Baggage for her isn't necessary. She has clothing at Mr Taylor's New York apartment.' And the fibber-of-the-year award should be presented to Richard Plantaine!

The driver launched into a monologue about his clever son, which lasted for the rest of the journey. And Richard sat silently exulting because he had got his beloved daughter back.

'I bought you some pyjamas and a toothbrush,' Janet told Amy when Richard returned with her to their hotel suite in Honolulu.

'I'd prefer to leave Hawaii tonight, Janet,' said Richard edgily. The ease with which he had done what he came to do seemed too good to be true.

'I tried to make provisional reservations for tonight,' Janet answered. 'There isn't a seat to be had until the day after tomorrow.'

'Then we could go and see Pearl Harbor, tomorrow,' said Amy. 'I've never been there.'

'Sorry, darling,' Richard replied. 'But we shall have to stay holed up here until we leave. We're still playing hide and seek with your grandfather. And I'd still like to avoid an unpleasant scene.'

'Okay, Daddy. How is your eye?'

'Better, thanks to you.'

How easily the child had slipped into her place in Richard's life, Janet thought, experiencing a pang because Amy was born of his love for another woman. 'That eye ought to be bathed,' she said.

Richard appeared not to hear her. His attention was riveted upon Amy, whose face had briefly puckered with distress.

'What's the matter, darling?' he asked her.

'I was thinking of Grand-daddy. When he gets back today he's going to be awful upset to find me gone. And I guess he'll come looking for me.'

'That's why I said we were playing hide and seek,' said Richard gently. 'But we don't have any choice, if unpleasantness is to be avoided.'

'I'm mad with him for telling me you were dead. And with Mommy for not telling me you weren't,' the child said. 'But I guess I'm sorry for Grand-daddy, too. Do you think it's very cruel of me to run off and leave him all alone?'

To Richard it was the punishment BT deserved. 'No.'

'He still has your mother, doesn't he?' Janet said kindly.

'Do you know my mommy?'

'I met her only once.'

'Then you know how beautiful she is,' said Amy with a poignancy that reminded Richard of how he had felt about Alison when he was a child – as though she were out of his reach.

'Mommy loves me, but she doesn't come home too often,' Amy went on. 'And I can't go with her when she's travelling, can I? I have to have my lessons.'

239

Travelling in and out of marriages, Richard thought.

'But she brings me lovely things,' Amy said.

Lee's way of expressing love, was Richard's reaction to that.

Amy showed them the wristwatch Lee had brought her from Switzerland, when she last put in an appearance in Hawaii, and both Richard and Janet thought how sad it was for a child to need proof of her mother's affection.

'I hope you like red, Amy,' Janet said to her with a smile. 'I went out and got you something to wear for the journey to England. That pretty sunfrock you have on wouldn't be warm enough.'

Amy was thrilled when Janet brought the wool dress and coat to show to her. 'How did you know my size?'

'I reckoned you'd be as big as your cousin Lottie, in England, who is your age.'

'I've got a girl cousin? Wow!'

'A boy cousin, too,' said Richard. 'Though they're not your first cousins, darling.'

'In our family that makes no difference,' Janet said, as Richard well knew.

'Any kind of cousins are better than none,' Amy declared. She gave Richard an impish smile. 'May I have some ice cream, Daddy? Even though I'm not having my tonsils out?'

They shared a laugh and Janet, who was not in on the joke, again experienced a pang she did not want to believe was jealousy.

Richard called room-service and ordered chocolate nut sundaes for three.

And three would be the operative number from now on, thought Janet. With Amy on the scene to absorb him, he was never going to open his eyes and see Janet as she wanted to be seen.

They were eating the ice cream when the telephone rang.

'It could be your mother, Richard,' Janet said.

'Or Grand-daddy,' said Amy apprehensively.

240

'He doesn't know where we are staying,' Janet told her.

Richard just stared at the phone.

'As we have the key, the desk knows we're in,' Janet prodded him.

'And it's unlikely to be my mother – it's five a.m. in England.'

Janet steeled herself to pick up the receiver and did not like what she was told by the desk clerk. 'Two gentlemen are asking for you, Richard. Representatives of Mr Bradwell Taylor, the girl said.'

Richard squared his shoulders and rose from his armchair. 'Ask her to send them up.' The all-powerful beef-baron hadn't the guts to do his own dirty work, but Richard would make short shrift of his side-kicks.

'Take Amy into your bedroom and lock the door, Janet.'

'I can spare you no more than a minute,' he said curtly, when a swarthy Hawaiian and an albino wearing dark glasses presented themselves at the suite door.

The albino, who had on a black suit and shirt, with a broad white tie, removed a speck of fluff from his sleeve. 'He ain't gonna invite us in, Pukui.'

'Tch, tch,' said his partner, regretfully, 'now that ain't polite, Jonesy.'

'So he can't expect us to be polite to him.'

'Would you please cut short the double-act?' Richard tersely requested.

Then he found himself gripped by his arms and frog-marched into the suite. In passing, the albino deftly kicked the door shut, as though he were well practised in this routine.

'We've come for Mr Taylor's grand-daughter,' said the Hawaiian.

'Let go of me!'

'Sure. When you tell us where she is,' the albino replied.

'As she is my daughter, that's no business of yours or Mr Taylor's.'

'Sez who?' they answered in unison.

241

'Sez me!' Richard rapped back, matching their style.

They still had him by the arms, and twisted them expertly until he could not restrain a cry of pain that brought Janet and Amy rushing from the bedroom.

'Hi, little lady,' the albino said to Amy.

'Your grand-daddy sent us to fetch his sweetie-pie,' said the Hawaiian, straightening his bright blue jacket and giving her an oily smile.

And they hadn't even needed to search the suite, thought Richard, whose arms felt as though wrenched from their sockets. Brute force wasn't in it and he was no match for such tactics.

Amy placed herself close to him and eyed the two men reproachfully. 'There was no need for you and Mr Jones to hurt my daddy, Mr Pukui,' she replied to the Hawaiian.

'You seem to know these gentlemen, darling,' said Richard, glancing at them with contempt.

'When Mommy's home, she sometimes brings me to Honolulu for a few days, and Mr Jones and Mr Pukui take care of us.'

Not just hoodlums, watchdogs also, Richard thought. And Amy was the one they were paid to guard, lest her father one day do what he now had.

'Why didn't Grand-daddy come himself?' she asked them.

'Who's gonna tell her, Pukui, you or me?'

'I guess I'll let you do it, Jonesy. I can't bear to upset her.'

Amy paled. 'Tell me what?'

Jones put a sorrowful expression on his colourless face. 'When your grand-daddy got back from LA and found you gone, he was taken very sick.'

'An' he ain't gonna get well again without his little sweetie,' Pukui capped it.

'Balderdash!' Richard thundered.

'Grand-daddy had a seizure once before,' Amy told him. 'When Mommy wanted to give one of her husbands another chance, before they got divorced.'

242

Richard could believe it. BT would stop at nothing to get his way.

'Did the doctor say Grand-daddy wouldn't get better without me?' she asked the men.

'I guess he must have,' Jones replied.

'We was told to tell you that,' Pukui endorsed.

Amy made her decision. 'I can't go with you, Daddy. Grand-daddy needs me.'

'So do I, darling.'

'But you're not old and sick, are you?'

BT had already got her back, and Richard knew it. She was too young to comprehend the emotional blackmail that was her grandfather's special skill, and by which he had kept her mother a captive. Lee's attempts to break free in pursuit of personal happiness always ended as Amy's was about to end.

It seemed to Richard now that only BT's death would cut the selfish bond with which he had tied them to him.

Amy had somehow remained unspoiled by his spoiling, Richard had noted, and he thought it remarkable that she had. She was a stronger character than her mother. But prey to grand-daughterly loyalty nevertheless.

She had taken to Richard immediately, but had no instinctive loyalty to him – how could she have, when he had not raised her?

Silence had fallen in the room. Janet was gazing through the windows into the hotel's exotic gardens, beyond which a picture-postcard sunset had lit the sky. Richard was aware of Amy staring disconsolately down at the melted remains of her ice cream, and knew that BT's men were waiting for his next move. There would be no trouble unless he made it.

Amy emerged from her momentary bleakness and gave him a smile. 'I guess we'll have to take a rain check on me coming to England, Daddy.'

'I'm not so sure about that,' he replied, and saw Jones and Pukui exchange a glance

'If I came with you, I would worry about Grand-daddy

243

all the time,' she said. 'He once told me he would die if I ever left him – but I didn't let myself think of it when I let you take me away from Napili. It was so lovely to find out I'd got you.'

'But if I was you, Amy, I'd keep remembering what your grand-daddy once told you,' said Jones gravely.

'And make sure it never happens,' Pukui advised her.

'I could use these two tragedians in one of my productions!' Richard exploded to Janet.

'But don't ask me to play opposite them,' she answered. 'I couldn't guarantee not to throw up onstage.'

'If we hurry, Amy, we'll just make the next flight to Maui,' said Jones, ushering her to the door.

'Take your hands off her!' Richard yelled, following them.

Pukui blocked his path.

'I have to go, Daddy,' she said forlornly before Jones whisked her from the room.

'Get out of my way,' Richard seethed to Pukui.

'Your kid went of her own accord, and don't you forget it,' the burly Hawaiian replied. 'And your ladyfriend here is a witness. But if you have to be knocked cold to make you see sense, here is more private than out on the sidewalk.'

When Richard came to, he was lying on the floor, and Janet kneeling beside him.

'I should have let Percy come with me,' he said with chagrin.

'He's no more cut out for fisticuffs than you are, Richard.' Janet helped him to his feet. 'All you've gained by coming to Hawaii is a cut lip and a sore eye.'

'Also a bruised nose,' he added, touching it gingerly.

'The size of that Hawaiian's fist, it's a wonder your face is still recognisable.'

'My ex-father-in-law knows how to pick 'em!' said Richard sourly, lowering himself onto a brocade *chaise longue* tthat epitomised the Royal Hawaiian Hotel's discreetly elegant decor.

'I'd better fetch a cold cloth and minister to you,' said

Janet. And remarked when she returned, 'Pukui doesn't speak like a Hawaiian.'

'He's probably spent time on the mainland – being trained by the Mafia! And I'd say Jones was born to his trade.'

'He gave me the creeps.'

'But injuries wasn't quite all I got for my trouble,' Richard said after she had tended them. 'I met my daughter – and she's quite a person.'

'Alison would adore her. They're two of a kind,' Janet declared with a smile.

'You saw that, too. So I got knocked cold, what of it? It was worth it.'

'I hope you're not thinking of staging a second round, as I've now seen for myself that you can't win,' Janet replied. 'When you told me what your ex-father-in-law was like, I thought, Who does the man think he is: God? But I wouldn't question Mr Taylor's omnipotence now, Richard. You stood no chance of getting Amy back. It didn't take him long to trace you here. And if you'd managed to get her to England, he'd have filched her from you there.'

She put a comforting hand on Richard's and said gently, 'What a goose you were to think that once you'd got Amy, all would be fine. You wouldn't have been able to let her out of your sight in England.'

'I wasn't thinking that far ahead.'

'In that respect, you too are like Alison. But in the end, Amy went back voluntarily – which if it weren't so sad would be funny.'

'But she's more intelligent and shrewd than her mother. Lee has never seen through BT. When Amy's older, she's bound to, and I'm banking on her coming to me then.'

'Let's hope you're right.'

'It's all I have to hope for, isn't it, kiddo? How I'll get by without her in the meantime is another matter.'

Janet went to gaze through the window. In the floodlit gardens, vacationing couples in evening dress strolled arm in arm before dinner. The palms were gently swaying, and she could hear the Pacific beating upon the shore. A harvest moon in an inky sky had replaced the glorious sunset, as though the scene shifters had changed the setting for the next act of a romantic play. Hawaiian music was drifting from the restaurant, adding to the ambience. There could be no place in the world more romantic than this – but she and Richard were discussing Amy; their relationship the same old camaraderie that it had always been.

'I'm thankful you're with me, kiddo,' Richard said.

Something in Janet snapped. 'I wish you would stop calling me that! I'm not the surrogate kid sister Fate didn't provide you with, Richard. I'm a woman, but you still don't see me that way. If you did, your life could have some meaning even without Amy.'

Richard was stunned and eyed her in confusion. Was she saying what he thought she was?

Janet left him in no doubt. Once unleashed, her pent-up feelings poured out of her. 'I'm still unattached at thirty-three because there's never been anyone for me but you. And if I'm a fool for telling you, you are blind as a bat for needing to be told!'

A moment of silence followed.

Richard had a dazed look on his face. 'You're very dear to me,' he said quietly.

'But now you know it's not in the way I want it to be, nothing can be the same between us, can it?' she replied. 'We can't go back to how we were. Nor can I go on being just a shoulder for you to cry on about Amy. It's time I took Auntie Clara's advice, before I am too old to have a child of my own. There's been no shortage of men who've wanted me.'

Richard noted her pocket-Venus shape. With the lamplight behind her, he could see her thighs outlined beneath her cotton mini-skirt, and her high breasts straining against her blouse.

He shifted his gaze to her face, and noticed that her mouth was as voluptuous as her figure, and it was as if he were seeing her for the first time. As the object of desire

246

she surely was to the men she encountered. The way a man did not see his sister. But Janet wasn't his sister – and blind he had certainly been, he thought, swallowing hard.

'When we get back to England, I'll make things easier for both of us by moving out of your mother's house,' she said before fleeing his presence.

Richard sat listening to the palms rustling outside the window. He could see from where he was seated a sliver of the moon, and became aware as Janet had been of the mysterious thrall of the Hawaiian night.

He heard Janet's bedroom door slam shut, and got up to pace the rug. Hawaii was for lovers, and he was alone in a hotel suite with a beautiful woman as rripe for the taking as the tropical fruit on the coffee table. He and Janet had not partaken of that, either.

Hawaii was, too, a double watershed in Richard's life. He had met and re-lost his daughter. Coming here had also led to his losing the comfortable relationship he had shared with Janet. As she had said, they could not go back to how they were.

Did Richard want to go forward with her along a different path? The hardening in his loins answered yes.

A moment later he was tapping tentatively on her door. 'May I come in?'

'If you wish.'

Richard hovered in the doorway. 'Is it okay if I come and sit beside you on the bed?'

'I don't recall you requiring permission to do so at home.'

If Janet was in bed when Richard came home at night, he often dropped into her room for a late-night chat. But a new tension was suddenly in the atmosphere.

'You were still "kiddo" to me then,' he replied, trying to keep his tone casual.

'And what am I to you now?'

He removed his gaze from her creamy arms and said thickly, 'I'm not sure.'

Janet wound them around his neck. 'Then let's find out.'

Richard needed no further encouragement and found her mouth with his. His hand strayed to her breasts – then he drew back. This was Janet, not one of the fast young women who accommodated his sexual needs in the absence of a wife.

'Does kissing hurt your split lip?' she asked tenderly. 'And your eye is still inflamed from getting the grit in it,' she observed.

Richard had momentarily forgotten his aches and pains, and Janet's concern served to emphasise that this was not one of his loveless one-night stands.

'How's your bruised nose?' she enquired. 'I picked a fine time to bring matters to a head!' she said with chagrin.

'But as you pointed out, there's no going back.'

They shared a long glance, and Richard knew that they had not lost what they had always had. Something had been added. From now on, Janet would be to him what the woman in a man's life should be. Friend and lover rolled into one, and he would be that to her.

All they had lost was time, he thought, gathering her close.

'I want you to make love to me,' she whispered.

Richard stroked her ash-blonde hair. 'Wouldn't you rather wait until we're married?'

Janet's whole being was transfused with indescribable joy. 'No to the question, and yes to the proposal contained in it,' she answered.

CHAPTER THREE

'RICHARD CALLED from Honolulu airport. They're on their way home,' Emma told Alison when she arrived back from the theatre looking pale and strained. 'The suspense is over.'

'Not for me – as you haven't told me if the outcome is good or bad.'

'Both.'

'How can it be both!'

'He isn't bringing Amy – but there's going to be a wedding.'

'Richard and Janet? Oh, how absolutely marvellous!'

Alison was overjoyed for her son and the young woman who had loved him for so long. But the happiness Richard had found in Hawaii was tinged with sadness, on account of his child.

'My mother's old friend Sarah Sandberg would call it the almonds and raisins of life,' Emma said when Alison voiced her thoughts.

'And it's a taste I've experienced many times,' Alison replied. 'But I must phone Conrad and tell him the good news about our children,' she said collecting herself.

'Don't you think you should let Janet do that?'

'Janet won't mind. And Conrad will be as delighted as I am.'

Alison was wrong in that respect. Instead of the excitement she had expected to mingle with hers on the line, a heavy silence followed her announcement.

'I hope you're not going to object because Richard is nominally a Gentile,' Alison said when she could bear it no longer. 'Richard is a quarter-Jewish, and feels part of the Stein clan, as I do.'

'You don't have to plead Richard's case, Alison.'

'Your silence made it seem necessary.'

'To Zelda and me, Richard is Richard. We fostered him, didn't we? – and the feeling for him that gave us will never change. There's no one I'd rather have for a son-in-law.'

'Thank you for saying that.'

'And after all he's been through, he ought to be spared any more trouble,' Conrad said. 'But if he and Janet marry, that will put him in the terrible position I was in years ago.'

Oh dear God, thought Alison, remembering now what Conrad had confided to her long before Janet was born. Though he and Zelda wanted a family, he had feared that the hereditary disease which Zelda had escaped might blight their children.

'You'd forgotten about it, hadn't you?' Conrad went on. 'And I put it from my mind after Janet was pronounced a healthy baby. But as she grew older, I knew I'd have to face up to it again when she married. I'm so sorry, Alison, that it could now affect a grandchild of yours, as well as mine.'

'Does Janet know anything about it?'

'There was no point in telling her. But she must be told now. And Richard must have the option of backing out, like Zelda's parents gave me.'

CHAPTER FOUR

In 1970, Alison agreed to make a film. Professionally, the last decade had rendered her disenchanted.

Her longtime wish to appear in a play by the now well-known woman author, Marianne Dean, had yet to be fulfilled. Miss Dean's agent sent all her work to Charles Bligh, who was only too eager to cash in on her success, having finally taken a chance on her first play.

Alison had attended that première and found it a warming experience. There was a no-nonsense quality about the writing, as though the author had no need of artifice to weave her dramatic spell. She was not surprised to read in the programme that Miss Dean was a northerner, and would have been interested to learn she was the granddaughter of Sarah Sandberg, whose words of wisdom Emma sometimes quoted.

The other new work presented in the Sixties had not – with a few exceptions – been to Alison's taste. Though she found Pinter's plays atmospherically riveting, she emerged after seeing one as foxed as the rest of the audience, and feeling cheated. For Alison, the first function of drama was to communicate. Which was not to say she enjoyed what Orton had communicated. She could not but deem him a brilliant playwright, but would not have lent her talent to the anti-social outrageousness that had made his name.

As for the Fringe theatre that had mushroomed during the decade, Alison had seen only one such production and found it enough. It had seemed to her then that theatre had divided into two camps.

It was to prod her from her apathy that Richard had suggested she make a film. A movie producer he knew

251

had just commissioned the screenplay of a novel set in Cyprus. The plot concerned a Greek legend and its effect upon the inhabitants of a convent. The role of the Mother Superior was made for Alison, he had declared.

Alison read the novel and agreed with her son. Her distinguished reputation, plus the publicity value attached to Alison Plantaine's first movie, ensured her the part.

Morton, who thought, as Richard did, that the change would refresh her jaded spirits, did not try to dissuade her. Instead, he rented a villa close to Limassol for the location period and went to Cyprus with her. Emma was persuaded to accompany them, and the venture took on for Alison the quality of a holiday in the sun with her two dear friends.

Not until she began work did she realise how strenuous film-acting was, that the disciplines and techniques were quite different from those to which she had all her life been accustomed. A play was performed all-of-a-piece, and built to its finale climax by climax, on an ever ascending plane. Movie scenes were not filmed in the natural sequence of the story's action. Nor was there the stimulus of an audience's reaction flowing towards the actors.

Being the professional she was, Alison coped, and stemmed the temperamental outbursts that threatened from within her when she was called upon to repeat what she had already done, for take, after take, after take.

When not required on the set, she would go for a solitary walk. The outdoor scenes were being shot at Paphos, where Aphrodite was said to have risen from the sea, and it was around that legend the novelist had woven his story. But contemplating the azure Mediterranean did not soothe Alison. Nor did the nun's habit she must wear in the heat, for hours on end, improve her sore feelings.

Emma and Morton occasionally went to watch the filming, though not at the crack of dawn when Alison must put in an appearance.

'It's too much for her. I ought not to have let her do it,'

Morton said one morning when he and Emma were shopping in Limassol's narrow, winding streets.

'Since when could you or I, or anybody, stop Alison from rushing into things headlong, Max?'

'And now,' said Morton crossly, 'here I am being dragged in and out of seedy little shops, so you can examine bits of lace!'

'You didn't have to come.'

'But I did – fool that I am! And how many lace mats and tablecloths do you need?'

'I can't go back to England without taking a piece of lace for every lady in my family.' Emma led the way into yet another shop and rummaged through a pile of bargain offers heaped carelessly on the counter. 'They would cost the earth at home, Max.'

'Then why not buy the lot, and have done with it!'

The storekeeper heaved her bulk off a stool to try to make a sale, and gave Emma a smile and a shrug. 'All husbands no like to go shopping.'

'He isn't my husband,' said Emma, turning pink.

To Morton the incident was meaningless and he wondered why Emma had suddenly lost interest in the lace and stalked out of the shop.

'This reminds me of the time I took Alison shopping for perfume on the Rue de Rivoli, in Paris,' he said, mopping the perspiration from his brow. 'By the time she'd had a hundred different kinds sprayed on the back of her hand, she couldn't remember which she had preferred.'

But I bet you didn't complain, Emma thought. Then she noted his weary posture and chided herself for keeping him out in the heat for so long. 'Let's go back to the villa now. I'll come into town by myself, another day.'

'I'll drink to that!' Morton glanced anxiously at his watch. 'I wonder how Alison is faring today? Shall we take a cab to the location and see?'

'No. You look worn out. And I'd rather not be there to see.'

'You think as I do, don't you, Emma? – that sooner or later she's going to explode.'

'And as I once told you, Max, all you and I can do is pick up the pieces. The only question in this case is when.'

Unlike the director, actors, and crew, Morton and Emma were not fooled by Alison's present veneer of cool professionalism. She had not succeeded in hiding from them that she was furious with herself for stepping out of her natural habitat – in her seventieth year – to do something she was not, to put it mildly, enjoying.

In the evenings, the three of them would sit on the villa terrace, listening to the nocturnal insects. Suffering them, too. Alison grumbled about the mosquitoes hovering around her face, but was never bitten. Emma, who was, scratched her bites in silence. Morton reacted with water blisters, and made no secret of his discomfort.

Added to this was the humidity for which there was no relief; even after a cool bath their clothing felt glued to them immediately they dressed. And hovering above the physical discomforts was Alison's unspoken dissatisfaction with what she was here for.

The explosion Emma and Morton were expecting came on the evening of the day they shopped in Limassol. The maid had cooked moussaka for dinner, and Alison, who disliked aubergine, had forced herself to eat it because she was hungry, and there was nothing else but cheese and fruit.

This did not help her mood. But Morton was the unwitting cause of her feelings being unleashed.

'I've been nibbled at again!' he said while they were drinking coffee on the terrace. 'Tomorrow, I'll have another damned blister.'

'I didn't ask you to come here with me, Maxwell – and you don't have to stay!' Alison lashed out.

'If we weren't with you, who would you shout at whenever you feel like it?' Emma answered.

'You weren't included in what I just said – but you're welcome to go back to England with him,' Alison flared anew.

'You're wishing you could do that, aren't you?' Emma said quietly.

'What I wish to do is one thing. My professional commitment is something else – as you well know.' Alison sipped some iced lemonade. 'Despite how I feel, it will be a good film. We're shooting a street scene in Limassol tomorrow, if you two would care to come and watch.'

Morton was relieved that the outburst had been only a small one, and thinking it was time he was abed. Suddenly, he felt drained of energy.

'Are you all right, Max?' Emma enquired with concern. 'You look a little pale.'

'Everyone looks pale in this lamplight,' said Alison, waving away a mosquito.

But to Emma, Morton's complexion looked waxy – and his shoulders more bowed than usual.

'I'm fine,' he said. 'Just ready for some peace and quiet, in my old age — '

Then he gave Emma a glassy stare and keeled over onto the flagstones.

Alison and Emma were down beside him so fast, they almost bumped heads.

'He must have fainted,' said Alison. 'Fetch some brandy, Emma, while I undo his tie.'

But Emma had his wrist and could not find his pulse. She placed her ear upon his chest and there was no sound or movement. 'Never mind the brandy, Alison. Get me the mirror from your evening bag.'

Alison went cold, but fetched her bag from the wrought-iron table. She watched Emma hold the mirror above Morton's mouth, and saw it slip from her fingers.

Then Emma got to her feet and they stood together silently gazing down at the man who meant so much to each of them, who was suddenly no more. Neither shed a tear, but each was prey to her private thoughts.

Emma had lost the one love of her life, who had died without ever knowing she loved him. And Alison her guiding light. Morton had been to her mentor, confidant, and protector.

Emma found her voice. 'We must call a doctor, and get a death certificate so we can take him home.'

Alison steeled herself to say what she must – and for Emma's reaction to it. 'I must stay here and finish the film. Maxwell would expect me to.'

'But I expect you to do the right thing.'

CHAPTER FIVE

RICHARD AND Janet had married despite the hereditary disease in her mother's family. Three years later, when she had not conceived the child she so dearly wanted, Richard wondered, as Conrad had when it seemed that Zelda might remain childless, if this was Nature's way of putting an end to an unhealthy family tree. Since Janet had no maternal cousins, the continuance of the line was dependent upon her.

As Conrad had in the early years of his marriage, Richard must live with the consequences of his wife's inability to conceive. With the passage of time, the initial radiance that love had brought to Janet had gradually diminished. And Richard knew that their home was an empty place to her without a child.

The moment when Conrad told them what they had to know returned to Richard's mind. Himself and Janet seated, hand in hand, on the sofa in her parents' living room, still cocooned in the dazed euphoria with which they returned from Hawaii. Conrad had waited until his wife retired to bed, before revealing the secret her parents had kept from her.

Richard could remember the clock ticking in the silence that followed, and the apprehension that rippled through him when Janet removed her hand from his.

When she spoke, it was of her mother, not herself, that she was thinking. 'How terrible it would have been for Mum, if I had been born with that disease. Even worse than if she had known it was possible,' she added with a shudder.

'Your late grandparents knew she was too highly strung

257

to live with that possibility,' Conrad answered. 'That was why they told only me.'

'But you had to live with it, didn't you, Dad?' Janet averted her gaze to the fire. 'I wouldn't blame Richard if he wasn't prepared to.'

'Nor me.'

Richard recaptured Janet's hand. 'We're in this together, sweetheart.'

Conrad's relief was expressed in a shaky laugh. 'Before I leave you two love-birds alone, I'll give you some advice. Try not to worry about what may never happen.'

It was easier said than done – as Conrad had learned for himself – and Richard detected a change in Janet from then on. Her habitual sunny smile began to look to him like a mask for her private thoughts, and there was often a faraway expression in her eyes.

When they had been married for a year, he suggested that settling for a childless marriage might be a wise decision.

'Since you are already a parent, it's all fine from your point of view for me never to be one!' Janet lashed out at him.

It was then that Richard understood that they were not sharing the same anxiety. His was that their children might be blighted by the disease. Hers was that her maternal need might never be fulfilled.

'You'll be late for curtain-up, darling, if you don't get ready and go to the theatre soon,' Richard said to her on the evening of Morton's funeral.

Janet was standing by the living-room window, looking out upon Hampstead Heath. 'I'm not like your mother, Richard. My work isn't my be-all and end-all. And had I not known it was to Alison, I would certainly know now.'

Alison's refusal to return to England for the funeral had shocked Janet almost as much as it had angered Emma.

Only Richard understood – as Morton would have, he thought now. There was a time when Richard would have viewed it as Janet and Emma did, but the aftermath of his breakdown, when Alison set aside her career to be with him, had given him a new insight into the complicated woman she was.

'You don't really know my mother,' he said wryly. And added, 'If she'd held up filming, which is what it would have meant, the director wouldn't be able to finish on time. It would have cost thousands over and above the budget.'

Janet was tightlipped. 'Which mattered more to Alison than being there when her lifelong friend was laid to rest! The man who has left his business to her son.'

'Uncle Maxwell had no relatives to leave it to.'

'That isn't the point. And he would still have left it to you, as you know perfectly well. He deserved better than your mother has finally meted out to him.'

'He always respected and admired her professionalism. It may interest you to know, Janet, that when I flew to Cyprus to arrange for him to be brought home, Mother was in a worse state than Auntie Emma.'

'Conscience!' Janet exclaimed.

'She told me her decision was painful to make, though she made it unhesitatingly. The film unit was dependent upon her, and it was futile to let down the living when doing so wouldn't help the dead, was how she put it.'

'But she will now have to live with the effect of her decision on her relationship with Auntie Emma,' Janet declared.

'How the two of them will manage without Uncle Maxwell is what worries me. For a long-time threesome to suddenly become a twosome won't be easy,' Richard replied.

'It will be easier for your mother than for Auntie Emma,' said Janet. 'Alison will just bury herself in her career.'

She glanced moodily around the spacious room, which she had made cosy with chintz-covered sofas and matching curtains. But sharing it with the husband she loved was no longer enough. Her imagination conjured up a little girl playing on the hearthrug, but – as always when she indulged in such fantasy – the child had Amy's face, and she blotted the picture out.

Richard had not heard from Amy since she was taken from him in Honolulu, but had not expected to. There was no way she could have found out his address. Though she was now thirteen, her movements would still be closely supervised. But the hope that she would come to him when she was older was one he had not lost. He no longer voiced it to Janet, warned by a sixth sense that doing so would not be wise.

Janet never mentioned Amy, nowadays. Though Richard had not divined her jealousy of his love for his daughter, he had come to recognise the expression in her eyes when she looked at him now. She was thinking of her own childlessness, and he was filled with compassion for her.

'If God grants my wish, I won't be like Alison. I'll retire from the theatre,' she said.

'But meanwhile, you have a performance to give tonight, darling. So you had better get your skates on!'

While Janet was changing for the theatre, Richard sat gazing into the fire. He had kept his own disappointment to himself, and was concerned that she now displayed little enthusiasm for her work. She had the talent to achieve stardom, but lacked the ambition.

What mischievous games Destiny plays, thought Richard, who could not have been Alison's son without her belief in fate rubbing off on him. Maternity had complicated his career-woman mother's life, but to his wife, her career amounted to marking time until her real need was fulfilled.

Janet came to kiss him before she left. The cab that took her into the West End each evening, when she was appearing in a play, was waiting outside the front gate.

'I hate leaving you,' she said as she always did. This was not Janet's idea of marriage. 'Why don't you pop over to Highgate and see Auntie Emma?'

'When we dropped her off at home after the funeral,

she wouldn't let us go in with her. She obviously wants to be alone with her thoughts.'

'That's a good reason for not leaving her alone with them. Have you ever known her not want company?'

'My wife is not only beautiful, but also wise!' said Richard, appraising her. But her beauty was more fragile these days. As though it would not take much for her to break. 'Would you like us to adopt a baby?' he asked gently.

Last year she had undergone surgery to help her conceive, and had since asked her gynaecologist to prescribe one of the new fertility drugs. Her age and family history, and the experimental nature of such drugs, had decided the doctor against it. If she conceived without help, and the child was born with the disease present in her family, nature could be blamed, he had said, but taking a risk via drugs was something else.

'I haven't given up hope,' she replied to Richard. And privately added: Of a child who'll mean as much to you as Amy does, who is yours and mine.

The cab driver honked his horn, and she sped away. Richard roused himself from the fireside and went to visit Emma.

This was a time when Emma and his mother should have been together, he thought while he drove to Highgate. But Alison's professionalism had deprived them both of the comfort they ought to have been to each other.

What would Alison be doing right now, alone in the villa where Morton had died? After her long day's work, she had probably given herself a brandy and gone directly to bed. But Emma was unlikely to seek comfort from a bottle, however deep her distress.

That she had suffered a double blow, Richard had no doubt. Morton's sudden death was coupled with the total disillusionment Alison's not attending his funeral was to her. She had sat stony-faced beside Richard on the plane carrying them and the coffin back to England.

When he let himself into the house the ticking of the grandfather clock in the hall heightened the silence that

261

greeted him, and a box of Morton's favourite cigars in the living room moved him to tears. They were kept there for when Morton dropped in, but he would do so no more. Nor Emma complain to him about the aromatic fug that remained in the air after he left.

As Richard would no longer have him breathing down his neck at the office. But owning Morton Theatrical Enterprises could not compensate Richard for the loss of the man who had bequeathed the fruits of his labours to him.

He stemmed his emotion and went to find Emma. The kitchen was empty, and, though the evening was chilly, Emma had not lit the fire.

'Where are you, Auntie?' Richard called on his way upstairs. 'Doing some spring-cleaning in June?' he made himself joke.

Emma appeared on the landing carrying a large old suitcase. 'I was up in the attic, Richard, getting this.'

'What for?'

'The one I took to Cyprus won't hold all my things.'

Richard followed her into her room, and noted that the wardrobe and drawers were open.

'I'm going home,' Emma said while she removed the cobwebs and dust from the old case.

Richard prickled with apprehension. 'This is your home.'

'Not any more,' she flatly replied. 'I've lived with your mother for forty years, Richard. Stuck by her through thick and thin. Clara told me the day would come when I'd see Alison in her true colours and leave her. It has.'

Richard watched with dismay when she began packing her winter clothing. 'Wouldn't it be better to wait until Mother gets back and have it out with her?'

'There's nothing to have out. Clara was right about her, and I was wrong. She's your mother, Richard, and I'm happy that all is now well between you and her. That you love and respect her, despite her deficiencies. So did Max – fool that he was! Me, too, and I still love her – but I'm not a fool any more. If I die before she does, she'll put her work before my funeral, like she did with Max's.'

262

Emma paused with one of the cardigans Morton had given her as Christmas gifts in her hand. 'When I think of all the sacrifices he made for her. The way he trekked back and forth to Berlin, trying to trace your father after he disappeared. And put up with her temperament because it wasn't possible for her to have you with her after you were born. That's only the half of it! Max required no thanks, and nor do I. What we did was done out of love and friendship – which has turned out to be so one-sided I feel now that I've wasted my life.'

'I'm here, to prove that you didn't,' Richard said with affection.

'But without me, your mother would have found some other mug,' was Emma's tart reply. 'And some other impresario to eat out of her hand, if she hadn't had Max. Her charm is her weapon and it's been my undoing since the day she came into my life, when we were both only fourteen.'

'Do you now regret not marrying the American who proposed to you during the war?'

'The last letter I received from him – and that was years ago – was to tell me he was getting married to the widowed lady next door,' Emma revealed.

'But it was you he really wanted, or he wouldn't have waited for so long. And you haven't answered my question, Auntie.'

'I'm too old for those kind of regrets, Richard. But I don't have to spend what's left of my life where all the memories have, thanks to your mother, turned bitter. I never want to see her again.'

'You don't mean that.'

'That's what she said, when I rang Cyprus to tell her I'm leaving. She thinks I'll change my mind, but she's in for a shock. Good old Emma has finally had enough!'

Though Emma would not have believed it, the day of Morton's funeral was torture for Alison. She had slept fitfully, and at dawn was pacing the terrace where her

263

friend had breathed his last. In her nostrils was the lemony scent she would henceforth associate with his death. In her ears, the shrill cacophony of awakening birds seemed a chorus of recrimination, as if they were chastising her for not being there when he was laid to rest.

It was still not too late to change her mind. If she caught the early plane, she could make it in time and return to Cyprus tomorrow. But it would mean losing two days' filming – and what would it achieve? Peace with Emma, an inner voice replied. But Emma would not stay angry with her for long.

Thus did Alison miscalculate the depths of Emma's feeling, as she watched the sun rise gloriously beyond the distant sea, and wept for Maxwell Morton who would feel its warmth no more.

Though the outcome of Alison's self-debate was never in doubt, throughout that long day, while take after take was filmed, she was prey to the painfully familiar private conflict between her professionalism and her heart – which Morton alone had understood. When she emerged from the shock of losing him, she would come to realise that he was the only person who had ever fully understood her.

Meanwhile, the world was for her an emptier place without him. He had loved and respected her. And she had taken him for granted, until he was gone.

CHAPTER SIX

WITH MORTON'S death, Alison's son was now her manager, a situation to which she did not easily adjust. Richard's modern approach to theatre was at variance with her own.

This was one reason why she declined Richard and Janet's invitation to live with them after Emma's departure. If she and Richard had a shared home life, their professional differences might spill over into their personal relationship. Alison preferred not to take that risk.

There was, too, her continued but diminishing hope that Emma would come back; retaining her own home was necessary on that account.

Emma was living with Percy and Beth, and seemed set to end her days in the house where they had begun. As Alison now appeared set to end hers alone with her fame, she reflected with mixed feelings when, in 1973, she was awarded the DBE.

Her proud son and daughter-in-law accompanied her to the Palace to receive the honour. But the medal bestowed upon her for services to the theatre could not dispel Dame Alison Plantaine's loneliness when she returned to her empty house after a celebration meal at the Ritz with Richard and Janet. And it seemed to her then that, though it might not be so for others, loneliness was in the end for her the real price of fame.

It was as though her life had turned full circle back to the point when her solitary state sent her fleeing north for comfort, and she brought Emma back to London to be her companion. Now, here she was again with only a cat for company and her work to occupy her. The difference was, that at seventy-three she was physically not up to appearing in one play after another. And her son's refusal to keep staging the classics, to which in her old age she affectionately clung, ensured her long periods of rest.

Richard's interpretation of her attitude towards modern theatre was that she had stopped moving with the times – and he's right, she thought as she put herself to bed. Perhaps this was Alison Plantaine's time to call it a day and devote herself to good works.

When he called her the next morning, she told him impulsively that this was her intention.

'In that case, I've made a wasted call,' he replied. 'I had just decided to stage some Shakespeare, to mark your DBE in the traditional Plantaine way. I had in mind *Romeo and Juliet*, as you made your Plantaine Players début in that play.'

'Since I'm long past playing Juliet, I presume you want to cast me as the Nurse?'

'But as you intend to retire — '

'The good works will have to wait,' Alison cut in.

Richard laughed. 'And will wait forever so far as you are concerned. You've been performing your own kind of good works for more than half a century, Mother, and you're never going to retire. Who are you kidding?'

'Nobody but myself!'

What kind of woman are you? Alison asked her reflection in the hall mirror, after she had rung off. That all it takes to set your adrenalin soaring is a professional challenge? The silver-haired old lady gazing back at her still bore traces of the girl she once was, and in that respect had not changed; in her eyes was the same gleam of anticipation that an exciting theatrical prospect had always put there.

The Nurse was a coveted role, and Alison had never in her long career played it. Part of the challenge was to bring to it her own interpretation, as every distinguished actress who had played it with the Royal Shakespeare Company at Stratford had memorably done.

266

She found her copy of *Romeo and Juliet* in the living-room bookcase, and took it into the kitchen to browse through while she drank her morning coffee.

If Emma were here, she would not have to make the coffee herself, she thought while doing so. But that was the least of Emma's absence – and she would not let herself think that the forty years they had shared had meant less to Emma than they had to her; that Emma had dismissed them as worthless and would never return.

CHAPTER SEVEN

WHEN AMY was sixteen, she called Richard from Maui.

'How have you been, my darling,' he said when emotion allowed him to speak.

'Fine, Daddy.'

'Why haven't I heard from you until now?'

'I wrote you several times.'

'I didn't receive your letters.'

'Then Grand-daddy broke his word. He said I could correspond with you on condition I didn't ever leave him again. He found out your address for me, and said he would mail my letters. When you didn't reply, I thought you'd made up your mind to forget me because I went back to Grand-daddy.'

'A man doesn't forget his own child, Amy.'

'But I would have understood why, if you'd tried to. It must have seemed to you that I'd chosen him instead of you. But it wasn't like that, Daddy — '

'I know exactly what it was like for you, Amy. I was there! And you need say no more about it, darling.'

'But after his not mailing my letters, I guess I'll never trust Grand-daddy again. You see I wasn't going to let you forget me – even if you wanted to. And when I can, I'm going to come visit you.'

'That's what I've been looking forward to, and I'll continue to do so, Amy.'

'But I'm calling you today for a very special reason. To tell you something I daren't tell anyone else. I'm in love, Daddy.'

Again Richard was overcome by emotion. His daughter knew she could trust him. 'Who's the lucky guy?'

268

'Kimo.'

'The boy who was with you on the beach?'

'Right.'

Richard recalled the slender, nutbrown boy who had not wanted Amy to leave him. He would now be a handsome youth – an educated one, also, if he had continued to share Amy's tutor. But BT would not think his Hawaiian housekeeper's son good enough for Amy. His daughter's need for secrecy was all too plain to Richard.

'Do you and he still have lessons together?' he asked her.

'Unfortunately not. When Kimo was twelve, he began going to Lahainaluna High School. Many pupils go on to college from there, if their parents can afford it; or they sometimes work their way through, which Kimo will have to do.'

'The cab driver, the day I came to Napili, told me his clever little son wanted to go to that school,' Richard recalled.

'The boys and girls who go there have a lot of fun together out of school hours,' said Amy wistfully. 'But Grand-daddy wouldn't hear of it for me.'

And what a lot Amy was being deprived of, Richard thought. The simple pleasures of mixing with other young people, for which living in the lap of luxury could not compensate. 'Do you and Kimo manage to be together often?' he said.

'Not too often on our own. But Kimo and his mother live in the house, so we are around each other a good deal. When Malia isn't making Kimo study,' Amy added with a laugh. 'He wants to be a lawyer, by the way, Daddy.'

'I wish him luck. What do you want to be?'

'An actress. But I guess you can imagine what Grand-daddy has to say about that!'

'Your grandmother, on the other hand, will be over the moon when I tell her.' Richard told Amy about Alison's DBE.

'Wow! Do you suppose I take after her, Daddy?'

269

'Time will tell. Janet will be pleased to hear about your ambition, too. She and I are now married.'

'Congratulations, Daddy! And the same to my pretty stepmother, I liked her a lot. I've had two more step-fathers since I last saw you. And Mom is heading for Reno again.'

'Don't let that put you off marriage,' Richard felt it necessary to say.

'Why should it? My mom is one on her own,' said Amy with a wisdom beyond her years. 'I'll call you again, Daddy.'

'Please do.'

Janet entered the living room as Richard was replacing the receiver. 'Who were you talking to?'

'My daughter – at last.'

'That accounts for your radiant expression.'

'I'm entitled to look radiant! It matches how I feel.'

'Did I say you weren't? Supper's ready and the table is laid,' said Janet, departing for the kitchen.

Richard was shocked by her disinterest in what was to him a momentous event. He had lived in hope of hearing from Amy for six long years, and Janet knew it. But she had not even asked how Amy was.

Nor did she while they ate their meal.

'Amy's hoping to be able to visit us before too long,' he said because he would not have his daughter the forbidden subject Janet's silence had made her.

'She'll always be welcome here,' was Janet's polite reply.

But Richard realised with dismay that the opposite would be the case.

CHAPTER EIGHT

KEEPING HER love for Kimo hidden was for Amy increasingly difficult, and no less a strain for him. He had not dared confide in his mother, lest Malia feel her position of trust with the Taylors was being jeopardised by her son.

Living under the same roof made it no easier. They had grown up together under Malia's motherly eye, and Amy still came and went freely to and from the servants' wing of the house, as she had when she and Kimo were child-hood playmates. Nor had her old nursery, now converted into a suite for her, become forbidden territory for Kimo. To their elders, nothing had changed.

The deceit of their situation marred their happiness. For Kimo, there was the added element of seeing no future in it, plus the irony of their having been raised together only to eventually separate and go their very different ways.

His view of life was a good deal more down-to-earth than Amy's. She took it for granted that the world was her oyster. He considered himself fortunate to have what he had. Had his mother not been the Taylors' housekeeper, Kimo's lot would have been that of his cousins, who spent their days labouring in the sugar-cane fields and went home at night to the poverty to which they were born.

Kimo sometimes wondered if he would have made it to high school had the accident of his mother's employment not singled him out. Though Lahainaluna was established by missionaries in 1831 to give local children the advantage their status in life might not otherwise have provided, in 1975 most of Kimo's classmates were the sons and daughters of tradesmen and artisans, who had elevated themselves from the primitive environs in which Kimo's

271

relatives lived. Others, though they were but a sprinkling, were from families that had migrated from the US mainland.

The school stood on a hilltop, a proud bastion of education for all to see. But Kimo knew that poverty dulled the minds of those like his aunts, uncles, and cousins, and deprived them of the incentive to do well. Who needed a good education to be a labourer? summed it up. And Kimo had no doubt that chance alone had saved him from that fate.

It was not surprising that cynicism mingled with the compassion he had for those less fortunate, hardening his attitudes.

Nevertheless, he was grateful to the missionaries for setting education in Hawaii on the right track, and when he passed the original pole-and-grass building they had erected, which still stood in the school grounds, he would mentally raise his cap to them for doing what they had long before Maui became part of the land of opportunity America was said to be.

Kimo, who had never been out of Maui, hoped there was more equality of opportunity on the mainland than on his homeground. New York was his goal. And his dream a cosy apartment which he would share with Amy.

Goals could be achieved, but his dream was an impossible one, he was thinking on a sultry September evening when he and Amy were window-shopping on Lahaina's quaint main street.

'If Grand-daddy knew we're in love, he wouldn't let you be my watchdog!' said Amy wryly when they paused to admire some examples of the ancient art of scrimshaw displayed in a store window.

Lahaina had changed since the days when Malia brought Kimo here to buy his first pair of shoes. Tourism was now making the shopkeepers prosperous, and its manifestations mushrooming everywhere. Richard's cab driver's worst fears had begun to materialise, though evidence that the developers had arrived was nothing compared with Waikiki, on Oahu.

272

To Kimo, the visitors from the mainland looked incongruous in the garments deemed by most to be part of a Hawaiian vacation. Colourful aloha-shirts, like the one Kimo had on, looked fine on him, but all wrong on the fair-skinned men hunting for souvenirs with their ladies; for whom the flowing muumuus meant for Hawaiian women did nothing, thought Kimo, surveying a stringy blonde, whose muumuu was flapping around her as though she were a pole and it a gaudy tent.

Amy was the only non-Hawaiian female who looked right in a muumuu, he decided, eyeing her olive-complexioned profile as she gazed into the shop window. She was not wearing one now, but sometimes did in the evenings at home and Kimo would think how well it set off her long, black hair – and imagine the voluptuous breasts and hips beneath it. The nearest to naked he had seen her was in her bikini beside the swimming pool. He was sure that she wanted him as much as he her, but as if by tacit consent they restrained their feelings.

How much longer he would manage to do so was anyone's guess, he thought, aware of an ache in his loins as they left the scrimshaw shop behind and continued along the street, which despite prosperity and progress had retained its character.

The tiny stores still had the crammed-together charm of an old whaling port, with their salt-bleached façades and upper-storey wood verandahs.

On the side of the street on which Amy and Kimo were walking, the Pacific pounded the rocks behind the shops and restaurants. The bracing scent of ozone was ever in the air, vieing with the sluggish heat that by day rose from the sunbaked pavements.

Even by night Lahaina could feel like an oven, and Amy and Kimo headed for the harbour where the old Pioneer Inn was still a meeting place for the men who sailed the fishing boats, and the cool breeze after sundown was a blessed relief.

But they were painfully aware that they could not stroll hand in hand, as other young couples were doing. They were liable to run into some of Kimo's schoolfriends, or his relatives from Napili giving their children a Saturday-night treat at the ice-cream parlour.

There was also the risk of encountering someone from the affluent community of retired mainlanders who was acquainted with Amy's grandfather. She went with him to the Sunday brunches that were part of their social scene, but enjoyed the polite socialising no more than he did.

Amy preferred the local Luaus, with their traditional dishes and entertainment, that were part of Hawaii's heritage. Her grandfather did not know that she had been to one with Kimo, or that she had learned to dance the hula, and feasted on succulent kalua pig, and poi, with those BT considered beneath him, on that memorable occasion. Amy had often wondered why he chose to live in Hawaii, since he eschewed the islands' way of life, including Polynesian food. Then one day he allowed her to go with him when he visited her namesake's grave, and the look on his face as he gazed down upon it had told her that he wanted to stay close to her late grandmother.

But it was not of this that she was thinking that evening, as she and Kimo wandered from the harbour to the Banyan Tree that was a major tourist attraction. Her thoughts were those of a young girl in love, and tinged with the desperation of her own predicament.

'I wish we could elope!' she said to Kimo impulsively.

He had not let himself think that she shared his unlikely dream, and discouraged her from doing so by abruptly changing the subject. 'It's hard to believe that's all one tree,' he said, studying the multiple trunk that gave the century-old banyan a freak appearance.

'If you tell me it's the biggest banyan on the islands, and its spread covers three-quarters of an acre, I'll scream!' said Amy with the tempestuousness she had inherited from Alison. 'I'm not a tourist, and you're not my guide!'

'I'm your watchdog, like you reminded me tonight,' Kimo replied stiffly. 'Your grand-daddy trusts me to take care of you – and I feel like a heel, Amy.'

274

'Is that why whenever I try to talk to you about us, you steer me to a different topic?'

'There is no "us". Not now we're grown up. We're already living on borrowed time.'

'You don't love me!'

'The hell I don't! Trust a woman to sidetrack a guy from the facts.'

'If we eloped, we could go to England,' Amy persisted. 'My father would welcome us.'

'And I'd end up in some crummy job. Oh no, Amy! I'm going to work my way through college and get to be a lawyer if it kills me,' said Kimo with feeling.

'Okay, so we won't elope. We'll wait. Grand-daddy can't disapprove of a lawyer, can he? It'd be handy to have one in the family – the kind of mom I've got!' she joked, though her mother's marital escapades distressed her.

Kimo felt like taking her by the shoulders and shaking some of his own worldliness into her. 'If I ended up a Supreme Court judge, Amy, I'd still be the son of a servant, with the wrong colour skin, to your grand-daddy. You and I were born to go separate ways, and you'd better believe it.'

'I'll never belieeve it.'

'And I guess I don't want to.'

They gazed longingly into each other's eyes, then Kimoo threw caution to the winds and held Amy close.

'I was talking off the top of my head,' she said wistfully. 'How could I elope? Grand-daddy would probably have another seizure, like the time I went off with Daddy.'

To Kimo, the emotional hold he knew the old man had on Amy was just another obstacle among the many.

'But he's getting very old, and he can't live forever,' she added, chiding herself for the thought. 'Promise you'll wait for me,' she whispered in Kimo's ear. 'That when you go to college, you won't fall for someone else. If you did, I'd — '

Kimo silenced her with a kiss, and it was thus that BT's chauffeur found them.

His ostentatious cough froze them in each other's embrace, then they sprang apart.

The chauffeur managed to keep his tone casual. 'When you two didn't show up, I guess I got worried.'

And with reason, he thought, driving them home in the white Rolls – and wished he had not gone looking for them after waiting a quarter-hour at the spot where he'd arranged to pick them up. He'd rather not have known what he now knew. Miss Amy necking with Kimo under the Banyan Tree! – as though she were just one of the local kids. Malia's boy should know better. Or maybe he was a deep one, like people said his dead father had been? If Kimo got BT's grand-daughter in the family way, he'd have to marry her and would be made for life, the chauffeur's thoughts raced ahead.

Kimo broke the awkward silence. 'I guess we owe you an explanation, Buck,' he said, thinking wryly that he was now back in his place – beside the chauffeur.

'It's Mr Taylor you owe one to, Kimo.'

'Haven't you ever been in love, Buck?' Amy asked from her privileged position on the back seat.

Since Buck was a stony, middle-aged bachelor, it was a futile question for the purpose for which it was intended. There was also Buck's prim and proper, Pennsylvania conditioning to contend with. And his loyalty to his long-time employer, who had selected him from a hundred short-listed applicants when he was a young man and the Taylors were living in Philadelphia.

Kimo followed Amy's lead nevertheless. 'I don't know what Amy sees in me, but I guess you know what I see in her, Buck.'

The Taylor billions, the chauffeur silently replied. 'Miss Amy is a fine-looking young lady,' he allowed himself to admit. 'I've known her all her life, and I always thought she respected her grand-daddy, as I do.' But she's turning out to be as feckless as her mother, he feared.

'People can't help falling in love,' Amy informed him. 'I guess you must know that, even though you're not married. And Kimo and I trust you to keep our secret.'

276

Buck glimpsed her pleading expression in the driving mirror and could not help but soften. Then he thought of his own position if his boss found out – which sooner or later he was bound to – and learned that Buck had been a party to it. 'That's more than my job's worth, Miss Amy,' he replied.

'Grand-daddy might have a seizure if you tell him,' Amy changed her tactics.

'I shall have to take that risk.'

'And ruin my life!' she declared dramatically.

Not to mention mine, Kimo thought. If BT fired Malia, which he was sure to, they would have to go live in a shanty with their relatives. And Kimo could forget college. He would have to work to help support himself and his mother, who wouldn't be given the references necessary to get another housekeeping job. Thanks to him, the sugar-cane fields would now be his mother's lot, and the best he could hope for was clerking in a downtown office for the rest of his days.

The outcome was to be very different from Kimo's expectations.

A few days later, Amy's breakfast was brought to her suite by a buxom Hawaiian woman whom she had never seen before.

'Who are you?' she enquired when she recovered from her surprise.

'My name is Peke, which in English is Becky. Call me whichever you wish, Miss. Would you like your breakfast in bed? Or outside on the patio?' The woman stood holding the tray, a friendly smile on her face.

But Amy could not return the smile. A premonition of disaster had immobilised her. Casual help was never employed in this house. 'Just put the tray down anywhere,' she replied.

'Can I hand you your fruit juice, Miss?'

'No, thank you. Where is the housekeeper?'

'That's me now, Miss. I started work this morning.'

Amy managed to stop her voice from trembling. 'Has our former housekeeper already gone?'

The woman nodded – and Amy's heart sank.

'Her and her son caught the plane to Honolulu that I flew here on. Mr Taylor's chauffeur dropped them at the airport with their baggage and picked me up. She seemed a nice lady,' Peke chatted on. 'And I guess she was excited about her and her boy going to live on the mainland. She said Mr Taylor has found her a job keeping house for someone he knows. I liked it on the mainland, myself – I had five years in LA – but when my man walked out, I came home to the islands.'

But Amy was no longer listening. She had heard all she needed to know, and paused only to put on her muumuu before going to confront her grandfather who was breakfasting on the terrace beside the pool.

'How could you do this to me?' she demanded.

'You ought to thank me, honeylamb.'

'For what? Banishing Kimo from Hawaii? What did you threaten him with, to get him to leave without even saying goodbye to me?'

BT's continued pleasantness to Kimo had led them to suppose the chauffeur had decided to keep their secret. But Amy's grandfather had known and kept silent until his plans were made. He had spent a day in Honolulu – interviewing candidates for Malia's job, as Amy now realised. And the *fait accompli* with which she was presented this morning must have been initiated last night, after she had gone to bed.

'You're a wicked and devious old man!' she seethed to him.

'And you are even more beautiful when you're hopping mad, sugar,' he replied with a smile. 'Devious I may be when necessary. But Kimo didn't have to say yes to my offer.'

'What offer?'

'To put him through law school. He's a clever boy, but every bright young Hawaiian doesn't get to go to Harvard – and that's where he'll be going. It will open a lot of doors for him.'

'By closing the door on me!'

278

BT sipped some of his papaya juice. 'It was never open to him, Amy. Nor would it have been in my lifetime.'

'Kimo knew that. But he loves me and was prepared to wait.'

'But it's amazing what the crackle of dollars will do,' BT answered.

Only then did the full significance of what had happened hit Amy. Kimo had been bought off.

'He'll go short of nothing while he's studying. I made sure of that,' her grandfather said, confirming it.

Amy felt like throwing up. She had taken wealth for granted all her life, but had only now seen its corruptive power. But the real corruption was in those who used their wealth to manipulate ordinary people's lives.

And her grandfather was an arch-corrupter in that respect. Was there nothing he would not stoop to? 'I hate you,' Amy told him. 'Because you are lonely and old, I felt sorry for you – even after I found out you never mailed the letters I wrote my father when I was a kid. But you didn't care if it hurt me when I had to believe his not replying meant he'd decided to forget me. All you've ever cared about is making sure, by whatever underhand means, that I stayed with you!'

BT had paled under the verbal onslaught, but showed no sign of having a seizure, Amy noted. Nor had she ever seen him really sick; his illness was just something he mentioned when it suited him to. Another of his ploys to keep her chained to him.

'I call my father often,' she enjoyed telling him. 'And I'm old enough now to choose where, and with whom, I live. All you've achieved by buying off Kimo is to show me he is weak. But I don't blame him, Grand-daddy. I blame you. As for me, I'm going to England as fast as I can get there.'

'Go right ahead. But you'll be disinherited,' said BT coolly.

'Now you're trying to buy *me*! But I'm not interested in my inheritance. From what I've seen of what money does to people, I'd rather you left your billions to a dogs' home. Suddenly, I'm able to understand why my mom's life has been one long mess. You raised her to think happiness can be bought. I guess I must take after my father and his family, because I never have and never shall think that.'

'You're still only eighteen – and as hot-headed as she is. But if you leave here now, that's it, Amy. Don't ever come crying to me.'

Amy eyed the small, hunched figure in the big, basketweave chair and briefly pitied him again. His daughter flitted in and out of his life like a moth with singed wings. Raising his grand-daughter had been his second chance, but he had blown it. All Grand-daddy had now was his wealth.

She hardened her heart against him – how else would she be free while he lived? – and listened for a moment to the sound of the ocean lapping the shore below the terrace. All around her was the exotic setting in which she had been raised, and its tropical fragrances in her nostrils.

She watched a yellow bird peck at her grandfather's uneaten breakfast, then switched her gaze to his face. 'I love Hawaii. But if I never see Maui or you again it will be too soon,' were her parting words.

Not until she reached the privacy of her room did she allow herself to think about Kimo, and shed some tears for what would never be. Then she squared her shoulders resolutely and began packing for her new life.

CHAPTER NINE

SEEING AMY was for Alison like looking at a picture of herself when she was a girl, and her grand-daughter's arrival as though a light had been switched on in the greyness of her old age.

The resemblance between them provided Janet with a topic of conversation when Richard brought Amy home from the airport. The words of welcome she had prepared had refused to issue from her lips.

They had arrived in time for lunch, and Alison was there with Janet. It was not just Amy she could not wait to see, but her son reunited with his child.

Richard had learned on the way from Heathrow what had precipitated Amy's sudden departure from Maui. The story had sickened him, as it had her, but she had told it in a way that led him to think she had put her first love behind her.

During lunch, Alison and Amy did most of the talking. Richard could not take his eyes off Amy, and was uncomfortably aware of Janet watching him.

'Your father told me you mentioned wanting to enter the traditional Plantaine profession, Amy,' Alison said while they were eating dessert.

'If she does, I'll be the outsider around here,' Richard put in with a smile. 'And deprived of Amy's company in the evenings, as I am of Janet's.'

'As you were of mine, too, when you were a boy,' Alison said. And added roguishly, 'Which you weren't too pleased about at the time!'

'I'm older and wiser now, Mother.'

'Aren't we all, darling?'

'If you're saying that a person lives and learns, that

281

doesn't include me,' said Janet with a smile that did not reach her eyes. 'I've been every kind of fool all my life.'

Alison had noted Janet's strained expression the moment she entered the house, but had made no comment and thought it wise to make none now.

Amy could not be expected to display such wisdom and asked Janet, 'What do you mean by every kind of fool?'

'Never mind.' Janet got up and went to the kitchen to make the coffee.

'Did I say something I shouldn't have, Daddy?'

'No, darling. Janet's a bit edgy, that's all. The play she's in has been running a long time.'

But Amy felt there was more to it than that. Her remembrance of Janet was of a friendly lady who had bought her a red dress and coat to wear for a journey to England that was never made. The Janet who was now Amy's stepmother was not that person. Something had changed her in the eight years between then and now. But it couldn't be marriage, Amy decided. Not when her husband was Richard Plantaine.

In the weeks that followed, Amy had cause to wonder over and again if she had said or done something to upset Janet, and to ponder over remarks Janet made that were as incomprehensible to Amy as the one about being every kind of fool.

Between times, Janet was warm and pleasant to her, and one day took her shopping for the winter wardrobe Amy had never before required.

After they had bought what Amy needed – for a tenth of what she was accustomed to spending on clothes – they lunched and laughed together at Fortnum's, and Amy was reminded of the Janet she had briefly met in Hawaii.

Janet was plainly enjoying herself – the way she never seems to at home, Amy reflected. Yet she obviously adored Richard. Her manner when under her own roof with him and Amy could not be attached to him. It's me she is on edge with when we're all at home together, Amy finally registered.

282

Janet finished relating what Carnaby Street was like during the Beatles era and said, 'This is the first time you and I have had an outing together. We must do it again.'

But why can't she relax with me when Daddy's there? Amy wondered. Janet's pattern of behaviour sure was a puzzle!

She would rather it had continued to be so than for the puzzle to have been solved for her in the shattering way it was. Amy's bedroom adjoined Richard and Janet's, and one night, after a more than usually strained evening, she heard them quarrelling about her.

'It isn't my fault I haven't given you a child,' Amy heard Janet shout.

Her father's tone was equally angry. 'Have I ever said it was? But you don't have to make my daughter feel unwelcome because of it.'

'I can't help it if her being here reminds me of how I've failed you! It isn't that I don't like her.'

'You just don't like what she represents. Well to hell with that! Is this the kind of home life we are all to have from now on? You hardly cracked a smile to Amy over supper. You were miserable enough before she came – I'd hoped having Amy around would cheer you up.'

'How can it? When she's yours and not mine. It's making me feel worse about being childless than I already felt.'

Amy had heard more than enough and pulled her pillow over her head. She loved her father and liked her stepmother, but felt at this moment as though she had stepped from a frying pan into a fire.

By morning, she had made up her mind to leave, though she would not tell them why. Her being here was not good for her father's marriage. Nor could she be happy here.

'I've enjoyed my stay with you,' she told Richard over breakfast. 'But it's time I began making my own life.'

'If it's the stage you're set on, Granny and I can help you.'

'It is. But I'd rather strike out for myself. In New York. Try my luck in the off-Broadway scene,' said Amy off the top of her head. But it was a good idea.

'Far be it from me to stand in your way, darling,' Richard said, though he was loth to part with her.

Alison, too, was bitterly disappointed, but hid her feelings. 'Your life is yours, Amy, to make of what you will.'

Amy had gone alone to see her play the harrowing role of the mother in Somerset Maugham's *The Sacred Flame*, and was electrified by Alison's performance. It was afterwards, backstage, that she told her grandmother of her intention.

'Your father revived this play for me,' Alison said, 'because it has a special significance for both of us. The last time I appeared in it he was six years old, and watched me from the wings. It was his first time in a theatre and he has never forgotten it – but I was playing the glamorous heroine then!'

'If I'm even half as good as you, Dame Alison, I'll be a big star,' Amy declared.

'But why in America, my dear? What's wrong with the British theatre? It was good enough for all your Plantaine ancestors.'

'I can't stay here, Granny.' Amy hesitated, then found herself telling Alison why.

Alison stopped removing her make-up. Had Janet's childlessness become an obsession, as it had with her mother before Janet was conceived? There was no other interpretation of what Amy had revealed.

Amy observed her compassionate expression. 'I'm sorry for Janet, too, Granny.'

'You also have reason to be sorry for yourself. I'm relieved you haven't taken it personally, Amy. It would be sad for your father to have to take sides between his wife and his daughter.'

'I guess he already has. That's why I'm leaving. So he won't have to any more.'

Alison rose from the dressing table to hug her. 'What a good girl you are! I certainly wasn't, at your age,' she reminisced. On the contrary, she had left her own father no option but to be her ally against her mother.

'I'll write you. And visit you when I can,' Amy promised.

'And remember I'm here if you need me,' Alison replied.

I haven't just found a grandmother, I've found a friend, Amy thought. And what a reassuring feeling it was.

CHAPTER TEN

ON HER seventy-eighth birthday, Alison was so eager to get to the mass of envelopes the postman had pushed through her letter box, she lost her footing and tumbled down the stairs.

When she tried to rise, a searing pain shot through her hip. Richard had told her to slow down, that she wasn't twenty-one any more, but she hadn't heeded the warning and it was too late now. The damage was done.

She had landed beside the hall table, and managed to pull down the telephone to where she lay trembling and exasperated.

'I've done something I'd like to kick myself for!' she said crossly when Richard answered his phone. 'But I can't move my leg.' Then a mist floated before her eyes and she passed out.

When she came to, she was in a hospital room.

'Would you mind telling me how I got here?' she asked Richard and Janet who were hovering at her bedside. 'The leading lady seems to have slept through the performance.'

'The doctor gave you an injection, Mother, to ensure that you would,' said Richard. 'So you wouldn't be in pain when you were moved.'

A hazy recollection of someone kneeling beside her in the hall and rolling up her sleeve returned to Alison. 'Oh well,' she managed to say with a wan smile.

'The ambulance men carried you with due reverence when they discovered the patient was Dame Alison Plantaine!' Janet told her, sounding more cheerful than she felt.

'We promised you'd give them a signed photograph,

after your operation,' said Richard employing the same light tone.

'What operation?' Alison had never been in hospital in her life – and now they were telling her she required surgery!

Her fury with herself was plain to see.

'Calm down, Mother,' Richard said gently. 'I'm afraid you broke your pelvis.'

'Damn my brittle old bones!'

'In three places,' Richard had to tell her.

'Emma used to say that trouble comes in threes. And she'll be admiring her birthday cards now. Where are mine?'

'At home. You received far too many to prop up on that bedtable,' said Janet.

'Emma's will be propped on the mantelpiece. She always had the mantelpiece for hers, and I the sideboard for mine. She didn't by any chance send me a card?'

Richard shook his head.

'I didn't send her one, either.'

Richard and Janet exchanged a glance. Her casual tone could not fool her son and daughter-in-law. Though eight years had passed without so much as a conciliatory gesture between them, Alison still clung to the hope that Emma would come back.

'Would you please make sure that the cards I received from my fans are replied to with thank-you notes,' she requested.

What a trouper she is, thought Richard. Lying in hospital, but still thinking of her public.

'And don't you two imagine for a minute that this is the end of Alison Plantaine,' she added. 'I'll be back onstage before you know it.'

If determination were all, there'd be no stopping her, Richard was thinking. Old age had not lessened his mother's indomitable spirit. But its hazards and their disabling consequences were something even she was no match for.

*

287

Emma found enough breath to blow out the candles on the birthday cake Beth had made for her, and thought herself fortunate to have so many people who cared about her.

When she first returned north, she had felt out of her element; like a plant suddenly transplanted back to the soil from which it had sprung. It had not been easy to re-root; but now, it was as though she had never gone away. Her life in London had receded like a dream. But had she really been back in Oldham for eight years?

She had only to look around her at tonight's family gathering to know that indeed she had.

Conrad and Zelda were as white-haired as herself. Clara – now a widow – was still blonde by artificial means, but her bejewelled fingers were crippled by arthritis. 'Little' Lottie and Lionel could no longer be described that way, and their respective parents were past middle-age.

Alison and I, thought Emma wryly, will soon be octogenarians! Only on their shared birthdays did Emma allow herself to think of Alison. And of the celebratory outings Morton had never failed to plan for them.

She cast remembrance aside, and went to telephone Richard to thank him for his card. What he had to tell her rendered her weak with shock.

Clara found her in the front parlour – in their mother's old home it had never been renamed 'the lounge' – where she had gone to be alone with her thoughts.

'Aren't you feeling well, Emma?' Clara asked, anxiously scanning her face.

Since Emma's return, Clara's sibling affection had emerged in full flow. Vindication had ensured it. Clara's judgement of Alison had at last been proved correct, and she had got her sister back.

'Alison needs me,' Emma said with distress.

To Clara, the words were as though she had been stabbed in the back by her long-time adversary. 'What kind of trouble is she in this time?'

'I'm sorry to hear it,' she said sincerely, after Emma

told her. 'But I'm not exactly a hundred percent fit, either, am I?' She glanced with distaste at her clawed fingers. 'I can hardly manage to dress myself. Or to hold a cup without spilling what's in it. The time may come when I need you, Emma.'

'I don't intend staying in London for ever.'

Clara eyed her in disbelief. 'Are you telling me that you are actually going?'

'If I hadn't left her to fend for herself, Alison wouldn't have had the accident. It was always me who picked up the mail from the doormat, and I took hers upstairs to her.'

'Don't mention doormats to me! It pains me to think you were one for Alison all those years. How can you even think of putting yourself in that position again? Have you never heard the proverb, "Once bitten, twice shy"?' Clara blazed.

'That wasn't why I left her,' Emma stiffly replied.

'You've never told me exactly why you did leave her.'

'And I'm not going into details about it, now.'

'But you suddenly saw her for what she is, didn't you?'

'Which includes many fine qualities, Clara. Alison is generous and loving, and loyal to a fault.'

'But she's never grown up,' said Clara with asperity.

'In some ways that's true. But it has nothing to do with why I left her. It was something she did that stuck in my throat and wouldn't go down.'

'But you've suddenly managed to forgive her, because she's broken her hip!'

'No. I'll never forgive her.'

'Then why are you putting yourself back in her clutches?'

Emma paused to think about it. 'I suppose because she is Alison, and I am me.'

Alison awoke after the operation to find Emma by her bed.

'Is it really you?' she said drowsily.

'Who else do you know who dresses from head to foot in brown?'

289

'I thought I might still be under the influence of whatever they used to put me out.'

An emotional silence followed.

Alison's gaze roved around the room. 'It's like a florist's in here.'

'Your dramatic journey downstairs got into the papers, and your fans reacted accordingly.'

'It's nice to know I'm appreciated.'

'Since when did your ego need boosting? That big basket of roses on the table is from the family up north.'

'They must have cost a fortune,' said Alison, admiring them. And added dryly, 'Which leads me to suppose Clara ordered them.'

Emma smiled. 'You suppose right. Though, needless to say, she disapproves of me coming.'

Alison's eyelids were drooping, but she willed herself not to slip back to sleep. This moment was too important. And it was necessary, too, to will herself not to weep.

'Why did you come, Emma?'

'Wouldn't you have come to me?'

'I wasn't the one who left.'

'What difference does that make?'

They fell silent, remembering all they had shared. The laughter and tears of a lifetime summed it up for both.

'I'll stay for as long as you need me,' Emma said quietly.

I'll always need you, thought Alison. 'Thank you,' she said.

Then Richard entered bearing more flowers, and gave them a beaming smile. Seeing them together again was a sight for sore eyes!

'Auntie Emma has come to wheel my bathchair,' Alison joked.

'You may have to be in one for a while,' he took the opportunity to convey to her what the surgeon had told him.

'And I'd rather Emma pushed it than anyone else,' said Alison with chagrin.

CHAPTER ELEVEN

AMY MAILED a get-well card to Alison on her way downtown. Since her brief stay in London they had corresponded regularly, and she knew that her famous grandmother was following her career with interest.

Such as it yet was! she thought on the subway train. And Granny probably disapproved of the kind of theatre Amy had gotten involved in.

Dame Alison was of the old school, and Amy of the newest. 'Theatre should hold up a mirror to life,' Alison had pronounced in her last letter – and had asked how an all-women company, staging plays without male characters, could fit into that definition.

But the off-Broadway scene was reflecting aspects of life that Alison might prefer not to know about, Amy thought wryly, imagining her grandmother's reaction to the gay musical, *Boy Meets Boy*. She was not to know that Alison had seen *The Boys In The Band*, when it transferred from off-Broadway to London in the Sixties, and had deemed it brilliant theatre with something moving to say about life.

Meanwhile, Black theatre and the Women's Movement were putting across what they had to say, and Amy felt part of an exciting and significant theatrical era.

She had thrown in her lot with the all-women company solely because she could not get any other work, but was now as devoted to the cause as to her art. Her earnings were meagre, but enabled her to share a small apartment on the Upper West Side with one of her fellow-actresses.

When she first arrived in New York, she had waited on tables in a coffee shop near to her grandfather's penthouse – and had thought that if he walked in for breakfast

291

and saw her in her waitress's uniform a genuine seizure would doubtless result.

Nor would BT enjoy seeing his precious grand-daughter squashed into this seedy subway train, with the sleazy characters some of those around her looked, Amy thought. Garlic and body odour respectively were drifting from the guys on either side of her. And there were times in the rush hour when it was difficult to know which particular guy had pinched her bottom.

For a girl from Amy's sheltered background, her first year in New York was both an eye-opener and a scaring experience. As discovering that Broadway was not wait-ing to warmly welcome Amy Plantaine had been a shock.

Had she stayed in England and auditioned for RADA, as Janet did, and Alison had suggested, the talent Amy knew she had would have been recognised long before now, she reflected, alighting at Columbus Circle to hasten to the part-time waiting job she still did.

But Amy did not regret that circumstances had cata-pulted her onto the hard road she had taken. It was good to feel she had got as far as she had without the nepotism her father's and grandmother's assistance would have been. And she was not just making a career, but living. Making her own decisions, and taking the consequences if she made a mistake.

The girl reflected in the store window she was striding past looked no different from the Amy Plantaine who was once in love with Kimo. But that girl no longer existed. The new Amy could be just as warm and friendly as the old one, but she had toughened – or she could not have survived alone in New York.

But her flatmate, she thought with a smile, was always telling her she was still a babe in arms. And it had to be said that Katy Blair, whose looks were angelic, was a tough cookie. They worked different part-time shifts at the coffee house towards which Amy was now heading. And occasionally double-dated. Unlike some of the actresses in the company, their feminism was not the kind that eschewed men.

It was through Katy that Amy met the man destined to change her life.

'I met a dishy Chilean, down by the river,' Katy said returning from a solitary walk one Sunday afternoon.

Amy was learning her lines for the company's next production; while the current play was running, the next was in rehearsal. 'Can't you even take a stroll by the Hudson without hooking up with a guy?'

'But this one is really something. He was telling me why he had to leave Chile. And I gave him the lowdown on Women's Rights.'

'It must have been some scintillating conversation! Did you buy the spaghetti you said you'd get on your way back?'

Katy ran a hand through her blonde hair and eyed herself in the mirror. 'I forgot. But I guess we won't need it, Amy. He invited us to a party he's throwing tonight – and he said there'd be food.'

'In that case I accept with alacrity. Chilean nosh will make a change from spaghetti without meatballs.'

'It ain't the nosh I'm interested in, honey,' said Katy, rolling her huge blue eyes.

'Where does he live?' Amy wanted to know.

'Even further uptown than we do.'

'The food had better be worth the subway fare!' Amy went to fill the kettle. In England she had acquired the afternoon-tea habit. 'In Hawaii, we had big flying roaches,' she said, flattening a couple of the smaller, creeping variety with which New York was plagued. 'But you could see them coming. They weren't the insidious kind that crawl into bed with you!'

'Talking of which,' Katy said, 'my dishy new guy has someone lined up for you.'

Amy put the kettle on the boiling ring and lit the gas. 'Oh yes?'

'You're too old to still be a virgin,' Katy informed her, while opening their shared closet to inspect Amy's assortment of garments. 'What're you going to wear for the party?'

293

'Maybe I should just go naked, then I shan't have to waste time undressing!'

Katy threw a shoe at her. 'May I borrow that Hawaiian thing of yours tonight, Amy? I'm in an exotic mood.'

'But they say Latins make lousy lovers, and that's what Chileans are,' said Amy with a grin.

'This is no time to quote Dorothy Parker to me!'

'You can tell me if it's true when you find out.'

Katy found Amy's old muumuu at the back of the closet and spread it on the still-good sofa they had acquired from the sidewalk, where the residents of Manhattan dumped their unwanted furniture.

'You can have it,' Amy said. 'I shall never wear it again. It's part of my young and innocent past.'

'I feel like you're presenting me with your chastity belt!' said Katy, with the fruity laugh that went with her personality.

'My chastity belt is in my heart and mind,' Amy replied. 'And it's going to take someone special to unlock it.'

The moment she met Daniel Gomez she knew it would be him.

'You aren't my idea of a Chilean,' she said after they had been introduced. Unlike their Latin-looking host, Alejandro, Daniel was fresh-complexioned and had fair hair.

'But you could be taken for a Chilean woman,' he answered, appraising her.

'My great-grandfather was Jewish,' she told him.

'And my great-grandmother Norwegian.'

They shared a smile, and Amy felt her blood tingle.

'Now that we've exchanged pedigrees, our friendship can begin,' he said humorously.

But it's going to be more than friendship, Amy knew in her bones. The feeling her puppy-love affair with Kimo had aroused in her was as water to wine, compared with the sensation just meeting Daniel's gaze produced.

'Your English is excellent,' she told him.

'It should be,' he said ruefully. 'I've been in New York longer than I would have wished.'

He glanced at his friend, who was greeting a crowd of guests who had just arrived – without removing his arm from around Katy's muumuu-clad waist.

'Alejandro is a fast worker!' he remarked with a laugh.

'How about you?' Amy asked impishly.

'I have neither his facility for meeting women, nor his ability to capitalise on the meeting *toute de suite*.'

But I prefer your kind to his, Amy thought.

'Alejandro is like a brother to me, and I to him,' Daniel told her. 'We were at school, and afterwards college, together in Santiago. But our studies were aborted when our lives had to take precedence.'

Amy, who knew nothing of Chilean politics, looked perplexed.

Daniel put her in the picture about General Pinochet's régime. 'Dissidents like Alejandro and me were disappearing day by day,' he added grimly, 'and have not been heard of again. Our parents begged us to leave Chile before we, too, were caught in the net. The few of us who were still in circulation were no match for the authorities. We would have ended up martyrs for an already lost cause. But it isn't going to stay lost – an underground movement is growing,' he said with feeling.

'And you're thinking of going back, I guess.'

'I already have my plane ticket,' he replied with the same intensity with which he had spoken of the oppressive régime.

Amy could feel his hatred of the oppressors and love for his country emanating from him, as though he were lit by an inner flame. It was why he had not needed to tell her he was going home.

'Alejandro thinks I'm out of my mind to risk it,' he revealed. 'But I've been exiled for almost five years, and if there's now a chance of freeing Chile, I want to be in on it. Also, my parents are getting old. I can't let them go to their graves without seeing me again. I'm their only child.'

'You two seem very wrapped up in each other,' Katy called, giving Amy a wink and brandishing the tortilla in her hand. 'Come and eat!'

295

'Are you hungry?' Daniel asked Amy.

She shook her head, though she had looked forward to sampling the hot, flat maize cakes that in Latin America were called what the Spaniards called their omelettes. There was chilli-con-carne on offer, too, she saw. But the thought that she was to lose Daniel, when she had just found him, had removed her appetite.

'I'm not hungry, either,' he said, as Alejandro came to join them.

'Having fun?'

'I leave that to you, my friend,' Daniel replied with a smile.

'I hope you like eggheads,' Alejandro said to Amy with mock despair.

'I like this one,' she answered. 'But I don't put labels on people – either I jell with a person, or I don't.'

Alejandro looked her over and appreciated what he saw. 'This is some dame I found for you, eh, Daniel?'

Amy was never going to jell with him!

'Okay, Daniel, you owe me,' Alejandro capped his matchmaking speech.

'Possibly more than you or I yet know,' Daniel replied.

'Then maybe she can persuade you not to go back to Chile – you fool!'

Amy intended to try, but doubted that she would succeed.

'Do you share this apartment?' she asked Daniel when his friend had drifted back to Katy.

'It would ruin Alejandro's love life, as there's only this one room,' he said with the dryness that was his style.

'Katy and I have only the one room. But it's much larger than this.'

'Mine is the same size as this one – and right next door. Would you care to be my guest for coffee?'

'Yes, please.'

Later, seated beside her on the divan that was both his bed and sofa, he showed her some snapshots of his elderly parents. 'My mother had given up hope – and then she had me!'

If only that could happen to Janet, Amy thought.

Some pictures of his home in Santiago told her that his family was comfortably off – though not in the Taylor bracket. But who was and who wanted to be?

While they drank their coffee, Amy re-lived for him the vicissitudes of her childhood and youth. She had not intended to mention Kimo, but found herself telling Daniel all there was to know.

'That boy will never be content,' he said thoughtfully. 'Those who want the wrong things never are.' He looked into Amy's eyes and smiled. 'But his loss was my gain.'

'There isn't a girl waiting in Chile for you?'

'If there were, I wouldn't be here like this with you. I'd be true to her. I'm that kind.'

'Me, too.'

A warm glance sealed their rapport.

'Now that is established, Amy, let me take you home. I imagine your happy-go-lucky friend Katy will be spending the night next door.'

Amy glanced around the room to imprint it upon her mind before she left, and thought it as restful as its occupant. Though, like her place, the seediness of the property in this part of Manhattan could not be disguised – most such apartment blocks needed to be pulled down before they crumbled – the simply framed prints and booklined walls lent it a quiet dignity.

They could hear voices and laughter, and the beat of music reverberating from next door.

'Alejandro is crazy about "10 c.c.",' Daniel said.

Amy listened to the vocalist singing 'Rubber Bullets', and shivered.

'I guess that's a modern ballad,' said Daniel grimly. 'That's why Alejandro likes that British group – and I have to agree that they don't just make music. In some of their songs they put out a message.'

He stared into space, and Amy knew he had briefly forgotten her, and was thinking of the military régime in his own country.

'Come back,' she said softly.

The faraway expression left his eyes and he glanced down at their interlocked fingers. 'If you're wondering why I haven't asked you to stay the night, I don't conduct my personal life like my dear friend conducts his. You're not going to be for me just someone to have fun with, Amy. Wanting you is the least part of the feeling you've stirred in me.'

But the passion with which he made love to her the following night belied his final words.

The tender endearments he whispered in her ear were spoken in his own language.

'Are you still going back to Chile?' she asked him, when they lay spent in each other's arms.

'A man's love for his woman cannot be his whole life, *querida*.'

But that didn't apply the other way round, Amy had learned through him. And so much for women's rights, she thought wryly. Equality versus Biology! And when a woman really loved a man, Biology won. The only way for Equality to win was to cut men out of your life, which must be why some of the liberated women she knew had chosen to be lesbians.

'I don't want you to go,' she said.

Daniel kissed her breasts, but his mind remained departmentalised. 'I must see for myself how strong the underground current is.'

'Then take me with you,' said the clinging vine Amy now knew she was.

'*Querida*,' he said huskily. 'If only I could.'

Amy slipped her hand between his thighs, and felt like Eve offering Adam the apple.

But Daniel proved to be stronger-willed than Adam. 'When Chile is again a free country, which I hope to help bring about, we'll plan our future,' he said.

Then passion again took precedence, and Amy knew it was useless trying to dissuade him. He had made up his mind, and was the resolute kind.

Alison could have told her there was more to it than

298

that. That in men like Daniel Gomez and Richard Lindemann, idealism burned as brightly as love.

Two weeks later, Daniel was gone.

'I'm grateful to him for deflowering you,' Katy joked in a futile attempt to cheer Amy up. And added, 'I can now talk sex with you without feeling I'm sullying an angel.'

'Please don't make wisecracks about it, Katy.'

'You haven't gone and fallen for your first lay, I hope!'

'If I hadn't, I wouldn't have let him lay me.'

'Kindly remember that in this day and age, a man and woman lay each other,' Katy replied.

'Well, it sure felt like male supremacy to me.'

'And some liberated female you are,' said Katy with a snort.

Just you wait until you really fall in love, Amy privately answered.

They had just come home from the decrepit old warehouse the women's company had, with their own hands, converted into a theatre for their shoestring productions, and were preparing an omelette to share.

'You missed two cues tonight,' Katy said, watching Amy beat the eggs with as little enthusiasm as she had shown for everything since Daniel left New York. 'And if the rest of the girls knew it was because you're pining for a guy, they'd throw you out,' she declared while she chopped a red pepper for the filling.

She put down the knife and went to place a sympathetic arm around Amy's shoulders. 'If this is love, count me out! I can't even remember who my first lay was – and that's how I intend to keep it.'

A tear plopped from Amy's eye into the bowl of beaten eggs.

'Now you won't need to add any salt,' said Katy. 'And oh my, have you got it bad!'

'I guess I have.'

'But you had better get a grip on yourself, baby,' Katy warned her. 'Alejandro told me that Daniel has taken his life in his hands by going back; when they left Chile they were wanted men.'

Amy let the fork in her hand slip into the bowl. 'Don't tell me any more! I'd rather not know.'

Katy took over the egg-beating. 'If you want to be an ostrich, go right ahead and be one. But this isn't a play you're appearing in. It's for real, and happening to you. And the too-true plot is that you've gotten emotionally involved with a guy you might never see again. Prepare to forget him, Amy.'

'I prepared myself to lose him when I saw him off at Kennedy. But forgetting him is something else.'

Some days later, she received a letter from Daniel. He was not staying with his parents, and she surmised that he did not want to implicate them in his dissident activities – about which he told her nothing. There was no return address on the envelope, which meant he preferred her not to write to him.

Several weeks passed by without her hearing from him again, and his silence became increasingly ominous. Alejandro had not heard from him either, and was by now hysterical with anxiety. But Amy retained an oddly philosophical calm. It was as though the love she and Daniel shared had given her a quiet strength.

August had slipped into September, and she would walk in Central Park, or on Riverside Drive beside the Hudson, thinking of her lover. In her imagination, he was beside her clasping her hand. By the time the trees in the park began shedding their golden glory, she was sure she was going to have his child.

'You sure were born yesterday!' was Katy's scathing reaction when Amy told her. 'I assumed you were already on the pill when you met Daniel.'

'Why would I take precautions for sex I didn't know I was going to have?'

'Because a girl never knows – and you're here to prove it. I stay on the pill even when I'm between affairs, like every modern woman does. I'm not about to get caught out.'

300

'But I'm not like you,' Amy replied. 'Sleeping around was never my scene. And when I met Daniel, everything but loving him went out of my head.'

'And look how you've ended up! What're you going to do? Get an abortion, or be a trendy single parent?'

Amy surveyed her friend's misleadingly cherubic countenance, now puckered with concern. 'Has Alejandro told you something he hasn't told me?'

'No. I'm just being more realistic than you're prepared to be. Could you get the money for an abortion from your father?'

'You still don't understand what Daniel means to me,' was Amy's response. 'If he doesn't come back, his baby is all I'll have of him.'

'Then I guess we'd better hotfoot it downtown to order the diapers,' said Katy with a resigned smile. 'And there sure is more to you than meets the eye.'

On the last Saturday in November, Alejandro came to the apartment.

'Katy's gone to the supermarket,' said Amy who was no more at ease with him now than at their first meeting. 'To fetch the quart of milk she's making sure I drink every day.'

'Katy's a kind girl. But it's you I came to see, Amy.'

She noted his haggard appearance, and tried to quell her own apprehension. Alejandro's shoulder-length black hair looked as if it had not been combed for days. His handsome face was wearing a set expression, and she could see a nerve twitching beside his mouth.

'That goddamn martyr has disappeared!' he burst out. 'I can't tell myself it isn't true any longer. All my efforts to trace him have failed.'

He thumped the wall with both fists, as though he must get anger out of his system before his tears of sorrow could be released.

Amy let him weep, but was dry-eyed herself. The moment she had dreaded had come, but her new-found strength came to her aid.

'Who are you angry with, General Pinochet or Daniel?'

she asked when Alejandro's sobs had ceased and fury again had him in its grip.

'Both!' he blazed while pacing the room like a tiger hunting its prey. 'One is a despot and the other a fool!' He halted and turned to look at Amy. 'But you and I, we love the fool – and now he is gone from us.'

'Disappearing isn't necessarily gone for ever,' she comforted him and herself.

'I wish I had your optimism. And I'm glad Daniel met you, Amy,' Alejandro said.

Then he came to embrace her emotionally, and she knew it was because she was to be the mother of his friend's child. Suddenly, the rapport she had been unable to establish with Alejandro was there, and how sad it was that her lover's disappearance from their lives had brought it about.

'We'll stay in touch,' she said when he was leaving. 'I'll call you from London. There's lots of space in my grandmother's house for a baby.'

Remember I'm here if you need me, Alison had said.

CHAPTER TWELVE

ALISON REPLACED the telephone receiver and smiled excitedly at Emma, who was waiting to wheel her back into the living room.

'Amy is coming to England!'

'I can't wait to meet her.'

'She's leaving immediately the play she's appearing in ends its run.'

'A true Plantaine,' said Emma drily.

'Except that her kind of theatre isn't mine,' said Alison tartly.

Emma foresaw sparks flying when Amy arrived.

'The play closes next weekend,' Alison told her, 'and Amy wants to stay with us.'

'Won't that upset Richard?'

'Of course. But it won't upset Janet,' said Alison with distress. 'There's something I haven't told you, Emma, there seemed no point. But now I must, as Amy is planning a long stay.'

Emma went on knitting the sweater she was making for Percy's birthday, while Alison explained why Amy's first visit to England had been no more than a visit.

'Poor Janet,' Emma said with a sigh. 'She's as maternal as her mother.'

'But Zelda was spared the sourness that Janet's continued childlessness has lent to her once sunny nature,' Alison added. 'And, I regret to say, the sparkle has also gone from her work.'

'Not everyone can forget their troubles when they're working, like you can, Alison,' Emma answered.

'And I've had all too many occasions to be thankful for that facility.'

'As I shared them with you, there's no need to tell me that.'

They exchanged an eloquent glance.

Emma had been back in London for three months and in all ways but one it was as though she and Alison had never parted. Their easy relationship had been resumed without difficulty. Each was back in her familiar place in the other's life.

Alison's inability ω walk more than a few yards, even with the support of two sticks, had not kept her offstage. She had just opened in *Ring Around The Moon*, which Richard had staged because one of the central characters was an old lady in a wheelchair. Janet was playing her mousey companion – a role for which she seemed well cast, nowadays.

'I always miss Maxwell at an opening,' she said. 'Not having him come to my dressing room before curtain-up, to wish me luck. And at the party, afterwards, standing beside me, po-faced, while everyone delivers the ritual platitudes. Fortunately, I haven't had a flop since he died – how I should get through the aftermath of one without him, I can't imagine.'

Emma missed Morton every minute of the day, and on a more personal level. 'I'll never get used to this house not reeking of his cigars,' was all she allowed herself to say.

They fell briefly silent, each with her own memories.

On winter Sundays, when they spent the day beside the fire as they were doing now, Emma would sometimes glance at the empty wing chair Morton had liked to sit in, and remember how, long ago, she had visualised the three of them together in their old age.

'The week before I had my stupid accident,' said Alison in the sour tone in which she always referred to it, 'Richard took Janet and me to Joe Allen's for supper.'

Emma emerged from her thoughts. 'Who is Joe Allen?'

'His restaurant is where a lot of theatre people go to eat, nowadays.'

'Max used to take you to the Ivy.'

'Yes. And going to the new rendezvous, with my son and daughter-in-law, reminded me of that – and made me feel that Maxwell and I were part of a bygone era.'

'I expect Max would have agreed.'

We can speak of Maxwell without strain, Alison reflected, but our break-up is never mentioned – because Emma would never come to terms with its cause. It was something they must live with individually and together, and had put between them an unspoken barrier that was never going to be removed.

She switched her mind to matters more pleasant. 'Which room shall we give Amy?'

'It would be nice for her to have the one that was her father's.'

'But Janet's old room overlooks the Heath.'

'Why don't we let Amy choose?'

After Amy's arrival, the question of which room would next year be the nursery took precedence. But domestic arrangements were far from Alison's mind when she first learned of her grand-daughter's plight.

Amy waited until they were alone before revealing her reason for coming to England, and was relieved that Richard had accepted without protest her wish to stay with Alison. The subtle change in him had dismayed her. He looked the same, but had lost the animation she remembered.

When he met her at Heathrow, his face had lit up at the sight of her. But it was like a candle briefly flickering, as though he had resigned himself to his lot, Amy thought.

That evening, after they had spent the day together, he took her to see *Ring Around The Moon*. Janet had afterwards pleaded exhaustion, and asked Richard to take her directly home. Alison had hoped to have them at a cosy family supper prepared by Emma, but Amy did not mind the way the evening had ended. She was by then struggling against jet-lag, and impatient for a private talk with her grandmother, with whom she had not yet managed a moment alone.

The cab home was not the place for so intimate a

matter, and Amy's first opportunity to raise it came after Emma had helped Alison to bed and herself retired.

Amy glanced at the silver-haired old lady, who looked distinguished even in a nightdress. Dame Alison had been born with the century – how would she take what her grand-daughter had to tell her?

Amy need have had no fears.

'Oh, my dearest child,' Alison said with compassion in which there was no censure.

Then she gathered Amy close and gently stroked her hair.

Her grand-daughter's story was like history repeating her own. Would the world never change? Forty-five years later, politicians and the military were still playing the same ruthless power games. And Amy's child might never know its father, as Richard had never known his.

'I love Daniel so much, Granny,' Amy said. 'He's very special.'

As my lover was, thought Alison poignantly. But a man had to be, to martyr himself to a cause. Richard had told Amy no more than that his father had died before he was born. Alison checked the impulse to tell her all. Now was not the time for Amy to hear a story similar to her own that had ended tragically. Within Amy's heart there was still the hope Alison had nurtured for so long, to no avail.

'You are fortunate to have met him, Amy,' was all she allowed herself to say. She cast emotion aside and switched her mind to more practical matters. 'The family – including those you haven't yet met – will help you in any way they can, my dear,' she said recalling her own out-of-wedlock pregnancy, most of which was spent hiding from the public eye in her Aunt Lottie's house. Conrad had even bought her a pair of dark glasses to wear if she ventured outside. Alison still had them – with the mementoes in her old trunk.

'It's good to feel I'm part of a real family, Granny,' Amy said. 'Tomorrow I'll tell Daddy my news. I wanted you to be the first to know.'

She rose from the bed and smoothed the counterpane.

'I must also start looking around for work. There's the equivalent of off-Broadway theatre going on in London.'

'It's known as alternative theatre, here,' said Alison without enthusiasm.

'Daddy called it fringe theatre. But whatever, that's my scene, Granny,' Amy said, giving Alison an impish smile.

'And who am I to argue with you?' Alison replied.

'Dame Alison Plantaine, that's who!'

'Who has begun to think that she and her scene have had their day.'

'How can you say that, Granny? You're still pulling in the crowds. The house was packed tonight.'

'But your scene is youthful and thriving. And youth is the future,' Alison resignedly countered.

'I can't wait to get in on the London end of it,' said Amy.

'When is the baby due, dear?'

'May.'

'Then it's hardly worth your looking for work now. It won't be too long before your condition shows.'

'That needn't stop me from working. Unmarried moms are all the rage nowadays.'

'I beg your pardon, dear?'

'I didn't mean to sound flippant. It's just that there's no stigma attached to it any more.'

'Are you sure, Amy?'

'Of course I am.' Amy gave Alison another of her impish smiles. 'I guess you've been hibernating during the Seventies, Granny.'

'I certainly seem to have been.'

It was a relief that no cover-up would be necessary. Nor the web of lies that had surrounded Alison's own pregnancy, with such devastating consequences for herself and her son.

'They call this the permissive age,' her grand-daughter told her.

'Though I welcome the change in social attitudes towards unmarried mothers, I don't like the sound of that,' Alison declared.

307

'But how could the change in social attitudes not lead to permissiveness?'

Alison begged the question. 'All that matters to me, my darling girl, is that it was not permissiveness, but love, that led you to your present plight.'

'And it isn't a plight, Granny.'

'In what *you* would call with-it circles, I don't suppose it is, Amy. But I have never mixed in them, and must accustom myself to all this. As for Emma, she'll have a fit at the mere thought of you venturing abroad in a maternity frock minus a wedding ring.'

'But my impression of her is that she'll eventually shrug and accept it.'

If she didn't have that capacity, she wouldn't have stayed with me all those years, Alison thought, with a dry smile.

'It's Janet I'm concerned about – and not on a moral level,' Amy said. 'I just hope the idea of me being a mother won't upset her.'

Alison's expression clouded. 'In view of her childlessness, how can it not?'

'That's why she didn't want me around; because I'm Daddy's child,' said Amy unnecessarily. 'But she couldn't be jealous of a baby, surely?'

'You're wearing the expression that used to be on my dear friend Maxwell Morton's face, when he had his thinking cap on,' said Alison. Amy's brow was furrowed in thought, and she was staring into space.

'I guess because I'm cooking something up, Granny. Something that could be good for Janet, and a big help to me. Do you think it would be a good idea to ask Janet to take care of the baby when it's born?'

'That could prove to be not just a good idea, but a positive brainwave, Amy.'

'Except that Janet, like me, is an actress and would have to take time out from her career.'

Alison sat up in bed and gave her clever grand-daughter a big smile. 'There's no need to give that another thought. *She* wouldn't, if a child came into her life.'

308

'You really think it would work?'

'I see no reason why not. And you would be free to pursue your art – like Emma's helping me to raise your father allowed me to pursue mine.'

Alison paused before saying firmly, 'But if I ever feel you are putting your career before your child, Amy, I shall have something to say to you on the subject. And frown upon you from the hereafter, if you forget it after I am gone.'

'I'm hoping to have you around for a very long time, Granny. What do you have lined up for when *Ring Around The Moon* closes?'

'Since there are not too many roles for severely disabled actresses, I must leave it to you to keep the Plantaine name in lights.'

'Mine isn't the names-in-lights scene, is it?'

'But metaphorically speaking, what I said still applies, my dear. It's your turn now, Amy – and knowing I can hand over the family heritage to my grand-daughter is a great comfort to me.'

CHAPTER THIRTEEN

DAME ALISON PLANTAINE graced the Edinburgh Festival with her presence in the summer of 1983. Her grand-daughter was appearing there in a Fringe production the critics expected would transfer to the West End – which Alison found amusing. The West End was to Amy and her ilk 'old hat'. Yet some of their offerings were now finding their way there. Artistic success was inevitably capitalised upon eventually, Alison reflected, and the West End was in the doldrums, with too many theatres standing dark due to the recession. She hoped Amy's lot would give commercial managements a shot in the arm.

She had flown to Edinburgh lest the play did not transfer, having seen too many slips betwixt cup and lip in her own career. Janet and Richard had accompanied her. Amy's little girl, too: Janet went nowhere without Daniela. Amy's brainwave had worked like a charm, and she and Daniela now lived under Richard's roof.

Alison was taking tea alone, in the lounge of the George Hotel, when a petite middle-aged lady who had been eyeing her with respect from a nearby table, came to speak to her.

'I'm Marianne Dean, Dame Alison – and I just couldn't miss the opportunity of saying how much I admire you.'

'How nice to meet you, Miss Dean.'

'I'm Mrs Dean, actually.'

Here, thought Alison, is one woman who has her priorities right. But that had not stopped her from having a successful career. 'I recall asking my late manager, many years ago, to try to get hold of one of your plays for me,' she said with a smile.

310

'I wish I'd known.'

'It's too late now.'

'But I bet,' said Marianne, 'that if you hadn't had that unfortunate accident you would never have retired from the stage.'

'Possibly not – but at my age, it was a good excuse to bow out and take things easy,' Alison said drily.

'If you don't mind my saying so, Dame Alison, you don't strike me as the taking-things-easy sort,' Marianne replied with Lancashire bluntness. 'And you could do radio plays, couldn't you? I'd love to write one especially for you. The producer I work with at the BBC would be thrilled to bits.'

'Thank you for the offer, my dear,' Alison answered. 'But an old horse doesn't find it easy to learn new tricks – as I discovered when I made my one and only film! And I'm a good deal more ancient now than I was then.'

'Are you enjoying the festival?' Marianne asked her. 'I'm here with my son and we've been doing the rounds. I'm worn out! Last night we ended up at the Fringe Club and were there till the early hours.'

'Such gallivanting,' said Alison, 'is no longer expected of me.'

'You're lucky.'

'I'm here to see my grand-daughter in a play that I shall probably not deem a play,' Alison told her. 'Amy calls me a square – and she's right!'

'It's the same with my son and me,' Marianne replied. 'He and his partner have written the lyrics and music for a way-out show that's on here. I sat through it expecting my eardrums to burst any minute. What we do for the younger generation of our families, sums it up, Dame Alison!'

'It does indeed. And I'm delighted to have met you, Mrs Dean.'

'If you change your mind about doing a radio play, please let me know,' Marianne urged before departing.

Alison watched the slim figure in a red linen trouser suit stride from the lounge with a purposefulness her gamine

311

appearance belied. Marianne Dean was the kind with whom Alison could have enjoyed a good working relationship. But Destiny had not thrown them together until now, and Alison would not change her mind about the radio play.

Not for anything would she put herself back in the trap from which retirement had released her; the ever-present strains and stresses that lived side by side with a career in the arts. She had earned her laurels and had found resting upon them more pleasant than she had expected.

Boredom had been her biggest fear, but time did not seem to drag. She and Emma took gentle walks on the Heath, though Alison still required a stick, and always would. They would talk of the past, as old people did, but neither lived in the past. They had Richard and his family to anchor them to the present.

Emma occasionally said it was time she went back to Oldham, where she belonged; that Alison was now quite able to take care of herself. But both knew that it was only talk. They belonged together. Emma's desertion had been just a hiatus in their shared life.

Richard interrupted his mother's musings to tell her it was time to change for the theatre. He would not have expected Alison to appear there in anything less than full evening dress. 'I hope you remembered to bring your white fox cape!' he teased her as they walked to the lift.

'I did. And my hope is that Janet has brought a frock for Daniela, instead of those jeans and tee-shirts she usually puts on the child.'

Richard laughed. 'At a Fringe show, be it Edinburgh or London, anything goes, Mother.'

'And if the auditorium is as makeshift as the last one in which I sat to see Amy in a play, it will take me a week to recover from the experience!'

'It was Janet and I who spent the evening seated on a backless bench. I seem to remember them providing you with a chair.'

'A hard one. In my day, audiences would not have paid money to put up with such discomfort.'

312

'But Amy's scene has pulled in a new kind of audience.'

'And they all wear jeans!'

'It's the modern uniform,' said Richard with a shrug. And added mischievously, 'In your day, the same could be said of evening dress in the boxes and stalls.'

'And I am now a dying breed,' Alison answered ruefully.

'What you actually are, and always have been, is one on your own,' her son told her with affection. 'And Janet was dressing Daniela to your approval when I left the room, to fetch you. The little one is so excited, it's hard to keep her still.'

'Of course she is,' said Alison. 'She's a Plantaine and this will be her very first time in a theatre. She is as unlikely to forget it as you have ever forgotten yours.'

Later, when they arrived at the venue, Alison found herself being treated like royalty by the brash young company.

'We're all in fear and trembling of something going wrong tonight, Dame Alison,' said the stage manager. 'Because you've come to see the play.'

'I have never been thought of as a jinx before,' she said, giving him a friendly smile. And was privately overwhelmed by the respect for her that was in the backstage air.

'A jinx nothing!' said the director, who was escorting them to Amy's dressing room. 'We just don't want you to think we're a lousy company – excuse the adjective, Dame Alison. Even Amy is nervous.'

'She is the only one of you who has cause to be, but I am not expecting her to let me down. Nor do I intend to measure new material with my old yardstick.'

The director halted in the wings, to allow Alison to appraise the set.

'Very interesting,' she said politely – there was nothing but a metal framework and a chair to appraise.

Daniela tugged impatiently at her hand, then ran onstage to inspect a big rag-doll that was on the chair. As with many Fringe productions, there was no curtain and those of the audience already in their seats laughed and gave her a clap.

The little girl responded with a curtsey – and Alison's heart skipped a beat.

Richard read his mother's expression. 'Shall we put Daniela's name down for drama college now?' he joked.

Alison laughed, and thought, We may as well. Remembrance of her grandmother, Jessica Plantaine, playing Desdemona, returned to her. And of her mother, Hermione, in the role of Titania. Theatre had changed since their day, and Alison had seen a plethora of new trends in her own time. Now, her grand-daughter was blazing a new trail, she reflected, glancing again at the set that old Gregory Plantaine would not have considered a set. And Daniela, in her time, would doubtless blaze yet another trail. Change was the lifeblood of theatre – and Plantaine blood would out. Alison's descendants would go on treading the boards long after she was gone. But she would not have those who came after her go through what she had to learn that it was human relationships, not achievement, that warmed the heart.